BLACK PYRAMID

HALLOWED KNIGHTS

BLACK PYRAMID

HALLOWED KNIGHTS

JOSH REYNOLDS

BLACK LIBRARY

For the Faithful.

A BLACK LIBRARY PUBLICATION

First published in 2018.
This edition published in Great Britain in 2019 by
Black Library,
Games Workshop Ltd.,
Willow Road,
Nottingham,
NG7 2WS, UK.

10 9 8 7 6 5 4 3 2 1

Produced by Games Workshop in Nottingham.
Cover illustration by Jon Cave.

A CIP record for this book is available from the British Library.

ISBN 13: 978 1 78496 930 1

See Black Library on the internet at

blacklibrary.com

Find out more about Games Workshop
and the worlds of Warhammer at

games-workshop.com

Printed and bound by CPI Group (UK) Ltd, Croydon, CR0 4YY

From the maelstrom of a sundered world, the
Eight Realms were born. The formless and the divine
exploded into life.

Strange, new worlds appeared in the firmament, each one
gilded with spirits, gods and men. Noblest of the gods was
Sigmar. For years beyond reckoning he illuminated the realms,
wreathed in light and majesty as he carved out his reign. His
strength was the power of thunder. His wisdom was infinite.
Mortal and immortal alike kneeled before his lofty throne.
Great empires rose and, for a while, treachery was banished.
Sigmar claimed the land and sky as his own and ruled over a
glorious age of myth.

But cruelty is tenacious. As had been foreseen, the great
alliance of gods and men tore itself apart. Myth and legend
crumbled into Chaos. Darkness flooded the realms. Torture,
slavery and fear replaced the glory that came before. Sigmar
turned his back on the mortal kingdoms, disgusted by their
fate. He fixed his gaze instead on the remains of the world he
had lost long ago, brooding over its charred core, searching
endlessly for a sign of hope. And then, in the dark heat of
his rage, he caught a glimpse of something magnificent. He
pictured a weapon born of the heavens. A beacon powerful
enough to pierce the endless night. An army hewn from
everything he had lost.

Sigmar set his artisans to work and for long ages they toiled,
striving to harness the power of the stars. As Sigmar's great
work neared completion, he turned back to the realms and saw
that the dominion of Chaos was almost complete. The hour
for vengeance had come. Finally, with lightning blazing across
his brow, he stepped forth to unleash his creations.

The Age of Sigmar had begun.

PROLOGUE

THE LAST PRINCE

Of the city's final hours, few stories remain. Tales of heroism, like the final charge of Count Vitalian, or the last stand of the High Executioner, who wielded her black axe in defence of the Great Gaol. And the doomed defiance of Tarsem the Ox, last prince and defender of Helstone...

– Ogwell Mancini
Nine Hundred Kings: An Expanded History of Helstone

Helstone burned.

The city was dying, circle by circle. The hounds of Chaos swarmed through the streets of the Ninety-Nine Circles, killing all who dared stand against them. Bodies choked the canals and aqueducts, and everywhere was the stink of slaughter.

Tarsem, Prince of the Fourth Circle, held the ragged hem of his cloak pressed tight to his mouth and nose, trying to block out the smell. He turned this way and that, gazing out over the edge of the balcony. Everywhere he looked, there was only fire. He wiped blood and smoke from his eyes and shifted the weight of his sheathed blade to his other shoulder.

He stood on one of the high, wide balconies that studded the immense support pillars known as the Hollow Towers. The towers had been the means by which the folk of Helstone moved between sky and salt. Now, they were a route of evacuation, as his people fled from the lower circles to the upper, seeking sanctuary. He suspected that there was none to be had, however. The enemy laid siege from above as well as below.

But there were safe places yet. His father, Tarsig, had foreseen such a need, and had constructed secret routes through the hollows of Helstone. Places where some of their people might survive the conflagration. It would mean hiding away in the dark, possibly for generations, waiting for the flames to burn themselves out – but they would survive. That was all that mattered. Helstone was its people, and Helstone would survive.

Even if he was not there to see it.

'Sigmar, grant me strength to do what must be done,' he murmured, tracing the sigil emblazoned on his breastplate – the twin-tailed comet, wrought in the shape of a stylised bull's head. The symbol of his house, and the heraldry of the Fourth Circle. He found comfort in it, even now. 'Grant me the strength to stand, whatever comes.'

Behind him, through the wide archway, he could hear the sounds of flight – whispers, weeping, muted panic. His warriors would be among the crowd, fighting to maintain some sense of order. Only when the last of them had fled would the great stone archway behind him be sealed, against what pursued them. Above, the secret routes were being readied. They too would be sealed, one after the other. Tarsem knew that he would not live to see it.

He had been marked for death, and a man could only run from death for so long. He traced the wet laceration that coiled about his neck – the mark of a barbed lash, belonging to one of the Huntsmen of Khorne. The daemon had called out his name, audible over the din of battle, and he had felt its lash twist about his neck, tightening as if to pop his skull from his neck. He could still feel it. Even now.

His fingers dug into the wound, and came away red. Behind him, a voice said, 'Leave it be, Tarsem. It will heal, eventually. But only if you let it.'

Tarsem smiled and turned. 'Are you speaking from experience, Mannfred?'

Mannfred von Carstein stood near the archway, the picture of lazy insouciance. If Tarsem hadn't known his friend was one of the soulblighted, he might have thought him a living man. Mannfred's bald head was streaked with blood. His black, ridged war-plate was stained with ash like Tarsem's own, and his great cloak was tattered and torn. His arms were bare and thickly muscled, the unliving flesh marked with an eternity of scars.

'Always, my friend,' the vampire said, grinning.

'Any word on Megara, or the others?'

Mannfred's grin faded, and he shook his head. 'I fear we are the last of the Ninety-Nine Companions standing. I saw Vitalian's head decorating a spear, and heard only the laughter of daemons where the Mistress of Doomcrag planned to make her stand. We are alone, brother. We are the last.'

Tarsem closed his eyes. If Vitalian and Megara had fallen, then what hope remained? He stood, remembering faces and names. Jests made and battles won, alongside men and women of renown. He thought of glories, now forgotten and trampled into the dust by the hooves of daemons and braying beasts. 'We were giants, once,' he said, softly. The wound on his neck ached, as if the barbs were still sunk in his flesh. He felt hot. Flushed. His fingers tightened on the hilt of his sword.

'Giants fall,' the vampire said. 'As will we, if we stay here much longer. The circles below have fallen, and even now drown in a rising tide of blood. Any who have not yet evacuated are lost.'

'We wait, just a few moments longer,' Tarsem said. Mannfred frowned but did not argue, for once. Tarsem smiled. 'Besides, I have an appointment to keep.'

'Rocha is not coming, Tarsem. The Great Gaol fell hours ago.'

Tarsem looked out over the city, and did not reply. Somewhere down there, his bride-to-have-been fought for her life. Rocha had refused his offer of sanctuary, with her customary stubbornness. It seemed only fitting to her that the High Executioner of Helstone be allowed to choose the place of her own death. In his mind's eye, he saw her, a pale woman, clad in robes of black mail and dark silks, headsman's axe in her hands. Handsome, rather than beautiful, with eyes like chips of ice, and a wide smile.

'A few moments more,' he said. Tarsem had not known of her intentions until it was too late. There had been too many innocents yet to be evacuated, the defences to see to... Too much to do, and no time to do it in. When he'd at last had a moment to seek her out, to explain, she was gone. And now it was too late. Too late to apologise, to tell her that it wasn't her fault. To tell her that she was not to blame for what had happened between them.

'It is not your fault,' Mannfred said, as if reading his thoughts. 'Love is a tricky beast, and even the most cunning hunter can miss his shot.'

Tarsem nodded. 'Perhaps.' Arranged marriages were the norm for those of his station, but he'd found little in common with the woman his father had chosen for him. Rocha was acerbic, with a sense of justice fully at odds with his own. For her, innocence was judged at the executioner's block. Those who came before her were guilty, else they would not have been there at all. Perhaps that harshness was why his father had chosen her – Tarsig had always bemoaned what he saw as his son's naiveté.

'Still, I've seen worse ways to avoid an arranged marriage,' Mannfred said. 'Though, frankly, having seen her fight, I'd be afraid of her carving herself a path back to your side, a daemon's head in one hand and her axe in the other. And knowing your soft heart, you'd be unable to resist such a proposal.'

Tarsem looked at him. 'Ever the romantic, Mannfred.'

Mannfred laughed and clapped him on the shoulder. 'Come. This battle is lost, but there are others to win. We can escape this place.'

'No.' Tarsem brushed Mannfred's hand away. 'You go, if you wish. But I must stay.'

Mannfred frowned. 'Tarsem, don't be foolish. If you die here, so too does any hope of organised resistance in this part of Shyish. Nagash is broken, the Mortarchs scattered. The Ninety-Nine Companions have fallen. We cannot lose you as well.'

'Then stay and fight beside me. Together, we might turn the tide.' Even as he said it, Tarsem knew it was a faint hope. He touched his neck again, and felt the warm trickle of blood, slipping down into his armour. Pain thrummed through him. He heard – no, *felt* – something roar, amid the cacophony rising from below. A sound of malign promise. He shook his head, trying to clear it.

Mannfred laughed incredulously. 'There is no stemming the blood-tide. I have tried.' He slapped his chest-plate for emphasis. 'Helstone is burning, Tarsem. All that is left now is to retreat – to regroup. We do not have to die here.'

'Perhaps you don't. But I fear my story is nearing its end.'
He held out his bloody fingers. Mannfred hissed and turned
away, as if he'd smelled something foul. 'I've been marked,
brother. There is no escaping what follows me. Not twice. And
well you know it.'

Khar'zak'ghul.

Khar'zak'ghul.

The words pounded on the air, like sword-strokes against
armour. His head ached with the sound, and he stumbled, suddenly dizzy. He heard Mannfred say something, but could not
understand the words. The air became close and sulphurous.

Khar'zak'ghul.

Khar'zak'ghul.

He looked up, and with stinging eyes saw a grotesque face
leering at him. Red and raw and twisted, with eyes like open
wounds and a mouth full of shrapnel teeth. Twisted horns,
capped with brass, rose over an inhumanly narrow skull. Mannfred shook him, shouting. The daemon held Tarsem's eyes with
its own. Its lipless mouth moved, chanting.

Khar'zak'ghul.

Khar'zak'ghul.

Tarsem drew his sword and lunged. The bloodletter's face
burst as his sword passed through it. A roar echoed up from
somewhere far below, shaking the balcony. All at once, he could
hear again.

'Tarsem, look out!' Mannfred roared.

As Tarsem retreated, sizzling ichor dripping from his blade,
more red-skinned daemons clambered over the edges of the balcony, hissing in eagerness. Mannfred flung out his hand, and a
bolt of eldritch energy punched one of the creatures backwards
in a gout of gore. The vampire drew his basket-hilted blade with
his other hand, parrying a blow meant for Tarsem's skull.

Tarsem returned the favour, plying his own blade with desperate skill. He swung his reinforced sheath up, using it to block a blow. A moment later, his sword looped out, chopping into a daemon's corded neck as it lunged for Mannfred. For a moment, they fought back to back against the snarling horde. Tarsem's muscles, honed in the fighting pits of the Fourth Circle, began to ache within moments, such was the ferocity of their opponents. Mannfred had no such difficulty.

The vampire fought with a savagery equal to that of the daemons. Fangs bared, face twisted into a feral mask, he moved like quicksilver, twisting under blows and spilling their ichor before daemons even realised he was there. Tarsem, in contrast, fought with stolid determination. His great two-handed blade swept out like a scythe, and daemons fell back, spitting and snarling, before him.

Far below, something bellowed. The daemons hesitated and drew back with guttural snarls. One by one, they slunk back the way they'd come, vanishing into the smoke. The roar came again, and Tarsem felt as if a spike of ice had been driven into his heart.

'My name… It calls my name.'

'The huntsman has come,' Mannfred said. 'We must go, Tarsem – *now!*'

Khar'zak'ghul. The name beat on the air like a hammer blow. Daemons clung to the edges of the balcony, watching with molten eyes. *Khar'zak'ghul*, they hissed.

Khar'zak'ghul.

Khar'zak'ghul.

Tarsem looked away. 'There is a place – the Hidden Circle. You know it?'

Mannfred hesitated. 'I do.'

Tarsem smiled. 'I had no doubt you would, though it was

13

one of our greatest secrets. See that my people make it there. The Hidden Circle will hide them. It's what my father designed it for. There are wards in the stones – the daemons will not see them. My people will live. Some of them, at least. And while its people live, so too does Helstone.' Tarsem felt the balcony shudder, and a wash of infernal heat enveloped him. The daemons had begun to rhythmically strike the stones of the balcony with the tips of their blades.

Khar'zak'ghul.

Khar'zak'ghul.

Tarsem raised his sword. The ancestral blade of his house, older even than Helstone itself. It had shed the blood of a god, or so his father had claimed. Perhaps it might do so again. 'Go. Please.'

Mannfred hesitated. 'Tarsem…'

'It is not your weird to perish here, son of night. It is mine.' Tarsem smiled and cast aside his sheath. He would not need it again. 'If I flee, it will simply follow, and slay those we seek to protect. And I am tired of running. Go, my friend. I will hold it back, so that you might escape and take my people to safety.' He glanced back. 'Go, Mannfred. Live to fight another day.' Then, more firmly, 'Bleed them, vampire. Make them pay for this victory, in blood and bone.'

Khar'zak'ghul.

Khar'zak'ghul.

He felt Mannfred's grip, tight on his shoulder. Then, the vampire was gone. Behind him, he heard the slow groan of the great stone passage sealing itself for the last time. A shadow of fire and smoke rose over him, blood and carnage made manifest. Khar'zak'ghul had come. Tarsem raised his sword in challenge as the daemonic shape loomed, great wings of ash spread, and a barbed whip coiling across the stones. The balcony shifted beneath the daemon's weight. He wondered that he felt no fear at the sight of it. Instead, there was only a strange sense of satisfaction.

'For Helstone,' he said, softly. 'For Sigmar.'

The daemon-huntsman roared, so as to shake the pillars of the heavens.

Blade in hand, the last prince of Helstone went to meet his death.

And was welcomed.

CHAPTER ONE

UZKUL

*The dust-barques of Caddow traders were well
known in Shadespire, and even the ports of the
Bitter Sea...*

– Tuman Wey
The Shadow-Routes: Trade in Eastern Shyish

Shyish was a place of bitter endings and silent decay.

Graveyards that had once been cities dotted a landscape
broken by war, their streets lost to shadows and dust. Carrion
birds circled the high places, and jackals haunted the low. And
everywhere was dusty silence.

The city of Caddow was no different. It sprawled across
the Sea of Dust like a broken corpse. Its once-mighty eyries
were reduced to jagged ruin, and the stones of its high walls
had fallen and lay scattered for leagues. Dust-barques that
had once carried holds of spices and damask lay forgotten in
dune-swallowed docklands, and the palaces of the mighty were

home now only to night-birds and hoofed beasts. A forest of stone rose where once a city had thrived. Silent and forgotten.

'*Uzkul-ha!*'

As the cry echoed over the broken city, the night erupted in fire. Long dragon-tongues of red-and-orange flame licked out, scoring the darkness. Startled flocks of carrion birds rose skyward.

'*Uzkul-ha!*'

Another crash of voices, another ripple of fire. Broken, twisted shapes slumped or were thrown back into the dust, their unnatural flesh steaming. Nightmarish creatures, part man, part animal, clad in rotting damask and tarnished gold, fell back from the high, steep steps of the black pyramid. They howled and gibbered as they retreated, sounding much like the beasts they resembled.

'*Gazul-akit-ha!*' A single voice bellowed, as the echoes of fire faded.

'*Uzkul! Uzkul! Uzkul!*' came the shouted response, echoing out over the shattered grandeur of the city. Fifty duardin voices, raised in defiance. Raised in prayer. The constant thump of a pommel stone against the inner rim of a shield accompanied the words. Funerary bells began to ring, slow and dolorous. Iron-shod feet stamped in a mournful rhythm.

The Gazul-Zagaz began to sing. A dirge of mourning, for the dead yet to be. Singing their souls to the deep caverns of Gazul, the Lord of Underearth, who was dead himself. All things died and walked in the deep, even gods. That was the way of it. But what was death to a god? 'Dust, and less than dust,' Gnol-Tul said softly, as he stroked the thick spade of salt-and-pepper beard that spilled down over his barrel chest.

Like all duardin, he was built like a cask of ale, with thick arms and legs. Age had not dimmed his vigour, though he'd seen more centuries than he had fingers. He looked on in satisfaction as his kinband shouted their song into the teeth of the enemy. Though there were only fifty of the Pyredrakes, they were worth three times that.

Clad in coats and cowls of burnished gromril, each of his warriors wore a steel war-mask wrought in the shape of a skull, and carried a baroque drakegun. Besides the hand cannons, each duardin was armed with a square pavise shield, which doubled as both bulwark and firing stand, and a heavy, flat blade, suitable for butchery and little else.

At that moment, the shield wall stretched across the southern tier of the ziggurat, protecting two lines of Pyredrakes. The first line would fire then step back to reload, allowing the second rank to take their place. A hoary strategy, but effective. Tul thought the old ways of war were often the best, and served against the disorganised rabble below well enough. Beastkin had little in the way of tactical acumen. They were savage and strong, but strength alone was as dust against iron and fire.

So had it always been, so would it always be.

Tul and his *bier*, his chosen companions, stood behind the firing lines. Armed with round shields, wrought in the shape of a scowling countenance, and carrying heavy runeblades, his bier was composed of proven warriors, those who had already sung their death-song and consigned their souls to the Underearth. Unlike the Pyredrakes, they wore white robes, and their masks were of silver rather than iron.

Tul himself wore the golden mask of an elder, and beneath it his skin and hair were marked with the sacred ashes of his ancestors. He carried a double-handed runeblade cradled in the crook of his arm. It was an old thing, hungry for death, and nameless, as was proper. To name a thing was to give it a will of its own, and a wilful weapon was one that could not be trusted. There were many named blades in the shadow-vaults of the Gazul-Zagaz, and there they would remain, until Shyish sank into the twilight sea.

Tul and his kinband had fought their way through the ruins and up the steps of the ziggurat over the course of several days, leaving a trail of dead and dying beastkin in their wake. The ruins were full of the creatures – thousands of them, breeding in the dark – and the duardin had roused them all as they advanced deeper into the city. But what were beasts, to the warriors of the Gazul-Zagaz?

'The gor flee, elder,' Hok, his *tolvan,* said. 'Our fire warms their bones overmuch.' His subordinate held a heavy stone tablet, upon which the names of the honoured dead would be carved upon victory – or just prior to defeat. Either way, their names would be recorded, and added to the Long Dirge of the Gazul-Zagaz.

'They will come again and in greater numbers,' Tul said, tugging on his ash-streaked beard. 'They are brief things, and determined.' The warriors of his bier nodded sagely at this. They were all veterans of a thousand similar skirmishes, their birth-swords grown dull on the bones of gor and *ik* – beastkin and daemons, as the Azyrites called them.

As he thought of their allies, a flash of silver, somewhere out in the dark below, caught his eye. He heard the sound of a hunting horn, and the shriek of one of the Azyrites' great beasts. Then, cerulean light sparked, and he heard the whip-crack of a boltstorm pistol.

'The Swiftblade is close,' Hok said, his disapproval evident.

Tul smiled sourly. Hok was referring to their ally, Lord-Aquilor Sathphren Swiftblade. Tul's mind tripped over the unfamiliar title. It had too many words, and unnecessary ones at that. Why advertise the swiftness of your blade to the enemy?

Surely it was better for such things to be a surprise. Then, there was much about the Stormcasts, and Sathphren in particular, that was confusing.

'As he promised,' Tul said. Hok bowed his head, accepting this chastisement with grace. Confusing or not, the Azyrite was an ally. He had helped the Gazul-Zagaz, and so, they would help him. An oath for an oath, a debt for a debt. 'By sorrow fail, and by sadness bound,' he murmured, reciting the ancient oath – the first oath and the last – made to the Lord of Underearth by his folk, in the days before the coming of the Undying King.

'An oath for an oath,' Hok said, and the others murmured agreement.

'As it was, as it must be,' Tul said, finishing the oath. He glanced up towards the pyramid's summit, where a massive, four-sided archway of carven stone topped the edifice. Shaped to resemble nothing so much as a great flock of birds, rising skywards to a single point, the archway sat atop a circular dais of curious construction, marked by runic sigils unfamiliar to Tul's eye.

Sathphren had called it the Corvine Gate. Once, the realm-gate had linked this part of Shyish to somewhere in Azyr, the Realm of Heavens. Tul let his gaze rise to the stars overhead, where Azyr bled into Shyish, and every other mortal realm besides. The Gates of Azyr had been sealed long ago, as the Ruinous Powers spread their baleful influence through the realms. Now, at last, they were opening once more.

Tul could not say whether that was entirely a good thing or not. But an oath was an oath, and he would pay his folk's debt, as he must. 'They've caught the gor,' Hok said, drawing Tul from his contemplation of the stars. Hok leaned over and spat. 'Will they drive them back to us? It is only fitting.'

Tul shook his head. 'No. They are selfish and careless, these

Azyrites.' Then, that was often the way of stars – heedless of all that they shone on. One could not expect them to hold to the niceties of civilised folk. 'Sathphren will take them for himself.'

His warriors grumbled at this, equal parts annoyed and amused. The Azyrites – these Stormcast Eternals, as they called themselves – were powerful allies. And faithful, in their own way, to their own god, Sigmar. The Gazul-Zagaz knew him as the Starlit King, and it was said that he had walked among them often, in days of antiquity. Before Gazul had fallen silent, his temples cast down and his folk scattered.

Powerful, yes, and faithful, to be sure. But like children. Careless and eager. But that was no bad thing, perhaps. For children soon grew up. Then, perhaps, they would truly be allies worthy of the Gazul-Zagaz, in fact as well as in deed.

He squinted, catching sight of more silvery flashes in the dark. Eerie cries echoed up from the ruins. The Swiftblade fancied himself a hunter, Tul knew. Well, he would find plenty of prey this night. He smiled: a hard, merciless expression.

Beast howls filled the night. A tide of filth flowed up the steps of the pyramid, surging forwards on hooves and claws. They made a great noise as they came, almost joyous in its intensity. As if they knew the oblivion that awaited them, and welcomed it.

'Uzkul-ha,' he said, softly. He lifted his sheathed blade over his head. '*Uzkul-ha!*'

'*Uzkul*,' came the response from his warriors. Death.

'*Uzkul! Uzkul! Uzkul!*'

Ghosteater lurched into the lee of a fallen pillar, his white fur smouldering. He snarled and rubbed at the bloody graze that marked his arm. He brought bloody fingers to his muzzle and sniffed, taking in the stink of fire powder. The stunted ones fought with iron and fire. There was little to be done against that, save die or drown them in bodies.

The only two tactics your kind knows, a voice within him hissed. One of his ghosts. They always felt brave when he bled. He growled softly and hunkered down as slugs of iron and lead whined off the stones around him. He would wait until they had stopped shooting, then see what there was to see.

Yes-yes, clever-clever, another ghost whined. Ghosteater snarled, silencing the chittering spirit. Even dead, it was afraid of him. They were all afraid of him, as they should be. He had eaten them, and they were his, now and forever. When he died, he would drag their souls with him to the scented bowers of the Absent God, and there, in the Glades of Silk, he would devour them again, for an eternity.

But for now, they served him in other ways. *Range is the key,* a harsh voice said, at his mental prodding. *They have it. The steep slope of the ziggurat slows advance, allowing them to deploy multiple volleys in the time it takes your warriors to recover from one.*

Another voice chimed in, *A mass rush might carry the day. Throw more bodies at them than they have shot for. Then it's just a matter of butchery. Even beastkin can do that.*

Ghosteater shook his head. 'Not enough warriors,' he growled. 'Not yet.'

But soon, perhaps. When a few more ghosts had been bent to his will. When a few more rivals had fallen to his blade and teeth. He glanced down at the sickle-like khopesh he carried. It was an old thing, made from beaten bronze in a time when such weapons had been valuable. He'd found it in the dust, alongside the bones of its owner. There had only been the tatters of a ghost left, clinging to those bones – just enough to teach him how to wield the khopesh with some skill.

Ghosteater studied his reflection in the curved blade. He stood head and shoulders above even the tallest gor, and resembled one of the dust-lions that haunted the deep canyons of the south, with a square head the colour of chalk, surrounded by a shaggy mane of the same hue. Red eyes blazed above a wrinkled muzzle, studded with thick fangs. Six bud-like horns rose through his mane, like a twisted crown of bone – a sure sign that he was blessed by the Absent God.

A daemon's blessing is nothing more than a curse, a voice said, weakly. Ghosteater ignored it. What did the dead know of blessings and curses? They were beyond such things. He lowered his blade and looked back at the ziggurat.

The stunted ones were chanting again. He heard the howling of the northern tribes in response. He caught sight of hairy shapes loping through nearby streets, bellowing and striking their blades against their wooden shields. He didn't need the ghosts to tell him that they would have no more luck than his own kin.

If you go, you die. Simple as that, gor. This ghost had a harsh voice, like metal on stone. A duardin, perhaps. *Run, like the beast you are. Live for another day.*

Ghosteater snarled, silencing the voice. Sometimes, the ghosts forgot who was meat, and who was the eater-of-meat. He watched as the northern tribes scaled the face of the ziggurat and were met by a deluge of fire. More bodies fell, rolling down the steps to join the charnel piles growing below. He felt a pulse of satisfaction at their failure. If his folk could not have victory, then neither should those they had spent years killing.

'Weak,' he growled, watching them flee. All the tribes were weak. They had made themselves weak, hiding in this forest of stone. They had been content to war among themselves, rather than seeking out worthy foes. Content to scrabble in the dust and drape themselves in tatters of carrion, rather than hunt living prey.

Ghosteater was not like the others. He was strong. He had fed on a hundred ghosts, and their voices lent him wisdom. That wisdom had let him rise, as surely and as swiftly as one blessed by the Absent God could do. His first ghost had been that of Twistjaw, his littermate, who'd tried to crush his skull in the dust for the offence of being an albino.

He had killed Twistjaw in the traditional fashion, and offered up his corpse to the Absent God after anointing himself with his littermate's blood. After Twistjaw had come Twisthoof, the tribe's shaman, who'd been resentful of his blessings. He had bitten through Twisthoof's skull and eaten his twisted mind, one handful at a time.

Every death after that had added to the sweet chorus in Ghosteater's head. Not just beastkin, but men as well, and duardin, ratkin and greenskins. The only foes whose ghosts he could not eat were the twice-dead – their souls were already claimed by another. But that didn't matter to the gor. There were plenty of ghosts to devour without scavenging Nagash's scraps and risking the ire of the God of Death.

He had taken his tribe and made them strong. They had eaten the other southern tribes, and grown large, adding the survivors to their ranks. He had abased himself before the Blessed Ones, who waited on the city's outskirts, and joined the fate of his tribe to theirs. Before the stunted ones had arrived, he'd thought to sweep west, and consume the tribes there. In time, the forest of stone would have belonged to him, and all the ghosts within it. And then, he might have turned his gaze south, to where the Blessed Ones lounged…

But no. The Absent God had chosen a different fate for his child. Ghosteater could feel the portents on the air. Twisthoof's ghost whined within him, showing him the myriad skeins of possibility – of what might be, and what must be. A door was opening, and a silver tide would spill down the sides of the great ziggurat, to flood the forest and drown his folk. Ghosteater shook his shaggy head, trying to clear it of the vision, and Twisthoof's whimpering. 'Be silent,' he snarled, cowing the ghost.

Stones shifted behind him. He turned and saw a group of his followers creeping towards him, shamefaced and muttering. He had been the last to retreat, and they knew it. Many of the beastmen bore wounds, but all of them still held their weapons. That was good. His folk were not cowards, whatever else.

'You live,' one growled. He did not sound happy. Wormeye was big, and built thick. A true gor, with high, spiralling horns and a long, goatish muzzle. One eye was covered in a filmy cataract, and many scars covered his tawny hide. He gripped a crude blade, neither spear nor sword, and wore a tattered tabard, stiff with grime.

'I live.' Ghosteater bared his fangs in a smile. Wormeye thought he should be chief. He was wrong, but that did not stop him thinking it. Until now, he had not acted on it, but Ghosteater could see him sniffing, tasting blood on the wind. 'How many?'

Wormeye glanced back, eyes narrowed. More beast-shapes crept close, regrouping among the fallen pillars and shattered walls. It had not taken them much time to regain their courage. Ghosteater was pleased.

'Enough,' Wormeye grunted. 'Many hands, still.' He twitched his fingers, for emphasis. 'We go again?'

'No,' Ghosteater said. 'Too much fire.' He slapped his chest, bloody from a glancing shot. 'No war-plate. We go, we die, like the rest. Nothing else.'

'Coward,' Wormeye snarled. The others murmured and shrank back. The accusation was as good as a challenge. Ghosteater looked at him and licked his chops, pleased by the outburst. Wormeye twitched back, suddenly realising what he'd said. He bared his fangs in what might have been an attempt at apology, but Ghosteater was in no mood for such gestures. Not now that he had an excuse.

He lunged, jaws wide, and bulled Wormeye back against a pillar. His fangs sank into the other beastman's hairy throat, and with a convulsive jerk of his head, he tore Wormeye's jugular open. Blood sprayed over him like a fountain as Wormeye gurgled and thrashed.

Ghosteater shoved the twitching body down. 'Eat. Quick.' As the others fell greedily on the body, he turned away, back to the ziggurat. Another tribe climbed the blood-slick steps, trying to fight through the fire, and failing. He watched the bodies rain down, and growled softly. What were the stunted ones up to?

They can't keep it up forever, one of his ghosts murmured. *No supply lines, for one thing. No support.*

None we can see, another added.

Ghosteater blinked, and growled low and long. Of course. It was a tactic his own folk used, and often. Let the prey fasten its jaws on bait, and pounce on them from behind. He turned, searching. If there were other enemies abroad, when would they strike? Now?

No, a ghost said. *They'll wait until most of you are in the trap – look!*

He did. He saw the broken remnants of several tribes gathering nearby, in what had once been a plaza. Chieftains snarled at one another, and came together in a flurry of blood and steel, each seeking to take command. Ghosteater considered following their example, but the whispered warning of his ghosts held him back.

A moment later, a flash of silver alerted him to the arrival of the enemy. He heard an eerie crackle, and saw beastmen drop. Bolts of snarling energy erupted from all around the plaza and cut through those gathered there. They died without seeing what killed them. Horns blew, somewhere in the ruins – not the crude instruments of the tribes, but something else. Clarion notes sawed through the clamour, and his head ached with the sound. Shapes moved in the distance – bestial, but not familiar. Strange cries sounded, and he felt his hackles stiffen. The wind turned, and he could smell them now – like clean water, and sand after being struck by lightning.

Something large and incredibly fast leapt down among his warriors a moment later. Silver war-plate flashed in the gloom as a crackling axe removed a warrior's head. His kin howled in surprise, and fell back. Ghosteater lunged towards their foe, khopesh raised. The attacker turned swiftly, lightning erupting from his hand.

Ghosteater howled in rage as bolts of azure pain struck his flesh and sent him stumbling into a broken pillar. He shoved himself back around with a roar, just in time to parry a blow meant to remove his head. His great khopesh shuddered in his claws as his opponent's axe whistled off course, to gouge the pillar.

The silver-armoured warrior leaned back, away from Ghosteater's rejoinder. He snorted and resisted the urge to fling himself on his foe. *Safely, softly,* one of his ghosts murmured. *He is strong-strong-strong...*

'Not stronger than me,' Ghosteater growled. His warriors circled them, growling and shouting, watching but doing nothing – if he failed, they would flee.

The silver warrior cocked his head, as if puzzled. 'No. But I am better,' he said, simply. He spun his handaxe in a tight circle and stamped forward. The axe hissed out, leaving a trail of blue sparks. Ghosteater swayed aside, agile despite his bulk. He reversed his khopesh, and let the barbed curve dance across his opponent's side. The silver warrior staggered and one of his ghosts snarled, *Now, beast, see – his leg is extended. Strike!*

Quickly, Ghosteater swept his blade down on his foe's knee, where there was a gap in the silver war-plate. There was a sound like breaking rock, and his opponent cried out. Instinctively, he sagged and reached for his shattered limb. Ghosteater caught him by the back of his helm and drove him face first into the pillar, hard enough to crack the stone. The silver warrior flopped down, unconscious.

Ghosteater raised his blade, ready to remove the fallen warrior's head. *No-no,* a ghost chittered. *Question-torture him, yes-yes! Information is useful-valuable, fool-fool!* He snarled in annoyance, banishing the shrill voice, even as he acknowledged the wisdom of its words. He looked at the others. They whined in confusion. As always, they needed his wisdom.

'We go – south,' he growled as he reached down, catching hold of the silver war-plate. His claws and palm tingled unpleasantly at the touch of it, but he ignored the sensation as he heaved his prisoner up onto one broad shoulder. Strong as Ghosteater was, his foe made for an awkward burden. 'To the camps of the Blessed Ones.'

Sathphren Swiftblade, Lord-Aquilor of the Swiftblades Vanguard Auxiliary Chamber, smiled as he watched duardin fire lance the night. 'As they promised, eh, Gwyllth?' He leaned forward in his saddle and patted his gryph-charger's feathered neck. The lean, cat-like beast gave a quiet chirrup of what he took to be agreement. Sathphren wasn't certain how much the beast understood, but he suspected it was a great deal more than most.

'Do we go now, brother?' Feysha murmured. The Pallador-Prime sounded eager, and Sathphren couldn't fault her. They were close now. He could feel it in his bones and in the air. It was the same sensation he got whenever he completed a successful hunt. The surge of triumph at seeing his quarry brought low.

But there was a time and a place for everything, and celebrations were best saved for after victory was certain. 'No,' he said. 'Third volley. Then we go.' Thalkun and his Vanguard-Raptors would be in position by then. As would Gullat and his Vanguard-Hunters. 'Precision, Feysha… It's all about precision.'

'As you say, Swiftblade.'

He glanced at his subordinate. 'Is that amusement I hear?'

'Light mockery, my lord.'

'Permission granted,' Sathphren said. It was his own fault. He'd never been one for chains, even those of command. He looked around, checking that the rest of his conclave was ready. The gryph-chargers of the Vanguard-Palladors crouched low in the ruins, waiting for their silver-armoured riders to give the signal to run. It had been no easy thing, sneaking through the broken city without attracting attention. Luckily, the Gazul-Zagaz had been willing to make plenty of noise.

Even luckier, the beastkin that inhabited the ruins were utterly disorganised, little more than squabbling packs. They had claimed the city centuries ago, and had, from what he could tell, spent most of the time since fighting over its dwindling resources, and eating each other. But the beastkin weren't the true threat in Caddow.

That would be the army camped on the far southern edge of the city. Gullat's scouts had reported hundreds of garish pavilions, scattered across the stony shores of the Sea of Dust, a forest of stakes encircling them. The stakes were heavy with the broken bodies of beastkin, and the grounds were stained black from spilled blood. Sathphren didn't know who they were, but he knew that there were more of them than his small force could handle. Even with the help of their allies.

He straightened in his saddle, peering south, wondering if they would have the time they needed to do what was necessary. Feysha caught his glance and said, 'Gullat would have alerted us if there was anything to be concerned about. They haven't so much as twitched since we got here.'

Sathphren shook his head. 'They're too close to the city for my liking. It doesn't make sense that they wouldn't investigate.'

'Maybe they're lazy. Or just used to the beastkin making noise.'

Sathphren gave a snort of laughter. 'Maybe so. It wouldn't surprise me.' He let his gaze ascend the black ziggurat, where the object of this entire exercise stood, uncaring of the slaughter carried out in its shadow. Legend said that the ziggurat had been carved in honour of the great pyramid of Nagashizzar, a sop to the ego of the Undying King by Caddow's rulers, in ancient days. And at its top, the Corvine Gate, one of the dwindling number of realmgates that directly connected Shyish to Azyr.

Most had been destroyed during the War of Heaven and Death, but there were a few left, scattered throughout the various underworlds – the Shimmergate in Glymmsforge, and the Lychway in the City of Sighs. The Corvine Gate was the last of these to remain in the hands of the Ruinous Powers, so far as Sathphren knew.

They had to take it. Hold it and fortify it. The honour of that task had fallen to the Hallowed Knights Stormhost. A full three warrior chambers waited on the other side of the gate, ready to pour forth and take the ruins of Caddow from the enemy, in Sigmar's name. If Sathphren Swiftblade could but clear them a path.

He grinned tightly, feeling old scars and new pull taut. He and his warriors had dared much to win this far. Memories of hard riding and dusty camps came to him, as well as other, darker recollections. Of desperate battles with the living and the dead alike, as well as things that had never been alive at all. Barely two-thirds of those who'd set out with him from Glymmsforge still rode at his side. The rest had returned to Azyr, there to be Reforged anew.

Shyish was deadly, even to those who meant it no harm.

But they were close, now. He could feel the aether twitch in anticipation of what was to come. All they had to do was hold on a bit longer, and kill as many of the foe as possible. The gate would open, and the city would be theirs.

Just a bit longer.

A roar sounded. He sighed in satisfaction. *Precision.* 'Third volley.' He thumped Gwyllth in the ribs and the gryph-charger heaved herself to her feet. The others rose as well, as the Palladors readied their weapons. 'Don't stop, or slow. Keep moving at all times. If they flee, let them go – Gullat's huntsmen will handle them. I want them broken and confused.'

A moment later, they were in motion. The gryph-chargers ran with a speed that put all other creatures to shame, even carrying fully armoured Stormcasts on their backs. The winds of Azyr flowed through their veins. Gwyllth leapt over fallen statues and bounded from broken pillar to broken pillar, her claws carving great gouges in the ancient stonework. Feysha and the others kept pace, spreading out around him in a crescent formation.

Around them, the ruins erupted with lightning. Thalkun was plying his trade from the heights, his Vanguard-Raptors forcing the disorganised foe into moving where Sathphren wanted them to move.

There were too many beast-tribes to break individually. Even the steady destruction rained down on them by the Gazul-Zagaz hadn't been enough. But the duardin had drawn them all in to a central location, and one they could not easily retreat from. Sathphren saw the lines of the city in his head, as clearly as when Gullat's scouts had reported back. Caddow revolved around the great ziggurat, like a wheel about its spindle. The city had grown outward from the massive edifice, and its main thoroughfares were shaped accordingly. And now, the enemy were caught by that wheel, trapped in its turning.

Lightning sparked and snarled, casting gouts of dirt and loose stone into the air. A tide of beastkin burst into view, fleeing their unseen attackers. Sathphren whistled sharply, and his warriors split up, the crescent breaking apart as individual Palladors readied their weapons.

'Remember, bloody them, but do not pursue,' he called out, loosening his starbound blade in its sheath. 'Leave some work for our brothers and sisters, when they finally arrive. Who shall ride the wind aetheric?'

'Only the faithful,' came the shouted response, as the Hallowed Knights fell upon the foe. Sathphren drew his blade and leaned low in his saddle. A beastman stumbled and fell, head tumbling from its shoulders as he swept past. He plied his blade like a scythe, letting the edge and his momentum do the work. He left a broken trail of bodies in his wake as Gwyllth leapt off the street and onto the top of a crumbled wall without slowing.

Silvery streaks carved through the massed beastkin, splitting the horde and funnelling the survivors down side streets and narrow pathways. Sathphren heard the whistle-crack of bolt-storm pistols as Feysha and the others blocked off pathways and sent chunks of rubble toppling onto the street, further scattering the demoralised foe.

It was all about precision. Keep your quarry guessing, keep them confused, and then harry them until they collapsed – or turned to make a stand. Either way, the end result was the same. A broken body at your feet, and meat for the feast.

Sathphren's smile was feral as Gwyllth pounced onto an unlucky gor, bearing the goat-headed brute to the street. The beastman squealed as the gryph-charger's claws opened it from nape to navel, and then she was moving again, leaving the creature thrashing in its death agonies. Gwyllth had played this game before, and knew it well.

A roaring beastman lunged towards them, crude axe raised. Sathphren removed its hands at the wrists with a looping blow, as Gwyllth carried him past, towards the ziggurat. 'Faster, sister,' he murmured.

Beastkin still sought to climb the edifice, hurling themselves into the guns of the duardin – hundreds of them. Heaps of hundreds more lay at the foot of the ziggurat, their ruined flesh still smoking. Erratic rivers of blood splashed freely down the wide, slabbed steps, but the creatures did not falter or cease their assault. They covered the southern slope, clambering over the dead, driven into a frenzy by the stink of death on the wind.

Without waiting for the others, Sathphren urged his steed towards the base of the ziggurat. Angles and rates of fire played across the surface of his mind. The duration between volleys was more protracted, allowing the beastkin more time to recover. The duardin were conserving their ammunition. Gwyllth took the steps two at a time, racing like a zephyr. Blade in one hand, he drew his heavy boltstorm pistol with the other, and clamped tight to Gwyllth's sides with his knees.

Gwyllth struck the rear of the horde like a thunderbolt, sending beastkin tumbling with the force of her arrival. Sathphren fired his pistol without bothering to aim. Lightning ripsawed through the enemy, hurling broken bodies away from him.

'To the top, sister,' he roared. An axe flashed, and he sent its wielder spinning away, headless. Beastmen turned as they became aware of his approach. Sathphren fired again and again into the howling mass of monstrous bodies. Gwyllth shrieked in rage, hooves and talons lashing out in a wide arc. Bones splintered and flesh was torn as she pushed forward, carrying him up the steps.

As they reached the uppermost tier, Sathphren saw that the Gazul-Zagaz shield wall was under threat. A wedge of beastmen, burly and battle-scarred, their hairy hides decorated with tattoos and trophies of battle, had managed to disrupt the line. A towering gor, with the head of a stag and a stone-headed maul in its talons, led the way, despite the bloody wounds that pockmarked its flesh. It smashed an unlucky duardin off his feet with a massive, sweeping blow, and turned as Gwyllth's shadow fell over it.

'Greetings, Tul,' Sathphren shouted, as Gwyllth bore the brute to the stones. The beastman thrashed beneath the gryph-charger's weight, squalling. Slowly, almost gently, Gwyllth bit her captive's head off. Nearby duardin drew back, muttering. Sathphren pretended not to notice as he holstered his boltstorm pistol. 'Good hunting, I trust?' he asked, as the shield wall reformed behind him, and another volley thundered.

'Hunting requires skill and effort,' Tul said. 'This requires neither. But our powder runs low. Soon we will be forced to kill them with our hands.' The duardin did not sound displeased by this prospect.

'So I see.' Sathphren turned. Beastmen fell back in a haze of powder smoke, leaving a shroud of bodies on the edge of the tier. But he could hear bellowing in their ranks, and knew that the respite was only temporary. Another rush, and they might well overwhelm the duardin. He could not allow that. He looked back at Tul. 'Retreat to the top of the ziggurat. I will buy you the time you need to regroup.'

Tul frowned but did not argue. A pragmatic folk, the Gazul-Zagaz. He shouted something in their grating tongue, and funerary bells rang out. The rear ranks of the duardin began to ascend. When they reached the midway point, they set their shields and levelled their drakeguns, creating an improvised gateway through which their fellows could pass.

A bird shrieked overhead. Sathphren looked up. Aetherwings circled overhead, trailing motes of starlight with every flap of their great wings. Thalkun was on the move. Sathphren nodded in satisfaction. It was a great comfort to him that his subordinates could act on their own initiative. Like him, they were hunters born, and knew their business.

Down below, Feysha and the other Palladors had reached the lowest tier of the ziggurat and were killing any beast they found. But there were still plenty between them and Sathphren. He grinned and slid from Gwyllth's saddle. The gryph-charger grumbled and he stroked her neck.

'Easy, sister, easy. Now is the time to meet our prey's final charge with steel and claw.' He unhooked his shock handaxe from the saddle and gave it an experimental swing. He turned, blade in one hand, axe in the other. Gwyllth growled and crouched behind him, tail lashing.

The last of the duardin stumped past, pulling back, leaving him alone on the tier, save for Gwyllth. The beastkin edged forward through the clearing haze of powder smoke. In a moment, their courage would return and they would charge. He did not intend to give them that moment. He scraped the edge of his axe against his sword, and laughed. Gwyllth screeched in challenge, her tail lashing.

Dozens of pairs of red eyes met his own. Sathphren grinned.

'Well? What are you waiting for?'

As one, the children of Chaos lunged forward, fangs bared.

Sathphren Swiftblade sprang to meet them.

CHAPTER TWO

NORDRATH

Nordrath the Proud. Child of the Great Mountain.
Long has Nordrath stood pre-eminent among the
great cities of Azyr, and its mountain clans are
famed for their hardy stoicism...

– Ogwell Mancini
Great Cities of Azyr

Gardus knelt before the celestial orrery in silence. The Lord-Celestant's runeblade and tempestos hammer sat crossed beside him, his helm placed carefully atop them, its stern expression turned towards the temple's entrance. The orrery was taller than a man, and twice as wide, swinging in an eternal rhythm, emulating the dance of the firmament. The Steel Soul watched the dance, seeking comfort in the familiar pattern.

The orrery was a masterwork of mortal craftsmanship. Fashioned from gold and brass, it was lit by but a single candle. Despite this, it somehow managed to cast its light to all corners of the temple. The spheres representing the mortal realms moved with a precision that he envied, each piece knowing where it was to go, and what it was to do. He wondered what it was like to possess such certainty, or if such a thing was even possible for one like him.

Once, he thought he'd known the limits of the world, and his place in it. But that assurance had evaporated the day he'd been forced to take up arms in defence of the dying. He closed his eyes, as the echoes of that moment reverberated dimly through him once more. He felt the weight of the candlestick in his hand, the moment of impact as the first of the Skin-Eaters had fallen. The savage tribesman had made little noise as he collapsed, skull staved in. But the others had screamed, oh yes – had howled and gibbered as they'd spilled across the marble floors of the hospice, stinking of slaughter.

As ever, the memory faded as suddenly as it had come, leaving his mind awash in red. His passing had not been easy, and he could still hear the screams of his patients as he fell. As he failed those he'd promised to protect, for the first time and the last.

'I am sorry,' he said, startling himself with the sound of his own voice. The words were almost a prayer. He looked up at the orrery. Unfortunately, there were no answers to be had in the dance of the spheres – at least none that were evident to Gardus. Then, few men, mortal or otherwise, found certainty in the stars. Instead, they found only possibilities. 'Perhaps that will have to be enough,' he murmured.

'It is beautiful, isn't it, my lord?'

'Yes,' Gardus said, glancing over his shoulder. 'And one of a kind, I am told.' He made the sign of the hammer, and rose to his feet. He tried not to notice how he loomed over the bent shape of the priest. 'Hello, Hulio. You are looking well.'

'A lie, my lord, but a kind one.' Hulio smiled. His voice was strong, despite his years. The priest was bent in the way of very old men, as if the weight of the world were too much for his shoulders to bear. His hair was threadbare and unruly, and his face was a mass of wrinkles. He wore pale blue robes beneath the ceremonial golden armour of a priest of Sigmar. Hulio had been lector in Nordrath for almost two decades. Before that, he had served as a war-priest, alongside a number of Nordrathi Freeguild regiments.

Gardus still remembered the young man the priest had been, all those many years ago. The strength of Hulio's devotion had shone like a star in his breast then, and he had fought with a righteous rage, the equal of any Stormcast. Now, those fires were dimmed, and the broad shoulders were bowed with age. Gardus felt a pang – a sense of time fleeing his grasp, of years passing in the blink of an eye. How many generations had passed since the death of Garradan of Demesnus? How many since Gardus Steel Soul had first set foot in Ghyran?

Hulio stepped past him and looked up the orrery. 'Made for this temple some one hundred years ago, by a visiting artisan. Uccello Grymwine. One of his celestial orreries adorns the great cathedral of Azyrheim. Much larger than this one, of course. And far grander in design.'

'You do your temple a disservice, Hulio. Size isn't everything.'

Hulio peered up at him. 'Helps, though, I'd say.'

Gardus laughed. The echoes of it filled the nave, and set the candle in the orrery to flickering. 'Perhaps.' He could hear the rattle of drums sounding outside the temple. Jubilation filled the streets. He had not noticed it earlier, so engrossed had he been in his prayers. But now it bristled about him, impossible to ignore. 'How long have they been cheering?' he murmured, somewhat taken aback.

Hulio turned towards the entrance to the temple. 'Hours, now. Much of the city has turned out to celebrate. And why not? A day long promised has come at last. Sigmar has answered our prayers.' He sighed. 'I wish – I almost wish I was going with you.' He sighed. 'Once, I might well have. But now...' He held out wrinkled hands. His fingers were bent and stiff. 'My fingers are too crooked to properly hold a staff, let alone a hammer.'

Gardus took the mortal's hands in one of his own. 'Rheumatism?'

'It comes and it goes.' Hulio smiled wanly. 'The perils of age.'

'I would not know,' Gardus said. He examined Hulio's hands gently, probing the joints and knuckles with his fingers. Old memories drifted briefly to the surface, the memories of a man long dead, and remade into someone new. Garradan had often massaged the joints of his older patients, easing their aches and pains. He heard Hulio gasp and saw light bleeding from the joins of his gauntlet. Hastily, Gardus released the priest. 'My apologies,' he said.

'They are right – you bear a holy light,' Hulio said, rubbing his hands. 'My hands – the pain is gone.' He smiled widely. 'Why, I feel I could almost wield a warhammer again!' He caught the look on Gardus' face, and his smile faded. 'You are not pleased?'

'I do not know,' Gardus said, softly. He curled his hands into fists and the radiance dimmed. 'Sometimes, I dream of being light. Of being nothing save light.' He shook his head. 'They are not good dreams.'

Hulio sighed. 'You bear a heavy burden, my lord. Would that I could remove it from you.' He smiled sadly. 'Alas, I fear you would consider my homilies quaint at best.'

Gardus chuckled warmly. 'Never that, Hulio. Not for nothing are your sermons transcribed and sold on street corners in Azyrheim.' He smiled. 'I have a book of them myself, you'll recall.'

Hulio flushed. 'Ah. I'd hoped you'd forgotten that bit of youthful folly.' As a young man, fresh to his posting in Hammerhal Ghyra, Hulio had made a gift of his collected sermons to Gardus. It had even been signed.

Gardus caught him gently by the shoulder. 'Never.' He glanced at the orrery and sighed. 'I must go. They will be waiting for me.' He bent to retrieve his weapons and helm.

'All of Shyish waits for you, I daresay.' Hulio bowed low, hands clasped before him in the sign of the hammer. 'Go with Sigmar, my lord. And know that the prayers of all Nordrath go with you, this day. For too long has our sister city lain silent. I would hear its song once more, before Sigmar takes me into his light.'

Outside the temple, the air throbbed with a celebratory clamouring. Musicians played on every corner, accompanied by jugglers and acrobats clad in colourful attire. Street vendors offered a variety of doubtful delicacies to the crowds that thronged the cramped lanes and cobbled streets of Nordrath. Over the slanted rooftops, Gardus could see the peak of the Great Mountain, wreathed as ever in clouds. Lightning flashed silently over the distant heights, and he could hear the faint boom of thunder beneath the tumult.

As he descended the flat, stone steps of the temple, he saw ranks of mortal troops marching past, heading south, towards the Plaza of Crows. They wore grey uniforms, trimmed in blue, and carried halberds, round shields and swords. Behind them came rank upon rank of handgunners, wearing the distinctive feathered caps common to the clansfolk of the Smoak Fens, rather than the round helms worn by the halberdiers. Each soldier was otherwise armoured the same, their slate-grey war-plate bare of all adornment save the sign of the twin-tailed comet. Too, each wore a black noose about his or her neck. It was from this emblem that they had gained their war-name – the Gallowsmen.

They were an old Nordrathi regiment, drawn from the hardy clans that occupied the mountains and fens of the region. The nooses were worn in honour of the first of their number – a band of criminals rescued from the gallows, in return for their swords, by Duke Lorcus, spokesman of the city's ruling conclave. The Gallowsmen had faithfully shed blood in the decades before the closing of the Gates of Azyr, and the regiment had prospered in the centuries since. The mountains and fens of Nordrath had been – and still were – home to monsters and bandits aplenty.

The regiment was made up of free men these days, rather than criminals, and led not by the Duke's executioners but by the sons and daughters of noble Nordrathi families. And the noblest of them all was Albain Lorcus, second son of the current Duke, and captain-general of the regiment. Gardus spotted the young commander as he rode along the street, keeping his men in formation – no easy task, given the ecstatic throngs pressing close on either side. Lorcus saw him as well, and urged his horse towards the temple steps.

'You have finished your meditations, my lord?' Lorcus had to shout to be heard over the commotion. Gardus nodded.

'I have.' He looked around. 'I see the city has turned out to see us off. Your father's idea?' The duke was an unsubtle man and took any opportunity to flaunt his wealth and prestige, diminished though it was since the days when the first duke had led the Gallowsmen to battle. This celebration would be the talk of Nordrath for weeks, if not months.

Lorcus had the good grace to look embarrassed. 'He is very excited, my lord. It is a day of days, or so he has often said, of late.' He swung down off his horse and fell into step beside Gardus. 'He believes this will be the reforging of us.'

'Perhaps he is right.' Gardus looked around. 'Though I hate to think what he's spending on all this.'

'Other people's money, mostly,' Lorcus said, lightly. Gardus chuckled.

'The others?' he asked.

'Already waiting in the plaza. Or so numerous messengers, each more harried than the last, have informed me.' Lorcus turned. 'My father insisted on a stately departure, so that Nordrath might have time to get to know the faces of its heroes.'

'You sound as if you disagree.'

'My father, and many of his generation, see war as a glorious endeavour. Our destiny manifest, meant to expand the borders of Azyr into the lower realms. He sees only the glory and profit to be had.'

'But you do not?'

Lorcus smiled. 'No. I see those things as well, both of which my family is in want of, at the moment. But I am the first Lorcus in three generations to take the field and share the hardships of the regiment. I learned the red trade with other regiments, and have dug latrines and set stakes in three realms. I have seen what awaits us, on the other side of the Corvine Gate, and I am not blind to the hardships ahead.'

Gardus studied Lorcus. He was young for his position, but that wasn't unusual. Many regiments operated under a system of purchasable commissions – an easy way to fill the coffers when not actively on campaign. He'd heard good things about Lorcus, though. It was one of the reasons he'd agreed to take on this duty, when the petition of reclamation had been approved and volunteers had been called for.

Such delegations were regularly sent to Sigmaron, to petition the representatives of the various Stormhosts – or even Sigmar himself – for the reclamation of this city or that ancient bastion. In his time, Gardus had gone to war on behalf of the Collegiate Arcane, merchant consortiums and determined heirs to lost kingdoms, as well as at the command of Sigmar himself. Many was the temple or holy city brought back to Azyr's light by the warriors of the Hallowed Knights.

Yet, while it was the duty of the Stormcast Eternals to drive back the Ruinous Powers on all fronts, arguments for preference could be made – and often were. Few Stormcasts would refuse the opportunity to free the lands they had known as mortals, however dim those memories. At other times, Stormhosts were petitioned by the conclaves of the trading cities of Azyr to help re-establish ties to their sister-cities in the lower realms. Many mortals insisted that trade was the lifeblood of civilisation, and that re-establishing the old routes would only help what remained to flourish.

'Hardships, yes, but rewards as well,' Gardus said, after a moment. Duke Lorcus had racked up a mountain of debt to fund this campaign, and no small wonder. The reclamation of a city was often a bloody affair, but inevitably profitable for those who invested in the venture. 'You will soon be the ruler of a city, and your family assured of primacy for generations to come.'

'If I survive,' Lorcus said, his smile crooked. By right of blood and claim, he would be the founder of a new ruling conclave. The other investors would be satisfied with rights of trade, construction or exploration. 'If we win.'

'We will.'

'Your certainty is admirable, Lord-Celestant.'

'Not certainty. Faith.' Gardus clasped the young man on the shoulder, careful of his great strength. 'Hold firm to that, and all things will align.' Ahead of them, he could see the pair of immense pillars, each carved from purest orichalcum to resemble a cloud of birds in flight, that marked the entrance to the Plaza of Crows.

Hallowed Knights Retributors stood on guard at the base

of each of the massive pillars, their heavy, two-handed light-ning hammers crackling with a harsh radiance. They dutifully inspected the line of troops passing into the plaza. Though they were all from the same Stormhost, they bore the heraldry of three different Chambers, including his own.

When he saw Gardus, the Retributor-Prime in charge stepped forward to greet him. His war-plate bore the markings of the Bullhearts warrior chamber – a stylised twin-tailed comet, resembling a bull's head in profile, covered one shoulder-plate, and a profusion of battle-oaths inscribed on auroch hide hung from his armour. 'My lord, it is good to see you. The Lady Cas-sandora has been asking after you.'

'A polite way of saying she's getting impatient.' Gardus waved Lorcus on ahead. The captain-general saluted briskly before moving off. 'Never mind, Iunias. Tell me, how is Ramus? If you're here, then I expect he has arrived as well.'

'He's waiting in the plaza, my lord.' Iunias hesitated. He cleared his throat. 'Though he will not say it, he is grateful to be here. We all are. For too long we have sat idle in Azyr, waiting to be called upon once more. You have my thanks, my lord.'

'Give your thanks to Sigmar, Iunias. For myself, I am glad to have your Chamber here. The Bullhearts have faced the horrors of Shyish before, and I cannot think of better warriors to have at my side when we pass through the Corvine Gate.' Gardus watched as the rear ranks of the Gallowsmen passed between the pillars. When the last of the soldiers had gone through, he followed them, with a parting nod to Iunias.

Beyond the pillars, the Plaza of Crows stretched from sun-rise to sunset. Once, it had been home to one of the greatest markets in Azyr. The stone berths of hundreds of long-disused aether-docks rose over the cobbled expanse, held aloft by swooping arches carved to represent the boreal winds or flying beasts, and connected to wide, spiral stairways by narrow viaducts of stone. Beneath them had been erected row upon row of tents, now being dismantled by the regiments as they readied themselves to march.

The plaza was banded by high bastions of stone, raised in those first fraught days after the coming of Chaos, before Sigmar had decided that the only way to save his realm was to isolate it. Lining the tops of these bastions was a battery of cannons, fixed on the massive archway that was the Corvine Gate.

Gardus stopped as two of the great, shaggy aurochs, common to the fens of Nordrath, clopped past, hauling a massive, multistorey wooden supply wagon. The wagon resembled a storehouse set on enormous wheels, and was topped by wooden observation platforms and rope walkways. As its large, iron-rimmed wheels rolled over the ground, they cast up a cloud of dust before him.

The great bulls that pulled the wagon were three times the height of a Stormcast, and covered in a thick coat of tangled hair. Long, curved horns sprouted from their square heads, and their hooves were heavy enough to flatten a block of sigmarite. A narrow wooden platform stretched across their broad backs, where a trio of drovers oversaw their progress. Two held long-barrelled rifles braced on their hips, and were passing a bottle of something back and forth over the head of their companion as he sang a lilting melody.

As the dust of the supply wagon's passage cleared, Gardus saw a familiar figure striding to meet him. The silver war-plate Lord-Celestant Cassandora Stormforged wore was much like his, save that hers bore a profusion of prayer-scrolls and sigils of purity. She held her helm beneath her arm, exposing round, dark features. She grinned and waved the last of the dust from the air. 'Finally. Done being maudlin, brother?'

Gardus smiled. 'I was praying, sister. I'd hardly call that maudlin.'

Cassandora snorted. 'No, you wouldn't, I suppose.' She extended her hand, and they clasped forearms. 'I see Lorcus has finally got those fat and happy parade soldiers of his on the move. The rest of the regiments arrived days ago. They've been asking to see you.'

'I'll speak to their commanders shortly,' Gardus said. 'What of the representatives from the Collegiate Arcane and the Ironweld? Have they shown themselves yet?'

Cassandora shook her head. 'I believe they're arguing over who gets to yell at you first. Something about mineral rights, I think. Give them time to get it sorted before you go looking for trouble. Or let Lorcus handle them. His father hired them, after all.'

Gardus nodded, frowning. 'We haven't even won the battle yet.'

'What can I say, brother – you inspire confidence.' Cassandora laughed heartily. 'They're not the only ones preparing for our inevitable victory, either.' She hiked a thumb over her shoulder, and he peered past her to see his Lord-Castellant, Lorrus Grymn, in close conversation with Octarion, his opposite number among the Stormforged, as well as Taltus, the Lord-Ordinator chosen to accompany them.

They stood in the lee of a supply wagon, studying a selection of maps, likely preparing themselves for the labours to come. Several gryph-hounds lounged at their feet, sleeping or staring at the silent realmgate with animal intensity. When he saw Gardus, Grymn raised his hand in greeting, before turning his attentions back to the maps.

Gardus looked around, taking in the sheer size of the army that occupied the plaza. All around him, mortal soldiers from three regiments readied themselves for the march, and he could hear the bark of officers and the laughter of rankers as they broke camp.

To the east, a dozen of the multistorey supply wagons waited. They would pass through the realmgate only after it had been fully secured. Within them was not just provisions and shot, but also the materials needed to erect palisades, construct bridges or repair structures. Alongside them sat several of the blocky, thickly armoured steam-wagons of the Ironweld, their boilers chugging softly as their crews readied them for travel. These carried the specialised equipment required by the human and duardin engineers accompanying the army.

And then there were the Stormcast Eternals. Not just his warriors but Cassandora's as well, arrayed in gleaming ranks before the Corvine Gate. The Steel Souls and the Stormforged had the honour of spearheading the assault. The Bullhearts would follow and act as support for the Freeguild regiments. It would be up to them to defend whatever gains were made in the initial assault.

He studied the realmgate where it towered over the far end of the plaza. The archway rose as high as the pillars directly opposite it. One side had been carved to resemble Sigmar himself, stretching his hand out towards a swirling pilaster of birds. Gardus gazed at the stony features of the God-King and wondered if he was looking down on them. He hoped so.

A large group of mortal seers and battlemages from the Collegiate Arcane stood before the realmgate, gesturing and chanting rhythmically. The mystic bindings that sealed it had taken days to remove, even with Sigmar's permission.

'Not much longer now,' Cassandora said. 'I can feel it in the air.'

Gardus nodded. A periodic blue glow flared within the cracks in the stones of the archway as the mages repeatedly struck the ground with their staves. Even from where he stood, he could feel the air knot and tense with every flash. 'You sound excited.'

Cassandora shrugged. 'It's a good day for a war.' She turned. 'Don't you agree, Dame Morguin?' Gardus followed her gaze, and saw the commanding officer of one of the other Freeguild regiments standing at attention nearby. She wore battered leathers and a shawl made from strung-together coins over a gilded breastplate. A golden helm, wrought in the shape of a gryph-hound's head, hung from her belt.

'I do, my lady. But even if it weren't, I'd be ready.' Dame Suhla Morguin swept off her wide, feathered officer's cap and gave a terse bow. She was a hard-faced woman, built tall and spare, after the fashion of folk from the Chamonian highlands. 'Twelfth Cohort is ready to march, my lord and lady – pike, shot and pavise. Whatever comes, whatever the ground, the Gold Gryphons will see Sigmar's will done.'

'I had no doubt, sister,' Cassandora said. 'Vindicarum is lucky indeed to have such soldiers. And we are lucky to be allowed their use.' The Gold Gryphons had a pedigree stretching back to the duelling fields of Azyrheim, though their scope and size had expanded significantly in the century. Now, like many of the older Freeguilds, they hired out individual cohorts, rather than the regiment as a whole. The Twelfth Cohort was almost the same size as the entirety of the Gallowsmen regiment, in terms of manpower.

Morguin took Cassandora's compliment with a shallow nod. Gardus wondered whether she was overawed by being in the presence of the two Stormcasts, or simply naturally taciturn. Perhaps both. The Gold Gryphons had a reputation for stubbornness in the face of incredible odds. The number of times their lines had been broken since the Gates of Azyr had opened could be counted on one hand. But if they were to win, they needed to do more than just hold.

Morguin made to speak, but a burst of off-key singing interrupted her. She grimaced. Gardus turned to see who had drawn her ire. A horseman, clad in a vivid red uniform beneath black-daubed armour, cantered towards them. The rider sang with more enthusiasm than skill, and what lyrics Gardus could make out were unabashedly licentious. He slipped off his lobster-tailed pot helmet and held it beneath one arm as he easily guided his cantering steed across the plaza with his other hand.

'My lord and lady,' he called out cheerfully. 'It's shaping up to be a fine day!'

'I trust then that your men are ready, Captain-General Cruso?' Gardus asked, as the horseman drew close. Captain-General Jon Cruso of the Nordrathi Red and Blacks was a short man, even mounted. Built sturdy, with a long, waxed moustache and a forked beard, he was the epitome of the Nordrathi aristocracy, as were all the warriors under his command.

The Red and Blacks were a specialised harquebusier regiment, smaller than most, but flexible. They were made up almost entirely of outriders, pistoliers and armoured cavalry, drawn predominantly from the city's aristocratic families. Billets in the Red and Blacks were hereditary, and most important families had at least one son or daughter serving with the regiment, if only for a campaign.

'Always up for a bit of blood and thunder, that's us,' Cruso said, as his horse came to a stop. The animal whickered as Cruso patted it fondly.

'Trust you to be cheerful about this, you bloody-minded Nordrathi bastard,' Morguin growled. She looked at Gardus. 'Damn cavalry – always eager for a fight, knowing the infantry have to do all the real work. You aren't even breaking your own camp – you're letting your servants do it for you.'

'Fighting *is* work, you sour-faced Chamonian witch,' Cruso said, leaning over in his saddle. 'Everything else is what you do between fights.' He grinned at her. 'As to our servants, well, that's what they're for, after all. My lads need their arms rested for the butchery ahead. Can't have them digging latrines and stacking rocks. Bad for morale, eh, my lord?' He looked at Gardus.

Gardus frowned. 'Bad for the infantry's morale, yes. Which is why your harquebusiers will do their share when it comes to digging and stacking once we pass into Shyish.'

Cruso sputtered as Morguin laughed harshly. Cassandora looked at her. 'We all will. Even those of us clad in sigmarite shall put our hands to the spokes.' She looked at Gardus, her eyes alight with merriment. 'The wheel of progress cannot turn unaided.'

'Indeed, sister,' Gardus said, fighting back a grin. 'All must see to the harvest, else all might starve. Such was decreed by Sigmar in days gone by, and so it must be.'

The mortals glanced at each other, uncertain as to how to reply to such an innocuous homily. The Hallowed Knights had come by their reputation for piety honestly, but mortals sometimes confused faith for dogma. Gardus let the silence stretch a moment longer, then said, 'You have spoken to Captain-General Lorcus?'

'Aye, shifty-eyed runt that he is,' Cruso said. 'Too smart by half, that one.'

'Good thing he's in command, then,' Morguin said.

'Yes, well, so he is,' Cruso said, sounding slightly aggrieved. Gardus suspected that his unhappiness had more to do with politics than with any real doubts about Lorcus' ability. Nordrath had its share of factionalism.

'Good. Then you both know what is required. Your forces will advance through the realmgate, supported by Lord-Relictor Ramus and the Bullhearts, only after the signal is given.' Gardus held their gazes. 'Do you understand?'

'Aye, my lord,' Morguin said, for them both.

'Then ready your warriors. The gate will soon open.' As they departed, he let his gaze drift across the silver-clad ranks of Stormcast Eternals standing ready some distance from the realmgate. Liberators stood at the fore, shields to the ready. Behind them, Judicators waited, ready to send the enemy reeling with crackling volleys. Seeded at intervals among the Liberators were cohorts of Retributors and Decimators, who would serve to break the strongest battle-line. Overhead swooped the winged Prosecutors of the Angelos Conclaves. They would be first through the gate, softening up the foe for those who came after. A strategy honed over the course of nearly a century.

'A sight to stir even a soul of steel, eh?' Cassandora said. 'The Steel Souls, the Stormforged and the Bullhearts. What foe could stand against us?'

'An overwhelming force to pacify one city.' Gardus looked at her. 'One Chamber would have been enough for this.'

'Yes, but three is a statement.'

'Maybe. Perhaps it's as simple as many hands make for quick work.'

'War is never quick, Steel Soul. You know that better than most.'

Gardus nodded reluctantly. 'We are entering uncertain times, sister. The enemy has been driven back, but the harder we push, the deeper they burrow into the flesh of the realms. Once, they would have hurled themselves at us, and died in droves. Now they retreat. They bar gates and raise walls. They make alliances, where once each sought to outdo the others. We have hurt them, but now they regroup.'

'And we consolidate.' Cassandora looked at him. 'We push the wilderness back and plough the furrows of civilisation in our wake. We do it again and again, as many times as we must. Until the war is won.'

Gardus nodded, not looking at her. 'Much is demanded,' he said, as he glanced back at the realmgate. The air tasted of iron, as after a storm. Something in him pulsed in time to the flares of cerulean light that limned the archway. There was a stirring in the ranks of the assembled Stormcasts. They felt it as well. It would open soon.

'To those whom much is given,' Cassandora replied, as she watched the light play across the stones of the realmgate. 'Or perhaps this gathering signifies something else. There is much speculation, you know.' Gardus, well aware of what she was referring to, didn't rise to the bait. She went on. 'You know of what I speak?'

Gardus sighed. 'Yes.'

'The post of Lord-Commander has been empty for too long.' She looked at him. 'Sigmar will choose someone soon.'

'Soon, to Sigmar, might be a hundred years from now, sister. You know that as well as I.' Gardus met her gaze. 'Unless you've heard something more?'

'I knew you were interested.'

'I'm merely making conversation. I am certain that whoever he chooses will uphold their responsibilities most admirably.'

Cassandora snorted. 'Our cousins in gold have all but elected theirs already.'

'Vandus is a fine commander.'

'How many times has he been Reforged, exactly?'

Gardus frowned. 'You might well ask the same of me.'

Cassandora waved his words aside. 'That is different.'

'I don't see how.'

'Vandus is not the man he was.'

'Are any of us who we were?' Gardus shook his head. 'Vandus is loved and respected among the Hammers of Sigmar. I can think of no finer warrior to lead them.'

'And what about us?'

Gardus looked away. 'Silus, perhaps. Or the Ironheart. Maybe even you, sister.'

It was Cassandora's turn to laugh. 'You left out a name, I think.'

'I do not believe so.' He looked at her. 'We have had this conversation before.'

'And we will have it again,' Cassandora said. 'I am not the only one who feels that you should be made Lord-Commander, Steel Soul.' She gestured about them. 'We have a full three warrior chambers waiting here, under your command. If that does not speak to Sigmar's intentions for you, I do not know what would.'

'We cannot know his mind,' Gardus said. 'Nor should we try. Faith is surety enough.'

'Do not quote the canticles at me, Steel Soul. I am speaking of faith. Faith that Sigmar sees in you what the rest of us do, whether some of us admit it or not.'

'And what of those against such a thing? For as you say, there are surely some.'

'They are fools. But even fools can be brought to the light, with patience and care.'

Gardus was silent for a moment. 'I have no interest in command, sister. I am content to be as I am, for so long as Sigmar wills. And then, when the war is done, I will be something else.'

Cassandora stared at him. 'Would you return to your hospice, and dress yourself in humble robes, brother? Would you have men forget the name of the Steel Soul?'

'In a heartbeat,' Gardus said. 'For if they forget, then that means they no longer need a warrior clad in sigmarite to protect them.' He looked at her as he pulled his helm on.

'And that will be a good day, indeed.'

Khela Sango, Lord-Castellant for the Bullhearts warrior chamber, sat very still as the children wove flowers into her tightly curled hair. They were the children of pilgrims, and they sang sweetly as they made her beautiful for the battle to come. The pale blossoms stood in stark contrast to her black hair and dark skin. She was at ease, one foot braced on her warding lantern, her hands in her lap. Her halberd lay nearby, close to hand.

She did not think she would need it here, though. Nordrath was as safe as it got, in the hinterlands of Azyr. There were beasts aplenty in the mountains, but few came down to the lower slopes these days.

She glanced towards the far end of the great plaza where the realmgate waited. She would need it there, though. Oh yes. She had never been to Shyish, despite her Chamber's history with that realm. In the early days of the war, more than one Chamber had split itself across many fields of battle. Such had been the case with the Bullhearts.

More pilgrims danced and sang hymns nearby, for the entertainment of mortal soldiers and Stormcasts alike. She watched and kept time with her fingers. She recognised some of the songs. The older ones, at least. Priests wandered among the mortal soldiers, doling out blessings and words of comfort, or absolution. Not all of them were Sigmarites. Even here, in Azyr, other faiths found rich soil.

She closed her eyes, listening to the music. She felt someone approach. The air smelled of lightning and burnt iron. The voice, when it spoke, was a harsh rasp.

'You should be readying yourself for war.'

Khela cracked an eye. 'I am, Ramus,' she said simply. The children had stopped, awed into stillness by the sight of the Lord-Relictor in all his dour glory. 'Are you?'

Ramus looked down at her. He made for an imposing sight, clad in his mortis armour, with its sigils of death and sanctity. His skull helm had been cracked once, and the resulting rift repaired with gold. A shield of mirrored silver, carrying a relief of a twin-tailed comet, hung from one shoulder-plate. 'I stand here, do I not?'

She nodded. 'So it seems.'

Ramus stared at her, and she met his gaze without challenge. Finally he said, 'Well?'

'The children aren't finished with their song.'

Ramus snorted. 'Send them away. We have matters to discuss.'

Khela turned to the closest of the children and smiled gently. 'Go, little ones. Carry the blessings of Sigmar's Own to your kith and kin. And thank you for the flowers, and the song.' The children scattered, laughing and singing. Her smile faded as she turned back to the Lord-Relictor. 'You frightened them.'

'Good. They should be frightened. We are not their friends, Lord-Castellant. We are their protectors.'

'So are hounds.' Khela caught up her halberd and used it to push herself to her feet. She scooped up her lantern and hooked it from her belt. 'And like them, we can be both. We must be both, else we lose sight of why we protect them.'

'Some of us do not require a constant reminder of our duty.'

'True.' She smiled humourlessly at him. 'But perhaps some of us do, whether they know it or not.'

Ramus studied her. 'Are you implying something?'

'Merely speaking my mind, brother.'

'You do that overmuch, of late.'

Khela's smile faded. 'You are not my superior, Ramus. Do not think to command me. We are equals, you and I. Only the Bullheart can tell me what to do, and you are not him.'

Ramus twitched, as if struck.

'No,' he said, after a moment. 'No, I am not.' His shoulders slumped, and for a moment Khela wanted to speak comfortingly to him. But the moment passed. Ramus would not thank her, and she had no words for him at any rate.

She caught up her helmet and settled it beneath her arm. 'Are we ready then, Shadow Soul? Has the time come at last for us to march?'

'Yes. The Corvine Gate will open soon. The Bullhearts go to Shyish. Come.'

He turned away, and she fell in step with him. 'And not just us – a full three Chambers of our Stormhost march. Truly a day of legend.'

Ramus grunted. Khela laughed. 'Would you rather we were doing it alone?'

'You know what I wish. It is not this.'

'Perhaps one will lead to the other. You must have faith, brother.'

'Do not speak to me of faith, sister. I have steeped myself in faith. I have drunk deep of it, and taken it into myself. I am full to bursting of faith, and yet...' He shook his head. 'And yet, here I stand. Here we stand.'

Khela sighed. 'Tarsus is gone, Ramus. He is dead, or beyond death. We must fight on, in his name. One of us must soon take up the mantle of Lord-Celestant in his name. The Bullhearts must become something else if they are to survive.'

'I do not wish to be anything else.'

'And I do not wish to be in charge of a sour wretch like you. But it must be one of us, or else...' She bit her lip. 'Well. You know.'

Ramus gave her a sharp look. 'No. Anyone but Osanus.'

'The Stormwolf is the only other one who's capable.'

'Capable?' he said, in disbelief. 'He can barely speak our tongue!'

'But he is popular. The others love him.'

'Because he's a bloody-minded savage who throws himself into the middle of every fight. He treats war as if it's a– a tavern brawl!'

'But he's never been Reforged. Unlike you.'

'Luck.'

'Luck or skill, he's popular. And not just with our warriors.'

Ramus threw up his hands in disgust. 'Not him. Even you're better than him.'

'Thank you, I think.'

'You know what I mean,' Ramus said, sourly. 'It does not have to be this way.'

'There is no other way it could be.'

Ramus looked at her. 'We could go to Nagash, as we did before, and make him return what he stole from us. With Sigmar's blessing...'

'You would die again, and take the rest of us with you.' Khela regretted the words, even as she said them. Ramus looked away. She caught hold of his shoulder. 'You know this to be true. We are strong, Ramus, but we are not gods. And Nagash is a god.'

'You sound as if you are admitting defeat.'

'I admit nothing. I merely state fact. Tarsus is gone. We cannot get him back. We must move forward. It is what he would want. You know this.'

Ramus was quiet. Then, 'I know only that I seemingly know nothing.'

Khela spotted Gardus and Cassandora standing nearby. The two Lord-Celestants were deep in conversation. She prodded Ramus with her elbow. 'There. We should pay our respects before joining the others.' Ramus grunted, but did not resist.

Gardus greeted them. 'Ramus, Khela, it is good to see you both.' He clasped hands with Khela, but Ramus did not proffer his own. Instead, he snorted.

'Somehow, I doubt that.' He gave a hollow laugh. 'I am only here because this venture requires a Lord-Relictor.' He pointed at Cassandora. 'Yours is seeing to matters in Hallowheart.' He turned to Gardus. 'And yours is still being Reforged after that… foolishness in Ghyran.' He leaned close. 'What were you thinking, as you pursued your Lord-Castellant into the foetid hell of Nurgle's domain, eh?'

Cassandora took a step towards the Lord-Relictor. 'Watch your tone, Ramus,' she said, grimly. 'What Gardus did, he did with the blessings of Sigmar.'

'Oh yes, I am certain he did. Gardus never acts against the will of Sigmar. Do you, Steel Soul?' Khela winced at the bitterness in the Lord-Relictor's voice. Cassandora made as if to speak, but Gardus waved her to silence.

'There are other Lord-Relictors, brother. Sigmar could have sent any of them.'

'Would that he had. As it stands, I cannot decide whether this is chastisement or mockery.' As Ramus spoke, Khela sighed in annoyance. He had never been able to hold his tongue. Many Lord-Relictors were models of restraint, taciturn and remote. But Ramus had always been immoderate when it came to his opinions – and his actions. Tarsus had encouraged such frankness, but not all Lord-Celestants were Tarsus.

'Say what you mean, brother.'

'Once before, I asked you to aid me,' Ramus said. 'You refused.

I see now that they were merely pretty words, with less meaning than the effort it took to produce them.'

Gardus looked at him. 'I meant no offence, brother.'

'Whether you meant it or not, you gave it. I asked for your help, and you refused. Then, you do the very thing you chastised me for.' Ramus looked away. 'Perhaps that simply shows your wisdom. You did not ask for permission, only forgiveness.'

'Why are you here, then?'

'I go where Sigmar commands.'

'And why do you think he commanded you here?'

'I told you.'

Gardus shook his head. 'No. The real reason.' Khela realised that the Lord-Celestant had begun to glow. Azure light slipped between the joins of his war-plate, and painted the air about him. Her breath caught in her throat. She had heard the stories, the whispers that Gardus' time on the Anvil of Apotheosis had changed him in some way, but had given them little credence.

Ramus did not turn away, despite the swelling radiance. 'I do not know.'

Gardus met his gaze. 'Then perhaps you should not make assumptions about what is permitted, and what is forgiven.' His voice resonated strangely. Khela felt it, and saw that the others did as well. It was as if, in that moment, Gardus spoke with the voice of Azyr itself.

Ramus stiffened, and his eyes blazed with anger. 'What are you saying?'

Gardus sighed, and the light dimmed. 'That is just it, brother. I said what I said, and nothing more. Sigmar denied your petition. And yet here you are. Perhaps... perhaps the time was simply not right. Perhaps this is the first step on the road to something more. Or perhaps the God-King knew what you will not admit – that there is no saving Tarsus Bullheart. And to attempt it would be to simply offer yourself up to Nagash once more. Only this time, there will be no Tarsus to aid you.' He swept a hand out. 'We are fighting a war on a thousand fronts, brother. Would you add one more?'

Ramus glared at him. 'How is it any different to what you did in Ghyran?'

Khela caught his arm. 'Enough, brother.'

Ramus tried to shake her off. 'No. I want – I demand – an answer.'

'And you know it already,' Cassandora said, softly. 'You're just too stubborn to admit it. You think because Sigmar let you have your way once, he should do so again. He already allowed you to go off on one wild hunt to satiate your need for vengeance. Who are you to demand he do so a second time, just because you failed to catch your prey?'

Khela felt Ramus stiffen. The Lord-Relictor stared at Cassandora. Lightning flashed suddenly about the bones mounted atop his reliquary staff. She quickly stepped between them. 'Ramus – *enough.*'

He looked at her. But before he could speak, there came a sound like rushes of grain, swaying in a high breeze. All four of them turned towards the realmgate, as amethyst light flared within the archway.

The sound became as the screaming of many birds, and the ancient stonework began to crack and shudder, as if gripped in a paroxysm. Wisps of pale mist rose from the stones leading beneath the arch, congealing into phantom shapes – the echoes of travellers past, which stretched and thinned, before vanishing entirely. The violet light swelled out over those gathered in the plaza, and the sound ratcheted higher, to the edges of mortal tolerance.

For the first time in centuries, the Corvine Gate opened.

CHAPTER THREE

THE JOYOUS REVELRY

*Oh, the mad cacophony, the whirling dance, the
desperate, joyous revelry...*

– Oswal of Thurn
The Mysteries of Pleasure

Bakhos, the Maiden's Son, the Leopard in Summer, Master
of the Joyous Revelry, reclined on his throne. 'Well. Isn't this
interesting?' he said, making it plain to his gathered courtiers
that it was anything but.

As the crowd muttered appreciatively, he peered down his
nose at the leonine beast kneeling before him. He knew the
albino by sight – given the rarity of such creatures, it would
be hard to forget. Most of the time, an albino was eaten by the
rest of the herd before it achieved adulthood. This one had
obviously avoided that fate and had grown into a magnificent
creature, clearly blessed in its own, simple way.

He yawned. It was already boring him with its crude attempts at civilised communication. Why did they insist on trying to talk? It wasn't as if they ever had anything important to say. He waved the brute to silence with a flapping gesture. He turned to the hooded figure who stood to the side of his throne. 'Vlad, my friend, can you translate, or something? Its voice grates on my perceptions.'

Vlad chuckled. Tall and lean, with a warrior's build beneath his robes, the sage stank of death and incense. He wore little in the way of decoration, contenting himself with only an odd, basket-hilted blade belted about his waist, and war-mask wrought in the shape of a stylised daemon's skull. 'Of course, O Radiant Prince. I shall plumb the depths, and return with a gem of purest understanding.' He descended the dais, stepping gingerly past the daemonettes clustered about the foot of Bakhos' throne, and stretched out a clawed hand to take the beast by one brawny arm. 'Come, my friend. Let us speak, as men.'

As they left the pavilion, Bakhos turned back to admiring himself in the heavy, mirrored shield to his right. The shield was held at a precise angle by one of his sword-eunuchs, so that it caught the light correctly. He reached out and idly stroked the head of a daemonette. Slim and hideously sensual, with androgynous features, it purred as the snaky locks of its hair curled teasingly about his fingers.

More eunuchs stood about his throne, fanning him with great feathers plucked from the gigantic carrion birds that inhabited the heights of Shyish. The ornate armour the eunuchs wore served less to protect them than it did to emphasise the comeliness of their forms. Each wore a mirrored helm, so that when Bakhos addressed them he might observe his own features as he did so.

Despite their aesthetic appeal, the eunuchs weren't only for show. They had been chosen for skill as well as beauty, and each had been trained by the deadliest weapon-masters in Bakhos' army. He even allowed some of them to bear scars, for a bit of novelty.

He stroked his chiselled jaw as he studied his reflection. He cut a fine figure. His war-plate, forged by the finest daemon-smiths of the Bale-Furnace, was the colour of midnight's last moment, edged in amethyst. Purple whorls and knotwork tattoos decorated his bare flesh where it was not hidden beneath loose robes of leopard-skin.

The Shyishan leopards were great, black things, the size of a man, and faintly spotted with grey. Their fur shimmered in the light. He thought the effect rather marvellous in its subtlety. A necklace of talons and teeth, from the same leopards, hung about his neck, and the scars they'd left him marked his arms and hands. A circlet of dark ivy crowned his head, holding back his unbraided hair.

His helm sat beside him, on a cushioned stand. It was reminiscent of those worn by the phalanxes of his native Semele, made to cover the wearer's head and neck, save for a t-shaped slit for eyes and mouth. A stiff crest of quill-like hairs, plucked from the heads of daemons, curved over it. The quills twitched and writhed, still possessed of the rudiments of awareness. He stroked them gently, causing their colours to change.

'Will you know me, when you see me again?' he murmured, idly. 'Am I as I was, when last we spoke? It is hard to remember, after so long.' He pushed the thought, and all it brought with it, aside. He was as he had always been, and would be. The Absent God had blessed him that much, at least.

He let his attentions wander across those gathered in the pavilion. Most were mere hangers-on – mad sages and hedge-witches, dissolute nobles from fallen kingdoms, and ambitious warriors seeking the favours of the Leopard in Summer.

They were a braying, pestiferous lot – good only for the mild diversion they occasionally provided. The stink of spilled wine filled the tent as they cavorted wildly or schemed their little schemes. A hurricane of joyous revelry, of which he was the eternal eye.

Once, such a thing might have pleased him. Now, it simply bored him. Indulgence without effort lacked a certain something. He looked up at one of the eunuchs. 'What point gorging on cooked flesh if one has not slain the beast themself?' he asked, lazily. 'Is any wine as sweet as that plundered by one's own hand?'

The eunuch did not reply, and, indeed, had no tongue with which to do so. Bakhos sighed. Ordinarily, he put such philosophical conundrums to Vlad. The masked sage was a cunning debater, and quick-witted. 'The answer is no, obviously,' he went on. 'Only a child thinks effort an enemy. All others understand that the joy of a thing is derived from the difficulty of its taking. But none understand this so well as the Three-Eyed King.'

At these words, the closest of his sycophants nodded, as if in agreement. Annoyed by their toadying, he pushed himself to his feet and descended his dais. The daemonettes who crouched on the steps scrambled from his path, tittering shrilly and clacking their crustacean-like claws in agitation.

'That is why I am proud to serve him as marcher lord here, waiting for the day that the dead of Caddow stir,' Bakhos continued, loudly. 'And have I not served faithfully and well? Have I not scattered the bones of deathrattle kings, and cast back geist-hordes?' He snatched up a jug of wine from a passing slave and unstopped it with his teeth. Spitting the cork aside, he lifted the jug. 'To Archaon – long may he reign!'

Drunken cheers filled the pavilion as hooves, claws and boots stamped on the ground. Bakhos looked around before taking a long drink. A Shyishan vintage, it was exceedingly bitter, suiting his current mood. He lowered the jug, wine dripping from his mouth and chin. Once, he had led the iron phalanxes of Semele into the fires of war. Now, he led monsters in an endless revel. He could not say which was more tiresome.

'Archaon?' someone slurred. 'Archaon is nothing.'

Music stopped and conversations ceased throughout the pavilion. Bakhos turned, eyebrow raised. A figure heaved itself to its feet, spilling a number of slaves to the ground. The warrior was a bloated hulk, with puffy, pale flesh spilling out between plates of black iron. His head was flat and lopsided, with rolls of flesh growing over one eye, and part of his mouth. Strands of lank, colourless hair clung stubbornly to his misshapen scalp. His hands were akin to flippers, and the loose flab of his neck and torso had been pierced in places by various hooks, studs and chains that acted to bind it.

Bakhos took another swallow from the jug. 'Is that your considered opinion, Magrise?' he asked, his tone mild. Magrise stank of ambition and stupidity. His appetite for indulgence was legendary, even among followers of the Absent God. He was a glutton among gluttons, a hedonist among hedonists. He was also as strong as an ogor, and enjoyed pain.

Magrise swayed on his feet, a rivulet of drool running down his distended chin. He snatched up his own jug, and took a long swallow. Most of it spilled down his doughy chest, but he didn't seem to mind. He swiped the back of his hand across his mouth and grinned. 'My... opinion, is that Archaon is a weakling. And a coward.'

Bakhos paused, as if considering this. There were more than a few heads nodding. It had been decades since either the Three-Eyed King or his representatives had last walked among them, and many, like Magrise, had short memories. To them, silence was as good as surrender. Victory was easiest to claim when the enemy barely noticed your existence.

'And what must you think of me, then?' Bakhos asked.

Magrise tossed aside his jug and shoved past several other warriors and slaves, reaching for a massive, two-handed stone maul lying on the ground. He wrenched the weapon up and extended it. 'I think... you are weak, too. And the time has come for a new master of this place.'

Bakhos emptied his jug and then upended it, teasing out the last few drops. Then, almost lazily, he sprang towards Magrise. The hulking warrior grunted in surprise, and swung his maul. Bakhos slid beneath the wild blow, and smashed the jug into Magrise's face. The hard clay cracked. He struck again, until the jug was nothing but jagged shards.

His grin widened. With each blow, he could feel his ennui fading. He'd been hoping the toast would prod someone into action. When he'd bent the knee to Archaon, it had been more out of boredom than any belief in the Three-Eyed King's superiority. But it provided him with an almost never-ending stream of challengers-by-proxy.

Magrise staggered, blood welling from the torn flesh of his face. His maul fell from his hands and he reeled, clutching at his head. Bakhos paced after him, smiling. Magrise tried to fend him off with a bloody paw, but he sidestepped the blow and drove a fist full of clay shards into Magrise's exposed chest. He twisted the shards, and ichor welled. Magrise tried to grapple with him, but Bakhos avoided his grasp and slashed a shard of clay across the warrior's exposed jugular.

Magrise sank to his knees, both paws clutched to his neck. His eyes bulged as blood spurted between his thick fingers. Bakhos circled the dying warrior, picking shards out of his palm. 'Is that all the fight there is in you, Magrise? Is this where your part in my story ends? How disappointing. I had hoped you might prove more interesting.' He flicked away a piece of clay as Magrise toppled onto his face with a strangled groan. 'But that is sadly the way of it, I have found. Another whose ambition far outstripped his ability.'

He looked around, smiling widely. 'Ah well. Enough of that. Troubadours – music! Slaves – wine!' He held out a bloody hand to the daemonettes clustered about his dais. 'Come, my sisters, dance for us.'

The daemonettes rose with languid grace and swayed towards him, stepping daintily through the spreading blood. The music started up again, and they started to whirl about him, unhurriedly. As they danced, the air turned thick and cloying, and more than one of his courtiers had a glazed looked in their eyes. Bakhos smiled and tickled one of the daemonettes under the chin. 'Sing for me, my sweet,' he purred. 'Sing to me of my grand victories, and glorious defeats. Sing of my generosity, my hubris and my love of slaughter. Sing the story of me, so that I might know peace in this harsh realm, for just a moment.'

The daemonette giggled coquettishly and smiled, revealing a mouthful of fangs. With infinite slowness, she began to sing. There was no joy in the sound, only sorrow, but even so, he recognised the song, and it brought back memories of sun-dappled glades and the feel of lyre strings beneath his calloused fingers. The daemonette's androgynous features changed, becoming those of something – someone – else. Someone as familiar as the song itself. Anger filled him. 'Stop. Be silent.'

'Is the song not to your liking?' the daemonette asked, its face half one thing and half another – a parody of the features burned into the deepest wells of his memory. Its voice, too, was almost hers. Just enough to elicit a shudder of phantom pain.

'That song is not for you,' he said, softly.

The daemonette laughed. 'All songs belong to us. As you belong to us, Hero of Thyrsus. As you have always belonged to us, though you hide behind the Empty Throne, and seek to curry favour with the Three-Eyed King.'

Bakhos caught the daemonette by the throat. 'Who are you, to speak to me as if we are equals?'

'Who is this, who asks? Is this Bakhos, Leopard of Semele, who came to the Realm of Death to search for the soul of his lost love?' The daemonette cackled, as Bakhos lifted it easily from its feet. 'Or is this Bakhos, cur of Archaon, who chained himself to the dullest of tasks all too willingly, in return for an empty promise?' It leered down at him, its claws clutching his forearm. 'Who demands it, O Maiden's Son?'

'The one who clutches your throat.' Bakhos' grip tightened. 'For they are the same man. I am him who came searching, and he who waits. That is the story of me, beginning and end. What are you, save a discordant note in my song?'

The daemonette's black eyes bulged as Bakhos lifted it higher. He felt its unnatural flesh crumbling in his grip, and smiled at the sudden consternation on its face. 'I am no puling prince-ling, content to endure the abuses of a lesser spirit. The Absent God may have fashioned you in his image, but you are not sacrosanct. None of you.' He cast a warning glare at the other daemonettes, and they drew back, hissing and snarling.

He flung the daemonette to the ground. 'Never imagine your-self anything more than what you are. A part of my story. A note in my song. Without me, you are as nothing.'

The daemonette glared up at him, and for a moment, he thought it might attack. Daemons were so terribly sensitive to even the mildest of insults. He smiled and spread his arms. 'Come, my sweet. But let me embrace you, and all will be forgiven.'

The creature rose and daintily stepped into his arms, defiance etched on its inhuman face. It stiffened as he embraced it, and then softened, crooning gently. He bit into its throat a moment later, before it could pull away. With an almost gentle tug he opened its veins, and it thrashed in paroxysms of agony. He held it, gulping at the hot, heady bouquet that spurted from its pallid neck. It burned through him like sweet fire and he kissed the top of its head with stained lips.

'Thank you,' he said.

Satisfied, he let the daemonette's dissolving form tumble to the ground. The remaining daemons quickly pounced on it, shrieking and fighting for a taste. He swiped the back of his hand across his mouth. 'Exquisite,' he murmured. He smiled as Vlad re-entered the pavilion. He held out gory fingers to the sage. 'Have you ever tasted daemon ichor, my friend? It is a rare treat.'

'I fear my palate is not so developed as yours, my lord. Such delicacies… disagree with me.' Vlad's tone was one of restrained distaste. The sage fancied himself an epicurean.

'Your loss.' Bakhos went back to his throne with a sigh, sucking ichor from his fingers. 'Well? What did the beast have to say? Something interesting, I hope.'

'Good news indeed, my lord. It appears we are under attack.'

Bakhos smiled.

Beneath his mask, Mannfred von Carstein mirrored Bakhos' expression. There was some genuine satisfaction to be had at the recent turn of events, which made it easier. His eyes fell on the body of Magrise, still lying where it had fallen. 'Ah. I see Magrise finally made his move. And I missed it. How disappointing.'

'Yes, it was.' Bakhos leaned forward in his seat. 'What do you mean we're under attack? This isn't another of your rhetorical flourishes, is it, Vlad? The last time you said "attack" what you meant was "a herd of deadwalkers has wandered into camp".

Mannfred grimaced slightly as Bakhos called him by his assumed name. He'd thought it clever, for some reason, when he'd first drawn it up out of the deep wells of his memory. But the more he heard it, the less clever it seemed. He'd come to hate it, though he couldn't say why. It mattered little. While he was here, among this conglomeration of monsters and madmen, he had little choice but to answer to it. 'No, my lord. I speak only honest truth. The beast-tribes are under assault even as we speak.'

'Excellent!' Bakhos leapt to his feet. Mannfred stepped back as he bounded back down the dais, as eager as a child on its Naming Day. 'Who dares come against us? The dead?' Bakhos shook his head, even as he asked the question. 'Anyone but the dead. I need living blood to spill. Even orruks will do.'

'Neither dead flesh nor green, my lord.' As Mannfred spoke, he caught the daemonettes watching him closely. Despite the protective glamour he'd woven about himself, he suspected that the creatures knew that he was not what he seemed. Luckily, they didn't seem to care one way or another. The Hounds of Slaanesh only bestirred themselves when necessary. They'd seen enough of him to know he'd provide them little sport for altogether too much effort.

Bakhos' expression brightened. 'Is it them? Have the hounds of Azyr come at last?' A murmur swept through the pavilion, and not a few looks of dismay. The latter amused Mannfred immensely. Many of Bakhos' warriors were far too certain of themselves, boasting constantly of their victories over beasts and hungry corpses, and puffing out their chests. Now, at the prospect of facing true opponents, they seemed to deflate.

But not all of them. Warriors heaved themselves to their feet with drunken awkwardness. Many brandished weapons and shouted questions. Bakhos silenced them with a sharp gesture. 'Tell me, man – who offers up their heart and marrow to the Maiden's Son?'

'Come, my lord, and see for yourself.' Mannfred turned and swept out of the pavilion, Bakhos following in his wake. He could feel Bakhos' interest reaching fever pitch. After all this time, he knew how to play on the Chaos lord's constant struggle with ennui.

It had been weeks since he'd inveigled his way into Bakhos' inner circle. He was beginning to tire of playing the dutiful sycophant, especially to a lunatic like the Maiden's Son. Bakhos was no simple brute, and he was cunning in his own way. That made him dangerous. Mannfred had little taste for danger, save when it pleased him to be otherwise. Something to liven the tedium of eternity.

He had played such roles before, of course. He was known by a hundred names in a hundred different kingdoms. While his fellow Mortarch, Neferata, might content herself with playing spymaster, Mannfred had always found playing the spy more entertaining.

To be in among the enemy, a dagger's stroke from victory at any given moment, that was true power. Neferata contented herself with murder from afar, at the hands of willing – and unwilling – tools. But Mannfred needed to see his enemies die. He needed to hear the consternation in their voices as they realised that it had been him all along, and to see the light leave their eyes as the blade went in.

He looked forward to that moment with Bakhos. Not because he bore the Maiden's Son any particular grievance, but simply because it would signal an end to the obstacles before him.

He glanced north, towards the ruins. He'd come far to find them again.

At its height, Caddow had been ruled by a fractious council of hereditary trading dynasties with a penchant for ritual mummification. There were armies of preserved corpses, arranged in artful slumber, in the great necropoli that stretched beneath the city.

Entire generations of the city's inhabitants, from those ancient nomads who'd first crossed the wastes seeking sanctuary to the knightly lords who'd conquered the Sea of Dust, slept the sleep of death and waited for the call of one who knew the ancient songs.

He'd come seeking an army, and he'd found one. Unfortunately, it wasn't the one he'd been looking for. Given recent events, it wasn't surprising that Archaon had decided to set a watch on one of the few remaining realmgates linking Shyish and Azyr. The Three-Eyed King feared nothing so much as a renewed alliance between the realms of Death and Heaven.

Finding Bakhos lurking on the southern edge of the city had forced Mannfred to adapt his plan. Subtlety was called for, else his new army would simply become bogged down in battle, before the time was right.

So he'd played the wandering sage, inveigling his way into Bakhos' good graces, waiting for the right time to seek out what he'd come for. For all his sophistication, Bakhos had a barbarian's fondness for sages, seers and witches. A few conjurer's tricks, a bit of haruspicy, and he'd won the warlord's trust. As Bakhos' chief advisor, he was in a position to take advantage of any opportunity to enter the city, and seek the entrance to the catacombs.

In the meantime, he'd played gentle games of manipulation to keep himself entertained. He'd stoked the fires of resentment among Bakhos' followers, and set the more gullible ones against each other. But now, thanks to this new turn of events, he might finally have the chance to achieve what he'd set out to do in the first place.

Outside, a crowd of the lost and the damned was already gathering. Ghosteater stood off to the side, long arms folded, watching as his followers restrained their prisoner.

The Stormcast tried to stand at the sight of Mannfred, but the beastkin shoved him to his knees. One of the brutes had torn his helm from him, exposing bloody features. Human, like all Stormcasts, but magnified somehow, as if a shard of the divine nestled within them.

'Do as you will,' he rumbled. 'I shall not beg.'

'Never say never,' Mannfred murmured, as Bakhos circled the captive.

'What is this?' he demanded. 'Just one?'

'More. In city,' Ghosteater growled. Bakhos glanced at him, and then back at the Stormcast. Mannfred stepped forward.

'From what our friend here has said, I gather they've come to open the realmgate.'

Bakhos paused. 'There's a realmgate here?'

Mannfred hid a sigh. 'Yes, my lord. At the heart of the city.'

'Sealed, I presume.'

'Yes, my lord, hence their need to open it.'

Bakhos nodded thoughtfully. Mannfred realised the questions were for the benefit of their audience. Bakhos was making sure everyone knew the importance of the ruins, and by extension, himself. After all, a realmgate was no small prize. Only the most loyal or the most powerful of Archaon's warlords were allowed anywhere near one. Even one that had been sealed for centuries.

'The beastkin caught this one?' Bakhos asked, doubtfully.

Mannfred gestured to the albino. 'Ghosteater is a singularly capable creature.' Which was true, as far as it went. Ghosteater was blessed by the Dark Gods in some strange way. It had more than its share of cunning to temper its obvious ambition.

'Is that its name?' Bakhos sank to his haunches before the Stormcast. 'How amusing. Do you have a name? Among my peers it is often said that you do not have names. That you are nothing more than constructs of metal and starlight.' He reached out and dabbed a bit of blood from the captive's face. He licked it from his finger and grimaced. 'You taste real enough to me. A most mundane vintage, in fact.'

The Stormcast spat in his face. Bakhos flushed and struck him, hard enough to send the silver-armoured warrior sprawling. Mannfred hid a wince. He needed the prisoner in one piece in order to interrogate him. Necromancy was little use when the dead evaporated like morning dew before you could so much as pose a question. But he said nothing. It was best to allow Bakhos to vent his anger.

As the beating continued, Mannfred turned away to study the ruins, just visible over the tops of the pavilions. Caddow rose from the Sea of Dust like a scattering of tombstones. Once, it had been a vibrant place, full of noise and colour. A city of merchants and adventurers, of sages and scholars. He'd visited Caddow often, before the end.

With the others. With Megara and Vitalian and… Tarsem.

Smell that? Dust-rat, cooked with Aqshian spices. A delicacy. Megara's voice – a harsh crow-rasp. He could hear her now, as clearly as he had then. The warrior-seer had been a hatchet-faced woman, clad in the dark robes and crimson armour of her order. Acerbic and quick-witted, she had matched him, insult for insult.

Mannfred closed his eyes. 'Only here,' he murmured, smiling slightly. 'Only to you.'

Rat's not so bad, but I prefer peryton. That was Vitalian. Bluff, bellowing Vitalian, in his amethyst war-plate, his beard dyed violet and black, and his eye of shadeglass. *How long has it been since we've eaten peryton, eh, Mannfred?*

'Too long.' Mannfred twitched his head, trying to banish the memories. One of the downsides of immortality was a preponderance of memories, like flocking crows. They gathered in the branches of the mind, croaking incessantly, demanding attention. Sometimes, he wished he could sear his mind free of all such distractions. At other times, they were all that made existence bearable.

He wasn't alone in this. The other Mortarchs had their own distractions. Neferata built her petty kingdoms, and played at being an empress. Arkhan busied himself cleaning up after their master, trying to repair all that Nagash inevitably broke in his madness.

Like clutching at sand, that.

Mannfred chuckled. 'Careful, Tarsem,' he murmured. 'You never know when he might be listening.' His smile faded as he thought of Tarsem and the others. The Ninety-Nine Companions of Helstone. There had never been that many of them, to his knowledge. A few dozen at most. But heroes all.

Heroes…

Behind him, the Stormcast groaned. Mannfred turned in time to see Bakhos kick the fallen warrior in the stomach. They'd torn much of his armour from him, leaving him exposed. Blows rained down, kicks and punches from others following their lord's example. They were eager to assuage their fear, to prove that the enemy was mortal after all. Mannfred shook his head. Time to end it.

'My lord, if you beat him to death, we will not be able to question him.'

Bakhos paused, his face dark with exertion. The Maiden's Son panted like a beast and shook himself. One of his few saving graces was that he could control himself, when necessary.

'And what question would you ask him, Vlad?'

Mannfred stooped and retrieved the Stormcast's helmet. 'For starters, I might ask how many of them there are. Are we facing a patrol – or an army?'

The Stormcast gave a harsh, wheezing laugh. He rolled over, bloody lips split in a smile. 'We are as many as the stars in the sky. We are the storm, come to wash the filth of you away.'

Mannfred sank to his haunches before the captive. 'Very poetic. But hardly helpful, for the purposes of gauging raw numbers. How many in your Chamber?'

The Stormcast's eyes widened slightly. Mannfred chuckled. 'Yes, I know your ways. How many? A hundred? Less?'

'More,' the Stormcast said. Then, with a grin, 'I do not know how many in the other Chambers, though. You'll have to see for yourself.'

Mannfred frowned. 'More than one Chamber?'

'And more besides,' the Stormcast said, holding his gaze. 'This city – this underworld – has been claimed. You would do best to retreat.'

Before Mannfred could reply, there was a sound like many birds screaming all at once and impossibly loud. He turned, staring towards the city. A beam of azure light, painful in its intensity, blazed upwards from the heart of the ruins, piercing the sky like a blade. A great cry went up from Bakhos' followers as beastkin and slaves cowered back.

'What is that?' Bakhos snarled.

Mannfred stood, mouth suddenly dry. The air pulsed with silent thunder. His flesh prickled, and he stepped back from the prisoner. 'I believe that the realmgate has opened, my lord. And there is very likely soon to be an army on our door-step.'

'But there is already an army in the ruins, if the beasts are to be believed.'

'Then it has just received reinforcements.' Mannfred turned. 'We must march on Caddow at once, my lord. There might still be time to stymie them.' Or at least reach the catacombs before the Stormcasts found them.

Bakhos shook his head. 'What's the point?' He turned away from the light, dragging the ivy crown from his head as he did so. 'I have failed.'

'Failed?' Mannfred restrained a snarl. Bakhos was moody – joy turned swiftly to sadness or rage in him, with little warning. Moments ago, he had been eager for a fight. But now he seemed defeated, before he'd even raised his sword.

'Failed, Vlad. Look – see for yourself!' Bakhos' voice took on a petulant sheen. 'Archaon sent me to prevent this from happening. But I have failed.' He tore at his robes with bloody hands, face mournful. 'Failed!'

Others, ever-attentive to their lord's moods, picked up the cry. Mannfred cast a wary glance at the crowd of warriors. He'd seen other armies shiver apart in similar circumstances. Bakhos was as much the heart of this force as he was its head. If he faltered, others like the unlamented Magrise would seize the opportunity to depose him, even with the enemy breathing down their neck. At any other time, Mannfred might have encouraged such in-fighting. Indeed, it was his favoured method of dispatching warbands such as this.

But he needed them in one piece, for the moment. And he needed them aimed at Caddow. If the Stormcasts had come in force, all that he'd worked for these past months would be for nothing. He had to act swiftly.

Mannfred stepped to Bakhos' side, formulating and discarding a dozen strategies in moments. There was only one that would snap Bakhos out of his sulk, and quickly. 'She might be among them, my lord,' he whispered. Bakhos stiffened. He turned, eyes narrowed. His hands flexed, and Mannfred was reminded of a leopard unsheathing its claws as it readied itself to spring.

'Speak plainly, Vlad. And swiftly.'

'There are but two places the one you seek might have gone. If she is not among the teeming dead, then perhaps she is with the stars?' Mannfred gestured to the dark skies above. 'For Nagash is not alone in taking what does not belong to him.'

Bakhos' eyes widened. 'What do you mean?'

'I am, as you know, something of a scholar, my lord. And it has been my experience that these Azyrites are, in truth, anything but.' He held up the Stormcast's helm. 'Sigmar hides their faces behind his own, but he cannot hide the truth. They are the dead, remade. The dead of a thousand kingdoms, given new life. And *she* may well be among them.'

Bakhos sagged slightly. 'Do you think – is that why I cannot find her here, then?' he asked, softly. He sounded almost a child, in that moment, Mannfred thought. Nothing more than a youth, trapped on an eternal precipice between love and madness.

Right where the Dark Gods – and Mannfred – wanted him.

'A possibility, my lord,' he said, sidling closer. 'Merely a possibility. But one to explore, perhaps, while the opportunity ripens?'

Bakhos nodded absently. 'Will she recognise me, do you think?'

'It is not for me to say, my lord. But if any man can break the spell which binds such a soul, it is you. Are you not the

Maiden's Son, the Walker-On-Shields, the Lord of the Lash?' Mannfred set a friendly hand on Bakhos' shoulder. 'Are you not the most faithful captain of an Absent God? Did not Archaon himself acclaim you Marcher Lord of the South?'

Bakhos looked at Mannfred's hand, and then at him. 'Aye.' He smiled, and there was nothing human in that smile. 'He did and I am.' He brushed Mannfred's hand off and straightened. 'Very well. Perhaps this will not be as tedious as I feared, after all.' He looked around at his gathered warriors. 'Time for a grand gesture, do you think?'

'It would not be inappropriate, I feel.'

'As wise as ever, Vlad.' Bakhos stepped forward, quieting the murmurs of the crowd with a gesture. 'Well, my friends. It seems our revelries are at an end, does it not? Silver legions pour forth to silence our songs and cast down the banners of joy. A sad end, don't you think?' He turned, arms spread. 'All our days, but dust. Will that be the story of us? Will that be the tale told in the feasting halls of the Varanspire?'

'No,' a warrior groaned, rending his silken robes with brass claws.

'No,' another hissed, through the grille of her cage-like helm.

'No!' Bakhos said. 'I don't know about you, but I have not come this far to see my story end so. I did not brave the horrors of the Varanspire to retreat without at least taking the measure of our foe.' He turned, his gaze feverish. 'I am the Leopard in Summer, who led the iron phalanxes of Semele into glorious battle. Sword-eunuch!'

At his cry, one of his mirror-helmed attendants hurried out of the pavilion, carrying a long blade in a sheath of calf-skin and gold. The eunuch knelt, hilt raised. Bakhos set his foot on the eunuch's shoulder and drew the blade with a flourish.

Forged from fyresteel, it gleamed with a crimson tinge. It had been a gift from Archaon himself, or so Bakhos claimed. It was possible that he did so simply because he'd forgotten where he'd acquired it, and calling it a gift made for a better story.

Bakhos struck his chest-plate with a fist. 'I bought a kingdom's freedom in blood, and then traded it for my own. I am the Maiden's Son, firstborn and last, and I have grown weary of drowning my boredom in wine!'

He spun, sword raised in both hands. The blow caught the prisoner on the back of the neck, severing his head in a single, powerful, motion. Lightning roared outwards and upwards as the Stormcast disintegrated, driving the crowd back.

Mannfred flung up a hand to shield his eyes, and glimpsed Bakhos standing unbowed, despite the lightning snarling about him. As the glare faded, Bakhos traced a finger along the smoking edge of his blade and flicked aside a mote of blood. Slowly, he extended the sword towards the ruins.

'To arms, my friends. We have guests to welcome.'

CHAPTER FOUR

TAKE AND HOLD

To effectively take ground from the enemy is an art few master. When done badly, the attempt alone can lead to defeat. But when done well, it inevitably spells victory.

– Arcudi Fein
A Soldier's Life

For a time, all was light.

It was beautiful and painful, all at once, like the radiance of a star stretched to its breaking point between the hands of a god. To Enyo, it was almost blinding in its intensity as she propelled herself on wings of lightning through the gap between realms. Beside her, the shimmering form of Periphas, her star-eagle, kept pace.

Around them, the corridor of light stretched and contracted. She heard a roar of impossible immensity as the distance between realms was folded into a space no bigger than the blink of an eye. She felt the grip of Azyr recede as a new, sour gravity took hold of her and Periphas, and drew them inexorably downwards, into the shadowed depths of infinity. Into Shyish, and the underworlds of the dead.

Sapphire bled into amethyst as the Knight-Venator burst from the shimmering surface of the Corvine Gate alongside the star-eagle, her silver war-plate reflecting all the colours of the universe. Even as the colours bled away, her hand dipped into her quiver of arrows.

Below her, the ziggurat was covered in a heaving carpet of beast-flesh. The malformed creatures scrambled up the steps on every side of the structure, hurling themselves towards the apex with desperate haste. Pinpricks of flame met those who reached the top, and the silver shapes of Vanguard-Palladors rampaged along the lower tiers.

It was an eerily familiar scene, one she had witnessed far too often of late, for her liking.

'Wherever we go, there we are, eh, Periphas?' she murmured. The star-eagle screeched and swooped around her in a tight circle. 'At least we will never want for work.'

The beasts had to be broken utterly and driven back before they overwhelmed the ziggurat's defenders. In a single, smooth motion, she selected an arrow and loosed it, even as her wings snapped out, carrying her upwards. Somewhere below, a beastman roared as her arrow struck home. She loosed two more crackling arrows as she climbed towards the dark stars above.

The city spread out below her like a series of immense rings. Each ring was a wall, or the remains of one, linked by hundreds of streets and alleys of varying size and shape. Clinging to the outer rings were the dust-wharfs, and the sprawling remains of the ancient, stone docklands. Hundreds of towering eyries loomed over the ruins, linked by high stone causeways, few of which were intact.

The eyries had once belonged to the ruling families of Caddow. They were as much ancestral homesteads as they were fortified bastions. Entire generations had lived and died in those enormous, swooping stone towers, or so she'd been told. Now, they were the haunt of beastkin and worse things. It would be a hard, bloody job, cleansing them. Thankfully, not hers. Being a Knight-Venator came with some benefits of rank, few though they were.

Her gaze was drawn back to the realmgate as the rest of the Steel Souls' Angelos Conclave erupted from it in a flurry of silver and lightning. Winged Prosecutors spread out across the city in blazing arcs, moving with singular purpose. Their orders were to take and isolate the plazas encompassing the ziggurat with all due speed and efficiency. That meant collapsing streets and passageways, cutting off the enemy's routes of advance and retreat.

Enyo and her huntsmen had a different task, and a more enjoyable one by far. Periphas screeched and she looked down to see a trio of silver shapes rising towards her.

'Tegrus,' she called out, in greeting. 'Mathias, Azar. I trust you are ready?'

'Always, Lady Enyo,' Tegrus of the Sainted Eye said. Besides the hammers he held in either hand, the Prosecutor-Prime had a heavy warblade sheathed across his back, its hilt rising over his shoulder between his wings, and a boltstorm pistol holstered on his hip. Mathias and Azar, for their part, were carrying shields as well as stormcall javelins.

'Yes, let us be about it,' Azar growled, scraping the blade of his javelin across the face of his shield. Mathias nodded, silent as always. All three had suffered from their Reforgings, but Mathias most of all. Whether he'd lost his voice entirely, or simply forgotten how to speak, Enyo did not know. But he was still one of them, and still served, if in silence.

Enyo nodded and looked at Periphas. 'Find us our quarry, my friend,' she said. 'Find us their hearts.' Periphas shrieked and shot off, trailing motes of starlight. She dived after the bird, Tegrus and the others following close behind.

The Knight-Venator had no doubt the star-eagle would soon find what they sought. Periphas was well experienced in this sort of hunt. While the rest of the conclave ensured that the foe's path was blocked or rerouted, she, Tegrus and the others sought out the enemy commanders, killing them from afar. A headless enemy routed soonest.

Sometimes the hunt was relatively easy. Other times, the enemy proved elusive. But Periphas found them all, in the end. From that point they were marked, harried and finally brought low by blade and arrow.

It was not an especially honourable practice, but it was effective. Without their chieftains and shamans to guide them, the beastkin would lose heart and quickly retreat. Battles were best won quickly, especially in the lands of Death. More than carrion birds haunted the sandy wastes of this realm, and the scent of war on the wind brought all sorts of scavengers to call.

Following Periphas, the hunters swooped away from the ziggurat and out across the streets of Caddow. Beastkin flowed towards the structure, their shrieks and howls filling every street and alleyway. The light and noise of the realmgate seemed to be drawing them out of hiding, the way a candle flame might draw moths.

Enyo fought the temptation to simply find a perch and deal death until her quiver was empty. As satisfying as such an act might be, it would have no more effect than throwing stones into the sea. The beastkin were not a united force, driven by a single will or strategy. This was simply a stampede. This was their territory, and they would fight for it as savagely as any animal.

'They're everywhere,' Tegrus called out. 'It's like someone kicked over an anthill.'

'Ants would be preferable,' Azar said, as he swooped past her, Mathias trailing in his wake. Below them, beastkin cater-wauled as they caught sight of the winged shapes hurtling overhead. Spears and arrows arced harmlessly through the air, unable to reach them.

Up ahead, the bright blur that was Periphas banked sharply. Enyo followed, the foul-smelling air whistling past her. A wide thoroughfare opened up before her, lined with towering statues. She sped past the weathered faces of old gods and forgotten kings, her wings trailing light.

The thoroughfare led back into one of the massive plazas that encircled the ziggurat. Whatever it had once been, it was a stag-ing ground now. A host of beastkin milled across it, eddying forth to battle in gusts and spurts, when the mood took them. Thousands of primitive banners rose over the seething horde. Some were made from wood, others from bone or less recog-nisable substances, and ragged flags of flayed hide or woven hair rippled in the wind.

Obelisks, carved from fallen pillars and broken statues, had been raised about the plaza. The beastkin were thickest around these, dancing and wailing. Drums thumped and hunt-ing horns groaned as balefires raged in makeshift pits dug by paws and hooves. Gors marked their flesh with soot and ash in preparation for the battle to come. Others brayed challenges to rivals, and spilled each other's blood across the stones in ritual combat.

Enyo's gut churned as she saw what hung from the obelisks, or dangled from the intermittent groves of rough stakes that jutted from the broken cobbles. Those sad remnants might have been human, once. Now they were desiccated reminders of what awaited any who fell into the hands of such creatures. Not that she needed such.

The sounds – the smell – it was all too familiar. The ashes of memory stirred, and she heard again the click of clockwork wings and felt the heat of that final, great conflagration that had claimed Cypria. She shook her head, clearing it of the scattered shards of remembrance.

'Never again,' she murmured.

Periphas screeched. The star-eagle had found their prey. With a snap of crackling wings, she banked. She spotted their quarry immediately – one of the beastmen's foul shamans, perched atop a fallen pillar.

The shaman was a twisted, hunched shape, clad in filthy robes, and clutching a staff of gnarled wood. Totems of bone and hair hung from its limbs and staff, and its goatish head was hidden by a hood, but the air about it pulsed with an ugly iridescence. The creature was snarling and gesturing with its staff as beasts cavorted about it in increasing agitation. More of the creatures were being drawn to the shaman's display, and soon, Enyo knew, they would frenzy forth at the creature's command.

'There,' she said, gesturing with her bow. 'We take it. Azar.'

Azar dived down, javelin at the ready, and skimmed low over the street. Bestial heads turned as the creatures caught sight of the Prosecutor. The shaman turned to follow Azar as he hurtled past, and began to gesticulate crudely, bellowing a guttural chant as it did so. The air took on an oily sheen as semi-visible shapes began to congeal about its hunched form.

'Lady Enyo,' Tegrus began.

'I see,' she said, calmly. She chose an arrow, sighted down the length of the shaft and loosed, all in a single breath. The arrow struck home with a snap of light, and the shaman threw back its equine head in a shrill shriek of pain. The half-conjured shapes of the daemons blew apart like a morning mist, leaving behind only frustrated wails. 'Tegrus – go!'

'Gladly,' Tegrus snarled. He shot forward, hammers whirling from his hands like Ironweld mortar rounds. The street bucked, and beastkin were hurled from their feet. Mathias followed suit, hurling his javelin with brutal speed. Azar joined him, and the shaman's followers died squealing as the Prosecutors swept past.

Atop the pillar, the shaman tore Enyo's arrow from its neck and flung it aside. Arcane energies crackled about its malformed paws as it tried to track its attackers. Tegrus was on it before it could find them. The Prosecutor-Prime crashed down behind the beastman, drawing his warblade as he did so. The shaman spun, eyes widening. Tegrus' blade hummed out, and the shaman's head fell away in an eruption of blood.

Howling beastkin raced towards him, eager for vengeance. Tegrus gave a snap of his wings and hurtled to meet them, blade held low. The tip of the sword drew sparks from the stones of the street as he slashed it out in a wide arc. Hairy limbs tumbled through the air as Tegrus rampaged among the creatures, a murderous blur of silver. His voice rose in a hymn of praise as he dedicated his kills to Sigmar.

Azar and Mathias joined him, and beasts died in droves. The creatures broke and scattered, causing undulations of panic and confusion to stretch through the plaza. Enyo loosed arrows with rapidity, filling the air with the hum of death. At her bark of command, Tegrus' hammers spun out, striking obelisks and shattering the street.

As the smoke and dust swelled up, filling the plaza, Enyo

whistled sharply, calling her huntsmen back. In moments, all three were rising towards her, their war-plate drenched in gore. Enyo felt something in her shudder at the sight. It was not the violence, but rather the joy with which it had been enacted. For a moment there had seemed little difference between Tegrus and the beasts they fought.

But the moment passed, and somewhere distant, she heard Periphas shriek again. She rose upwards, wings burning the air, her hand falling to her quiver.

'Come, brothers. Let us continue the hunt.'

As Gardus stepped from Azyr to Shyish, he paused to take his bearings. A great clamouring enveloped him – the crash of steel, the cries of the dying. The hateful threnody of war. After more than a century, he was almost used to it.

The world around him shook with a great, groaning sigh. The four facets of the Corvine Gate blazed with light as silver-armoured shapes emerged and readied themselves for war. He heard the clarion call of a war-horn echo beneath the low thunder of the realmgate. Kurunta, the Knight-Heraldor of the Steel Souls, was making his presence known.

'The Lion of the Hyaketes roars,' Feros, the commander of his self-appointed bodyguard, rumbled. Gardus glanced at the Retributor-Prime. Feros of the Heavy Hand had fought at his side for longer than many. He had also been one of the first to fall, to be Reforged anew.

'He sends the foe our greetings,' Gardus said.

Feros laughed, harshly. 'They do seem eager to welcome us.' Around them, the cohort of Retributors moved into position. Clad in heavy bastion armour, and wielding massive, two-handed lightning hammers, the Retributors were eager to be where the fighting was thickest.

'Orders, my lord,' the Retributor-Prime said.

'Hold fast,' Gardus said. Feros gave an impatient grunt, but nodded. Unlike some, the Reforging process had seemingly done little to change Feros. The Heavy Hand was still the same bellicose yet comforting presence he had always been. At least on the surface. Who knew what changes had occurred within him. Did he too feel the call of distant stars when his attentions wandered? Gardus had never asked, and did not intend to now.

He turned his attentions back to the matter at hand. Before him, Liberators pressed beastkin back, taking control of the top of the ziggurat. The cohorts shifted position around the four sides of the realmgate, moving with drilled precision. The shield walls of the Hallowed Knights were not static emplacements but living things, always in motion and ever-growing. An unwary enemy could soon find themselves isolated, trapped by a cordon of silver, as the battle-line enveloped and bypassed them.

'My lord,' Feros said. Gardus turned, and saw several strangely armoured duardin moving cautiously through the ranks of his Retributors. The rest of their number had retreated behind the Stormcasts' shield wall, where they now tended the injured, and sang dirges for the dead. Though he had never seen them before, Gardus knew who they were. Lord-Aquilor Sathphren had sent word to Azyr of his alliance with the Gazul-Zagaz, though their presence here was something of a surprise.

Gardus met them, leaning forward slightly to be heard over the roar of the gate and the clamour of battle. The duardin were broad, like all their folk, and clad in white robes beneath their armour. They wore silver death-masks, save for one, who wore gold instead. He carried a sheathed blade in the crook of his arm, and made a complicated gesture of greeting. Gardus pressed his fists together, and bowed his head. '*Ofgrontalaf,*' he began, haltingly.

'Your accent is awful,' the duardin said, his voice a harsh rasp, like one rock scraping continuously against another. His companions chuckled dourly. 'I speak *umgali*.'

Gardus frowned. Umgali sounded similar to *umgi*, a duardin term meaning 'ill-made'. He decided to ignore the insult. 'I am Gardus. You are Gnol-Tul?'

'I am Tul. It is good you are here. We thought our dirge would go unheard.' Tul looked past him. 'The Swiftblade was right. You have brought many warriors.'

'There are more yet to come.' Gardus held out his fist, in the way of the Fyreslayers. 'You have our thanks, for holding this place.'

Tul studied Gardus' fist, and then set his own atop it. 'We swore an oath.' He pointed past Gardus, towards one of the lower tiers of the ziggurat. 'The Swiftblade – did he survive? He held them back as we retreated. Alone. I lost sight of him as the gate opened.'

Feros shook his head. 'That is like him. Always playing hero, that one.'

Tul nodded, in agreement. 'Indeed. He is very excitable.'

Gardus stifled a chuckle. The two of them sounded very alike in their disapproval. 'If he has not already gone back to Azyr, we shall find him. Ready yourselves.'

The duardin stepped back as the Retributors formed up around Gardus. Lightning sparked from the heads of their weapons, and danced on the air.

'Let us play them a hymn, brothers,' Feros said. He struck his hammer against that of another warrior, eliciting a fat spark of cobalt. Hammer slammed against hammer and sparks crawled across their war-plate as the ringing cadence filled the air.

Gardus studied the ebb and flow of the battle, noting where the beasts fought the hardest, judging the merits of a counterthrust.

Pick the wrong moment, the wrong place, and the beastkin would not break, and any attack would be overwhelmed. But when the right moment came, you had to seize it immediately.

He saw a beastman stagger, arrows jutting from its chest and throat. It fell, and for a moment, there was a gap in the press. 'Now,' he said, and advanced, pace quickening with every step. Feros and the Retributors followed, weapons wreathed in crackling bands of energy. As they drew close, Liberators stepped aside, and the shield wall split.

Gardus hurtled through the gap. A beastman rose up before him, bellowing. His tempestos hammer arced out, and the beastman toppled away, skull pulped. A moment later, Feros and the others joined him. They struck the enemy like a battering ram. Lightning cascaded down the side of the ziggurat as the Retributors went to work. Surprised beastkin scrambled from their path, some too slowly. Hairy bodies were flung into the air, broken and ruined, as the Stormcasts descended.

Feros laughed, swinging his hammer with casual grace. 'A good day's work, this, Steel Soul! The work we were forged for, eh?'

Gardus did not answer. His gaze was fixed on the next tier down, where something silver flashed among the heaving masses of the foe. He heard the shrill shriek of a gryph-charger, and a voice calling out Sigmar's name. Sathphren – and still alive. He extended his runeblade. 'There. Clear me a path, Feros.'

'Gladly,' Feros said. 'Hamu, Dakut – with me.' The three Retributors moved down, clearing the way with wide sweeps of their weapons. 'Make way, beasts,' Feros roared. 'Make way, for the Heavy Hand has come, and you will not bar his path. Make way!' Hamu's starsoul mace crashed down, sending a convulsion through the stones. Beastmen stumbled and fell, and were made easy prey for Feros' hammer.

Gardus followed in their wake, the remaining Retributors forming up around him. Feros and the others were a bulwark of silver and azure, grinding forward relentlessly. A trail of pulped and broken bodies was left in their wake. Beasts fell back before them, or streamed away, scrambling down the side of the ziggurat in a panicked rush.

As the press lessened, Gardus spotted a gryph-charger crouched over the body of its rider, beak and talons wet with blood. The creature snarled, but stepped back as he drew close. Feros and the others moved past them, to the edges of the tier, hammers swinging. 'Do you yet persist, brother?' Gardus asked, reaching down to help the fallen warrior to his feet.

'I think you'll find I'm quite persistent, Steel Soul. Annoyingly so, some might say.' Sathphren rose heavily, despite the lightness of his tone. His silver armour was streaked in gore, and his weapons were thick with it. 'Gwyllth?'

Gardus gestured with his hammer to where the gryph-charger crouched, tail lashing. 'She lives. And did a damn sight better a job keeping her feet than you, Swiftblade.'

'I can kill as easily on my back as on my feet,' Sathphren said. Gardus could hear the grin in his voice. Sathphren's faith was a bloody thing, weighed in scalps and foes slain. 'Still, your timing was impeccable.'

'Precise, even,' Gardus said, looking back up the steps. Cohorts of Liberators were already descending in the wake of their charge. Behind them, Judicators followed suit, ready to loose another volley into the ruins below. They would advance slowly, until the foe had lost their stomach for battle. 'Your Chamber?'

'Doing Sigmar's work.' Sathphren sank his axe into a beastman's carcass and used the tattered remnants of his cloak to clean his sword. 'They'll keep them from massing long enough for you to set up a proper shield wall below.'

'We'll take the city plaza by plaza,' Gardus said.

'We might have competition. The beastkin aren't the only slaves of darkness about. There's an encampment to the south.'

'Large?'

'Larger than I like.' Sathphren sheathed his sword. 'Large enough that I suspect that they're here at someone's behest, rather than because they like the scenery.'

Gardus frowned. 'Archaon,' he said, softly.

Sathphren nodded. 'The Three-Eyed King's servants have claimed much of Shyish as their own. We've run across them more than once since arriving. And if you were him, wouldn't you leave watchdogs here, just in case?' He hiked his thumb over his shoulder, indicating the Corvine Gate.

Before Gardus could reply, the roar of a war-horn pierced the din, and a crackling volley broke the last of the beastkin clinging to the ziggurat. A moment later, Liberators advanced past him, down the steps of the ziggurat. As they marched, they sang a low, sad hymn – a song of loss and fading memory. The song slipped from cohort to cohort, carried back upwards to the indistinct, silver forms still emerging from the blazing depths of the Corvine Gate.

But as the first Liberator reached the enemy, the song changed, becoming martial. Harsh, rather than sad. A paean of challenge. Sigmarite shields slammed into the beastkin, knocking them back. Hammers and warblades came next, smashing and stabbing. Blood slopped down the wide steps and bodies tumbled in tangled avalanches. The beastkin retreated in disarray, abandoning the wounded and the berserk.

Behind the Liberators, the Judicators had taken up the song, even as they loosed volleys after the enemy. Crackling arrows slammed into the horde, driving them into a frenzy of fear.

'We are war's millstone,' Gardus said, absently.

'And peace our grain,' Sathphren said. He drove the side of his fist against Gardus' arm. 'Who shall walk proudly in red fields, brother?'

'Only the faithful.' Gardus grimaced. 'Red fields. An unpleasant saying.'

'War is unpleasant, Gardus. That is why I take what small pleasures I can from it.' Sathphren chuckled and caught hold of Gwyllth's reins. 'Speaking of which – can't let your warriors have all the fun.' He swung himself up into the saddle. 'Care to join me?'

Gardus shook his head. 'I have my duties, Lord-Aquilor. And you have yours.' He reached up, and they clasped hands. 'Go with Sigmar, brother.'

'I always do,' Sathphren said, laughing. He thumped the gryph-charger's flanks and she shot down the ziggurat's slope, winnowing through and around the advancing cohorts like a blur of starlight. His Vanguard-Palladors joined him as he reached the bottom of the ziggurat and raced into the ruins, where they were soon lost to sight.

Gardus stood for a moment, watching as a tide of silver filled the space below. 'Who will carry light into the dark?' he said. 'Who will walk unafraid into the deepest shadows?'

'Only the faithful,' Feros replied, his hammer held across his shoulder. 'But we'd best be quick about it, else there'll be no shadows left to walk in.'

In Nordrath, the shadows grew long as the last of the Stormforged marched into the flickering depths of the realmgate. Khela watched the procession from where she stood some distance away. Part of her wished she was going with them. She had been looking forward to it, though she found battle to be, at best, a distraction from her true purpose – the creation of something lasting. A new city, greater by far than the ruins it would rise from.

Beside her, Lord-Relictor Ramus watched the procession with ill-concealed impatience. 'The last of them are through,' he said. 'The battle begins. And we are still here.' His gaze was fixed on the shimmering surface of the realmgate, as if by sheer will he might discern what was happening on the other side.

Though she could not see his face, Khela imagined the Lord-Relictor was scowling. Ramus was always scowling. He had ever been a dour presence, and had only grown worse since the Bullhearts had first journeyed to Shyish.

'Not just us. Lord-Castellant Grymn is here, as well as Lord-Castellant Octarion. And the Lord-Ordinator as well.'

Ramus did not look at her. 'Details,' he muttered. 'I should be there.'

'We, you mean.'

'Of course.' He shifted his weight slightly, cloak rustling. 'It is an insult. A calculated one. Cassandora's idea, I have no doubt.'

'Really?' Khela asked. 'Gardus is in overall command. It was his decision.' She turned, looking at the forces still arrayed before the realmgate. The Gallowsmen would be next to march through the gate, their lines bolstered by the warriors of the Bullhearts. Lorcus sat at their head on his steed, seemingly at ease. She studied him for a moment, wondering if he was up to the task ahead. To Khela's way of thinking, battle was easy. Building something afterwards was hard.

'He reminds me of Tarsus,' Ramus said. She turned back.

'Really?'

'In some ways. Gardus has more common sense.' Ramus stiffened. 'Is that... singing?'

Khela listened. She could hear it now, over the sound of the realmgate. 'Osanus,' she said. A cohort of Hallowed Knights from their Chamber were crossing the square towards them, led by their Knight-Heraldor, Osanus. He was singing as he came, his voice booming out like thunder. She heard Ramus snort in discontent as Osanus caught sight of them and lifted his war-horn in a gesture of greeting.

'Hark, I have come,' Osanus bellowed. 'Mine brother and sister in storm, yes!' He waved eagerly, nearly knocking over the warrior beside him. 'I come, and we go, yes? Yes! We go as the storm, with much lightning and thunder. Zig-mah-HAI!' He threw back his head and howled, pounding his chest-plate with a clenched fist. The warriors around him gave the Knight-Heraldor space as he filled the air with noise.

The Stormwolf was not quite as massive as his voice led one to believe. He was broad, rather than tall. His hair and beard were long and spilled out from beneath his helm, when he bothered to wear one. He had lived and died among a nomad clan of the Amber Steppes of Ghur, the Vurm-tai. Or so he claimed, whenever he sang the bellicose sagas of his people. Which was often, despite frequent requests to the contrary.

Ramus disliked him, Khela knew. Not truly, but with the sort of ever-present infuriation one might feel towards a singularly disobedient dog. Osanus was primitive, even by the standards of such warriors as the Astral Templars. But his faith shone like a star when he fought, or sang, or laughed. The Stormwolf *believed* with an intensity that put others, including herself, to shame. For him, faith was not a philosophical conundrum, but simply a thing that was. He believed, and nothing could shake that belief.

Perhaps that was why Ramus disliked the Knight-Heraldor so. Osanus took as a given the things Ramus questioned, and all with a smile. If the other Stormcast had been less good-natured about it, the Lord-Relictor might have found it more bearable.

As it was, Khela liked the Stormwolf. He was boisterous, true, but not entirely lacking in wits. Whatever Ramus thought, there was a keen mind under all that hair, and other Chambers had done worse out of more civilised commanders. But convincing Ramus of that was a war she had little interest in waging. She had faith the problem would be resolved one way or another, if not to everyone's liking.

Ramus bestowed a withering glare on Osanus. 'Calm yourself, Knight-Heraldor. We go when the time is right. Not before.'

Osanus bobbed his head, grinning. His teeth had been filed, and holy runes carved into those that were visible. Similar markings scarred his round cheeks and brow. 'As you say, brother, yes? Osanus is here. He goes where you tell him, and sings when you say.' He glanced at Khela and punched her in the arm, rocking her on her heels. 'Hello, sister!'

Khela laughed and returned the gesture, striking him in the shoulder. Osanus laughed.

'Be silent, the pair of you,' Ramus snarled. 'The mortals are coming over.' He swept his reliquary staff out, indicating Albain Lorcus and several others as they walked over. The mortals approached hesitantly. Only Lorcus seemed unafraid.

'Lord-Relictor,' Lorcus said, bowing his head respectfully. 'I wished to personally convey my thanks for assisting us in this endeavour.' Khela studied his hangers-on. Two were obviously officers, going by their uniforms and armour. The rest were scribes, money lenders and what appeared to be a priest, in blue cassock and golden sigil.

Ramus looked down at Lorcus. 'That is not necessary.'

'Even so,' Lorcus said. He turned to the realmgate. 'How long will we wait?'

'Until Gardus and the others let us know that the way has been cleared,' Khela said. 'They must drive the foe back and gain us the space we need to begin erecting defences.'

Lorcus looked at Khela. 'You have my thanks as well, Lord-Castellan. Without your aid, I'm certain our efforts to rebuild the city would be doomed from the start.'

'It is my duty,' Khela said. The mortal met her gaze without awe or fear. Lorcus had a core of steel to him that few mortals possessed. His subordinates, on the other hand, stared at the Stormcasts – especially Ramus – in awe. The Lord-Relictor was something of a legend, Khela recalled. The stories of his dogged pursuit of the vampire Mannfred von Carstein were favourites of the feasting halls in Azyrheim and Nordrath.

'It is *our* duty,' Lord-Castellan Grymn said, as he and Lord-Ordinator Taltus joined them. They were accompanied by Lord-Castellan Octarion, who nodded silently to Khela. She knew Grymn only by reputation. Like Ramus, he was a legend among legends. It was said that he, like his Lord-Celestant, had faced the Ruinous Powers in their own realm with only his faith to shield him, and had emerged all the stronger for it. Too, he was among an ever-dwindling number of Stormcasts who had yet to be Reforged even once.

Taltus was another whom she was unfamiliar with. She had heard the Lord-Ordinator's name, and seen the results of his labours in the Mortal Realms, but had never fought alongside him. He was a lean warrior, his muscular arms bare of sigmarite, revealing the profusion of knotwork tattoos that coiled about his biceps. His scalp was shorn clean, save for a single scalp-lock of braided black hair that hung down across his chest-plate. Long moustaches decorated his upper lip, and he tugged on them as he spoke.

'And one we are pleased to fulfil.' He looked at the realmgate.

'The real work begins on the other side.'

'We are ready when you are,' Lorcus said. Khela looked around, taking in the continuing preparations. While the Gallowsmen were ranked up before the realmgate, the rest of the army was still in a state of confusion. Or so it appeared to her. The great wagons were still being loaded, and horses fed. The rows of tents were still being broken down, and the non-combatants herded a safe distance from the realmgate. It seemed, to her eyes, that everywhere was noise and disorder.

The march of a Stormhost was a thing of brisk efficiency. Stormcasts only rarely required supply lines or support, save that provided by their own cohorts and conclaves. But a Freeguild army was a different beast entirely. It required supplies and preparation. A warrior chamber was ready for war at a moment's notice. Mortals required considerably more warning. They needed food, ammunition, alchemists, horse-leeches, mule-skinners and various other necessities.

Khela did not recall such things from her own brief two decades as a mortal, but then she had been an artisan rather than a warrior. A builder of bridges and causeways, with no interest in swordplay. Not until those last, savage days. She pushed the thought aside.

'It all seems so... messy,' she said. Lorcus laughed.

'I suppose it does at that, my lady.'

Ramus made a sound of discontent, and Khela glanced at him, wondering what he was thinking. Nothing pleasant, most like. The Lord-Relictor was many things, but pleasant wasn't one of them. 'If the army is not ready, it will be left behind. Speed is of the essence.'

'We all know our business, Ramus,' Grymn said.

Ramus turned away. 'I hope so, Lord-Castellant. For your sake, as well as ours.'

CHAPTER FIVE

SONG AND SHADOW

*Like all cities in Shyish, Caddow possessed its share
of necropoli and catacombs, stretching for untold
leagues beneath the dust-dunes...*

– Palento Herst
The Corvine Gate and Other Edifices

The march of the Joyous Revelry was akin to a celebration.

There was no discipline, no order to Bakhos' forces – order
was anathema to servants of the Absent God. Every warrior
fought for themselves, with no concern for anything save what
glory they could find. Some ran on bloody feet, howling out the
name of Slaanesh, while others careened through the streets
on gilded chariots pulled by serpentine daemon-beasts. None
marched, where they could run. None ran, where they could
ride.

It was a sort of heaving, convulsive advance that shook the
ruins from eyrie to cellar. A flood of bodies, pouring through

the streets, moving unerringly towards the sounds of battle. Beastmen, fleeing the fighting, were crushed underfoot by the celebrants as they met them coming the opposite way.

Bakhos laughed as he urged his steed forward over the twitching bodies of beastkin.

'Faster, Ucepha,' he shouted. The warhorse was big and black, its glossy coat more metal than flesh. Wolfish fangs filled its jaws, and its mane was more akin to brambles than hair. It shrilled and reared, clawing at the air with barbed hooves. Bakhos hauled on its reins, fighting for control. As ever, the daemon-steed had its own ideas about where they were going, and it was a constant battle to ensure that it went where he told it.

His followers spread out behind him in a riotous cavalcade – chariots and wild horsemen, daemon-riders and loping beasts. There was no commonality to the battle-line, beyond a mad lust to reach the foe. Once, such a thing might have offended Bakhos' sensibilities, but those days were long past him.

'Ride on, ride on,' he howled. 'Ride to ruin and glory!' He thumped his steed's flanks, urging Ucepha into a breakneck gallop. His horse bugled a challenge as its hooves tore gouges in the street. A wall of silver and azure rose up before the Maiden's Son, and in its mirrored surface he saw the glory of himself reflected a thousand times.

The Stormcasts were waiting for them.

The enemy might as well have been the automatons that some insisted they were. They marched in lockstep, azure shields presented as a solid wall. A wave of silver and blue, ever encroaching, albeit steadily rather than swiftly. They filled the street ahead from one side to the other, blocking any attempt to get around them.

His followers gave a ululation of delight at the sight of them and raced forward. Arrows of light hummed through the air to meet them. Ucepha screamed as one took the beast in the eye, and Bakhos was hurled over the dying horse's head. He rolled to his feet, drawing his sword as he did so. He slashed out, carving a gash across the face of a shield. The force of his blow staggered the Stormcast, and Bakhos lashed out with a foot, knocking the warrior to the ground. Another took his place almost immediately.

Bakhos retreated, sliding his mirrored shield from his back as he did so. The shield wall advanced with a rattling of steel. The ground trembled beneath his feet as his followers drew close. He met the calm, flat gazes of his foes, and grinned a leopard's grin. He was stronger. Faster. Better. The Absent God had whispered the truth of the world to him in his dreams, and had purged him of all weakness. Burnt him inside and out, so that what remained was mighty indeed.

'Well then,' he said. 'Let us begin.'

He took a single, fluid step and launched himself full at the shield wall. His blade danced out, quicker than the eye could follow. A Stormcast staggered, shield split in twain, silver armour stained red. Bakhos pursued his prey, hungry for death. He had enjoyed the taste of that strange lightning, and wished to do so again. He surged into the line, using his shield as a battering ram, knocking Stormcasts off balance.

He brought his shield up as arrows snarled home. He felt lightning crackle over its mirrored surface, and laughed. He lashed out, to the left and the right, widening the gap as the Stormcasts drew back to better defend themselves.

He caught sight of the one he'd wounded. The others were trying to shield him, but Bakhos' warriors had followed their lord into the fray, and the Stormcasts' attentions were soon diverted. The first of Bakhos' followers struck the shield wall with a wild cry. It was taken up by others as they closed in. They fought without discipline, every warrior a battle-line unto themselves. They selected their prey and went after them with all the savagery at their disposal. It was not the most efficient way of waging war, but it was fun.

It felt good, this. For too long, he had sat idle, fighting foes who provided little to no challenge. Nomads, beasts and the occasional would-be rival with delusions of grandeur. But these Azyrites were worthy foes indeed – strong and tough. Tough enough to take some killing. Tough enough that he could take his time and enjoy himself.

He swept his sword out in a glittering arc, driving the Stormcasts back. His shield met theirs, and he matched them strength for strength, glorying in the test. If only Vlad were there to experience this with him. But his advisor had insisted on shouldering the inglorious burden of playing the shield to Bakhos' sword. Vlad had led a contingent of his forces south, to ward Bakhos' flank from the advancing Stormcasts.

He thought, briefly, of Vlad's warnings as they'd set out from camp. That the Azyrites had to be thrown back quickly and the realmgate retaken, else they would soon face more than just Stormcasts. The enemy would come slinking down from the stars, carrying fire and death such as few of Bakhos' followers had seen.

He'd made Vlad tell him all about those weapons and the destruction they could wreak. Several times, in fact. He longed to possess such things, though their manufacture seemed a tedious process. For the moment, he was willing to settle for another taste of sacred lightning. Just a bit, to clear his head of the last dregs of boredom.

As the shield wall heaved and thrashed like a wounded beast, Bakhos caught sight again of the warrior he'd wounded with his first strike. He fought his way towards his quarry, suddenly possessed of the desire to finish what he'd begun.

'Why do you always run?' he growled. 'Answer me that, eh?' He slammed his shield into the injured Stormcast, knocking him to the ground. 'You are in the land of death already. Where is there to go?'

The warrior rolled aside as Bakhos' blade descended. Bakhos laughed and followed. 'Struggle all you wish, it only makes your death all the sweeter.'

The Stormcast surged to his feet, his armour stained red, his breathing laboured. Bakhos lunged smoothly. His sword pierced the warrior's chest-plate as the fell magics woven into the blade ate through the silver metal. As he wrenched his weapon free, the Stormcast erupted. Lightning washed over Bakhos, singeing his hair and scorching his armour and cloak. He breathed it in, luxuriating in the brief agony.

When the glare of the departing soul faded, he blinked and shook his head. 'Exquisite,' he murmured. He needed to taste it again. He turned, seeking new prey. The Stormcasts' battle-line had broken up into struggling knots of silver, surrounded on all sides by his warriors. He could see them attempting to fight their way to each other, to rebuild what his charge had broken. He licked his lips and started towards the closest knot.

He broke into a sprint, leaping over the broken bodies of his warriors, and launched himself at the Stormcasts. His first blow knocked aside a shield, and his second removed a head. He danced through the lightning with quicksilver steps, striking as they turned, moving more quickly than they could see. His exposed flesh was raw and smoking by the third, but he paid it no mind. He felt the hands of the Absent God upon him, driving him forward to greater agonies and pleasures. It was everything he had yearned for, for so long.

He knocked a Stormcast back against a pillar and closed in, almost singing his delight. Dust swirled about him as his opponent came apart in a cascade of crackling magics. Only when the echoes of that dissolution had faded did he realise that the ground was shaking. He turned as, behind him, towers toppled, blanketing the street in a cloud of dust.

Bakhos looked up and saw silver shapes streaking overhead, trailing lightning in their wake. Another building collapsed, slumping across the street, burying his warriors. More importantly, it was changing the shape of the city around them. He thought of a cage, and bars slamming down. He dismissed the image. A fancy, nothing more.

Thunder rumbled from elsewhere in the city. Lightning streaked upwards, tearing holes in the sky. And the dust clouds grew. He turned back to the battle at hand, and saw the Stormcasts retreating. Not in disarray, but in orderly lockstep. Back and back and then the shield wall reformed, as if it had never been broken at all. Perhaps it hadn't.

This shield wall was smaller than the first. Compact, with shields held not just to the fore, but overhead as well. Arrows hissed through makeshift slits, punching into his warriors, buying the Stormcasts time to regroup. Not into a battle-line this time, but something else. As one, they began to sink down, like a tortoise retreating into its shell.

Again, his eyes were drawn upwards, to the silver shapes circling overhead like great birds of prey. What were they waiting for?

He got his answer a moment later.

Ghosteater snarled and ducked aside as a crackling arrow passed over his shoulder and killed the beast behind him. He flung himself behind a chunk of fallen masonry as more arrows followed, reducing the solid wedge of Bakhos' followers to rags and tatters.

He and his herd had claimed the honour of the vanguard for themselves, a reward for bringing the captive to the Blessed Ones. Only now, he'd realised that it was less a reward than a sacrifice. In his head, ghosts laughed at his naiveté. *Their sort never rewards your kind, gor,* a harsh, deep voice rumbled. *They hate you as much as my folk do.*

Fool-fool. Stupid beast-thing, another ghost chittered. *Never-never go first. Slaves go first. Leaders go last.*

Ghosteater growled low in his throat, silencing the shrill spectre. Its words were more an annoyance than a help. As he scrambled to his feet, he heard the screaming of horses and daemon-beasts as they were cut down by the Stormcast archers. *Smart,* a ghost murmured. *Kill the horses, and you slow the advance. And look – above!*

Ghosteater did. Silver shapes hurtled overhead, but did not slow to attack the horde below. Where were they going?

To cut off your retreat, beast. Watch...

Thunder rolled, and the great stone lairs of mankind collapsed. Dust filled the street, choking the air. Ghosteater whined in sudden realisation. If they were cutting off the line of retreat, which meant that what was waiting for them at the other end was worse than any shield wall. He clutched his khopesh, wanting to lash out, to kill something. But there was nothing in reach.

Calm yourself, beast. Panic and bloodlust are weapons in your enemy's hand. Look. Think. You have time – more time than you know. The ghost spoke calmly, fastidiously. The scratch of a quill over parchment echoed beneath every word. Ghosteater remembered this one, an old man, dying even as Ghosteater's pack had set upon his caravan. What was his name? He shook his head. It didn't matter.

It mattered to me.

Ghosteater grunted. He swiped dust from his stinging eyes and searched for his warriors. Many of them had followed his example, going to ground as arrows filled the air. The rest of the horde continued to flow after Bakhos, drawn in their warlord's wake.

Ghosteater had been awed by the Maiden's Son at first. He was powerful, and frightening, strong with the spirit of the Absent God. But perhaps not so wise. None of them were. He had thought the Blessed Ones to be greater than himself; only with his ghosts could he hope to match them. But they were as much blood-drunk fools as his own rivals.

They were brutes. Weak. He licked his chops, watching as they reached the enemy line at last. Only the first ranks had done so. Everyone else was caught in the press and flow, trapped by the narrow street.

Like a chunk of meat, caught in the belly.

The buildings to either side might as well have been mountains, rising upwards forever. Each was riddled with alcoves inhabited by massive statues, which glared fiercely down at the tide flowing beneath them. More statues lined the streets, crouched atop high plinths or standing at the crossways where another street intersected the main path.

Statuary is a vice of Shyishan cultures – Shadespire, Oskirian, Helstone – all the same. Where there is a street, there are statues. This street was known, colloquially, as the Street of Scribes–

Ghosteater twitched, trying to banish the old man's voice. Some of the ghosts shared what they knew, even when he didn't force them. He didn't know whether to be pleased or infuriated at the tide of useless knowledge.

No knowledge is useless.

'It did not help you here,' Ghosteater said, closing his eyes.

I came here to see Caddow with my own eyes before I died. To see the wonders I had only written of previously. And I did. I do not begrudge you a meal, though it was an unpleasant experience – oh, look! That archway is a classic example of neo-Settrosian–

'Quiet,' Ghosteater snapped. He shook his head, trying to clear it of the smell of dusty books and ink. 'Don't care. Buildings… not important.'

Oh, but they are. Take these buildings here – look at them. They are composed of heavy slabs of stone. The first families of Caddow enslaved a tribe of dust-gargants to build many of these structures for them, and buried the poor beasts beneath them when they were done. The old man's voice was patient. Dry. *These buildings are now little more than immense deadfalls… which, I'd guess, your foes are well aware of.*

'What?'

Thunder. The street shook. The cobbles cracked as fissures raced along unseen fault lines. He heard howls of alarm, and smelled the sudden acrid odour of fear rising from his warriors. A great, bone-deep groan shivered through the street as it began to twist in on itself. Ghosteater backed away as a statue toppled and shattered, crushing a Chaos warrior beneath it. Slabs of stone peeled away from crumbling structures and fell towards the street and the forces trapped along its length, crushing them.

Chaos warriors and devoted mortals stumbled back towards Ghosteater, blinded by dust and disorientated. He howled, calling his followers to him. A Blessed One, clad in pastel-daubed war-plate, stumbled, and Ghosteater caught him without thinking. The warrior stank of strange spices and unguents, and his armour was slick to the touch.

'Trap,' the warrior coughed. His eyes were glazed within his helmet. 'It was a trap.' Ghosteater growled low in his throat. That much was obvious. Bakhos had led them into an ambush.

A pillar slammed down, nearly knocking them from their feet. Ghosteater heard his warriors howling and screeching as they scrambled for safety. Dust coiled about him, blocking the Blessed Ones and their foes from sight.

If you value your skin, it's time to go, the old man murmured. A map of the city unfurled in Ghosteater's head, showing him the way to safety. 'Come,' the beastman snarled, forcing the pastel-armoured warrior upright. 'Follow, if you want to live.'

Mannfred von Carstein grimaced and ducked aside as lightning sawed out and cut through the ranks of warriors behind him. Cerulean flames washed over the dying, consuming them even as they screamed the name of their god. They died in ecstasy, but succumbed all the same. Their patron could not protect them here. Indeed, he suspected that even had Slaanesh been able to do so, it would have chosen otherwise.

The left flank of Bakhos' advance had utterly collapsed, thanks in no small part to Mannfred leading them directly into the hands of the enemy. It hadn't been difficult. The fools wanted a fight, and Mannfred had obliged.

Silver shapes swooped overhead, splitting the night with fire and fury. The Stormcasts were as monstrous as he remembered – they were more akin to a millstone than an army. They ground on, always moving, regardless of what was in their path. Obstacles were crushed underfoot, whatever their size or ferocity. And through it all, that mindless chant, echoing through the very stones.

'Only the faithful,' Mannfred muttered, as he cast aside his mask and slipped into the shadows. He moved swiftly, ignoring the flow of battle. It didn't matter who won here, so long as he reached his goal. He could hear the rumble of collapsing buildings and felt the street buck, nearly tossing him from his feet. Great columns of dust rose into the sky as towers and temples fell.

It was as he'd feared. The Stormcasts were using the city as a weapon. Not just to trap, but to kill as well. They were more cunning these days – more willing to think beyond the obvious tactics. A part of him yearned to face them across the field and match them gambit for gambit. But that too was a trap.

It was the same reason they wore such gaudy war-plate. They challenged the smart as well as the stupid, baiting them into open conflict. Sigmar was more clever than even Nagash gave him credit for. The God-King had created a weapon his enemies could not ignore, that they would focus on to the exclusion of all others. When the Stormcasts took the field, Khorne could not help but attack, and even Nurgle interrupted his gardening. And the less said about Nagash, the better.

But Mannfred was not Nagash. He was not blinded by fury or obsession. And he knew better than to allow himself to be distracted from his true purpose. Even so, it was difficult. The Stormcasts were everywhere. Around every corner, bulling down every avenue. Wherever he turned, there they were – a silver millstone, grinding Caddow into dust.

In the moment, he wished he hadn't sent Ashigaroth to skulk in the nearby hills. But the dread abyssal would have attracted the wrong sort of attention. Nonetheless, he was tempted to summon the beast. But that could wait. He ran, slipping from shadow to shadow, avoiding confrontation. Warriors he'd laughed with, drank with, died. He felt nothing.

Not even a bit of shame, then?

'They are monsters, Tarsem.'

They are still men. Men who looked to you to lead them. As my people did.

'More fool them, then.'

Where are my people, Mannfred? What has become of them?

Mannfred paused, shaking his head, trying to clear it of ghosts. 'They lived,' he said, finally. 'I did that much, at least.'

The memory of Tarsem fell silent. Mannfred heard a thunderous boom, as something heavy collapsed nearby. He could hear the wailing of beasts and wondered whether Bakhos was still alive. He hoped so. As long as the Maiden's Son was savaging their flank, the Stormcasts would be too preoccupied to notice what was going on beneath their feet.

He slipped down a narrow side street, dragging shadows in his wake. It was a simple enough enchantment, and one he could enact with but a gesture. It wrapped about him like a cloak. The shadows also muffled sound and dimmed light. He felt as if he were covered in a thick shroud, and found the sensation oddly comforting. As if it were part of him.

At the end of the street was a slim, square archway set into the base of a squat, onion-domed structure, squeezed between the buildings that rose to either side. The archway was topped by funeral carvings – bones, vines and crows – and was barely wide enough to contain the inset stone door. Mannfred paused as something flashed overhead – more Stormcasts. He was confident that they couldn't see him, thanks to his shadows. But even so, there was little sense in tempting fate.

When he was sure they'd passed on, he went to the door. The catacombs had several proper entrances in this part of the city, most of which were sealed by magics and duardin artifice. But there were also the lichgates – smaller paths, known only to the ancient mortuary priesthood of Caddow. And to Mannfred.

The door had no visible handle or lock. Supposedly, the priests had been able to open the lichgates with but a touch. Like as not, there was some cunning mechanism. But he had neither the patience nor the time to discover it. Instead, he set his shoulder against the flat surface of the door and shoved. Ancient hinges warped and burst.

He stepped into the dark, leaving the din of battle behind. A set of steps wound down into the depths. While the main entrances to the catacombs were for pomp and ceremony, the lichgates had been for more clandestine interments – those no one was to know of, or the ones that everyone wished to forget.

Once, masked and hooded priests had carried carefully wrapped bodies down these wide, winding steps, to place them in the waiting vaults. The walls were marked by warding sigils, meant to calm the spirits of these unfortunates, and lull them into an eternal lassitude. Mannfred could feel them, like lions slumbering in the dark. The souls of despots, merchants and murderers, drifting aimlessly. They were bound in chains of ritual, rendered harmless by the rites of that long-extinct priesthood.

He smiled. 'Soon,' he murmured. He felt the air twitch at his words, and knew that the dead had heard him, if only subconsciously. Body and soul, the dead of Caddow would rise at his command. And then–

And then you ride forth once more, to the aid of an egomaniacal god.

'Quiet, Tarsem,' Mannfred muttered. 'You are dead.' He continued down the steps until he reached the passageway at the bottom. The passage was lined with alcoves, each containing a mummified form, or the remains of such.

So are you.

'Not my kind of dead.' At the end of the passage was a larger alcove, this one containing another slab-like door. To Mannfred's gaze, it radiated power. Faintly glowing sigils covered its surface. They squirmed beneath his gaze, as if somehow aware of him.

Only I'm not dead at all, am I? Not really.

Mannfred closed his eyes. It was an old argument, and one he'd had before. More than once. Memories were tenacious, and no matter how fast one ran, they were impossible to escape. When he was certain Tarsem was gone, he opened his eyes, and studied the flickering wards once more. Like the main entrances, this one had been mystically sealed.

I'm not dead, Mannfred.

Mannfred cursed and thumped the wall with his fist. 'I know that. Don't you think I know that? I warned you, if you'll recall. Twice, I tried to save you from your own vainglorious idiocy, and twice you refused me.'

His voice echoed through the catacombs. He fell silent, suddenly all too aware of the battle raging overhead. He was running short of time. He turned his attentions back to the wards. They were cleverly designed. Unravel the wrong one, and the entirety of the catacombs might collapse, or worse. It required the utmost concentration to–

You could still save me, you know.

Mannfred growled. 'Be silent. You are nothing more than a figment of memory, lodged in my consciousness. You are not here. Vitalian is not here. Megara is not here. None of you *are here*. So, please – stop talking.'

Silence. Blessed silence. Mannfred grunted, annoyed with himself. He was increasingly haunted by the angels of his better nature. They gathered in the dark of him, and sprang when his defences were at their lowest.

Mannfred rarely gave thought to the morality of his actions, in service to the Undying King. That Nagash was inimical was unquestionable. So too was a desert scorpion. Both had their place in the Great Work, as did Mannfred.

And yet, at times, he found himself wondering what might

have been. If he had not followed his nature, not done as Nagash had bade him. Just once. If just once, he had truly been the treacherous jackal his fellow Mortarchs thought him, what might have been accomplished?

He shook his head, annoyed with himself. 'I am but that I am,' he muttered. His lot had been chosen for him, long before he had drawn breath or tasted blood. He could not defy the will of the Undying King, whatever his own wishes in that regard.

Have you ever truly tried?

He stopped, as Tarsem's voice echoed in his head. 'I…' he began.

The ceiling of the catacombs collapsed in an explosion of dust and stone. Mannfred staggered back. A moment later, something silver raced towards him, through the billowing dust. Mannfred cursed and drew his sword, interposing it at the last moment. A blade connected with his own, as the Stormcast – a Prosecutor – drove him back through sheer momentum. Mannfred grunted in pain as his back connected with the wall.

He lashed out, beating aside his opponent's blade, and drove a fist into the side of the Prosecutor's head. The winged warrior stumbled and swept a crackling wing out. The shimmering feathers sliced across Mannfred's chest, scoring his armour with a white-hot gouge. He backed away, one hand pressed to his chest.

'I knew I had seen something,' the Prosecutor boomed, shaking his head. 'A rat, crawling in the dark.' The Stormcast stalked after Mannfred, wingtips scorching the walls to either side. The corpses in their alcoves caught fire as the edges of the shimmering feathers brushed across them. The Stormcast shot forward with a snap of his wings.

Mannfred snarled and lunged, battering the Stormcast to his knees with a flurry of blows. When the Stormcast sank down,

Mannfred lashed out, kicking him in the head. The Prosecutor fell backwards, sword clattering from his grip. Mannfred planted a boot on the Stormcast's chest, pinning him to the ground. 'Say hello to Sigmar for me,' he crowed, raising his blade in both hands.

An arrow pierced his forearm. A second followed it, piercing his other forearm. His sword fell from his suddenly nerveless fingers. Mannfred staggered, hissing in pain. Two more arrows hummed towards him, puncturing his palms and pinning his hands to the wall. Another sank into his thigh, and he howled in pain and frustration.

'You can tell him yourself, vampire.'

He looked up and saw a second silver figure advancing towards him, down the slope of rubble created by the Prosecutor's entrance, her wings folded behind her. The Knight-Venator nocked another arrow, and he ceased his struggles. The Stormcast studied him over the length of her arrow.

'I know you,' she said. Behind her, the Prosecutor rose unsteadily to his feet and retrieved his blade.

Mannfred attempted a smile. It was difficult, given the pain. 'I am sorry I cannot say the same. Would you believe I meant him no harm?'

'Kill him and be done, Enyo,' the other Stormcast growled.

'I wouldn't, Enyo,' Mannfred said, quickly. 'I'm fairly certain your God-King wants me alive.' She cocked her head, and he grinned weakly. 'You know what I mean.'

'Yes.' She lowered her bow and slid her arrow back in its quiver. 'Perhaps you are right. We shall let Gardus decide what to do with him. Tegrus, get him down.'

'Yes, Tegrus, quickly. These arrows burn terribly.' Mannfred hissed as he was freed, none too gently. He stumbled, and the Prosecutor caught him by the throat.

'If you try to escape, vampire, I will remove your head.'

'Point taken,' Mannfred croaked. He held up his bloody hands in a gesture of submission. 'I am your prisoner. I place myself in your hands.' He smiled. 'Take me to your leader.'

CHAPTER SIX

THE PRISONER

The eyries were at once a source of pride and terror for the common folk of Caddow. Fortresses and prisons in one, the shadows of these great towers stretched across the city like the bars of some immense cage.

– Palento Herst
The Architecture of Eastern Shyish

The wind cast the dust into strange shapes.

Gardus wondered if they were ghosts as he watched them twist and dance through the ruined streets. He used a scrap of cloth to clean the ichor from his runeblade, then cast it into a nearby pyre. Dozens of the great sapphire bonfires lined the street ahead, kindled by the magics of the gathered Lord-Castellants' lanterns. The bodies of the foe provided the fuel that would keep those fires raging through the night.

'We caught them by surprise,' Lorrus Grymn said, from

where he sat on the head of a fallen statue. The Lord-Castellant stroked the head of his gryph-hound, Talon, as he spoke. 'They'll regroup, once they finish licking their wounds.'

Gardus sheathed his sword. 'We'll be ready for them. The mortals are already setting up camp.' He gazed out across the broken ground of the market plaza. There were twelve of the great plazas encircling the ziggurat. Each had once played host to traders from not just Azyr and Shyish, but across the width and breadth of the realms. Now, they had become the campgrounds of an invading army. Everywhere, the ruins were full of activity.

Palisades were being erected at the mouths of streets and alleyways by straining Freeguild soldiers as heavy emplacements of stone and gromril were dropped into position by duardin labourers. Street by street, Caddow would be partitioned, each district isolated until it could be cleansed of the foulness that had overtaken it.

Stormcasts tramped past, dragging the broken bodies of beastkin to the great pyres. Others worked alongside mortals to investigate the ruins closest to the ziggurat, and ensure that no enemy managed to breach the cordon that was being erected. Ironweld artillery, newly arrived, bombarded the farthest streets, reducing buildings to rubble and creating makeshift killing fields in anticipation of future attack.

'How soon, do you think?' Grymn asked.

Gardus shook his head. 'It is hard to say. They may well already be on the move. They've had centuries to prepare for this, after all.'

'So have we.' Grymn rose to his feet. 'And speaking of preparation, best ready yourself. Look who's coming this way.'

Gardus turned and sighed. The representatives of the Collegiate Arcane were making their way towards him across the broken ground. There were three of the battlemages, led by the tall, thin form of Reconciler Ahom. Ahom was clad in the dark azure robes of a master astromancer, the hems decorated with astrological and astronomical sigils. He wore silver gauntlets and a ceremonial breastplate that seemed to all but swallow him up.

Gardus didn't know the names of the other two battlemages. One was a thickset, burly practitioner clad in heavy furs, with a full beard that would put even a duardin to shame. He wore a necklace of animal fangs and his belt was made from the hide and skull of a wolf. The other was a short, round woman in robes of amethyst and cerulean. Her silver hair was pulled back in a tight bun, and her cheeks were tattooed with strange glyphs. Neither spoke, seemingly content – or resigned – to let Ahom do all the talking.

'Lord-Celestant? Lord-Celestant!' Ahom called out as the three approached, trailed by a gaggle of scribes and apprentices.

'Yes, Reconciler Ahom?' Gardus looked down at the battle-mage. Out of the corner of his eyes, he saw Grymn hurrying away, Talon trailing in his wake. Gardus restrained a smile. The Lord-Castellant had always known when to make a strategic withdrawal. 'Is there something I can help you with?'

'There is still the matter of our territorial claim, Lord-Celestant. I have signed documentation to the effect that–' Ahom waved a handful of scrolls, sealed with wax, in a vaguely threatening manner. Gardus silenced the battlemage with a curt gesture.

'I would prefer to deal with such matters after we've won the day, reconciler.'

'And I would prefer not to risk the lives of my colleagues without first ensuring that any sacrifice we might be called upon to make is suitably repaid.' Ahom drew himself to his full height. 'I am no fool, Lord-Celestant. I know full well what might be forgotten in the confusion of victory.'

A harsh voice interjected, before Gardus could reply. 'Aye, because you've forgotten it yourself often enough, you old skinflint.'

Ahom whirled. 'Mahk,' he said, making the name sound like a curse.

'That's right. It's me. Your worst nightmare.' The duardin was heavyset, even for one of his folk, and clad in rich robes and runic armour. He wore a shapeless hat decorated with a cogwheel pin, and a strange, multi-lens monocle. An ornate drakefire pistol was holstered on his hip, and he rested one be-ringed hand on the grip. He grinned. 'A duardin who knows what he's worth.' He glanced at Gardus. 'That goes for you too.'

Gardus inclined his head respectfully. 'Cogsmith Mahk. A pleasure, as always.'

Mahk snorted. 'You almost sound like you mean it.'

'I was speaking to the Lord-Celestant,' Ahom said, looking down at the duardin. 'Wait your turn, you grease-stained... labourer.'

'What'd you call me?' Mahk's grin faded.

'You heard me.'

Mahk's finger tightened on his weapon, as if to draw it. Gardus thrust an arm between them. 'Enough. Did you wish something, cogsmith?'

'Territorial rights and duties,' Mahk said, pugnaciously. 'The Ironweld won't be cheated out of its fair share of the plunder, no matter what this *wazzock* thinks!'

'Plunder,' Gardus said. The battlemage and the duardin paused, and shared a look. Gardus straightened to his full height. 'There will be no plunder, my friends. Caddow is a sister-city of Azyr. This is not a campaign of conquest, but reclamation.'

'Reclaim what? There's no one still alive in this pile of rubble.'

Mahk shook his head. 'That ruin might as well be fresh territory.'

'But it isn't, my lord,' Albain Lorcus called out, as he strode towards them. 'It is *my* territory. By right of blood and iron. By the shadow of the Great Mountain, and the authority of the God-King himself.' He smiled thinly as he came to a halt. 'Even so, I am fully prepared to honour all documents, oaths and promises made, in good faith.' His smile became knife-sharp. 'So long as you both uphold your ends of the bargain.'

Gardus seized the opening Lorcus had provided. 'Indeed. While it is my task to reclaim this city and all its territories for Azyr, Captain-General Lorcus is responsible for the dissemination of all consequent rights and duties, as he sees fit. He will be lord here when the day is won, and it is to him you must make your petition.'

Ahom glanced at Mahk, and then at his subordinates. The battlemage frowned, but nodded. 'Very well. I shall take you at your word, Lorcus.'

'Captain-general,' Lorcus corrected. 'Or my lord. Whichever suits you.' He smiled. 'We must maintain the proprieties, reconciler.'

Ahom turned with a huff, and stalked away, trailed by his followers. Mahk chuckled and looked up at Lorcus. 'Well, you put him in his place, manling.'

'The proprieties extend to you as well, cogsmith.' Lorcus glared down at the duardin. 'I won't have you, or Ahom for that matter, attempting to renegotiate your contracts mid-campaign. Do you understand?'

Mahk leaned over and spat. His grin never wavered. 'Aye. We'll do the job we were contracted for. So long as you guarantee that we'll be paid.'

'One way or another, you'll be compensated for your efforts,' Lorcus said. He spat into his hand and held it out. Mahk copied the gesture and they shook hands. The cogsmith left them, whistling cheerfully as he stumped away.

'Madness,' Gardus said. 'To worry about such things before we've even won.' He looked at Lorcus. 'My thanks for your intervention.'

'I thought you looked in need of reinforcements,' Lorcus said.

Gardus smiled. 'Is that what you call it?'

'Conversations with men like Ahom and Mahk are battles waged with words, rather than steel. Each seeks to take as much territory for himself as possible. You must hold the line and keep them to their own territory.'

'I shall keep that in mind for next time.'

'I fear that you simply do not have the knack, my lord. No offence meant. Best leave them to me.' Lorcus tapped his fingers tunelessly against the pommel of his sword as he studied the ruins. In the light of the fires, he looked startlingly young. 'My grandfather used to tell me stories – stories his grandfather had told him – of the days when Caddow and Nordrath traded freely with each other. When they were sister-cities not only in name, but in blood.' He looked at Gardus. 'I would see those days come again.'

'As would I,' Gardus said. 'And we will do so – together.'

Lorcus nodded. 'Unfortunately, that means dealing with individuals like Ahom and Mahk. I – we – need the Collegiate Arcane and the Ironweld to make something of this place. I need sorcery and shot to tame this land.'

'You will have it, one way or another.' Gardus turned as someone called out his name. Cassandora strode towards them, her war-plate stained with soot and blood. Like Gardus, she had taken the fight to the enemy, leading the Stormforged into the thick of battle. She pulled her helm off as she joined them, and nodded to Lorcus.

'You will excuse us, captain-general. I must speak to the Steel Soul.'

'Of course. I have matters to attend to myself.' Lorcus bowed low and departed.

Cassandora waited until he was out of earshot before speaking. 'We have a prisoner.'

Gardus blinked. 'What? Who?'

'He says he's Mannfred von Carstein.'

Gardus stiffened. He knew that name. All Hallowed Knights did. The vampire who had betrayed Tarsus Bullheart and his Chamber into the hands of Nagash. The survivors had spent months after their Reforging attempting to track the beast down, only to lose him, at the last. 'Does Ramus know?'

'Not yet, but I doubt that'll hold true for long.'

Gardus nodded. 'Take me to him. Quickly.'

Ramus leaned against his reliquary staff and watched smoke climb towards the new dawn. He stood atop one of the few intact eyries that dotted the city. The immense towers had supposedly belonged to the city's noble families – looming spires of stone that were, for all intents and purposes, independent citadels. Each possessed gardens, armouries and cisterns in abundance. No two were alike, save in general verticality.

What he had seen of this one, as he led his warriors in cleansing it of the beasts who had used it as a lair, did not impress him. It reminded him of nothing so much as a vertical rat's warren, with tiny chambers and black gardens. Nothing of any value had been left unsoiled, and even the stones stank of corruption.

He turned, gaze sweeping across the canopy of shattered rooftops and towers. It was almost impossible to tell what Caddow had looked like when it still lived. The city was a desiccated corpse. The sooner it was torn down and rebuilt, the better.

There had been little fighting to do, once they arrived. The Steel Souls and the Stormforged had driven the foe back, barring a few of the more cunning beasts. Hunting them down was easy enough work, though Ramus had little taste for it.

So instead he'd set his warriors loose to see to it and retired here, hoping for a new perspective. Shyish was much as he remembered it. Looking out over the city and the wasteland beyond, he saw only a sea of endings. What sort of city could grow here, in so arid a place? Nagash had blighted the realm with his madness, and it withered day by day.

He looked up, towards the stars. They seemed impossibly distant, here. 'Why did you send me here? Is this punishment?'

As ever of late, the stars were silent. Ramus sighed and set his staff against the balustrade. He removed his helm and hung it from his belt. The wind felt coarse against his face, full of grit and smoke. He remembered what it had been like, the day he and Tarsus and the rest had first arrived in the Vale of Sorrows. A day of blood and madness. Then, it seemed that was every day in this benighted realm.

It had all gone wrong that day. From the moment they'd arrived and found the prisoner, hanging in his black sun. 'Mannfred,' he murmured. The name tasted like poison, even now. It was Mannfred who had led them to Stygxx, and Mannfred who had betrayed them to Nagash. Mannfred who had escaped again and again, his tally of victims ever increasing... Tarsus... Vandalus... the innocents of Cartha, and how many more besides? The vampire's span stretched across centuries.

Ramus touched the silver shield hanging from his shoulderplate. He unhooked it and weighed it in his hands. A sign of Sigmar's trust, or so he'd thought at first. Now, he wasn't certain.

He wasn't certain of anything save the gnawing feeling of failure that tinged his every waking moment. *He had failed.*

He had failed Sigmar. He had failed Tarsus.

He had failed himself.

'Much is demanded of those to whom much is given.' The words brought no comfort. They had not, for some time. But he said them regardless, hoping they might help him see the way ahead.

'Lord-Relictor.'

Ramus stiffened. 'Sagittus, what is it?'

The Judicator-Prime's expression was unreadable. Sagittus had acted as his second-in-command more than once during the hunt for Mannfred. A heavy boltstorm crossbow was strapped to his back, and he held his helm under one arm.

'He's here, Shadow Soul.'

Ramus did not ask who Sagittus meant. The Judicator-Prime's tone revealed all. 'Where?' he growled.

Cassandora studied the prisoner with interest. Mannfred wasn't the first vampire she'd encountered, but he was the first Mortarch. He sat on the cot in his cell, seemingly at ease. As if he were the one in charge, and not being held captive.

There were dozens of similar cells on the uppermost tier of the eyrie. It was set back into the rear of the chamber, and took up half of the available space. Each cell on the tier was the same – alcoves with bars and stone cots, and narrow flues set where the back wall met the floor. The flues were for the disposal of waste, she assumed. Some of the cells were still occupied, albeit by the long-dead.

She was not certain of the purpose of these cells. They were not a dungeon in the conventional sense, but rather reminded her of the cells beneath the Consecralium in Excelsis. A place to keep those too important to be executed out of hand, but too dangerous to be allowed to roam free. She could almost hear the whimpered moans of the forgotten dead, still echoing from the stones.

Mannfred smiled, as if reading her thoughts. He looked away, as the argument outside the chamber rose in volume. 'I recognise that voice,' he murmured.

'I expect you do.'

He looked at her. 'I don't recognise you, though.'

'A shame I can't say the same.' She removed her helm and Mannfred blinked.

'A woman.'

'Surprised?'

'No,' Mannfred said, smirking. 'Just stating the obvious. Might I inquire as to your name, my lady?'

Cassandora hesitated. Dim memories of mortal life told her that telling a creature like this her name was tantamount to an invitation. She tapped one of the prayer scrolls on her armour. 'Cassandora. Lady Cassandora to you, leech.'

'Oh, I would refer to you no other way,' Mannfred grinned. It was the sort of expression a tiger might give a particularly courageous hound. An acknowledgement of strength, but nothing more. He tapped one of the bars and winced as the air crackled. 'Mystic wards?'

'I thought it wise,' she said. She'd had Lord-Ordinator Taltus inscribe sigils of warding and protection on the cell walls and bars before they'd thrown Mannfred in. She had no doubt that the vampire would eventually find a way to squirm free, if they left him to it. Once they'd questioned him, however, she intended to see that the mystic wards were redoubled. There would be no chance of the creature escaping then.

Mannfred frowned. 'Is there still a bounty on my head, then?

How much is the God-King willing to pay to claim my scalp?' He ran a hand over his shorn pate.

'It is my duty and my honour to bring you to Sigmar in silver chains.'

He snorted. 'How noble.'

Cassandora smiled. 'I didn't say there wasn't some small pleasure in it, though.' Her hand fell to the pommel of her runeblade. 'And you should be grateful. There are some among our Stormhost who would prefer to send you back to Azyr in pieces.'

'Do not speak to him,' Ramus bellowed, as he flung the door to the chamber open and stomped in. 'He is a snake. He can charm with a word or a glance. We should take his tongue and his eyes, lest he endanger those set to guard him.'

'Case in point,' Cassandora murmured.

'Hello, Ramus,' Mannfred said, waving with mocking cheerfulness. 'Good to see you too. It's been some time since last we spoke.'

'Silence!' Ramus struck the bars with his staff.

'You should heed yourself, and lower your voice to a dull roar,' Cassandora said, rubbing her ear for emphasis. 'We may be the storm incarnate, but that does not mean we must speak with thunder and fury. Especially indoors.'

Ramus turned. 'What did he say to you?'

'Hello,' Cassandora said.

'I have no patience for inane pleasantries. I asked you a question.'

'And I answered it.' Cassandora prodded the Lord-Relictor in the chest. 'I am not one of your warriors, Ramus. Do not think to order me about.'

Ramus made to reply, but stopped as Gardus entered the chamber. 'Both of you, lower your voices,' he said, calmly.

'Ramus, I have allowed you in here only because it would be a waste of effort to try to keep you out.' He looked at Cassandora. 'Please try not to provoke him.'

'I make no promises,' Cassandora said, somewhat irked by his tone. Gardus had an unfortunate tendency to play the part of the patriarch. He doled out advice and guidance regardless of whether anyone had asked for it.

He shook his head, a slight smile on his careworn face. 'I ask only that you try, sister.' He looked at Mannfred. Cassandora's annoyance grew as she saw the smirk on the vampire's face. He had enjoyed watching his captors argue.

'Maybe Ramus is right,' she said. 'Maybe we should ensure that he cannot work his wiles on us. Shall I hold him down?' She was gratified to see Mannfred's sudden consternation. The vampire stiffened.

'Surely you would not allow a helpless prisoner to be tortured so?' he asked, looking at Gardus. Cassandora almost laughed, to see the vampire's expression of injured innocence.

'Is it torture, or merely a necessary precaution?' Gardus said. 'I have heard the stories. I know full well what you are capable of.'

'My fame precedes me.' Mannfred sat back.

'Infamy, more like.'

The vampire laughed out loud. Ramus bristled, thin sparks of lightning dancing across his war-plate. Cassandora half thought he might attack the creature, cell or no cell. Gardus interceded before the Lord-Relictor could do anything rash. 'Why are you here, vampire? Why were you skulking beneath the city?'

Mannfred shrugged. 'That is my business, surely?'

'And now it is mine.'

Mannfred bared his fangs and leaned forward. 'I'll tell you nothing. I know your reputation, Steel Soul. Soft Heart, more like. The kindly warrior...'

Gardus was on him before he'd finished speaking. The Lord-Celestant thrust his hand through the bars of the cell and caught Mannfred about the throat. He hauled Mannfred forward, slamming the vampire against the bars. Mannfred yowled, but couldn't find the leverage to break free.

'You will tell me everything, or you will burn.' As Gardus spoke, light seeped through the joins of his war-plate. Cassandora was forced to shield her eyes as the light swelled, filling the chamber with an almost unbearable radiance.

'I'd heard…' Ramus began, his voice a whisper.

'But it is something else to see it, yes,' Cassandora murmured. 'Like the light of Sigendil itself.' Mannfred had begun to shriek. Through the glare, she could see the vampire twisting and writhing in Gardus' grip. Smoke rose from Mannfred's flesh and his armour and cloak blackened, as if exposed to a great heat. For an instant, she almost felt pity for the vampire.

Abruptly, Gardus released his hold, and Mannfred sagged to the floor, face cradled in his hands. The light dimmed, faded and was gone. Cassandora felt curiously empty at its passing, as if something were lacking from the air about her. Gardus sank to one knee and stared at Mannfred's huddled form. 'Speak. Or burn.'

'You – you would not kill me,' Mannfred growled, pulling his hands away from his seared flesh. His eyes had gone crimson, as if filled with blood, and his countenance had shed all pretensions of humanity. His face was that of a beast – a night-prowling hunter, hungry for flesh and blood. 'Threaten all you wish. Sigmar would not allow it.'

'Who is to say what Sigmar would or would not allow,' Gardus said, his voice mild. 'Perhaps this moment was pre-ordained. I have faith he will make his wishes known, should I diverge from them. Speak. Or burn.' He gripped the bars, and his hands began to shimmer.

Mannfred grimaced and raised a hand in surrender. 'Fine. Yes. I should know better than to argue with fanatics, I suppose.' He hauled himself to his feet with as much pride as he could muster. 'I came on behalf of Nagash.'

Cassandora tensed. If the Undying King knew of what they were doing here, he might view it poorly. Fighting the servants of the Ruinous Powers was one thing. Having to fight the dead as well... That could mean disaster.

'He sent you,' Gardus said.

'Not quite.' Mannfred chuckled. 'I am here on his behalf, not at his command.'

'What's the difference?' Ramus snapped.

'Nagash isn't aware of our presence yet,' Gardus said. 'Is he?'

Mannfred spread his hands. 'If he were, we would not be having this conversation. No, his mind is elsewhere, these days. Pondering some great work, to which mere servants such as myself are not privy. No, I came hoping to earn his favour, nothing more.'

'How?'

'How do you think?' Mannfred grinned. 'I intended to bring the armies of Caddow to Nagash. A fleet of dust-barques, bearing the dead of a hundred generations. An army, appearing from nowhere, to strike the enemy where he least expected.'

'Why does Nagash need this army?'

Mannfred shrugged. 'He doesn't need this one in particular. He simply needs an army. He is hard-pressed, far to the south. There is... a bridge. Of sorts. An entrance to Nekroheim. One of many, and currently under attack.'

'Archaon,' Gardus said.

Mannfred nodded. 'Or one of his servants. It amounts to the same thing. Bakhos – that is the name of your foe, by the way – was ordered here to keep watch over the realmgate. To say he never expected it to open would be an understatement. I saw an opportunity to take advantage of his confusion.'

'You failed,' Ramus said.

Mannfred looked at him. 'Thanks to you Stormcasts, yes.' His gaze slid back to Gardus. 'But it doesn't have to end that way. Let me go, and I'll sweep aside the servants of Chaos for you. I'll raise the dead and march them right through Bakhos' camps, and away from here. You can win this war without losing a single Azyrite life. Imagine how pleased Sigmar will be.'

'If you think we would trust you…' Ramus snarled. He subsided at a glance from Gardus. Mannfred laughed, as if he had expected that reaction.

'I had to try. I hold the eternal hope that one day I will run across a sensible Stormcast. Not you, Ramus, obviously.' Mannfred gestured dismissively. 'Never mind. The dead of Caddow will remain at rest a bit longer, I suppose.'

'For an eternity,' Gardus said. He looked at Ramus. 'I want those catacombs opened and everything within consigned to peaceful oblivion.'

Mannfred laughed. 'You lack the wit and strength both to break those seals alone.'

'Then you will help remove them,' Cassandora said.

'That is beyond my power, I'm afraid.' Mannfred sprawled back on the cot and set one boot up against the frame of the cell. He examined his claws. 'No, you are out of luck, my silvery friends. Those vaults will remain sealed until such time as Nagash wishes them opened. Which might be sooner than you think, if he gets word of this… endeavour of yours.' Mannfred twitched a finger. 'Tsk-tsk. Pride goes before a fall, I'm told.'

'If you cannot open them, why were you attempting to sneak down there?' Ramus growled. 'I will know if you are lying.'

Mannfred shrugged. 'I thought I could open them alone. I was mistaken. Your warriors interrupted me as I was preparing to leave.' He smiled. 'It would have made a pretty trick, though. I played the part of Bakhos' dogsbody for months, all for a chance at those burial vaults. I intended to sweep south with a fleet of dust-barques, and drive the foe before me. Archaon's curs would have fallen like wheat before the scythe.' He laughed again and inter-laced his fingers behind his head. 'Ah well. Nagash will simply have to make do with the numberless legions already at his disposal.'

Ramus stared at the vampire. Cassandora, in turn, watched Ramus. To a mortal, Ramus would have seemed a stone, but to her altered perceptions the Lord-Relictor was almost trem-bling with rage. He hated Mannfred, that much was plain. It was understandable, but worrisome in its intensity.

She turned to Gardus. 'The representatives from the Collegiate Arcane might be able to open those vaults, with the proper motivation.' Ahom was a greedy soul, eager to plumb forgotten knowledge and improve his standing among his fellows.

'A good thought,' Gardus said.

Mannfred chuckled. 'I doubt that.'

'Be silent, leech,' Ramus snarled.

'Or what? I am already interred in this skyborne oubliette. What more can you do to me?' The vampire spread his arms. 'Will you lop off my head, or split my heart? No. I am too val-uable a prize to discard so readily, despite your threats to the contrary. Burn me if you wish, but I know you will not truly consign me to the pyre. So I will laugh and talk and there is not a thing you can do about it, you morose, overbearing–'

Ramus slammed his staff down. Lightning snaked across the floor and through the bars. Mannfred yelped as it coiled about him. He fell from the slab, flesh smoking. He rose and lunged, snarling. Ramus struck the floor again, and Mann-fred screamed as lightning ripsawed through him. He fell, but

Ramus struck the floor a third time, causing the vampire to convulse in obvious agony.

'Ramus, that is enough,' Gardus said. When Ramus appeared not to hear him, he caught the Lord-Relictor by the shoulder and spun him around. 'Ramus! Cease.'

Ramus shook his head. 'Not until he is ash. Not until he has paid for his crimes.'

'He will pay, brother,' Cassandora said. 'But not like this. We are not savages, to execute a beaten enemy in the heat of anger.'

Mannfred, smouldering on the floor, gave a weak laugh. 'No, no, it's much better to execute them after a mock trial, in the cold dawn of new day.' He hauled himself to his feet, his blistered flesh already healing. He grinned. 'So civilised, you Stormcasts. To hear Nagash speak of Sigmar, one would not expect his chosen to be so... *merciful.*'

Ramus took a step towards the cell, but Gardus pulled him back. 'Leave him, brother. Let his adder's tongue wriggle in the dark, unheard and forgotten. Come.'

'We could just pull it out, as Ramus suggested,' Cassandora mused. 'It would grow back, but the problem would be solved for a time.' Mannfred glanced at her, but thought better of commenting. He returned to his slab, and faced away from them.

'He's lying,' Ramus said, as they left the chamber.

Gardus nodded. 'Of course he's lying. Everything I know about him says that he lies as readily as we breathe. But the end result is the same. We will open the vaults without him, and consign what resides within to cleansing flame and honoured burial. This city will belong to the living.'

'What will we do with him in the meantime?' Cassandora asked. 'I'd feel better if he were elsewhere, under heavy guard. Should we send him to Sigmaron in chains? Let the God-King decide his fate?'

Gardus shook his head. 'We'll keep him under guard for now and send him on as soon as the entirety of our forces have come through.' He sighed and ran a hand through his hair. 'This… Bakhos worries me. If Mannfred is to be believed then our foe is not simply some idle warlord, but one of Archaon's slaves.'

'We defeated him,' Ramus protested.

'No, he withdrew.' Gardus looked at the Lord-Relictor. 'He felt our steel, and fell back to regroup. Archaon would not have sent a complete fool to guard this place. They will muster and come again.' He frowned.

'We must be ready.'

CHAPTER SEVEN

WARRIOR POETS

*The fall of Semele was due more to a failure of
philosophy than any weakness in its phalanxes.*

– Cadwell Gern
Leopards in the Smoke: A History of the Six Republics

Mannfred lay on his stone cot, listening to the sounds of a city
returning to life. Caddow echoed with the thrum of industry.
The stones reverberated with it. 'The music of Azyr,' he murmured. He sat up and ran his palms over his scalp.

He stared at the bars of his cell, watching the interplay of
mystic wards that held him confined. To his eyes, it was as if
a swarm of cerulean fireflies were clustered about the bars.
The hum of Azyrite magics made his fangs itch. He gestured,
attempting a minor unbinding spell. A fat spark of light burst
before his eyes and he jerked back with a curse.

Blinking tears away, he shook his head. 'Damnation.' The

wards were strong. It would take both time and concentration to break them.

The Stormcasts were taking no chances this time. He could sense the skeins of magic that had been strung throughout the chamber. Not all of them were to prevent him from leaving. Some were there to alert the Stormcasts in the event of an escape attempt. 'Clever,' he murmured, tracing the lines of enchantment. They stretched out of the chamber and beyond his sight. He reached up as if to pluck them, but restrained himself.

He could escape, if he put his mind to it. But there would be a cost. And the inevitable pursuit. He settled back on the stone cot, frowning. He closed his eyes and immediately felt a surge of discontent and hunger pulse through him. Ashigaroth was close. The dread abyssal had sensed his predicament through their soul-bond, and come a-hunting.

'Open your mind to me,' he murmured. 'Let your eyes become mine.'

As ever, Ashigaroth resisted his intrusion. Mannfred could feel the dread abyssal thrash and snarl as the vampire's thoughts overlaid his own. But, as always, the creature eventually subsided. It was akin to sinking into a sea of silver razors. The dread abyssal's thoughts were not those of a normal beast – there was a dreadful power to them, and unless Mannfred was careful it would sweep him away.

Through Ashigaroth's eyes, he saw a flash of silver, as Stormcasts marched along a street below. Ashigaroth was crouched somewhere far above, clinging to the side of an eyrie. At his urging, the creature turned. He could see smoke and hear the roar of artillery, and in the distance he spied the pavilions of the Maiden's Son. 'Go,' he said. 'I wish to see.'

Ashigaroth shrieked in protest, but leapt into the air and swooped towards the distant encampment. The dread abyssal moved more swiftly than any living creature, and the pavilions swelled from pinpricks on the horizon to great splashes of gaudy colour, stretching beneath him. From above, the pavilions more resembled the fortress they were meant to be.

The great tents sat atop high, sloped earthworks, protected by dry moats filled with thick stakes and jagged debris. Palisade walls had been erected here and there, mostly between the outer pavilions. The walls were less a means of defending the encampment than they were a way of delineating the territories of Bakhos' various subordinates.

Smoke rose thick and foul from many of these outer areas as warbands fought each other. Champions met blade to blade amid screaming crowds of warriors and slaves as each sought to replace a fallen war-leader or to usurp control in the wake of battle. That was only to be expected, whether in celebration of victory or acknowledgement of defeat. The servants of the Ruinous Powers needed little reason to turn on one another.

Ashigaroth swooped low, scattering a flock of carrion birds. Music rose from the inner pavilions, and through the dread abyssal's senses Mannfred could smell spilled wine and blood. Too, he could feel Bakhos' presence. There was a monstrous weight to creatures like the Maiden's Son, as if the accumulations of their sins had bent the realms out of shape around them. The aether trembled when they moved.

That the warlord had survived came as some small relief. Without Bakhos, the army would tear itself apart and prove little distraction to the Stormcasts. As long as Bakhos was alive, he was a threat and a bargaining chip in one. Mannfred intended to buy himself time with the only coin he had – information. About Bakhos, about the size and composition of his forces. Anything to delay being sent to Azyr.

The thought of being interred within the celestine vaults of

Sigmaron elicited a rare thrill of fear in Mannfred. The wrath of men could be endured or turned to more amenable ends. But the wrath of a god… There was little chance of surviving that, even for one as cunning as himself. Sigmar was more like Nagash than his followers admitted. The God-King was no less vengeful than his opposite number, but where Nagash often allowed cold calculation to guide his reprisals, Sigmar was more tempestuous.

But if he could delay that moment, buy himself a day, or a week, then he might be able to come up with a way to escape his predicament, and perhaps even leave Caddow with what he'd come for. He needed to remain observant and seize whatever opportunity presented itself.

Ashigaroth shrieked suddenly and wrenched himself away from the pavilions. Hunger bloomed and Mannfred found his control slipping. He cursed himself for allowing his mind to wander. The dread abyssal spotted something near the edge of the encampment and dived towards it with a screech of anticipation. A slave, Mannfred realised, as the wretched creature looked up, scarred features twisting into an expression of mortal terror. The slave screamed, but the sound was swallowed in the ugly noise of its demise. Ashigaroth slammed the ragged shape hard into the ground, claws tearing at paper-thin flesh.

Mannfred blinked, breaking the connection. He could still taste the echo of the slave's blood and fear on his tongue. He rubbed his temples, trying to ease the ache of prolonged contact. Being in Ashigaroth's mind as the dread abyssal fed was unpleasant, even for him. The creature had no interest in flesh, save as an appetiser. Ashigaroth's preferred provender was the mortal soul. He would devour what was left of the slave's shrunken spirit, leaving its ruined body for the birds.

Despite the suddenness of the broken contact, he had seen

enough. The city was far from won, and where there was conflict, there was opportunity. Mannfred settled back, eyes closed. There was always an opportunity, if one but had the wit to see.

He just had to be patient.

'Loose,' Bakhos said, his voice loud in the stifling confines of the pavilion.

Arrows flew, some with more accuracy than others. Few of those who followed him were natural archers. Those who were rarely used bows in battle. But this was not battle, or even a hunt. This was divination.

In Semele, as a youth, he had seen the art practised. There, accredited sages and seers had counted the arrows, and divined patterns from their falling. Here, he had only a few cackling hedge-witches, culled from the tribes that haunted the wastes, to read the portents, malign or otherwise.

Arrows thudded down, several of them catching slaves too slow to avoid the deadly rain. They fell, screaming piteously. One of his eunuchs glanced at him for approval.

'Very well,' Bakhos said, with a sigh. The eunuch made a sound that might have been a laugh and flung out a hand, signalling a nearby kennel-master to release his hounds.

The Chaos hounds gave yowls of pleasure as they slipped their chains and shot towards the wounded. The hounds were an unnatural medley of bestial traits – some had once been pure-blooded hunting dogs, while others might have been men. They fell on the wounded slaves, biting and tearing until their screams were silenced, to be replaced by the sounds of eating.

Hedge-witches mumbled and crept through the field of arrows, plucking up this one and waving their tattooed hands over that one. None of it was particularly illuminating. 'If only Vlad were here,' Bakhos murmured. He glanced at his guest.

Ghosteater crouched nearby, gnawing on a length of bone. The gor looked up, as if alerted to Bakhos' attentions, and bared his fangs. 'Is that a challenge or a smile, I wonder?' Bakhos said, as he rose to his feet. 'Or both, eh?'

Hands behind his back, he descended his royal dais, trying to churn gold from his sluggish thoughts. It had been so long since he had fought a proper war. He had forgotten how fast one's fortunes could turn, and how little plans meant in the face of the enemy.

His survival had been a matter of luck.

It was not the failure itself that rankled, but the swiftness of his defeat. He had allowed himself to be led into a trap, and had lost almost a third of his forces to stones and timing. It irked him. That he had escaped was only a small comfort. Others had not been so lucky.

Vlad was gone – dead or lost, he could not say. That was the hardest blow. He'd come to rely overmuch on Vlad. Being in command was tedious. Vlad had provided the necessary bulwark between Bakhos and the dreary scheming of his subordinates. Now, he would be forced to deal with it himself.

He turned as something screamed somewhere outside the pavilion. The sounds of raucous battle were audible. He had no doubt that a host of new champions would present themselves to him in the morning. But tonight was for the drowning of sorrows in wine and blood. While his hedge-witches busied themselves reading the arrows or plumbing the guts of unlucky slaves, he would seek answers elsewhere.

Bakhos frowned, studying the beautifully illustrated map of Caddow and the Sea of Dust that adorned one side of his pavilion. It stretched from post to pole, and it took several moments to walk from one end to the other. He'd made it himself, crafted the inks from daemonic ichors and plant dyes and tanned the hides of a hundred beastkin to a supple softness, before stitching them together. He'd spent years exploring the territories Archaon had so generously gifted him, and had waged thousands of mock wars against every conceivable foe across the width and breadth of the region.

His eunuchs had helpfully marked the map for him on his return. It now showed the positions of his forces and those of the invaders, as reported by those among his forces observant enough to take note of such trivialities. The invaders were consolidating their forces in the heart of the city, no doubt even now making it a bastion upon which he would break himself. That was what they did. And he would have to attack it – his followers would accept no less. Again and again, until either they were destroyed, or the enemy was.

Suddenly annoyed, he drew his sword and hacked at the map, reducing it to ragged ruin. Panting slightly, he turned away.

'Waste of time,' he said, softly. 'All such a waste. All that preparation, and for what? No grand duel of stratagems or carefully deployed tactical acumen. Instead, nothing but a stalemate. As if two obese champions were engaged in a shoving contest. First one to fall loses.' He snatched a jug of wine from the trembling hands of a slave and gulped half of it down. 'Where is the glory in that?' he bellowed. 'Where is the release from tedium?'

The warriors in the pavilion watched him warily. For his part, he studied them with disgust. They were out of condition. Sluggish. They had grown fat and lazy out here with no enemies save the dead and each other. Only the beastkin were strong, but they had not a brain between them, more was the pity. He glanced at Ghosteater, who was watching him, without fear. Only interest. Like an animal, sizing up potential prey. He hid a smile.

There might be some brains there, after all.

He tossed the empty jug aside and stabbed his sword into the ground. Leaning on the pommel, he surveyed the assembled war-leaders. Only a few had answered his call. The rest were too busy fighting among themselves or putting down revolts in their own ranks. Most of those before him were mortal – hill-men and sellswords. Brigands, whose only loyalty was to the Absent God. But some few were like him, blessed by Slaanesh.

The hulking Chamonian, Etax the Maw, and the slim, androgy-nous Ghyranite, Lemerus of the Sibilant Glade, stood out among these. Etax was a massive brute, clad in golden war-plate that had been fitted to his swollen form by his legion of bond-slaves, with a flat, wide head that was little more than an oscillating maw of hooked fangs. A pair of pale, heavily tattooed slaves stood to either side of him, draped in golden chains that hooked to Etax's chest-plate. These were his translators, Etax being no longer capa-ble of human speech.

Lemerus, in contrast, was slim and sylphlike. It did not resemble a human anymore, if it had ever been one in the first place, instead being almost aelflike, with delicate features and wide eyes of purest black. Wormlike tendrils of braided hair hung down from Lemerus' head, and its mouth was a wide, red slit, held open by a series of hooks set into its pale flesh. It wore a set of dark, scaly armour, resembling the skin of a fish, and held a long-hafted maul wrought in the shape of a woman's face. It met Bakhos' gaze with a sharp-toothed smile.

Bakhos frowned. Etax and Lemerus were his strongest sub-ordinates at the moment, as well as the most influential. He trusted neither of them. Vlad had played the balance, keep-ing them preoccupied with their own rivalry. But Vlad was gone, and he needed a new second-in-command. One of them would have to do.

Decisions, decisions.

Bakhos sighed. 'I led phalanxes once – squares of iron and

flesh. None could resist us. And yet, here I now stand, master not of disciplined legions, but of raucous monsters.' He took another swig. 'Frankly, I wouldn't have it any other way. Discipline is boring. It is simply a cage by another name. But cages have their place, on occasion.' He lowered the jug. 'We must remember our cunning, my friends. Those skills which brought each of us here must now once more be put to use. We must think. We must see a way forward.'

'We should sweep them from the city in a wave of blood and joy,' a great brute, shrouded in leather and iron, roared. Others cried out their assent. Bakhos took another drink. When the cheering had died down, he looked around.

'Are your memories that short?' he asked, gently. 'Or are you simply idiots?'

A few scattered cheers answered the question for him. He sighed and nodded. 'Our numbers are indeed great, but they work against us on occasion. This is one such time. Charging in heedlessly – amusing as it was – got us bloodied and little else. Discipline is the key. Hateful, I know. But it is the only way.'

'We await your wisdom with breathless anticipation, O Maiden's Son,' one of Etax's translators said, in a high, thin voice. 'But speak, and Etax shall race to obey.'

'That is good to hear, my friend.' Bakhos turned. 'For too long, I have let you play at war. Now you must learn the truth of it. The hard labour of battle.' He made a fist. 'Forget all that you know. Forget your traditions. From here, there is only one tradition. Mine.'

'Would you make us phalanxes then, O Maiden's Son?' Lemerus looked around as it spoke, as if judging support. Bakhos could almost smell the ambition rolling off the champion. He knew that scent well. The need to prove oneself was strong in those who danced in the shadow of the Absent God.

'No. But I would make you an army.'

'But we are many armies already, my lord,' Lemerus purred. 'Any one of which might throw back the invader, if given the chance. Will you deny us our due glory?'

'I would ensure victory.' Bakhos emptied the jug and tossed it aside.

'Whose victory, O Leopard of Semele?' Lemerus spread its long arms, as if it were an actor upon a stage, playing to an audience. 'Yours, or ours?' There were murmurs at this, though whether at the champion's audacity, or in support of its state-ment, Bakhos could not say. He felt a moment of unease. Defeat had stolen some of his grandeur. Lemerus would not be the only one questioning his fitness to lead.

'It is one and the same,' Bakhos said. He looked around. 'Unless... someone has an alternate strategy to propose?' In his youth, he had seen the commanders of the armies of Semele use a similar tactic to undermine dissension. 'Come, come, speak up... Etax?' He motioned to Etax. 'Your campaigns in the Sellarn Gulf are legend. What would you do?'

One of the translators began to speak, but Lemerus cut them off. 'Why ask a brute to explain subtlety?' it asked, challengingly. 'What will Etax suggest save the most straightforward of ploys?'

Etax turned, his great mouth flexed in an unsightly fashion. One of the translators pointed a shaking finger at Lemerus. 'Who are you to question our subtlety, Lemerus? We were waging war when you were but a puling infant, suckling poi-son milk from your mother's withered teat.'

Lemerus' hand fell to its sword. 'Age is no proof of wis-dom, brute.' The two champions squared off as around them, the others chose sides. Bakhos had known they would. He stepped back as the first punch was thrown. A marauder, cov-ered in furs and feathers, brought both meaty fists down on the neck of a hunchbacked swordsman, dropping the mal-formed warrior flat.

'Idiots, fools and monsters,' Bakhos muttered, watching as brawls broke out across the pavilion. The Absent God was too generous at times, bestowing his gifts upon those not fit to bear them. He snatched another jug from a fleeing slave and turned away from the confusion. There was no point in attempting to restore order. Better to let them fight, and deal with the sur-vivors afterwards.

He drank, letting the sour liquid burn down his gullet. As he gulped the wine, he thought of Semele, of the city-states and the people there. So different to those he led now, and yet so alike. His own folk had had seasons devoted to many deities, includ-ing the Absent God. In the summer, when the grapes ripened, and wine flowed, the folk of Semele had danced to the music of pipes and engaged in orgiastic ceremonies designed to please the Dark Prince. And Slaanesh had smiled to see such debauchery.

But there was discipline too. The cage of ritual and train-ing, that had seen the phalanxes of Semele conquer a thousand fields of war. He missed it, sometimes.

He missed many things.

The vessel cracked in his hand, slopping wine to the ground. He cast the broken shards away and snapped wet fingers. A slave hurried forward, jug lifted over her bowed head. She was pale, after the fashion of the local nomad tribes. The waste-folk travelled the Sea of Dust on slim dhows, following the ghost-winds. Sometimes, those winds led them too close to Caddow, and then they were nomads no more.

He stroked her scarred cheek. 'You are lovely,' he murmured. 'She was lovely, as well.' She did not look at him, did not make a sound. Her passivity irritated him, and he snatched the jug from her trembling hands. 'Go. You bore me.'

She hurried away, and he turned back to the brawling. Every champion and chieftain in the pavilion was involved now. A scrum of ambitious nonentities, each hoping to scavenge a few crumbs of divine notice. He laughed softly, worked the stopper loose and swigged from the jug. Sometimes, it seemed the only way to get through life was by dulling his senses with wine. He wondered if even this pathetic excess pleased Slaanesh.

He caught sight of a familiar white shape watching him. The beastman, Ghosteater. The creature stood apart from the rest, seemingly content to let others spill blood for a chance at glory. He met the beast's gaze, and the creature approached.

'Teach,' Ghosteater grumbled, slapping his scarred chest. Bakhos lowered his jug and fixed the beast with a curious eye. 'What was that?'

'Teach. Teach Ghosteater.' The beastman sank down onto his haunches, flipped back one of the rugs covering the parched earth and began to draw in the dirt with a claw. 'Phalanx. Teach... Show. Need to learn. Good to learn.'

Bakhos crouched opposite the beast and watched in growing delight as he scratched out what might have been crude lines and formations. 'How do you know of these things?' he asked, wiping the excess wine from his mouth.

'Ghosts teach some,' Ghosteater said, tapping the side of his head. 'But not everything. Need to know more.'

'Why?'

Ghosteater looked at him, and Bakhos realised that the creature was actually considering how best to answer. He grinned, pleased. It was all but unheard of, in his experience, for such creatures to show any concern for such things. They were beasts in mind as well as body. But this one was different. Smarter. Or at least wiser.

'To conquer,' the beast said, finally. 'Many little tribes. Too

152

many. Must be one. Mine.' Ghosteater bared his teeth. 'Ghost-eater's tribe.'

Bakhos sat back on his heels and took a long drink. Then he handed the jug to Ghosteater. 'Yes, I can see why that might be tempting, my friend.' He sat down and crossed his legs, nomad-fashion, as Ghosteater drank.

'Very well. Let us discourse as true warrior-scholars, eh?'

Ghosteater listened as Bakhos spoke, and did not interrupt. Despite his earlier foolishness, it was clear that the Maiden's Son was wise, in his way. And Ghosteater needed wisdom. The voices in his head had quieted after his escape from the city, and now huddled sullenly at the base of his skull. They had no words for him, no advice. In time, that would change, but he was too tired to wring it from them now.

So instead, he turned to the living. He listened, blocking out the noise of the fighting around him. It was difficult. Every instinct compelled him to join the bloodletting. But he knew it would earn him nothing. It was a trick, and one he had used himself on occasion. Bakhos had pitted his angry followers against one another. They would tire themselves out and forget why they had been angry in the first place. Or, at the very least, they would lack the strength to challenge him directly.

'War is not about survival. That is the first lesson.' Bakhos gestured to the markings Ghosteater had made on the ground. 'War is a game – move and countermove. You must think of it that way, else you lose sight of victory.'

Ghosteater nodded. 'Phalanxes,' he growled.

Bakhos smiled widely. 'A bundle of sticks.'

Ghosteater blinked in confusion.

Bakhos gestured. 'One stick might be strong, but it can be broken easily. Ten smaller sticks, bundled together, can better resist breaking than one alone. One warrior might win great glory, but die as the enemy overwhelms him. But ten warriors, fighting together, will push the enemy back. There is less glory for each, but a greater chance of victory.' He gestured to the fighting around them. 'Each of them, worth five of the enemy. But the enemy will send six. Do you see? The enemy does not care about glory, or survival – only victory. We must think as they think, and fight as they fight, else we will be chewed to pieces. An army of heroes, beaten by slaves.'

Ghosteater considered this. 'Who are the sticks?' he asked, finally.

'Many little tribes, made into one.' Bakhos upended the jug, found it empty and tossed it aside. He gestured to the champions brawling around them. 'They will not learn. Too set in their ways, too far along their own path. But you… You could learn, if you wished. With the right teacher.'

He means to use you, one of his ghosts said. A rough voice. Another stirred. *Trick-trap you, yes-yes. Hurt-kill you.*

Ghosteater restrained a snarl. Something about Bakhos had set the ghosts on edge. They feared for him, because his death meant their doom. But he was no fool. He saw what they saw well enough. Bakhos wanted to use him – use his folk – as his kind always had. But there was opportunity in being used, if he was cunning enough to grab it. 'You?' he asked.

Bakhos shook his head. 'I cannot be seen to show such favouritism. Not yet. For now, I have another in mind.' He motioned to one of his eunuchs, hovering nearby. The mirror-helmed warriors had taken up positions all around them, without Ghosteater noticing. 'Find the Unborn. Bring him to me.' The eunuch nodded and ducked out of the pavilion.

Bakhos looked back at him. 'You saved one of my warriors. Do you recall?'

Ghosteater grunted. 'Maybe.'

Bakhos smiled and stood. Ghosteater scrambled to his feet a moment later. As he did so, a warrior approached, following one of the eunuchs. He dimly recognised the newcomer by his pastel war-plate, with its strangely slick surface. The warrior had his helm under one arm and his features were strangely youthful.

'Ah, Chaell – welcome. You wished to thank your saviour, I understand. Well, here he is, in all his barbaric splendour.' Bakhos stepped aside and gestured invitingly. He turned, and Ghosteater followed his gaze. The fighting in the pavilion had begun to die down. Bakhos' lips thinned. 'I shall leave you both to it.'

He left them, his eunuchs falling in around him. Ghosteater looked at Chaell. He bared his fangs in half-threat, half-greeting. 'Talk,' he growled.

'I am Chaell, called the Unborn by some,' the warrior said. His voice was soft. Almost musical. Ghosteater looked at the extended hand, and then at the warrior's oddly unlined face, seeking some hint of mockery. Finding none, he clasped the warrior's forearm. The plates of Chaell's armour tensed like flesh in his grip.

'Ghosteater.'

'I know. There is only one of you, in the entirety of this land. As there is only one of me.' Chaell smiled. 'And speaking as that one, I must convey my thanks for your timely intervention, earlier. I might well have perished, had you not aided me.' He paused. 'Why did you aid me?'

A good question, beast, a ghost asked. *Never known you to be altruistic.*

Ghosteater flicked away the spirit's question. He shrugged and looked away. 'We do not always eat our own. No matter what you say about us.'

Chaell's smile became quizzical. 'I assure you, I have never spoken of your folk. Indeed, I had never even thought of your kind, until you pulled me from the jaws of that trap.' He laughed. 'My mind is full of nothing else, now.' He turned away as another warrior called out to him. He waved in greeting and glanced at Ghosteater. 'I look forward to our continuing acquaintance. Something tells me that it will prove... interesting.'

As Ghosteater watched him go, a dry voice spoke up, accompanied by a familiar quill scratch. *If a man like that offers you his hand, it's best to make sure it's not got something nasty in it,* the ghost said. He remembered its voice. The one that liked to talk about buildings.

The ghost that helped you escape, you mean?

Ghosteater snorted. Then, careful to let no one hear, he said, 'You don't help – you serve. Your ghost, your wisdom... mine.'

Only if you bother to listen.

'Don't need to know about buildings. Need to know about phalanxes. About tactics and strategy.' The words felt strange in his mouth. For most of his kind, there was only one strategy. That of the ambush. Strike swiftly, and fight until the foe was dead. That was how all wars were conducted in the stone forests of Caddow. Ambush and counter-ambush.

But there were other ways. Better ways.

Ghosteater growled, softly.

'We just need to learn them.'

CHAPTER EIGHT

DIRGE

There are over four thousand lines in the Great Dirge of the Gazul-Zagaz. Each a story in and of itself, commemorating the slow decline of their clan...

– Grund Hakkisson
Folksongs of the Forgotten Clans

Thalkun stroked the aetherwing's feathered neck and murmured softly to the bird. A moment later, it was gone, a flickering streak, carving across the dark sky. The Raptor-Prime turned, surveying the ruins below. The sounds of battle had long since faded, and now the only sounds to be heard were the clatter of the Ironweld's great machines. He sighed and removed his helm, exposing tanned features to the chill wind.

The air stank of death. It always did, to some extent. It was Shyish, after all. But this was new death. Recent. There were bodies in heaps and piles, smouldering still. The Huntsmen of

Azyr left few survivors in their wake. He'd seen them, at a distance. Killing like lightning, and hurtling away.

Eventually, when the Ironweld pyre-gangs reached them, the bodies would be burned in cleansing sweeps of flame, so that their foulness would not taint the foundations of the new city that was to come. From what Thalkun had seen of it, he was of the opinion that it would be better to consign the ruins themselves to the fire, and build over the ashes.

The city had belonged to beasts and monsters for too many centuries. Only dark things could flourish here.

'They've retreated,' one of his Vanguard-Raptors said. The warrior crouched nearby, balancing herself easily on the ancient slates. Like all of his cohort, her silver war-plate had been darkened with ash, so as not to give away their position. Four more warriors crouched in sight on the broken roof, and others were scattered nearby.

Thalkun nodded and set his longstrike crossbow aside. 'But not far,' he said. He reached into his armour, retrieving his pipe and a bag of smokepinch. Carefully he began to fill the bowl of the pipe with a layer of crushed leaves.

'The scent will give us away,' another of his warriors said, disapprovingly.

'If they get close enough to smell it without us noticing, then we're dead already,' Thalkun said, setting the stem between his teeth. He took the thin-bladed knife from his belt and scraped it along a finger of his gauntlet, summoning a spark. A moment later, the smokepinch took and he sucked in a lungful. It was harsh, like a tumble of ashes, but there was an underlying sweetness. It was a vice left over from his mortal life, and one he cherished. Puffing gently, he sent a smoke ring wafting through the air.

Down below, the sounds of mortal labour had grown louder.

Temporary emplacements of celestine and steel were being set across thoroughfares and boulevards, even as cogwork watch towers were erected. He could smell the smoke of cooking fires and the less pleasing stink of Ironweld boilers.

'They make too much noise,' someone murmured.

'They aren't alone in that,' Thalkun said. He peered south, towards the pavilions of the enemy. He'd only seen them at a distance, but that was enough. He could hear music, of sorts, and screams. Someone would be punished for their failure today. That was usually the way of it with such creatures. There was always someone to blame, some flaw in an otherwise perfect stratagem.

Thalkun had made a study of his prey in the months since the Swiftblade had brought them to Shyish. Like any hunter, he'd learned their habits, their strengths and weaknesses. They had plenty of both. Raw courage, balanced by a distinct lack of discipline, save in rare cases, made them more akin to a natural disaster than an army. Like orruks, in a way.

But there were differences. Unpleasant ones.

Orruks could be cruel, but they lacked imagination. The greenskins got bored quickly. They might eat you, laughing all the while, but they wouldn't keep you alive while they did it. They might torture you, but not for long.

The followers of Slaanesh, on the other hand, were monsters. From the lowliest slave to the mightiest lord, they supped on agony as if it were their meat and drink.

Thalkun had come to hate them. Not passionately, but fiercely. Of all the servants of the Ruinous Powers, he hated them the most. Even Nurgle's putrid slaves sought something beyond mindless debauchery.

He tensed as metal scraped rock somewhere below. 'Gullat,' he said.

'Who else would it be, brother?' Gullat swung himself onto the roof, moving lightly despite his war-plate. The Hunter-Prime's helm hung from his belt, and he carried a shock handaxe in one hand. His features were lean and unshaven, and his eyes were the colour of the night sky. He waved a hand in front of his face. 'Are you smoking again?'

'It relaxes me.'

'On this wind, it carries.'

'That's what I said,' a warrior piped up.

Thalkun pointed at him, without looking. 'Quiet.' He looked at Gullat. 'I know my business, brother. And you'd do well to remember it.'

Gullat raised his hands in surrender. 'Fine. Don't say I didn't warn you.'

Thalkun grunted. 'Your Vanguard-Hunters?' he asked, changing the subject.

'Close by. The Swiftblade wanted to keep an eye on our neighbours after that attack.' Gullat smiled crookedly. 'We're setting up a welcome for them.'

Thalkun raised an eyebrow. Gullet chuckled. 'Deadfalls, mostly. A few spring traps. A wolf-pit or two.'

'When did you have time to cut the stakes?'

'Didn't have to – they left behind a lot of spears.' Gullat gestured and Thalkun handed over his pipe. The Hunter-Prime inhaled deeply and handed it back, coughing slightly. 'Smoke-pinch?' he choked out.

'From Excelsis.'

Gullat nodded. 'Good leaves.' He coughed again and wiped his mouth. He pointed. 'Only two major thoroughfares from the northern districts. Both wide enough for troops to pass through in great numbers. Everything else is akin to a forest path – cramped, dark and too convoluted to find your way through without a compass.'

'Tricks and traps won't stop them.'

'That's why you're here, brother. You and your Raptors can help us pick off their scouts, if they even bother with them. If we can prevent them from massing, we might stand a chance.' He smiled thinly as he spoke.

Thalkun frowned. 'That many of them, then?'

Gullat sat back against the slope of the roof and ran a hand through his hair. 'More than we anticipated. Did you count those tents, brother? Hundreds of them, scattered across the southern wastes.' He held up three fingers. 'There are more than thirty distinct beastherds in the city itself. We spent days watching them...' He trailed off and shook his head. 'If they ever truly unite, we'll be facing several thousand warriors, at least.'

'And how likely is that, given the beating we just gave them?' Thalkun knew the answer. He was asking for the benefit of his warriors. Not all of them had his experience, and this was as good a moment as any to teach them.

Gullat grinned. He understood why Thalkun had asked such an obvious question. He had done the same, with his own warriors. 'Very. We killed the stupid, and the stupidly brave. That leaves the smart ones – the ones too wary to charge at an unknown enemy. They've been spoiling for a real fight with only each other to kill. Now they've got it.'

Thalkun puffed on his pipe. 'It'll take a few days for them to figure out who's in charge. That's if those to the south haven't already taken the matter out of their hands.'

Gullat nodded. 'Listen,' he said, softly.

Thalkun did. Drums thumped, somewhere in the city. Horns blared, distantly. Other, less recognisable instruments whined, out in the dark. It almost sounded as if the enemy were celebrating. Perhaps, in their twisted sensibilities, victory and defeat were almost one and the same. That was as close as Thalkun could come to understanding them.

'Are they coming again?' someone asked.

'No,' he said. 'But they will.'

The Gazul-Zagaz were easy to find. One simply had to follow the singing.

The Shyishan duardin had kept to themselves in the hours after the opening of the realmgate. Gardus had half expected them to melt away into the night, their oaths fulfilled. Instead, they had taken over one of the old buildings near the ziggurat, and begun to sing. The sound of it drifted eerily through the streets, carried on the night wind.

The structure had once been a temple, Gardus thought. One of a hundred in this district of the city, and one of more than a dozen on this street alone. A street of small gods, whose names and rites were now but dust on the wind. It was square, save for the cracked remnants of an onion dome, and the broken leftovers of ornamental pillars lined its outer walls. A semicircle of flat, rough steps led up to a set of double doors, set into an archway carved to resemble a pair of great cats.

Gardus led his delegation up the broken steps. Sathphren walked beside him, while Ramus and Cassandora trailed behind, the Lord-Relictor carrying a cloth-wrapped bundle. At the top of the steps, two of the duardin Pyredrakes stood sentry. They studied the approaching Stormcasts for long moments, saying nothing. Gardus glanced at Sathphren, who stepped forward.

'We would speak with Gnol-Tul,' he said.

'He leads the dirge,' one of the guards rumbled.

'The dirge cannot be interrupted,' the other added.

'We will be as quiet as mice, my friends,' Sathphren said.

'Big mice,' the first guard said.

'Very big mice,' the other said, doubtfully.

'But quiet ones,' Sathphren said, hand over his heart. He glanced back at Gardus and the others. 'We loom large, but tread softly.'

From inside the building, the sound of singing faded, for just a moment. The guards glanced at one another, shouldered their drakeguns and stepped aside. 'Enter and be welcome,' one said. Sathphren bowed low and gestured for Gardus and the others to follow him. As they stepped through the doors, the dirge began anew.

The temple was small and cramped. Beyond the entry hall was a single, wide chamber, its walls decorated with fading murals. Stains that might have been blood marked the floor, and the smell of drakeguns hung on the air. Whatever had used this place as a lair had not surrendered it willingly. But it belonged to the Gazul-Zagaz now.

The bodies of their fallen lay in neat rows, each covered by his or her robes. The rows stretched from one side of the chamber to the other – nearly a third of their number. Members of Tul's bier walked along the rows, murmuring prayers and writing on clay tablets. The rest of the duardin were grouped in the centre of the chamber, their hands linked, their voices raised in a groaning, rumbling dirge.

The dirge ended as the duardin spotted the newcomers. Tul stepped from their ranks, his golden mask gleaming in the light of the torches that illuminated the chamber. He came to greet the Stormcasts, his sword in the crook of his arm. 'Be welcome, children of Azyr,' he said, his voice carrying easily through the chamber.

Gardus bowed to him. 'Gnol-Tul.'

Tul returned the gesture. 'Lord-Celestant.' He nodded to the others. 'Have you come to join the dirge?' The question seemed less an invitation than a greeting. Gardus shook his head, regretfully.

'I fear my singing voice is not what it was, Gnol-Tul.'

Sathphren removed his helm. 'I would be honoured to do so, Tul, if the invitation stands. It has been some time since I raised my voice in song.' Tul's eyes widened slightly in evident surprise, but he nodded and gestured.

'Gazul welcomes all voices.'

'Very accommodating of him,' Ramus said, as Sathphren went to join the duardin. Tul looked up at the Lord-Relictor.

'Yes. He is an obliging god.'

'And dead.'

'That too.' Tul looked at Gardus. 'If you have not come to sing, why are you here?'

'Sathphren says that you intend to leave soon.' The dirge had begun again, though softer this time. Gardus watched as the Lord-Aquilor joined his voice to that of the duardin. Though he could detect little difference between them, Tul evidently could. The duardin nodded in seeming satisfaction.

'We do. The journey home is long, and best started soon, once the last song has been sung, and the names and deeds of the dead recorded.'

'Will you need an escort?'

Tul laughed harshly. 'It is not necessary. Our enemies are more concerned with you at the moment. We will slip out unnoticed easily enough. We long ago learned how to avoid the attentions of the living.'

Gardus nodded. 'You have our thanks, Gnol-Tul, and that of Sigmar. Without your people, we would not have been able to find this place and do as we have done. To show our gratitude, we have brought you a token of our esteem.'

He gestured and Ramus stepped forward. The Lord-Relictor

unwrapped the bundle he held to reveal a gleaming runeblade. Bones had been set into the length of the blade, and the hilt was crafted from a femur. Each of these morbid additions had been covered in intricately carved mortuary sigils, and they hummed softly with power.

Tul took the sword gingerly. 'This blade – it sings.' He barked a command, and one of his subordinates hurried forward to take it from him.

'In a sense,' Ramus said. 'It was crafted from the bones of a saint, and the remains of the blade that slew him. Should your folk have need of us, drive it into the earth. The blade will call out and the Hallowed Knights will answer – whatever the distance, whatever the threat. Call, and we will come.'

'That is our oath to you, Gnol-Tul,' Gardus said. 'We swear it on our faith.'

Tul ran a hand along the blade. He looked at Gardus and nodded. 'An oath for an oath,' he said.

'As it was, as it must be,' Gardus said.

Cassandora sighed as they left the temple. 'What's next, then?' She took her helmet off and ran a hand through her short, shaggy hair. 'Anyone else that needs seeing off?'

'We left the Swiftblade behind,' Ramus said. They started back towards the ziggurat, which rose over this section of the city like a lodestone.

Cassandora motioned dismissively. 'He's fine. Let him sing. The Swiftblade is useless at anything that doesn't involve blade work.'

'He's not that bad,' Gardus said, mildly.

'Have you seen his requisition orders?' Cassandora scoffed. 'He can barely spell his own name. Superfluous vowels *everywhere*.'

Gardus laughed. 'That is why we have scribes.' His smile

faded as he looked around. 'Still, I wish the Gazul-Zagaz were staying. We could use those drakeguns of theirs. And their knowledge of the surrounding terrain.'

'You worry too much,' Cassandora said. She swung a hand out, indicating the streets around them as they walked. 'Our armies already occupy the surrounding plazas. From there, we can press out into the city's outer districts. It will take weeks, perhaps months. But with the realmgate secured, supplies and reinforcements will not be hard to come by.'

'It's not supplies I'm worried about. There's still an army camped on our doorstep. Not to mention the potential one below us.' Gardus shook his head. 'There's still much that can go wrong. We must be vigilant.'

'Have some faith, Steel Soul,' Cassandora said. Gardus snorted, and she smiled. 'Besides, we'll soon turn this city into a bastion that no king, whether Three-Eyed or Undying, can break.' She pointed down a side street. 'And there's the proof.'

Gardus stopped. 'Is that Taltus?' The Lord-Ordinator had kept to himself since their arrival, always on the move, overseeing the preparation of the city's defences as Grymn and the other Lord-Castellants saw to the construction of the Storm-fort surrounding the ziggurat.

'Hard at work as ever,' Ramus said. Cassandora glanced at him, wondering whether he meant it as a compliment or a jibe. It was hard to tell, sometimes.

The Lord-Ordinator stood nearby with Mahk, Lorcus and a group of Ironweld engineers, both human and duardin. Gardus nodded in satisfaction. 'Good,' he murmured. 'Lorcus is proving singularly adept.'

'He's a canny one, that mortal,' Cassandora said, as they continued past the group. Taltus raised a hand in greeting, and she returned the gesture. 'Calmer than most.'

'Which is why he was chosen for this. If he is to rebuild this city, to make it flourish anew, then he must have the heart and mind for it. Not just on the battlefield. A city is a mechanism of many moving parts, with no one more important than the other.'

'Apt, if not poetic.' Cassandora looked around. 'Though if this city is a mechanism, it is a decidedly broken one.'

'And that is why we stand here. To repair what has been broken.'

Cassandora smiled. 'Ever the optimist, Gardus.' She stopped, watching as a workgang of Freeguild soldiers set up ropes and pulleys in order to haul sections of wood up to the broken terraces of a ruined building. 'It is a strange thing, fighting alongside mortals.'

'You have done it before,' Gardus said.

'Only duardin – and Fyreslayers at that,' Cassandora replied. 'They are more akin to a force of nature. But this – by the time the mortals arrive, we will have already erected defences and Stormforts. Our task is all but done as they begin theirs.'

'Perhaps it is past time that we worked alongside them, then. And not just on the battlefield.'

'We do.' She looked at him. The light was back, gleaming between the joins of his war-plate. It suffused his face, rendering his features almost formless. As if there were no face there at all – only light. She felt a flicker of unease as she looked at him, and could tell from his expression that Ramus felt the same.

'Do we?' Gardus asked. 'Or do we hold ourselves separate from them? I see it in our brothers and sisters – in the Knights Excelsior, among others. This assumption of superiority, as if we are greater, somehow, than those from whom we came. It is a weakness to see strength in isolation.' He gestured, and light washed across the nearby buildings. Startled mortals turned, squinting against the sudden glare. Cassandora saw several fall to their knees, murmuring prayers. Others made protective gestures.

Gardus continued, unheeding. 'Look around – under the sky, under the stars, there is but one people. This I believe. All are one in the eyes of Sigmar. All are worthy of life. And perhaps one day, they will realise it. *We* will realise it, and–'

'Speaking of which, what of our guest?' Cassandora asked, heading off the sermon before it could get started. 'When will we send him back? The sooner he's gone, the better.'

'We should kill him now,' Ramus said, harshly. 'We have shown him mercy too many times. Let us be done with him now, and forevermore.'

'That is not Sigmar's will.'

'Sigmar has been wrong before,' Ramus said. He glared at them, as if in defiance. Ramus was bitter at the best of times, but this was different. Cassandora glanced at Gardus and saw what she thought might be worry in his eyes.

'Ramus, there is no sin in questioning the gods.' Gardus shook his head. 'For a time, I sought certainty, the way the river seeks the sea. I thought that once I found it my journey would be done. But I see now that it was only the beginning.'

'What do you mean?'

'Faith must always renew itself. There is no end, no final answer. Only the eternal search, and the dance of starlight on the surface of the water. But even if there are no answers to be had, the questions must be asked. Lest we become complacent... or worse.' Gardus looked at the Lord-Relictor. 'Your doubts are ours. Your questions are ours as well. You do not have to suffer them alone.'

Ramus stared at him. 'What do you know of anything, Steel

Soul? What questions could you have? Nothing has been denied you. Sigmar's hand is on your shoulder for all to see. His light cloaks you.' He laughed bitterly. 'It is the rest of us who are left in the shadows. The rest of us who are left to wonder at the intentions of our god.'

'What a spirited theological debate.' Cassandora laughed sharply. 'Don't bother trying to improve his mood, Gardus. This one enjoys marinating in his own misery.'

The Lord-Relictor glared at her. 'I enjoy nothing about this, least of all his pious blithering. Sparing those creatures was simply another mistake, added to a very long list.' He pulled his cloak about him. 'I will endeavour to do better. If you will excuse me.' He turned and stalked away, shoulders stiff, head held high.

Gardus made to call out to him, but Cassandora stopped him, shaking her head. 'Leave him to his gloom, Gardus. I'll make sure he doesn't jump off the ziggurat. Go, attend your duties. Leave this one to me.'

Gardus hesitated. 'Be kind, sister,' he said, softly.

'I am always kind,' Cassandora said. Gardus raised an eyebrow, and she smiled and made the sign of the twin-tailed comet over her heart. 'I swear, brother. I will treat him as gently as a ghyr-lioness treats her cub. Now go.'

Ramus stalked along the street, away from the others, cursing himself silently. Ruined structures rose to either side of him, casting jagged shadows across the pockmarked street. The fires of the workgangs were visible between buildings, and he could hear the sounds of the mortals at their labours.

They would work through the night, and every night to come, until the defences were deemed suitable. Then would begin the slow expansion, one street at a time. Thus were the realms tamed by Sigmar's chosen. Ramus frowned and touched the mirrored surface of the shield hanging from his shoulder-plate.

He'd thought himself chosen, once. Now, he knew better. He had been a tool, nothing more. Sigmar had taken his rage at Mannfred's betrayal and put it to use. And in the end, it had resolved nothing. Tarsus was still gone. Mannfred had escaped. And Nagash's promises of alliance had dissolved like a morning mist.

Failure had compounded failure. A litany of collapse, from beginning to end.

That was why Gardus' homilies grated so. In truth, Ramus bore the Steel Soul no real ill-will. There was much to admire in him, and few in the Stormhost spoke of him with anything save praise. That was why he'd hoped Gardus would be the one to see sense, that he would agree to help Ramus crack the vaults of Shyish and rescue Tarsus from whatever hell Nagash had consigned him to.

But Gardus had turned him down, just like all the others. Sigmar had decreed that it be so, and the faithful followed. 'Much is asked, of those to whom much is given,' Ramus murmured. How often had he said those words? How much was too much? How many souls had been lost, for some advantage known only to the God-King?

He stopped and looked up. In the centre of the street, a statue rose – a figure in thick robes, holding a scroll in one hand and a bird on the palm of the other. Time had worn the statue's features to nothing, but something about it rang familiar.

Ramus had few memories of who he had been before he had become what he was. Part of him did not wish to know. He feared that the man he had been might be disappointed in who he had become. He chuckled sourly. 'Haunted by my own ghost,' he muttered.

He heard footsteps behind him. 'I wish to be alone,' he began.

'Idiot.'

Cassandora's blow caught Ramus by surprise. Her palm struck the back of his head, and he spun, eyes wide.

'You dare...?'

'Obviously. I just did it.' Cassandora met his glare with one of her own. 'He was trying to help, fool.'

'Then he was doing a singularly poor job of it.'

'Or maybe you are too mired in the mud of your own dissatisfaction to see a helping hand for what it is.' She looked up at the statue. 'It is not easy, losing a friend,' she said, after a moment.

'You do not know how I feel,' Ramus snarled.

'I know exactly how you feel, fool.' Cassandora shook her head. 'I was not always Lord-Celestant of the Stormforged, or have you forgotten? I was merely a Knight-Vexillor when Artos Stormforged fell, leaving our Chamber leaderless in the midst of battle.' She looked at him. 'I saw him, saw my – my *friend* die. I saw his soul rupture into a thousand azure shards, to be trampled under the wheels of his slayer's chariot.' She fell silent.

Ramus hesitated. 'I... I had forgotten,' he said, softly. 'Forgive me.'

'There is nothing to forgive, brother. But you are a fool.'

'What?'

'Your hubris knows no bounds. You think that you alone have felt the pain of loss. But that is the story of every Stormcast, from Liberator to Lord. And many of us have had to hammer a sigmarite spike into the great pillar in the Sepulchre of the Faithful in the name of a lost comrade. Of a lost friend.'

Ramus looked away. 'He was the best of us,' he said, softly.

'Maybe. But he is gone and you now stand in his place.' She looked away. 'Do not let anger eat you hollow, brother. Do not throw away the gift Tarsus gave you, in the name of anger. There was a saying among my folk, when I was mortal – set the wolf free.'

Ramus chuckled. 'The wisdom of the steppes, is it?'

Cassandora laughed. 'If you like. It's a good saying, regardless.' She caught him by the shoulder. 'Let your anger go. Move forward. Leave the past to the past, and set your eyes to the future.'

'That would be easier if the cause of my anger were not still among the living.' Ramus glanced towards the distant shape of the eyrie where Mannfred was being held. The thought of the vampire sitting in his cell, with his head still attached, sent a thrill of fury through him. His grip on his reliquary staff tightened, and he wanted nothing more than to storm the eyrie and hurl Von Carstein from the highest balcony.

'He is our prisoner now, brother,' Cassandora said. 'He will not escape. There are guards on him day and night. The wards on his cell have been reinforced. He will go to Azyr and face Sigmar's justice.'

The thought brought Ramus little pleasure. He had seen enough to know that while Sigmar still hoped to form any sort of alliance with Nagash, Mannfred's survival was almost certainly assured. The vampire would become a bargaining chip. He growled softly and thumped the ground with his staff.

'As you say, sister,' he said, concealing his unease.

'I pray only that Sigmar lets me carry out the sentence myself.'

CHAPTER NINE

DECISIONS

The minds of the damned are a maze of unspoken decisions.

– Karl Logrim
Memoirs of a Witch-Finder

Well. Were you planning to escape, or…?

Mannfred closed his eyes. 'Patience is the key to any victory.'

That would explain why you've been taken prisoner, I suppose.

'The same could be said of you, Tarsem. Be quiet please. I'm trying to think.' Mannfred lay back on his stone cot and massaged his temples, waiting for the obvious rejoinder. But his memories remained stubbornly silent. He sighed.

Outside the cell, he could hear the Stormcasts speaking softly to one another. He could smell the scented oils they rubbed into their war-plate, and the acrid odour of the energies that coursed through their weapons. They prayed often, one standing on guard while the other knelt. As they murmured, the

173

wards about his cell flared and crackled. The prayers strengthened the mystic barrier in some way. Or perhaps renewed it.

It had leached into the walls, stretching azure filaments between the stones. Slowly, level by level, the Stormcasts were sanctifying this place. It made his flesh crawl, but there was no way out that did not bring with it the risk of his own destruction. They would be ready for it. Indeed, some, like Ramus, probably wanted him to try.

You make enemies the way a gambler creates debt.

'No one asked you, Megara. And you weren't exactly beloved, yourself.' The Mistress of Doomcrag had built her tiny fiefdom on the blood of its former ruler – literally, in some cases. He flexed his hand. Megara had been possessed of a fierce spirit, an unquenchable thirst for mystic knowledge...

Flatterer, the memory of her whispered. He felt her cool hand stroke his cheek, as she had so often done in life. He banished the memory with a twitch of his head. Megara was dead. Had been dead for centuries. Truly dead.

While we are remembered, can we be truly said to die?

'How very philosophical of you, Tarsem. I shall keep that in mind.' Mannfred sat up and swung his legs over the edge of the cot. He ran his hands over his head, trying to silence the ghosts that murmured in his head. 'Of course, if you keep bothering me, I'm never going to escape. I will be executed, and then we'll all be well and truly dead.'

Past time, probably. Vitalian laughed. Mannfred could almost imagine him, leaning against the wall, arms crossed. *To outlive one's legend... not healthy, that.*

'My fame is eternal. So long as Shyish exists, the name of Mannfred von Carstein will be remembered. There's even a kingdom named after me.'

Didn't you name it?

'That's not the point.' Mannfred jabbed a finger at the phantom Vitalian. 'I have outlived nothing.'

Save those of us who called you friend, Vitalian said.

Or lover, Megara murmured.

Or brother, Tarsem whispered.

Mannfred lurched to his feet, fangs bared. 'More fool you, then, for ever thinking those things. I am who I am. I am who I have always been. Whatever comes, I am always true to myself.'

'But who are you?'

The question brought him up short. Mannfred turned, eyes narrowed. Gardus Steel Soul stood before the bars of his cell, watching him. 'How long have you been standing there?' he snarled.

'Long enough to hear you arguing with ghosts.' Gardus took off his helm. His features were ordinary. Plain. Not handsome, or ugly. The face of a forgotten man. White hair, colourless and shaggy, covered his head. And his eyes...

Mannfred turned away. The Stormcast's eyes were unsettling. Too calm by half. Too centred. It was like looking into a sacrificial well to find every skull on the bottom looking back. There was no anger there. No bitterness. Only calm acceptance. The way Tarsem's eyes had looked that last day, before it had all turned to ash.

'What do you want, Stormcast?'

'Information. On the forces arrayed against us.'

Mannfred turned back, a smirk on his face. 'Ask, and receive enlightenment.' Before Gardus could speak, however, Mannfred raised a finger. 'But... I require something in return.'

'What do you want?'

'Freedom.'

'No.'

'An alliance, then. Sanctuary. I help you, you help me.'

'No.'

'Then I'm afraid that we're at an impasse.' Mannfred shrugged. 'I have no reason to help you. You've already decided my fate, and your success or defeat here means little to me.' He crossed his arms and leaned against the wall. 'But, if you bend a bit… perhaps we can come to some… arrangement?'

Gardus frowned. 'That you still live at all is a compromise.'

Mannfred laughed. 'Then we are halfway there!' He scratched his chin. 'Have you managed to breach the wards about the catacombs yet, out of curiosity?'

Gardus ignored the question. 'Bakhos is attacking piece-meal – why?'

'He's bored,' Mannfred said. 'This is a game to him, at the moment. A way of enlivening the tedium of his existence. Or else he's attempting to winnow out those among his forces who intend to supplant him. Or both.' He leaned forward. 'But it'll only stay that way for so long. One way or another, they will come for you in strength, and the forces you have mustered here will not be enough to contain them.'

'We did so once, and easily.'

'Because of me. I led them into your volleys and onto your swords because it made my task easier.' Mannfred smiled. 'Bak-hos is not a fool. There is a keen strategic mind there, though buried under centuries of decadence. Once he has taken your measure, he will devote himself fully to your destruction. He might not be able to kill you himself, but he knows one who can.'

'Archaon.'

Mannfred nodded. 'It will take him time to come to that realisation. Days, weeks, months… Eventually, he will swallow his pride and send for aid. And in the meantime, he will bleed you. He will throw whole tribes at you, just to amuse himself. You will not be able to build, to expand, because you will be preoccupied defending yourselves.' He gestured. 'But release me, and I will wipe him out for you.'

'You said that before.'

'And I will keep saying it, until one of you listens.' Mannfred shook his head. 'The problem with you Stormcasts is that you see compromise as weakness – as a failing.'

'Not all of us.'

Something in Gardus' tone brought Mannfred up short. He said nothing as Gardus continued. 'Tarsus compromised. Trusted you when you could obviously not be trusted. I have often wondered why. What did he see in you, Mannfred von Carstein?'

There was no mockery in the question. That was a surprise. Mannfred found himself at a loss. 'I don't know what you mean.'

'What possessed him to listen to you?'

Tell him, brother. Tell him why I listened to you.

Mannfred tried for a sneer. 'I'm sure I don't know. Perhaps he was just a fool.'

Gardus nodded. 'Perhaps. Or perhaps he knew something that we don't.'

Mannfred looked away. 'He knew nothing. We made a bargain, and I fulfilled it. What does it matter to me that he suffered for it? As you say, it is obvious that I cannot be trusted.' He waved a hand. 'Better to be rid of such a fool, I feel. I'm sure Sigmar agrees – else he would have cracked the vaults of Shyish and saved him.'

'And yet, here we are.'

Mannfred looked at him. Gardus was frowning, but not in anger, he thought. Rather, as if he were pondering some thorny issue.

'Yes, here you are.' Mannfred licked his lips. He twitched, try-ing to shake free of the sudden feeling of weight that had settled on him. 'Bakhos will come, and you will be driven back. That is not prophecy, but hard fact. Unless you free me.' He turned away, suddenly unsure. 'That is my final word.'

Gardus departed, without saying anything more. Mannfred stood in the centre of his cell, wondering at the unsteadiness of the world about him. His earlier certainty had vanished. 'What did you see in me?' he murmured.

Nothing that was not there, Tarsem said.

The realms moved in strange ways. Fate carried men as swiftly as a river, and drowned them just as surely. He felt it now, lapping at him, threatening to pull him from his feet.

As if he were on the cusp of some great opportunity.

No, my friend. A decision.

Mannfred looked up. 'What do you mean?'

Silence. He frowned and looked at his hands. How much blood was on them? He had never before considered it. Or if he had, he had forgotten the question and answer both. He curled his fingers into fists.

Mannfred went back to his cot and sat.

He had much to ponder, and a feeling that there wasn't much time left to do it in.

Bakhos studied the ruined map with a keen eye. His slaves had attempted to repair it, to the best of their meagre abilities. In gratitude, he had slain them with only a single blow apiece. Their bodies now hung in the camp's larder, to be salted and stored against a harsh winter. He ran a finger along the tat-tered edge of a sword-stroke, smiling thinly.

'Adequate,' he murmured.

Behind him, the victorious soon-to-be-dead awaited his

decision. They were the winners of the latest blood-bouts to determine those who would be given the honour of leading an assault. The bouts provided amusement for his grumbling subordinates, and further pruned his ranks of those too dangerous to be controlled.

Bakhos tapped three places on the map – areas where Ghost-eater's scouts had spied enemy forces building up their defences. 'Maygrel, you will lead your horsemen along the eastern thoroughfare, on the morrow. Tabbisa, you and your tribesmen will take the southern ramparts. And to you, Hulmean, I leave the central plaza.'

He turned, facing the three champions. Maygrel and Tabbisa were mortal – scarred tribal leaders, marked with ritual unguents and carrying the crude tools of their trade. Maygrel was from some distant steppe, his lanky, bow-legged frame built for a life in the saddle. Tabbisa was a muscular woman wearing a high, horned headdress and armour that had been beaten into shape, rather than forged. One of the oathbound tribes, sworn to the Three-Eyed King's service.

Hulmean, on the other hand, was not mortal, not any longer, but a brute, sealed in his black war-plate by the whims of the Dark Gods. He stank of rot and spices, and tangles of greying hair emerged from the gaps in his armour. In other places, growths of what might have been bone or callus pushed through the metal and gleamed wetly in the torchlight.

'You honour me, my lord,' Hulmean growled, striking his chest-plate with his fist.

'As you honour me with your unquestioning fealty, my friend.' He turned, playing to the audience. 'As you all honour me. It does my heart good to see you here, rather than brawling amongst yourselves. We are stronger together than apart.'

Bakhos caught Etax's black gaze and held it. Lemerus tittered.

The two champions stood apart from the others, surrounded by their sycophants. Surprisingly, they hadn't killed each other yet. Instead, they'd used the brawls and challenges to solidify their own power bases. Factions were forming about them. Etax nodded, perhaps in recognition of the unspoken chastisement, and gently stroked the head of one of his slaves.

With the war-leaders chosen, the informal meeting splintered into the usual raucous revelry. There was still enough wine to drink and songs to sing yet, despite increased consumption of both. Things would become more difficult when they ran out of one or the other. But that was a problem for another day.

Bakhos stood in silence, watching as his subordinates played their games of influence and status with each other, vying for his attentions or the favour of those of higher rank. There would be more duels tonight. More murders. And tomorrow, three new champions would request the honour of attacking the enemy. As it should be.

He motioned to one of his eunuchs. The mirrored helm twitched and the eunuch glided away. The rest of his eunuchs followed suit. They would spread out among his followers and spy unobtrusively, taking the pulse of his army. A lesson he'd learned early on – it paid to know what warriors were saying when they thought no one was listening.

Bakhos snagged a jug of wine and a goblet from a cowering slave. He tore out the cork with his teeth and spat it at the map. Though he was loath to admit it, defeat was a possibility. The enemy had access to a realmgate, weapons that could reach great distances, and seemed well led. Were they to meet on open ground, his phalanxes against theirs, he was certain he could break them.

But this way, this straining tug-of-war, did not favour him. He needed an edge. He needed to bloody them and break their defences. The probing attacks he arranged would do little more than distract them. He needed something more. He caught sight of the white shape of Ghosteater lurking near the map, and smiled. 'Yes, something more,' he murmured.

Bakhos strode towards the beast. The creature was studying the map as if he understood what it was. Maybe he did. 'What do you think, my friend?' he asked, as he filled his goblet. He handed the jug to the creature, and Ghosteater slurped wine thirstily.

'You will not conquer the city this way.'

Bakhos nodded. 'No. That has never been my aim. I did not come here to rule, you know.'

'Why come, then? Why take what was ours, if not to rule?'

The question brought Bakhos up short. He looked at the beast with new respect. As he'd suspected, there was a mind there. A barbaric one to be sure, but keen. Here was a beast who could learn, and in learning, perhaps become more useful than others of his savage kind. After a moment, he answered.

'I came into the underworlds in search of someone I lost.' He smiled thinly. 'I fought my way through legions of the unliving, and parcelled out my soul a piece at a time, but I never found her.' He paused. 'I have not found her yet,' he corrected.

He gestured about them. 'This, all of it, is simply flotsam and jetsam. The accumulation of adventure. It is of no more importance to me than this cup.' He hefted the goblet and crushed it. Wine spilled over his fingers and dripped to the ground. He whistled, and two Chaos hounds ambled over. He extended his hand and the beasts licked at his fingers, cleaning them.

'Why stay then?' Ghosteater growled. Another keen question. A hint of resentment. Bakhos' smile widened, and he felt a flush of pleasure. Not just a mind, but ambition as well. He'd seen a flash of it earlier, but here it was again.

'Vanity. I sought Archaon's aid in my quest and was given a

duty in turn. Guard this place, while his spirits seek my love in remote realms. But it has been almost a century, and no word from the Varanspire. No word from the Three-Eyed King, or his servants. A more cynical man might suspect that he had been forgotten.' He gazed at the map. 'Still, it has not been without its pleasures.'

Ghosteater grunted. Bakhos could not say whether it was a noise of agreement or not. He looked at the albino beast. 'How many tribes of your sort lurk in those ruins? A dozen? Two?' He paused. 'What would you do with them, if I gave them to you?'

Ghosteater licked his chops, eyes narrowed. 'Why would you?' he growled.

'Call it a gift.' Bakhos gestured to a slave, who brought him a new goblet. 'It was laziness, you see. That is why I left your folk to their own devices for so long. I see now my mistake. This is why Archaon set a watch here. I should have devised fortifications and traps. Instead, I wasted time planting vineyards in the hills and taking slaves. But that changes now.' He drained his cup and held it out for a passing slave to refill. 'I have sent messengers to the herds lurking in the hills, and those on the outskirts of the city. The chieftains will come, because I have commanded it. And when they come, I will see that they bow to you. Would you like that, my friend?'

Ghosteater peered at him, as if suspecting a trick. Bakhos smiled. It was a trick, just not the sort of trick the beast was used to. The beast shook his shaggy head. 'I must think.'

Bakhos lifted his goblet in salute. 'Take all the time you wish.' He turned back to the map. 'I have no doubt you will come to the right decision, when the time comes.' He gestured. 'Now, leave me. I have a war to plan.'

* * *

Ghosteater licked his chops and turned away, leaving Bakhos to his contemplations. He felt the eyes of champions and slaves alike on him. Weighing him. Gauging his importance. None had challenged him yet. They would, in time.

But for now, he was nothing. Just meat.

If you are wise, that is what you will stay, a ghost murmured. *It is the highest stalk which is first cut. An old Shyishan saying.*

Ghosteater grunted. The old man who liked to talk about buildings. What was his name? It tickled the edges of his consciousness. Most of his ghosts had forgotten their names, forgotten everything but what he needed them to know.

The study of buildings reveals the innermost thoughts of their builders. And my name is Herst, brute. Palento Herst. Scholar and gentleman. My name is known from the academies of Hammerhal to the salons of Glymmsforge–

Ghosteater flicked the words away. Buildings were for men. Soft men, too soft for living in the wild. Beasts were not soft, not weak. Beasts built nothing, raised no statues, imposed no order on the chaos of the world. Such things were anathema to Ghosteater's folk.

And what of herdstones, then? What of the great fanes of bone and flesh your kind assembles in darkened glens?

'Different,' Ghosteater muttered.

How?

'Gods command. Beasts obey. That is the way of it.'

Why?

Ghosteater paused. Such a question had never occurred to him. He growled softly, irritated. 'That is the way it has always been.'

Yes... but why? The first lesson a scholar must learn is to always ask... why?

Ghosteater growled again, silencing the old man. 'Not a scholar. Meat.'

Who? Me, or you?

'Both.' Ghosteater shook his head.

Oh, I think that you do yourself a disservice, beast. The inside of your head is a labyrinth of intricate construction. I look forward to exploring it, as my soul crumbles to a whisper. Perhaps I shall even teach you something, before the inevitable darkness.

'Teach me nothing,' Ghosteater growled.

We'll see.

Herst's voice faded back into the constant susurrus of whispers. The ghosts were growing agitated. Of them all, only the old man's voice held no fear, no hate. Ghosteater didn't know what to make of it, or why the old man had chosen now, of all times, to assert his presence. Regardless, he remembered Herst now, more fully than before. As if, by talking to him, he had kindled the fading memories to a new vibrancy.

The old man had not been frightened. Not of Ghosteater, or the sounds of death rising from the rest of the caravan. He'd had a pistol, but had not fired it. Instead, he had simply held Ghosteater at bay as he scratched the final words onto the parchment before him. 'Wait,' he'd said. 'Wait a moment, please.' When he'd finished, he'd set his quill back in its pot of ink and turned to look at Ghosteater.

'Aren't you a fine beast,' he'd said, softly. And then, he had set his pistol aside, and smiled. It was the smile that Ghosteater remembered most. While the expressions of men were often an enigma to him, this one had seemed almost… joyful.

It was that smile that had prompted him to devour the body, after. Curious, he had hoped to learn something from the old man's ghost. Instead, Herst had remained silent. Until now.

Ghosteater shook his head, and made his way across the pavilion towards the great avalanche of cushions which occupied an out-of-the-way corner. Daemonettes and mortal warriors lolled among them, passing thin pipes full of some rancid herb back and forth among themselves. The air was thick with a cloying fug, and Ghosteater waved a hand before his muzzle, attempting to clear the air.

Chaell the Unborn sprawled among them, stroking the quill-laced skull of a daemonette. He held a pipe in one hand, and streamers of multicoloured smoke slipped between his lips as he spoke. 'Ah, my friend. Come. Take a pipe. Relax yourself.'

'Foul,' Ghosteater growled, snout wrinkling. 'I need to speak to you.'

'I regret that I am otherwise preoccupied,' Chaell said, lazily. He gestured to the daemonette. 'Why not have a dance, eh?' He caught the daemonette's quills and pulled its head up to look at him. 'K'rst'il, my dear, why not dance with my friend, eh?' He blew it a kiss and released it.

The daemonette rose, its every movement a lesson in languid hauteur. It circled him, tracing his scars with the tip of a crustacean-like claw. 'I smell souls on you, little beast. So greedy. Give me one.'

Ghosteater jerked away from its touch. 'My souls. My prey.'

'Greedy, greedy, greedy,' it murmured, androgynous features twisted into a pouting expression. 'Why are you so greedy? Be nice. Let me have one.' It leaned towards him in a parody of affection, needle teeth flashing behind thin lips. 'Just a little one. Just a taste.'

Inside him, some of his ghosts fluttered in terror. Others raged. Only one remained silent. Watchful. Ghosteater was almost grateful to the old man's soul, in that moment, else he might have been overwhelmed. The daemonette caressed his muzzle, black eyes staring into his own. Seeking weakness. They made men tremble. Made wise men foolish, and the fearful brave.

But Ghosteater was not a man. He shoved the creature away, with a snarl of contempt. He felt, rather than saw, the others bristle and rise to their sister's aid. His hand fell to the hilt of his khopesh. A hand closed on his wrist. Ghosteater turned, teeth bared. Chaell released him and stepped back. 'Easy, my friend. No need to start a brawl.'

'Talk,' Ghosteater growled. 'Not dance.'

'Very well.' Chaell waved the agitated daemonettes back. 'I see you are in no mood for relaxation. Come.' They strode away from the cushions and foul-smelling smoke. 'Well? What did he say?'

'He calls the chieftains to gather. He says they will be mine, if I wish.'

Chaell frowned. 'Do you?'

Ghosteater shrugged. 'Don't know.'

'There are many here who would jump at such an opportunity, were it offered them. To lead such an army... A rare thing.'

'He gives me what is mine by right,' Ghosteater growled. 'As if we are meat, to be shared. We must be more than meat.' He shook his head. 'We rule, but only where you – where the Blessed Ones – do not wish to. You take our kingdoms from us when it suits you, and devour our young. You herd us into battle, and take the eyes of the gods from us.'

Chaell frowned. 'That is the way it has always been.'

Ghosteater looked at him. 'That is not the way it should be. We are more than meat.' He slammed a fist into his chest. 'More than beasts. We are the children of the gods, no less than you.' He snarled and flexed his claws. 'Now we will prove it.'

'He's using you, you know,' Chaell said, softly, after a moment. 'He's bored, whatever his claims. Looking for an excuse to leave. That's what Etax and the others say.'

'Then why not just leave?' Ghosteater growled. It was the

same question he had asked Bakhos. He wondered if Chaell would have a different answer. The Chaos warrior was wise in the ways of the Blessed Ones.

'Archaon, obviously. Bakhos swore to sit sentry here. If he fails or abandons that duty, then there is nowhere in the realms he will be able to hide from the Three-Eyed King.' Chaell tugged on one of his braids. 'But, if he can pawn that duty off on another...'

Ghosteater grunted. 'Me.'

'An unexpected choice, but I can see the wisdom. Your kin now outnumber us, especially if these seemingly ill-planned assaults he's conducting continue. They are wise enough to retreat to their territories and wait, rather than charge out, looking for trouble. But united...' He trailed off and smiled. 'You can't do worse than us, at least.'

'No. We will do better,' Ghosteater growled. '*I* will do better.'

CHAPTER TEN

SIEGEWORKS

The weaknesses of a city may be seen in the placement of its streets.

– Vorrus Starstrike
Meditations on the Sacred Duties

Lord-Ordinator Taltus unrolled a hastily sketched map of Caddow before him, pressed against the wall of a building. He tapped a spot on it, a tangle of narrow streets to the west of their position. 'These streets here are in deplorable condition. I suggest erecting a stationary emplacement across them until we can begin repairs.'

Around him, the city rose wild. It had gone feral in the centuries since its fall. Streets had buckled, leaving gaping pits where thoroughfares had been. Many of the great towers had fallen, creating impromptu mountain ranges. Ornamental gardens had either withered away or flourished with savage abandon. A thick latticework of roots now winnowed through the city, and strange trees grew around the great cisterns that fed each district.

Taltus turned as the whistle-crack of a Judicator's bow echoed along the street. At the eastern end of the avenue, a silver battle-line of Hallowed Knights advanced into one of the immense cul-de-sacs that dotted this district. The sounds of a skirmish echoed a moment later. He paused, waiting to see if he would be needed. When he was certain his presence wasn't required, he turned back to the map. 'If we place stationary emplacements to the south and the west, we can create a secure corridor through this district.'

'That'll leave us with a gap in our lines, once we begin the advance,' Albain Lorcus said, with a doubtful glance at the cul-de-sac. He leaned around Taltus and traced the streets on the map with a finger. 'And what about all these side streets?' Taltus nodded approvingly. The young commander of the Gallowsmen had a keen eye for the little details.

'Collapse them,' Mahk suggested. He stood nearby, peering through the eyepiece of an ornately wrought rangefinder mounted on a heavy tripod. 'Better to knock it all down and start fresh. Turn that whole district into a killing field.' The duardin cogsmith made an adjustment to the rangefinder. 'We could start now,' he added, rubbing his hands together. 'Flatten this entire block, scrape it back to the bedrock.' The leader of the Ironweld forces had a fondness for destruction that Taltus found vaguely unsettling.

'I don't recall giving permission for that,' Lorcus said, mildly. Mahk looked at him.

'I don't recall asking, manling.'

'Given that I'm paying for your powder and shot, I assumed that I had some say in how it was deployed.' Mahk burst out laughing. Lorcus raised an eyebrow, but maintained his temper.

'Also, I'm sure I don't need to remind you of the terms of the contract you signed?'

Mahk stopped laughing. The duardin scowled at Lorcus. 'No,' he said, sourly. 'No true duardin needs reminding about such things.' He huffed and turned back to his rangefinder. 'It was just a suggestion. No need to bring up contracts.'

Taltus hid a smile. Lorcus was proving more than competent at managing his assets. That was good. Raising up a fallen city was always a difficult process. If it wasn't the Ironweld wanting to turn everything into one big foundry, then it was the Collegiate Arcane wanting sole rights to everything between the horizon and the stars.

Not to mention the various factions and interests who would follow the army through the realmgate sooner or later. Guild traders, tithe-collectors, representatives of the Church of Sigmar, and more besides. All looking to have a hand in how the city developed.

Taltus shook his head, glad that such petty distractions bypassed him entirely. Lord-Ordinators were responsible only for the form of the city, not its function. It was up to mortals like Lorcus to make good use of what Taltus designed.

He sighed and looked around. This was the best of moments – before construction began, when the city was a blank canvas. There was potential here, in these broken streets. Beauty slumbered, awaiting his touch to awaken it. He would make wonders here, if he was given a chance. He looked at the map, imagining a band of gardens, ringing the heart of the city. A rebuilt temple district, centring on Sigmar's fane, with all others orbiting it.

Lorcus coughed politely. Taltus blinked and glanced at him. 'My apologies, captain-general. I was lost in thought.'

'I said, have you seen something we've missed, Lord-Ordinator?'

'No. Just daydreaming about glories to come.' Taltus smiled

thinly. 'I am glad to be here. It has been a few decades since I last turned my hand to such sustained creation. Of late, I have been preoccupied with the construction of celestial observatories in the Nevergreen Mountains. It is… nice to do something different.' He placed his palm against the wall, feeling the ancient strength in the stones. Magics had been used in much of Caddow's construction, and he could still feel the faint echoes of it. 'When I was mortal…' He trailed off.

'What?' Lorcus pressed.

'I built dreams,' Taltus said, after a moment. 'I built what I saw in my head – cathedrals and keeps and habitations for rich and poor alike. Towers that caught the sun, and walls that could trap moonlight. I was one of the foremost architects in the Lantic Empire.' He smiled sadly. 'I was among those summoned to repair the Gilded Steamgird in those last, savage days.'

'Did you?' Lorcus asked.

Taltus frowned and shook himself free of his memories. 'We would not be having this conversation if I had, young lord.' He sighed and rolled up his map. 'Still, the past is in the past, and we have much to look forward to. Isn't that right, Aetius?'

He directed the question to the Liberator-Prime who strode towards them, blood stains on his silver war-plate. The Storm-cast ignored the question. 'I've organised an irregular patrol pattern along the southern canal, Lord-Ordinator. We're coordinating with Thalkun and Gullat, to make periodic street-by-street sweeps along the canal. So far, resistance has been minimal.' Aetius Shieldborn was, as ever, stiff and formal in the presence of mortals. Gardus had seconded the Liberator-Prime to Taltus in order to oversee the cohorts under the Lord-Ordinator's command.

Taltus nodded appreciatively. 'We can probably declare the area secure.' He looked at Mahk. 'If we can get the cisterns cleansed, how long until your engineers can get fresh water cycling through this part of the city?'

Mahk rubbed his chin thoughtfully. 'A day, maybe two. That's a full day, mind. If we have to break off to man the guns, it'll take longer.' He frowned. 'The sewers are going to be a problem, though. They've been left to themselves for centuries. Grungni alone knows what's lurking down there, in that jungle of filth, and that's not even getting into the repair-work that'll be needed.'

'I could second a few cohorts from the Gallowsmen – some of them have worked the undergangs in Nordrath. They have experience in such tunnels.' Lorcus studied the map. 'I suggest a static emplacement here.' He drew a line across a scattering of streets. 'That's a warren if I ever saw one. My patrols have reported strange sounds and lights in those alleyways. Best to isolate it now, and aim a few Helblasters at it.'

Mahk nodded. 'Agreed.'

Taltus smiled, pleased. Things were always easier with competent partners. They weren't always easy to come by. He had lent his expertise to the design of any number of cities, including Hallowheart and Glymmsforge. In some cases, the whims of his mortal associates had prevented him from completing his task in as efficient a manner as he wished.

There was an art to designing cities. Even the simplest of defences could be made all but impregnable, with the proper care.

He looked at Aetius. 'We'll also need to send patrols to the docklands, to secure what we can before the first load of cartographers and archivists arrive.'

The Liberator-Prime nodded. 'Easily done.'

'And I want you to lead the guard detail for the cartographers personally.'

Aetius frowned. Taltus headed off his protest. 'Those maps are of the utmost importance, Aetius. They are as necessary as Mahk's artillery. If we are to make this place more than a ruin, we must know the scale of the undertaking ahead.'

'With respect, Lord-Ordinator, I am not well suited to guarding mortals. Surely someone else might–'

'Just do it, Aetius,' a new voice intruded. 'That way we know it'll be done properly, at least.' Aetius turned stiffly and bowed his head.

'Lord-Castellant,' he said.

Lord-Castellant Lorrus Grymn nodded his greetings to the others. He looked at Taltus. 'I trust I'm not interrupting anything?'

'Nothing that can't wait. What news?'

'We've got the foundations set, at last. The engineers from the Zhu'garaz are more than adept. Their workgangs are swifter than any I've seen.' Taltus nodded, pleased. He'd worked with the duardin of the Zhu'garaz before and found them a briskly efficient folk. Less stubborn than some, at least when it came to the construction of Stormforts.

'Concentrate on the palisades to the north and west,' Taltus said, tugging on his moustaches. 'I want them raised before the next attack.'

'The ground's uneven on the western approaches to the ziggurat,' Grymn said, shaking his head. 'We'll need to scrape it flat and rebuild the substructure, else it won't take the weight of the palisades. That'll take time.'

As he spoke, war-horns sounded, somewhere to the north. They all turned. A moment later, the thud of artillery echoed through the narrow street. 'That's *Black Josef* – one of our Helstorm rocket batteries,' Mahk said, softly. 'On the north-eastern emplacement.'

Taltus frowned and looked at Grymn.

'Time, brother, is something we may not have.'

Gardus frowned. 'You can't breach the wards,' he said. He studied the entrance to the catacombs beneath the city. Around him, servants and soldiers clad in the livery of the Collegiate Arcane worked to clear the rubble from the tunnel. He glanced at the latter, eyeing their gilded hauberks and colourful uniforms with mild curiosity.

While the arcane colleges were not allowed to maintain their own standing forces, they often hired smaller Azyrite Freeguilds on long-term contracts. The soldiers were ostensibly merely escorts for the battlemages, to protect them in the field. In truth, they also ensured that the interests of the Collegiate Arcane were not disregarded by those who availed themselves of the battlemages' services.

Reconciler Ahom glared at Gardus. 'I didn't say we couldn't. Merely that I counsel against it.' The battlemage passed a hand over the wall. The air wavered, and sigils were briefly illuminated. 'Any attempt to open these catacombs without the proper spells will result in their complete destruction.'

'That might be for the best.'

Ahom snorted. 'Only if you want to lose half the city.' He folded his arms. 'My professional opinion is that we quarantine these catacombs. Seal them off, set up wards of our own, and leave whatever resides within them to their rest.'

Gardus glanced at Ahom's fellow representatives from the Collegiate Arcane. Neither looked especially happy with Ahom's conclusion. The burly, bearded battlemage, in his furs and rawhide, coughed something under his breath. Ahom glanced at him. 'You have something to add, Jerob?'

Jerob flushed. 'Nothing you want to hear.'

Ahom grimaced. 'This again? Your methodology is flawed. These wards extend in all directions. Trying to breach them from either a lower or higher plane is doomed to failure.'

'In your humble opinion,' Jerob snapped.

The silver-haired woman in her amethyst robes gave a bark of laughter. 'His opinion is anything but humble. He's as arrogant as you are unhygienic, Jerob.'

'Stay out of this, Ilesha,' Ahom said, as Jerob swung a baleful glare towards her. 'Your suggestions were equally ridiculous. Shadeglass is a charlatan's dodge, and you know it! We're not here to indulge your mad theories.'

'I am telling you, with the proper placement of mirrors, we can dilute the magics,' Ilesha said sharply. Ahom waved her statement aside.

'It's always mirrors with you. No, until we can bring the full wisdom of my fellow astromancers to bear on this problem, I judge it best to leave it be…'

'You mean until you can claim the treasures in these vaults for your own, don't you?' Jerob growled. 'Blasted star-kissers, always so greedy.'

Ahom made to retort, but Gardus intervened. 'No one is claiming anything. If these catacombs cannot be opened, then it is best to leave them be for the time being.' He raised a hand, to forestall their protests. 'And I will set a guard on them – Stormcasts,' he said, before Ahom could claim the responsibility for himself. 'In the meantime, you can…' He trailed off and turned towards the wards. He'd heard something. A soft sound, barely audible. 'What was that?'

'What was what?' Ahom said, puzzled.

'I heard something. Quiet.' He gestured to the workers. 'Keep them quiet.' Jerob turned to bellow an order at the soldiers. They stopped what they were doing and stood, watching.

Gardus closed his eyes, listening. The soft sound was intermittent, like the scuffle of unseen vermin. When he opened his eyes, he said, 'They are stirring.'

Ahom blinked. 'Impossible. The wards…'

'Like calls to like,' Ilesha said. 'Death feeds death.' She pulled her amethyst robes tight about her. 'We should have anticipated this,' she said, glumly. 'The dead of Caddow may well awaken, even if no one is there to call to them.'

Ahom cursed. 'The battle. Of course.' He looked at Gardus. 'Death magic… It inundates this place. The more who die here, the stronger it blows.'

'And the stronger it blows, the more likely they are to awaken,' Jerob growled.

Gardus looked at them. 'Will the wards hold them?'

Ahom shook his head. 'They're meant to keep us out, not them in.' He frowned and traced the wards, causing them to spark and glimmer. 'We could strengthen the wards. Add our own, overlaying the originals.' He glanced at Ilesha. 'Ilesha – what about that spirit trap theory of yours?'

'There are a few shamanic rites from the Ghurdish lowlands that might be helpful as well,' Jerob said, as he peered at the wards. He stroked his beard thoughtfully. 'Or the Invocation of Narshan?'

Ahom looked at him. 'Third translation?'

Jerob snorted. 'Second, obviously.'

'What about the Harkwell charm?' Ilesha asked. She adjusted her spectacles. 'It's ordinarily for elementals, but we could adjust the fifth and tenth lines and make it fit for purpose. Or the Rite of Salazar?'

Gardus looked back and forth between them for a moment, and then left them to it. He climbed the slope of rubble, left behind by Tegrus' descent into the catacombs, up to the street. Cassandora awaited him. 'Well?' she asked.

'The dead stir.' Around them, this part of the city was a hive of activity. Workgangs erected barricades and reinforced weakened buildings. Patrols of Gallowsmen and Gold Gryphons walked the streets, alongside cohorts of Stormcasts. The air hummed with the sounds of sawing and hammering, the shouts of engineers and the curses of duardin. A wagon, full of loose stones and broken timbers, rumbled past, pulled by one of the Ironweld's clockwork horses.

'I expected as much. Never easy, is it?' Cassandora hiked a thumb over her shoulder, in the direction of the ziggurat. It loomed over the nearby buildings, casting its shadow over the centre of the city. The Corvine Gate flickered and shrieked as it opened. 'The bureaucrats have arrived, right on schedule.'

'Lorcus?' Gardus asked.

'Already there, with the Swiftblade. I came to fetch you.'

'Where's Ramus?'

'Where do you think?'

Gardus frowned and turned. He looked up, at the eyrie looming in the distance. 'And what of our guest?'

'He's been quiet since you talked to him.' She shrugged. 'Ramus demanded to speak to him alone. I managed to extract an oath that he wouldn't do anything foolish. Whether he keeps to it or not…'

'He will. Much as he may wish to, Ramus will not break an oath.'

'One of his few virtues.' Cassandora glanced at the flickering realmgate. 'We should go. They'll be expecting us.'

Gardus sighed. She was right, but he wasn't looking forward to the tedium of the next few hours. 'Yes. Did you ever think, all those years ago in the Gladitorium, that so much of our time would be taken up with talking, rather than fighting?'

Cassandora snorted. 'If I had, I wouldn't have fought so hard.'

She dropped her fist onto his shoulder. 'Cheer up, Steel Soul. It could be worse. I'll take talking to mortals over trading barbs with a vampire anytime.'

Ramus stepped into the chamber at the top of the eyrie, his gaze cold. 'You haven't tried to escape yet. How unlike you.' The Stormcasts on guard duty closed the door behind him, leaving him alone with the prisoner. His grip on his reliquary staff tightened as once again he resisted the urge to fry Mannfred where he lay.

'I wondered when you would come to check on me.' Mannfred sat up and swung his legs off his cot. 'I didn't want to disappoint you.'

'That you continue to exist is a disappointment.' Ramus stared at the vampire. 'Why haven't you tried? What are you waiting for?'

'You.' Mannfred laughed. 'If I wished to escape, I could. But you would pursue me. And I know from experience that you are a most assiduous huntsman.' He flexed his hand. The wounds he'd taken had already healed. 'I have had many days to think on my next course of action. Escape by conventional means is so difficult as to be impossible, so instead I have decided to offer you a chance to help me.'

'Help you?' Ramus lifted his staff. 'I ought to kill you.'

'Then you will never free the soul of your friend, and mine.'

Ramus paused. 'Speak,' he said, hoarsely.

Mannfred leaned forward. 'You were right, earlier. I was lying. I did not want the army to help Nagash. Nagash needs no aid. And the spirits of Caddow – well, let's just say that the Undying King was no friend of theirs. No, I intended to invade Nekroheim while Nagash is otherwise occupied.'

Ramus laughed. 'You truly are an adder, biting all who come within reach.'

Mannfred snorted. 'The venom in your words warms my heart, Stormcast. It is gratifying to know that men of sigmarite can hate as passionately as the dead.'

'I am nothing like you.'

'No. You are not. You gave up, after all.'

Ramus paused. 'I did not give up on him. I have not given up.'

'Oh, but you have. Else you would not have allowed your master to call you off. You hate me because you blame me. But in truth, I am nothing more than a scapegoat. You called me an adder, Ramus. Are you then surprised when I strike?' Mannfred gestured dismissively. 'No. I will not play this game with you, Stormcast. Blame yourself for not saving him, if you must blame someone.'

'I should kill you.'

'So you keep saying.' Mannfred spread his hands. 'Here I sit. Incinerate me. Dash my brains upon the floor. Impale me and sweep off my head. Anything to relieve this tedium.' Ramus stared at him. Mannfred met his gaze and smiled. 'But before you do, you should know that the wind has turned. The fetters of chance have become brittle, and things once thought impossible are now made possible, if one but has the wit to act in a timely fashion.'

'What do you mean?'

'The Three-Eyed King turns the full fury of his legions upon the lands of the dead. He fears Nagash, and seeks his end. Shyish is become the next, great battleground. And Nagash is distracted by his own schemes. He shores up his defences and gathers his armies, hoping to weather the storm until he can enact whatever plan he's brewing. Disaster breeds opportunity.' Mannfred's smile slipped, for an instant. 'And I have waited for a long time for this moment.'

Ramus stared. 'Is that remorse? Are you capable of such a thing?'

The smile returned, sharp and gleaming. 'No. But the debt Tarsem – Tarsus – thrust upon me is one I find most unbearable, and I would be rid of it. I would owe nothing to no one. Better a lender than a debtor be, as they used to say.'

Ramus was silent for long moments. 'What do you want?' he asked, finally.

'Free me, and I will lead you to him. Bring every warrior you can muster, and together, we will burst the gates of the underworld and release Tarsus Bullheart from his torment.' Mannfred clasped the bars of his cell, his eyes gleaming crimson. 'Decide quickly, Lord-Relictor, for there is no telling how long Nagash will remain preoccupied with other matters. Soon enough, he may turn his attentions back to the soul of our friend, and then there will be no salvation for any of us.'

Ramus stared at the vampire for long moments, and then turned and left without another word. Sagittus was waiting for him in the passage.

'Did he say anything of use?' the Judicator-Prime asked.

'Nothing he hasn't already said,' Ramus replied, after a moment. He glanced back at the door leading to the cell and frowned. 'Set the wolf free, she said,' he murmured. Despite her often acerbic tone, Cassandora was no fool. Indeed, she was perhaps wiser than she knew.

'What?' Sagittus asked.

'Nothing.' Ramus turned back. 'Come. Let us leave this place.' He paused and looked up at the bones of his reliquary standard. The skull set there seemed to grin at him in some secret understanding. He looked away.

'I must pray.'

CHAPTER ELEVEN

WILL OF THE GODS

To the strong, the crown. To the weak, the grave.
That is the will of the gods.

– Nechris Litharge
The Canker of Civilisation

Bakhos gestured, and the slave's throat was opened. The wretch died without complaint, his blood filling the stone trough. Out in the dark of the wastes, something sighed in anticipation. At Bakhos' command, two more slaves were brought forward, and their blood added to the long trough.

He frowned, staring into the dark. The dead had grown restless since the opening of the realmgate. One slave a night was no longer enough to propitiate the hungry ghosts who stalked the Sea of Dust. But unless they were fed, and regularly, they would ravage the encampment, stealing away his warriors and bleeding his forces white.

'My forces.' He laughed softly. A rabble, by any other name.

Hulmean and the others hadn't launched their attacks yet, but he could hear the boom of cannon-fire from the city. Someone had attacked without his permission, hoping to win glory for themselves, or his favour. Or perhaps they'd simply grown bored. He knew that feeling.

He inhaled the fresh, cool air and shook himself. The wine sang in his veins, lending energy to his step. He felt as if the lethargy of the past decades was now truly gone. The cobwebs had been shaken out, and he could see the way ahead with almost perfect clarity. It had been a mistake to come here, to allow Archaon to chain him like a dog.

But here was the way out, possibly. If Archaon cared only that an army was here, then it would be a simple matter to switch one guard dog for another. Then, the Leopard would be free to prowl once more. 'And where would you go?' he murmured to himself.

That was the question that had come to him, like a thief in the night. He felt as a man caught for so long in the press of battle that it had become his world – and now, just for a moment, there was a gap. A way to freedom. But what to do with that freedom? Resume the quest that had drawn him here? Or seek out new lands and experiences?

Or, simply run. Run far and fast, before word reached Varanspire. He turned and gazed at the pavilions rising over the wastes – a city of gaudy pleasure, inhabited by monsters and the mad. It had started with a bare few hundred. But it had grown, over the centuries. More and more warriors, seeking purpose, sent by Archaon or driven by the whispers of their own daemonic patrons. Three hundred had become six, then a thousand. He did not know the final tally now. A hundred chieftains and champions graced his private debaucheries, and three times that celebrated among themselves, in their own encampments.

'Will you give it all up, O Maiden's Son?' he asked himself. 'Will the Leopard change his spots?' He flexed his hands, wanting to draw his blade, to kill something. Someone. To feel the pull of muscles, the shock of steel meeting flesh. To indulge his appetites. 'Walker-on-Shields. Man-of-War. Spear-King and Slaymaster.' He recited his titles to himself, seeking to calm the urge building within him. He felt someone approach, but did not cease his recitation.

'How many is that now? Fifty? A hundred? How many names, O Blessed One?'

'My names are as the grains of sand in the wastes, Lemerus,' Bakhos said, as he turned to face the champion. Lemerus gave a shark-like grin. 'I trust you know them all?'

'Of course. They are as the lyrics of a great and terrible song, my lord. I sing them to myself, when my courage wavers.'

'Then you do not sing it often?'

Lemerus laughed. A soft sound, like leaves rustling in the wind. 'No oftener than some.' It held its maul over one narrow shoulder. It brought the weapon around and Bakhos saw again how it resembled a woman's face. For a fleeting instant, that face was one he recognised. But then, in a flash of old pain, it was gone.

Lemerus tapped the maul against Bakhos' chest. 'There are whispers, Bakhos. The wind murmurs that you are weak. That you fear a challenge, so you distract us with games of war, wine and song.' The gesture was disrespectful. Almost a challenge. A lesser warrior might have taken it as such. Bakhos, however, merely smiled.

'If you do not remove that gaudy trinket from my person, I will take it from you and add your blood to the ghost-trough.'

Lemerus hesitated. Then, it swung its maul down. Bakhos' smile widened. 'That was not a proper challenge, Lemerus.

I am disappointed. Do you fear that the Absent God will be angry with you if you fail to kill me?'

'The Absent God is lost. He speaks to no one. Can be angry with no one.'

Bakhos laughed. 'The Absent God is not lost. We merely have not found him yet. His absence is a test, Lemerus. We strive, we seek our own desires, for only in satiating ourselves can we reach his realm. To want, is to seek. You and I, we have been searching for our god from birth.' Bakhos smiled. 'That we have not found him yet is merely a sign that our own desires are not yet fulfilled. You see?'

Lemerus shook its head. 'Nonsense,' it said, prettily.

Bakhos laughed. 'Well, I thought it sounded good.' He looked at the champion. 'What do you really want, Lemerus?'

'I want it all.'

'I meant specifically. At this moment.'

'Your head.'

'As much as I admire your attempts at humour, I am in no mood for it this day,' Bakhos said, putting an edge to his words. 'Speak your mind.'

Lemerus sighed. 'There are beasts approaching the outer pavilions.'

'And?'

Lemerus looked at him. 'Should we kill them?'

Bakhos gestured loosely and strode past the champion. 'Why would you do that? I invited them.' He could hear the horns, now, warning the indolent inhabitants of the encampment that someone was approaching. As the echoes faded, he heard the clatter of armoured bodies rising lazily to their feet, and bellowed questions. He glanced at Lemerus, who was following in his footsteps.

'Go make sure the others keep their hands and their blades

to themselves. These beasts are my guests. It wouldn't do to slaughter them.'

'We could use the meat,' Lemerus said, laughing softly.

'There are plenty of slaves, if you're feeling hungry. Where is Etax?'

Lemerus shrugged. 'Somewhere. Plotting. Why?' The champion's seeming lack of concern was obviously a front. Lemerus knew damn well where Etax was, even as Etax knew where Lemerus was. They circled each other like hungry megalofins, drawing weaker predators into their orbit with every flick of their tails.

Bakhos smiled. 'Merely curious. Don't worry, Lemerus. You're still my favourite.'

Lemerus stopped, a puzzled expression on its face. 'What?'

Bakhos didn't reply. Lemerus would gnaw over that statement for days, wondering if it was true. The thought pleased him. The champion was entirely too certain of itself. Like Etax, it thought itself his lieutenant and his primary rival. Granted, that was mostly due to his own laziness. But things were going to change, soon. One way or another.

His army had swelled to an unmanageable size – too many disparate warbands, too many sycophantic champions. He had relied on Vlad overmuch, and left creatures like Etax and Lemerus to their own devices, when he should have disciplined them. He knew that now. There were no phalanxes to be found among this rabble. No iron core to strip back to, no salvaging the mess that had been made of things. But the press of battle had thinned, and freedom was at hand.

And victory, of sorts, could still be had.

The sky was the colour of the flowers that grew on graves. Night was drawing on and it was cold. The dying season was here, and soon snow would begin to fall, covering the grey stones in a white shroud. Ghosteater inhaled the scent of it, and let it fill him.

The dying season was the great enemy of his folk. Prey sought shelter, and food became scarce. Many herds turned to eating the weak in this season, and their battles made the white snows red. Even here, among the pavilions of the Blessed Ones, the bite of cold was evident. Slaves shivered, their bare flesh pale and blue. Warriors clad themselves in furs, if they possessed them, or stole them if they didn't. The tribes who camped on the fringes made sacrifices to the little gods of winter, attempting to placate their unending hunger, even as Bakhos spilled blood to hold the ghosts at bay.

Eat or be eaten. That was the first law of the gods. Make meat of your foes, or be made meat. The first rule a cub learned, at the hooves of his elders. How many of his litter had been made meat by his father? How many had he himself eaten, in the days that followed? Their ghosts were still with him, whimpering and whispering. Sometimes, in the dark of night, he felt a flicker of something that might have been regret. Other chieftains surrounded themselves with their litter-mates, and the progeny of their litter-mates. Kin could only trust kin. The pack, the herd, was bound together by blood.

But Ghosteater had no blood. No progeny. His warherd was a thing bound by strength and challenge. Outcasts and weak-bloods, held together only by his will. That would have to change.

'You are not listening.'

Ghosteater blinked and shook his head. 'Thinking,' he said. Chaell the Unborn stood across from him, sword in hand. The Chaos warrior had removed his helm. His features looked older, in the gloom. As if he aged as the day wore on, and became a youth again with the dawn. Maybe he did. The Blessed Ones were peculiar.

'Talking to ghosts, you mean?' Chaell asked.

'No. Just thinking.'

'Well stop. You asked me to help hone your skills and that is what we are doing. Thinking will only distract you.' Chaell lifted his blade. 'Now, mark me. Watch your footing. That khopesh of yours is more axe than sword, but there are some universals to the wielding of both.' He moved gracefully, lighter on his feet than Ghosteater would have believed. With each slash, he changed position slightly, manoeuvring himself closer to an imaginary enemy. 'There's a rhythm to blade work. Think of each sword as a song – play it properly, and applause will follow. Play it badly, and… well. Don't play it badly, eh?'

Ghosteater tried to follow his movements, but it was all but impossible. Chaell and his sword were one – lethal and graceful. *Don't watch him – anticipate him,* a dry, dusty voice murmured. The khopesh's former owner. All but gone now, subsumed by Ghosteater's hunger to know.

Chaell stepped back. 'Now, you try.'

Ghosteater did. Chaell laughed. Ghosteater spun, fangs bared. Chaell lifted his blade in warning. 'Don't be a fool. A bit of mockery has never hurt anyone.'

'Don't laugh,' Ghosteater growled. 'Teach.'

'I am teaching you. You are copying, not learning. Do not copy. You weigh more than I do, even unarmoured. Your reach is greater, especially with a weapon like that. You are not as fast, but you are stronger. Think. Adapt.' Chaell tapped the side of his head. 'Use what little brains the Dark Gods gave you, my friend.'

'Insults, now,' Ghosteater rumbled. He turned away, infuriated with himself. 'I am not a fool.'

'No. You are most assuredly not, else Bakhos would not have taken an interest in you. But you must know how to fight properly, or you will be slaughtered by the first halfwit to challenge you. And they will challenge you.'

Ghosteater turned back. 'Who? Which ones?'

'Saladar of Guin. Waro Lustbane. The Shivering Maiden. A dozen others – wretches and fools. Minor champions, seeking to attract Bakhos' eye.'

'Like you.'

'Like me.' Chaell smiled. 'But I am not so foolish as they. Besides, I owe you a debt.'

Ghosteater snorted. 'You owe me nothing.'

'My life is not nothing,' Chaell said, extending his blade. 'Raise your sword. Come.'

Ghosteater turned and raised his khopesh. He nudged his ghosts into awareness. Murmurs filled his head. *He favours his right side – no injury, just preference. Might be a feint. Don't try and match him, skill for skill.* The murmurs grew into a babble, until he was forced to silence them with a snarl. He darted forward.

Their blades met with a screech. Chaell grunted, as he was forced back a step. Ghosteater hammered at him, trying to overwhelm him. The Chaos warrior retreated steadily. For a moment, Ghosteater thought he was winning. Then Chaell ducked aside, and thrust his sword out. He pulled his blow, and the tip of his blade skidded across Ghosteater's muzzle. Ghosteater roared and spun, khopesh slashing out.

Chaell ducked, and pressed the tip of his blade to Ghosteater's chest, just below his heart. 'You weren't listening, then,' he said, in a disappointed tone of voice.

Ghosteater made to reply, when the wind brought a familiar scent. He lowered his blade and turned, sniffing the air.

'What is it?' Chaell asked.

'The others are here. As he promised.' Ghosteater sheathed his khopesh and followed the scent, weaving through the sea of tents. Chaell followed.

Bakhos was waiting at the edge of camp, where pavilions gave way to the shattered remnants of the city walls. Towers of stone and wood loomed like jagged teeth, casting thick rivers of shadow over the broken ground. Among these shadows, the chieftains waited, growling and muttering to themselves. They glared warily at the Chaos warriors who stared back, hands on their weapons.

Bakhos turned as Ghosteater approached, and held out a hand. 'Ah, there you are, my friend. Even as I promised, I have gathered them, and I am just about to make my case.' He smiled widely, and Ghosteater repressed an instinctive snarl. Bakhos' smile was like the edge of a blade, a promise of pain yet to come.

Bakhos turned back to the chieftains and spread his arms. 'My friends – it has been too long. That is my fault, not yours. For too long, I have been lax in my duties to you, as subjects of this kingdom of mine.'

'Not your kingdom,' a chieftain snarled. Ghosteater didn't recognise him. A leader of one of the smaller herds, from the eastern districts. The big gor stepped into the open, all muscle and hate. Curving horns rose above a shaggy mane, and equine jaws tensed. The gor swept out the cleaver-blade it carried for emphasis. 'Ours. Always ours.'

'No, no, no,' Bakhos said, as if to a child. 'This kingdom belongs to the Three-Eyed King, and he has given it to me, to rule in his name. You are his subjects – and loyal ones. Let it not be said that the children of Chaos are not loyal to the one the gods have invested with their authority, eh?'

The beastmen murmured at this. Ghosteater could smell

their nervousness. For generations, the Blessed Ones had been a remote presence. Occasionally, a warlord or champion would enter the ruins to hunt them, or demand aid in attacking some nearby settlement. But beyond that, the Blessed Ones rarely paid any attention to them at all. And now, they were in the presence of the greatest of the Blessed Ones.

Some of them looked at Ghosteater. These, he knew. Wyrm-hoof and Blacktongue, shamans and seers. Scarbelly, the eld-est of the northern chieftains, with his fur almost white and his horns gnarled tight like knots of stone. Ancient, by the standards of their folk. Beside him, but not too close, was Manglepaw, who had given himself over to the gods, and stank of blood. Onehorn and Spliteye, lesser chieftains, both of whom Ghosteater had fought before, huddled close, with their faces almost like those of men. He showed them his teeth, and they looked away.

Ghosteater paid no attention to Bakhos' words. They were not for beasts, but for men. A show, for the champions and warriors who had gathered to watch. Instead, he watched the shamans, creeping among the chieftains, whispering into their ears. The shamans spoke with the voices of the gods, more so than even a being like Bakhos. And like the gods, they played their own games. Wyrmhoof leaned forward and murmured something into Manglepaw's ragged ear. The burly chieftain's red-eyed glare slid towards Ghosteater, and then away.

Wyrmhoof will resist, Twisthoof's ghost whined. The long-dead shaman shuddered. *The Changer holds his soul, and he cannot help himself. Blacktongue is as a leaf in the wind. Which-ever way it blows, he will follow.*

Ghosteater silenced the shaman's shade with a flick of his mind. The ghost told him nothing he had not already guessed. He glanced at Bakhos. The Maiden's Son was still speaking, layering the air with flowery nonsense. Appealing to them as equals, when all knew that for the lie it was. *It is prelude, nothing more,* Herst's voice said, suddenly. *All prelude. You are to be his sacrifice on the altar of compromise. They do not trust men, but they may trust you. And since you trust him...*

Ghosteater growled. Bakhos turned, in mid-speech. 'You have something to add, my friend?' he asked, lazily. Before Ghosteater could reply, Bakhos turned back to the others. 'You see him, here? This one is the wisest of you, for he came to me, and woke me from my slumber. He did not hide in the ruins, but came to me – came to us – and demanded action of his sovereign!' He laughed. 'Here is one to emulate, if you would rise in the eyes of the gods. See, he is blessed, even as I am blessed...'

Manglepaw gave a bellow of laughter. He towered over most gors, his ursine features pockmarked with scars earned for the glory of the Blood God. He was covered in slabs of fat and muscle, and his hooves were shod in brass. He wore scavenged war-plate, modified to fit his bulk, and wielded an axe he'd fashioned with his own fists. He brandished it now. 'Let us hear it from him, then. You wish us to fight as one tribe, under your banner? Let him tell us.'

'A trap,' Chaell murmured, from behind Ghosteater.

Ghosteater said nothing. Chaell was right. Manglepaw seethed with violence. He would challenge Ghosteater, and try to use his death to bind the weaker herds to his own. To show that Ghost-eater wasn't the only one blessed of the gods. Other shamans had tried the same, before Wyrmhoof. Always urging on this chieftain or that to take the head of the albino. Like Twisthoof.

Twisthoof whined in protest. *Only just. Only right. Eat or be eaten.*

Ghosteater silenced him and stepped forward. 'You wish me

to talk? I talk. We go. Away from the ears of men.' He glanced at Bakhos and saw uncertainty in his eyes. Then, the Maiden's Son nodded and smiled.

'By all means. We shall wait here, for your decision.'

The chieftains rose as one, and faded into the shadows of the ruins with an ease no human could match. Ghosteater followed them. He felt eyes on him – the chieftains had not come unescorted, and their warriors watched from all around, unseen and unnoticed by the Blessed Ones. Ghosteater laughed softly.

They underestimate you, a ghost murmured, almost admiringly. *They call the ruin a forest of stone, but they do not understand what that means. Not truly.*

Caddow belonged to the beast-tribes, whatever Bakhos claimed. They had made it their own, feeding the ground with blood and bones, and the forest sheltered them in return. Such was the second law of the gods. To make the ground holy, and fit for their tread. Eat or be eaten. Bless the ground. And the third law... The third law was the most important of all. The third law said you must always strive to earn all that the gods gave you.

The broken stones of the city wall rose tall about them, hiding them from the sight of men, as it had always done, and always would. Ghosteater looked around. 'I am here. You will listen,' he growled. His voice echoed among the stones.

'Speak,' Scarbelly said. As the oldest, it was his right. Even Manglepaw stepped lightly around Scarbelly. Only the cunning lived long enough to see their muzzle turn the colour of the stones. And the others respected him. Many of those gathered here were his progeny, or else the spawn of his by-blows.

'They wish us to become one herd. They wish me to lead. I am blessed, they say. Not as much as them, but enough.' He looked around. Growls of denial echoed through the stones. This was a day long feared, by all. The loss of autonomy that was as inevitable as winter. As the moons rose, what beasts made, men took.

'I will do this thing. But not for them,' Ghosteater growled, thumping his chest with a fist. 'The Blessed Ones use us. We all know this. They use us until we break, and then cast us aside for their greater glory.' Growls of assent greeted these words. The eldest among them understood. There was not one of them who did not wear the scars that came from the Blessed Ones' wars. 'But we are the true children of the gods, made in their image.' He looked around. 'Why then do we content ourselves dying for the glory of men?'

'It has always been thus,' Scarbelly grunted. The ancient chieftain scratched at the pale marks that had earned him his name. 'It is the will of the gods.'

'No,' Ghosteater snarled, startling the old chieftain. 'It is not their will. Else we would not be given cunning to question it. We can be more than chattel.' He struck his chest again. '*I* will make us more than chattel, if you follow me.'

'Blasphemy,' Wyrmhoof brayed. The shaman stamped in fury. 'The gods give us glory – we bleed to show our thanks!'

'What glory?' Ghosteater spun to face the shaman. 'We bleed for their glory, not our own. We die for them, and they walk a path of our bones.' His muzzle peeled back from his fangs. 'They will not walk on me. I will lead you, but not into death. Not for them.'

'The gods will punish you, kin-eater,' Wyrmhoof said, eyes flashing. He looked around. 'As they will punish any who follow you.'

'Let them punish me now, if they wish.' Ghosteater spread his arms. 'Come. Strike me down. I will not die for the glory of men, only my own!' He threw back his head and roared a challenge to the sky. He thumped his chest and hurled his words to the sky with all the strength he could muster. 'Come, you gods – come and slay me, for I will bow to men no longer. Either raise me up, or strike me down, but do it now.'

Thunder rumbled in the distance. To his ears, it sounded like the satisfied purr of some great beast. Ghosteater counted six beats of his heart and lowered his arms. He looked at Wyrmhoof. 'I still live,' he said, in the silence that followed. 'Will you challenge me?'

Wyrmhoof stepped back, head lowered. He grunted, and Manglepaw rose from his crouch. Manglepaw met Ghosteater's gaze and snarled. 'I will challenge. You are a pale thing. A grub. A maggot. Not fit to lead beasts into war. If we are to be one herd, it will not be led by you.'

Ghosteater snorted and drew his khopesh. 'Come then. Come and kill me.'

Manglepaw roared and charged. Ghosteater stepped aside, avoiding the bite of his foe's axe. His khopesh scraped across Manglepaw's war-plate and the brutish gor spun, nearly taking Ghosteater's head. His ghosts urgently murmured advice.

…favours his left hoof…

…axe-haft is splintered…

…get inside his reach, fool…

Their voices tumbled over one another, becoming a roar. Ghosteater shook his head and focused on Chaell's lessons. He had to use his head. He could not win this battle with his blade. Manglepaw had no skill, but he was stronger and nearly as fast. Ghosteater leapt back, as the axe whistled down. His khopesh snapped out and was turned aside again by Manglepaw's armour.

The pillar – there, to your left – see it? Herst's voice echoed suddenly in his head. *It's made from gloomstone – ornamental, rather than durable. Heavy, though. Incredibly heavy. And its base is weak – see the cracks?*

'Stop running and fight,' Manglepaw howled as Ghosteater backed towards the pillar. The other chieftains were cheering and stamping, excited by the battle. He could see Wyrmhoof watching, hunched against his staff. The shaman wouldn't interfere, no matter how much he might wish to. Scarbelly and the others wouldn't stand for it.

Ah, there – you'll only have a moment, Herst murmured. *You'll have to be quick.* The pillar was taller than Ghosteater, and wider. It creaked slightly as he touched it. He could feel its weight, and bared his teeth. 'Come then,' he roared. 'Come and get me!'

Manglepaw loomed over him, slaver dripping from his jaws. His eyes bulged wildly. Ghosteater waited until the axe had begun its downward stroke, and then lunged aside. Manglepaw's axe struck the base of the pillar, and the stone ruptured. Ghosteater turned in time to see the pillar crash down atop his opponent. The chieftains fell silent.

Manglepaw was still alive, in the rubble of the pillar. His armour had once again saved him, but only just. It hadn't prevented his bones from being broken, and his innards pulped. Blood spattered his muzzle, and one of his horns had been snapped off. He clawed at the stones, trying to drag himself free. 'Cheat,' he wheezed. 'Cheat.'

'Blessed,' Ghosteater corrected. He stepped over Manglepaw and caught hold of his remaining horn. He wrenched the gor's head up, exposing his throat. Manglepaw brayed in protest, bloody froth spattering Ghosteater's chest and face.

But as Ghosteater set the curve of his blade against Manglepaw's throat, the other beast calmed. 'Do not... do not eat my soul,' he grunted. 'I have offered it up on the Blood God's altar.' There was no hint of fear in the plea, no intimation of mercy. Merely an honest appeal. 'Leave me my ghost.'

Ghosteater looked down at him. 'I will leave it,' he said, loudly, so that all could hear. 'To the gods, what is theirs. But your flesh shall feed us all in the celebrations to come.'

'As it has always been,' Manglepaw whispered. He closed his eyes.

Ghosteater jerked the khopesh across his throat, spilling the rest of his blood across the stones. He turned. None of the others would meet his gaze. Not even Scarbelly. He set his bloody khopesh across his shoulder and looked around.

'I still live,' he said. 'Who will challenge me?' When no one answered, he growled in satisfaction. 'You will follow me. We will be one herd, as the Blessed Ones wish. But not their herd. My herd. Ghosteater's herd.' He raised his blade, and one by one, the chieftains began to howl and stamp, in approval. 'We will not be meat,' he roared, and they roared with him, filling the forest of stone with the sound of their exultation.

'We will not be eaten. And the gods will see us, and know us for their own, at last!'

CHAPTER TWELVE

ASSAULT

*The best offence is a good defence. React swiftly,
with forethought.*

– Archime Dashos
The Middle Span

'It is not safe here, woman,' Aetius Shieldborn grumbled. He
and his cohort had been ordered to escort a small group of cartographers and archivists through the secured areas of the city,
alongside soldiers from the Gallowsmen. The maps of Caddow were centuries out of date, and the mortals were to craft
new ones, as well as survey those parts of the city in need of
reconstruction. Unfortunately, one of the mortals had insisted
on leading them into the tangled warrens of the city's harbour.

The mortal in question was Tulla Mir, a preceptor of the
cartographer's guild, and a senior official of the civilian contingent. Nordrathi by birth, she was tall and pale, her light hair
streaked with silver. A daughter of the mountain clans, she had

jagged tattoos, reminiscent of distant crags, marking one side of her narrow features. She was clad in loose, pale robes and blued steel war-plate. The latter bore little sign of use, and had been etched with celestial sigils, including stylised representations of the realmspheres. A satchel of delicate instruments and bundles of rolled parchment hung across her chest, and a finely wrought duardin pistol was holstered on one hip.

'Do you know where we are?' she asked, excitedly, her accent rough and drawling. She turned to look at Aetius. 'These are the famed docklands of Caddow.' She gestured to the immense wooden frames that rose over the stone wharfs like the skeleton of some great leviathan. 'Legendary, even in its heyday!'

Aetius looked around. Whatever they had once been, the docklands were now a jungle of collapsed beams, torn sails and spillages of rope. A canopy of broken walkways and gangplanks rose overhead, leading back to the upper storeys of the ruined warehouses and storage yards on the other side of the street. Opposite them, massive stone wharfs jutted out into the Sea of Dust, and had been all but buried by the encroaching dunes. The signs of some long-ago fire marked the area, and twisted trees grew from the street. Their withered branches tangled up with the walkways and rotted pulley-lines that had somehow survived the centuries.

Dangerous terrain. Aetius could smell the years of beast-stink clinging to the stones. There were still beastherds loose, wandering the high walkways and deep cellars of the docklands. But the scribe was heedless of all save faded grandeur.

'There are dust-barques, still in their berths!' Tulla spread her arms, as if to encompass the docklands. 'Once, they plied the Sea of Dust, carrying cargos of silks and spices from Azyr to the cities of eastern Shyish. Even as Tuman Wey wrote, in his seminal treatise on the southern trade routes…'

She continued in this vein for several moments, and Aetius tuned her out. Instead, he concentrated his attentions on his cohort, checking their positions. Judicators stood sentry every twenty paces, and Liberators every ten. A Stormcast could cross thirty paces in moments. Spread out as they were, they could form a battle-line instantly.

They were not alone in acting as escorts. Soldiers of the Gallows-men, in their grey and black, patrolled the edges of the docklands. They were efficient, for mortals. These were armed with crossbows, swords and shields. Aetius caught the eye of their commander, a tall woman, after the fashion of all Nordrathi. He gestured surreptitiously and she marched towards him.

'Regretfully, it appears I must confer with my opposite number,' he said, interrupting Tulla in mid-flow. She frowned, but before she could speak, he turned and signalled a nearby Liberator. 'Liberator Serena will escort you wherever you wish to go.' He looked at Serena. 'Stay in sight of the others. This area is still unsecured. We may need to fall back.'

Serena nodded. She glanced at Tulla. 'Shall we?'

Tulla clapped her hands, cheerful once more. 'Excellent! You have my thanks, Liberator-Prime.'

'And you have mine,' Aetius murmured to the mortal officer, when Tulla was out of earshot. He studied her. Her hair was clipped short, beneath her helm, and her face was hawk-keen. She radiated a simmering displeasure; whether at him, or the situation, he couldn't tell.

'You're the Stormcast in charge, then?' She looked up at him, frowning.

'Yes. You are a… lieutenant?' Aetius had a fascination for the varied ways the Freeguilds signified rank. In this case, it was the colour of her noose – a deep azure meant an officer. Bare rope meant a ranker. Other colours meant other, less obvious, things.

'Dashos. Lieutenant Dashos. Tenth Cohort.' She saluted, tugging on her noose.

Aetius nodded. 'Liberator-Prime Aetius, called by some the Shieldborn.'

'Sounds like a low-realm name.' She said it with the sort of casual dismissal a native Azyrite used when talking about the realms below Azyr. He took no insult. He had no more emotional connection to the lower realms than she did.

'Regardless, it is my name.' He looked down at her. 'You look familiar. Have we met before, mortal?' He emphasised the last word, slightly. She frowned again, and he had it. She resembled the Gallowsmen's commander, Lorcus. A blood relation, then. The Nordrathi had made an art of nepotism. The Freeguilds from the country around the Great Mountain were often family affairs, at least when it came to the officers.

'Not to my knowledge,' she said.

Aetius let the matter drop. He turned back to the docklands, watching as the Gallowsmen escorted the scribes along the ancient wharfs. 'Your soldiers seem proficient.'

'They bloody well should be. I've drilled them often enough.' She sniffed. 'Got a reputation to maintain.' She watched Tulla Mir rambling cheerfully to her escort, and snorted. 'Be easier to maintain it on the emplacements, though.'

'I am told that this duty is an important one.'

'Yes, every duty is important.'

They shared a brief look that only veterans would recognise. 'I heard she's writing a book,' Dashos said.

'They're all writing books, I imagine.' There were books everywhere now. It seemed to Aetius as if every mortal with access to ink and paper was gripped by the urge to scribble down their thoughts – whether anyone was interested or not.

'My grandfather wrote a book once,' Dashos said, idly.

'Oh?' Aetius said, more to be polite than out of any interest.

Dashos nodded, not looking at him. 'It was awful. All about strategy and tactics. Utter rubbish.'

'Was he not a warrior, then?'

Dashos laughed. 'Not so as you'd notice.' She smirked. 'More of a thinker than a doer, my old grandy. Lots of brains, not a lot of muscle.' She tapped tunelessly against the pommel of her sword.

'Intelligence is often considered an asset,' Aetius said, doubtfully. He'd never agreed with that conclusion. Asking questions – thinking – instead of obeying orders had seen many under his command sent back to the Anvil of Apotheosis.

'So is doing as you're told,' Dashos said. She sucked on her teeth for a moment, and then spat. 'Can't be looking at the clouds when the enemy is in the mud.'

'Very sensible,' Aetius said, approvingly. He was beginning to like this Dashos. She seemed efficient.

She looked at him. 'They say the Steel Soul is soft-hearted, as far as your sort goes.'

Aetius frowned. 'You speak too freely, mortal.'

Dashos looked away. 'My apologies.' Then, a moment later, 'Is he, though? Soft-hearted, I mean.'

Aetius laughed harshly. If she was brave enough to press the point, he owed her an answer. 'No. He merely wields mercy the way a swordsman wields a blade.' He paused. 'I once saw him spare the life of an orruk war-chief, in Ghyran. Not a thing we normally do, for obvious reasons.'

'Can't trust the greenskins,' Dashos said, in agreement.

'But he did. And somehow, he brought an army of greenskins to its knees, just by that one act. They departed the field that eve. He had shamed them, you see. Shown them they weren't worth killing. And thus, a glorious battle was averted by his soft heart.'

'That must have been irksome.'

'Far from it. We are made for war, but we are not berserkers. Some of my brothers and sisters, perhaps even myself, would have perished in that battle. Though death is not our end, it is not pleasant, and we do not seek it.' He paused. 'Not all of us, at any rate.' He peered at her. 'You understand?'

Dashos nodded, and then shook her head. 'Not really.'

'The Steel Soul's heart does not bleed. Sigmar's hand is on his shoulder. He does not spare an enemy because he is soft of heart, but because it is the right thing to do. The thing that the God-King demands, in the moment. Now do you understand?'

'I do.' Dashos frowned. 'I tell a lie. I don't, but I have faith that someone else does.'

Aetius laughed. 'Mud and clouds, eh?'

Dashos smiled. 'Mud and clouds, Liberator-Prime.'

Satisfied, Aetius turned back to watch Serena escort Tulla to the dust-barques, sitting in their berths. The barques reminded him of the galleys he'd seen in Ghyran – long, low-hulled ships, with prows like axe-blades, and curved oars, meant to help propel the vessel across the Sea of Dust. Each had a high aft-deck, and tall masts, and sat upon a curious, raised bed of horizontal timbers, which slanted downwards at a steep angle. From what little he could see, Aetius assumed that the arrangement of the timbers allowed the barques to roll down into the sands, giving them enough momentum to catch the wind.

'They say the winds that blow across the Sea of Dust would strip a man to his bones,' Dashos said. 'Must have been a special sort of hell, sailing across it.'

'One does what one must.' Aetius paused. He glanced around, and saw a Judicator raise his hand in silent warning. The other Stormcast had seen something. He leaned close to Dashos. 'Gather your men.'

Dashos didn't waste her breath asking why. Aetius raised his shield, signalling the rest of his cohort. He started towards the barques, where Serena and Tulla were. As he did so, he heard the hum of a bowstring, and a bleat of triumph. 'Sunstrike,' he shouted. 'Watch yourself!'

He winced as Serena caught hold of the back of Tulla's cuirass and yanked her back, as an arrow flew past. It sank into a support beam, shivering slightly. Tulla gawped at it. She turned. 'What was that?'

'An arrow,' Serena said, drily. She turned. 'Liberator-Prime, we are under attack!'

'How good of you to notice. Fall in, Liberator. Shields east,' Aetius bellowed. 'Protect the scribes.' As Serena hurried a protesting Tulla towards safety, Aetius took in the street at a glance.

Liberators turned in the direction the arrow had come from, raising their shields as they formed up. More arrows came, hissing through the dark, to shatter on the shields. Ululating cries filled the air. Judicators loosed arrows into the dark as they fell back towards the shield wall. Behind the line of shields, Dashos' soldiers set their own shields and readied their crossbows.

Before them, beastmen spilled out of the alleyways and side streets, howling for blood. Aetius made a quick estimate of their numbers, and cursed. Too many for his cohort to beat back, even with the aid of the Gallowsmen. He caught hold of a Liberator. 'Ravius, fall back to the last staging post. We need reinforcements – go!'

Enyo sat on her haunches atop a broken pillar. Her realm-hunter's bow was braced across her lap, and her helm hung from her belt. She tilted her head back, eyes closed, tasting the wind. The smell and sound of the Ironweld's war-engines reminded her of Cypria. If she kept her eyes shut, she could almost imagine that no time at all had passed. That the world was as it had been, rather than as it now was.

She murmured a brief prayer, asking for forgiveness for her momentary indulgence. To live in the past was to lose sight of the future. So said the tenth canticle of the Hallowed Knights. 'We are the light, cast forth into the dark to show the path ahead,' she said, to herself. Shouting from below broke her from her reverie, and she opened her eyes.

Down below, the cogsmith, Mahk, was berating one of his engineers. Workers and soldiers in the colours of the Ironweld busied themselves across the square, erecting emplacements and reinforcing the foundations of the few nearby buildings that were still structurally sound. The square was close to the dock-lands, and had been claimed as a staging post by the Ironweld. It provided easy access to the eastern district, and the engineers were in the process of blocking off the side streets, in order to create an easily defended corridor for troops to pass eastwards.

'That's what we have the fire-pumps for, you wazzock,' Mahk growled, jabbing the other engineer in the belly with his finger. 'Now go burn them out or get eaten trying. Either way, stop whinging and get on with it!'

'Trouble, cogsmith?' Enyo called down.

Mahk peered up at her. 'Nothing my lads can't handle, Stormcast. Just a few troggoths, holed up in the valve-ways. Once we burn them out, we can get the cistern system for the eastern district flowing again.'

Enyo stepped off the pillar and dropped lightly to the street, her bow across her shoulders. 'Are you certain that I can't be of assistance?' She smiled. 'I have not hunted troggoth since the Fellwater.'

'By all means, go ahead,' Mahk said, dismissively. 'I warn you though, those wings won't do you much good down there. And

I won't have your warriors using those hammers of theirs to break those tunnels. I need them intact.'

Enyo laughed. 'Never fear, cogsmith. I will not add to your labours.'

Mahk snorted. 'Then you'll be the first.' He frowned and reached into his robes, extracting a cheroot case. Taking one, he lit it. The cheroot stank of some musty weed, and Enyo waved a hand to disperse the odour. Puffing on his cheroot, he eyed her. 'How goes the hunting, then? I notice your warriors aren't hanging about like idle crows.'

'Tegrus and the others are close. The Steel Soul commanded the Angelos Conclave to see that your efforts here weren't disturbed. So that is what we are doing.'

'And what are you standing here for, then?'

'I am on sentry duty,' Enyo said. She turned as a cohort of Prosecutors flew overhead, following the corridor west. She raised a hand in greeting.

Mahk watched the winged shapes vanish over the rooftops. 'More of the city falls to our efforts every day. Soon, these emplacements will stretch all the way to the docklands.'

'A city is more than defensive works.'

Mahk blew a cloud of smoke into the air. 'But every city begins with a palisade.' He turned. 'What's this, then?' Enyo looked past him, to see a lone Liberator stumbling towards them, supported by a Prosecutor. She recognised Azar, one of her huntsmen. She started forward, followed by Mahk.

'Azar – who is this?' she said.

'Ravius,' Azar said. 'One of the Shieldborn's warriors, I think.' Enyo helped him set the injured Liberator on the ground. His war-plate was scored by marks, and a dozen or more broken arrows jutted from between the silver plates. Clearly, he had fought his way through long odds to reach them.

'Speak, brother. Tell me what has transpired.'

She sank to one knee, and the Liberator caught her arm. 'Shieldborn – Shieldborn requests aid,' he gasped. Blue lights spun behind his eyes, and she could smell the storm, seeping from his wounded flesh. She touched one of the arrows, and he shuddered. The beastkin often dipped their arrows in filth. Motes of light and heat rose from Ravius as his shudders grew worse. He would return to Azyr soon. She looked up at Azar.

'Where are Tegrus and Mathias?'

Azar hiked a thumb over his shoulder. 'Covering our escape. They should be just behind me.' He glanced back the way he'd come. 'There are beastkin everywhere out there. It's as if every herd in this district has decided to attack at once.'

'Impossible,' Mahk growled. 'We would have seen some sign!'

'The beastkin have lived in this city for centuries. Do you truly think they cannot move through it unseen, if they wish?' Enyo said. Ravius coughed, and went still. She rose and stepped back. His body erupted into a flash of lightning, and his soul was carried back to Azyr in a clap of thunder.

As the glare faded, Tegrus and Mathias arrived, their weapons bloody, and the war-plate marked by signs of battle. They dropped to the ground, startling a number of mortals, and strode quickly towards her. 'Lady Enyo,' Tegrus began.

'Azar told me,' Enyo said, cutting him off. She raised her hand. 'Periphas,' she called out. The star-eagle swooped low and landed on her proffered forearm. The bird met her gaze, head tilted. There were stars in his eyes, an infinity of space that drew her in. Periphas was old. Older than her. The beasts of Azyr aged as the stars themselves. He had hunted the heights since before mortals had first scraped stones to make flame. He would hunt them again, long after she was gone.

'Go,' she whispered, after a moment. 'Show me where they

are.' Periphas shrieked and leapt upwards with a flap of his powerful wings. The star-eagle was faster than any Prosecutor, and with a keener gaze. The bird rose over the plaza and swooped out in a wide circle, over the nearby streets.

'What's going on?' Mahk demanded, glaring at her.

Enyo watched the star-eagle, ignoring Mahk's questions. Periphas screeched once, circling. Enyo drew on her helm. 'Ready your guns, cogsmith. The enemy have already arrived. I and my huntsmen will buy you what time we can. Tegrus!'

'Lady Enyo?' Tegrus said.

Enyo gave a flap of her wings and rose upwards. 'Carry a message to the Steel Soul. I fear this may well be the prelude to something larger.'

Gardus strode along the avenue leading east from the ziggurat. Around him, the city echoed with the thunder of civilisation. Workgangs of duardin laboured to rebuild the streets closest to the realmgate, so that the Ironweld could safely transport their war-engines. He heard a roar and saw a duardin, clad in a leather smock and a curious metal mask, drop a flask of something down a hole in the street.

He stopped to watch. The duardin scrambled back and azure flames shot up through the cracks in the street. More duardin, wearing similar protective vestments and armed with drake-guns, moved up. Briskly, they descended into the hole. A moment later, he heard the muffled bellow of the drakeguns. He turned away, leaving them to their business.

Up ahead, he saw several newly erected field hospices. The mortals were making use of the more stable ruins, stretching new canvas roofs over broken walls. Gardus ducked through an archway and into one.

Inside, he saw tall pillars holding up a mostly non-existent roof, and tiled floors, newly cleaned. The walls were covered in faded murals. The ruin had been a bathhouse, once, he thought, though the baths themselves had long been dry. The duardin were working to get water running. Clean water was essential for a field hospice.

It was not as busy as he'd feared. There weren't many wounded yet, though the unhygienic conditions were proving a trial – unless they could get the cisterns repaired, dysentery might become an issue. Cots lined the walls, and grey-robed priests and priestesses moved among the wounded, tending to their injuries or illnesses.

The Order of the Dove were a mendicant brotherhood within the Church of Azyr. They worshipped Sigmar in his aspect as caretaker of humanity, and often acted as healers for armies in the field, in return for permission to set up hospices within newly taken territory. But they were not the only members of the clergy present. Gardus saw an azure-robed warrior-priest kneeling next to a nearby cot, head bowed and hands clasped.

Gardus cleared his throat. The priest started, and rose, robes swirling. 'My lord,' he said, in surprise. Gardus studied him. He was young, as mortals judged such things. He wore the golden war-plate of his order, and his head had been shaved. A two-handed hammer hung across his back, and several books were chained to his waist. 'My apologies, I…'

Gardus shook his head, silencing him. 'Who are you?'

'Cullen Twayn, my lord,' the young priest said, bowing. He looked down at the man who slept in the cot. 'Prayer seems to bring them some comfort.' He looked across the chamber. 'So many of them, and the battle only just begun.' He shook his head. 'I did not think it would be like this.'

'You are new,' Gardus said. 'Have you just arrived?'

Twayn nodded. 'I came with the latest supply shipment.' He hesitated. 'Lector Hulio sends his regards. He asked me to pass them along, if I were lucky enough to meet you.'

'You know Hulio?' Gardus asked, pleasantly surprised.

'Of course, my lord. His sermons are legendary, among the lay brethren.'

Gardus smiled. 'Do you recall the one about bringing light to the darkness?'

Twayn hesitated. 'I know it well, my lord. I requested to join this campaign for that very reason.' He watched as a priestess carefully wound bandages around a soldier's ravaged face. From the look of his wounds, Gardus suspected that his handgun had exploded. 'I had hoped to take his sermons – and mine – into the dark of Shyish. There are tribes in the surrounding regions who know not the light of Azyr. I would carry Sigmar's word to them.' He sighed. 'Foolish, I know, when there are souls in need, closer to home.'

Gardus was silent for a moment. 'Not so foolish, I think. Every action plants a seed. What fruit might spring from such a planting? Will it sour on the vine, or provide nourishment for years to come?'

'Heady questions, my lord,' Twayn said, softly. 'I cannot, in good faith, answer them. Some among my order would make the attempt, I have no doubt. But I am not so certain in my faith as that.' He looked at Gardus. 'I know only that there must be more than this.'

'That is my thinking as well,' Gardus said, softly. He set his fist on Twayn's shoulder. 'Pray for them. Pray for me. And perhaps your prayers might reveal the way forward.'

Cassandora was waiting for him outside, talking quietly with the mortals there. She had her helm under her arm, and ran a hand through her hair as he appeared. 'I knew I'd find you here,' she said. She fell into step beside him, as he walked back towards the ziggurat.

'What do the Swiftblade's scouts report?' he asked.

'Beastherds are gathering on the periphery of our lines. A few warbands of mortals have made attempts on the eastern emplacements. Also, a nest of troggoths was discovered lairing in the eastern sewers by Mahk's engineers. Nothing serious.'

'Yet.'

'Yet,' Cassandora agreed. 'We should push forward. Strike those encampments before they decide to do the sensible thing and attack en masse.'

'Not until the defences have been completed,' Gardus said. 'Defeating Bakhos' host will mean nothing if beastherds or worse are running rampant behind our lines.'

Cassandora sighed. 'But once that's done...'

'I promise, sister – you and the Stormforged may take the fight to the foe.'

Cassandora knocked her knuckles against his chest-plate. 'I'll hold you to that, Gardus. Don't think I won't.' She looked up.

A silver shape fell to earth like a comet, shaking the street and sending mortals scrambling. Tegrus of the Sainted Eye rose from the small crater created by his landing and dropped to one knee before Gardus. 'Lord-Celestant – we are under attack. All along the eastern emplacements and the docklands. It's as if every beastherd in the city has been summoned to war...'

Gardus glanced at Cassandora and said, 'Rise, brother – carry word to the other emplacements. Find the Swiftblade, and Lord-Relictor Ramus.' He looked east, listening to the echoes of battle, only now becoming perceptible.

'We have urgent matters to discuss.'

CHAPTER THIRTEEN

WATCH AND WAIT

In denial, every soul finds its secret truth.
– Oswal of Thurn
The Mysteries of Pleasure

'It is ever thus, the impatience of mortals,' Bakhos said, saluting the distant sounds of war with his goblet. He glanced at Hulmean. 'Then, you have been remarkably tardy, my friend. Maygrel and Tabbisa have attacked without you.'

Around them, Hulmean's encampment readied itself for war. Warriors clad in black war-plate fed and watered their steeds, even as their mortal blade-slaves readied chariots for those lucky enough to possess them. Hulking ogors, their pasty flesh scarred by slave-brands and ritual markings, howled impatiently, awaiting the order to march. Their mortal overseers attempted to keep them in check with barbed whips and gifts of bloody meat.

Hulmean looked at him. 'My lord, you said I was given

233

the centre. No word was made of when I had to attack.' The black-iron reaver crouched beside one of the horses that would pull the towering war-altar his slaves had constructed. The animal deigned to allow him to check one of its six silver-shod hooves, but snapped at him with wolf-like teeth as he stood. Hulmean struck the beast, staggering it in its traces. It whinnied in frustration, and he gave it a fond pat on the neck. He turned.

'Besides, my lord, Maygrel lives in the saddle, and Tabbisa's warriors are nomads – they need only what they carry. For them, war is as instinctive as breathing. But I am an artisan of murder, not some howling savage.'

'Here here, kindly Hulmean,' Lemerus called out, from where it stood nearby. Bakhos frowned in irritation. The thin champion had been shadowing Bakhos for days, watching his every move. 'There is no reason to rush, eh?'

'No reason at all,' Bakhos murmured. 'You've built quite the warband, Hulmean. Impressive chattel.' Not just ogors, but gargants as well. There were three of the looming, gangly limbed monsters. Their bodies were slathered in slabs of iron, tied on with chains or hooked into their flesh, and their malformed skulls were encased in heavy helms.

'I bought the ogors from the slavers of the Furnace Lands, in Aqshy. The Furnace-Kings raise the brutes in pens, and feed them on scraps of their mothers' flesh.' Hulmean eyed the ogors with satisfaction. Each of the beasts was clad in crude war-plate, and carrying a serrated, cleaver-like blade, capable of chopping an armoured warrior in half. 'I send them in first. They make for a suitably belligerent beginning to any battle.'

'The best kind,' Bakhos said. He looked up as a shadow passed overhead. Screeching daemon-shapes, part bat, part wolf, swooped and dived, tormenting slaves and warriors alike. 'Furies as well. You are taking this seriously, my friend.'

'You say that word so often, it has little meaning.'

Bakhos took a sip from his goblet and looked at Hulmean. 'Have I insulted you, Hulmean? I must have, for I cannot reason why else you would dare speak to me so.'

Hulmean gave a gurgling laugh. 'No, my lord. No insult. It was merely an observation. We are not your friends. We are your servants. We are as much your blade-slaves as those mirror-helmed eunuchs who ghost your path.' He gestured to one of Bakhos' eunuchs, standing silently nearby. 'Lemerus and Etax may not admit it, but I am not so foolish as they. I do not pretend to have free will.'

'What is will, next to glory?'

'Nothing,' Hulmean said. He turned, staring at the city. 'Nothing at all. Listen – the thump of crude drums. The beasts go to war.'

Bakhos nodded in satisfaction. Elevating Ghosteater had accomplished all that he had hoped. The albino led his new forces into battle, disrupting the enemy all along their defences. The beasts would die, of course. But all in good cause.

He took another swallow of wine, contemplating the future. Soon, his forces would have shed all the dead weight accumulated over the decades. Then, only an iron core would be left. An army in truth, rather than merely in name. And then – well. The world was open to him. The beasts numbered in the hundreds of thousands in the city alone. Properly motivated and led, they would hold Caddow for months, if not years. There was little need for him here, save to send the most foolish champions to their deaths.

He looked east, eyes narrowed. Nagashizzar was there. And Archaon. The Three-Eyed King waged war on the holdings of Nagash, striking everywhere at once. The armies of Varanspire laid siege to every wall and port, holding the dead trapped in their tombs. At least for now. That was where the glory was. He just needed an excuse. A reason. Something that would keep Archaon from removing his head.

Laughter sounded, echoing through the encampment. Bakhos turned, and saw a cluster of daemonettes watching him. Their oil-black eyes were fixed on him like arrows, ready to be loosed. They knew what he was thinking. He suspected that they approved. The Handmaidens of the Absent God were things of desire and impulse. This place wore at them, and made them seek oblivion almost gladly.

They would follow him, when he left. He knew it, as well as he knew his own name. Proof enough that he was blessed by the Absent God. He raised his goblet, and they laughed again, sweetly. He turned away. Hulmean was watching him.

'They love you, O Leopard.'

'Because I am the truest son,' Bakhos said. 'I have ever followed my own desire in all things. I am a slave to it. Eaten hollow by need, and unfilled, as yet.'

'And what need is that? Not glory, I think.'

'No, not glory,' Bakhos said, after a moment. 'I had enough glory for a hundred men before I ever set foot in the Glades of Silk.' The daemonettes laughed again, and began to sing, softly. He did not look at them. The song they sang reminded him of soft light, and welcoming shadows. Of the sound of her voice, and the way she had plucked the strings of his lyre, when she thought he wasn't looking.

He closed his eyes. Her face was still there, etched on the cave walls of his mind, if barely. How many years had it been since he had last recalled her clearly? Would he forget her entirely, in time? A desire unfulfilled soon turned sour. Became something else.

Archaon had promised him that he would see her again, if

only he did his duty. But duty was a millstone, wearing away his desire and memory both. He had allowed himself to be lulled, to be caged. The Leopard, leashed. But not for much longer.

This was the story of him, and he would see it through to its glorious conclusion. Not this sad, dull anticlimax. The Hero of Semele would march again, and set himself on the pathway of desire.

He emptied his goblet and tossed it to Hulmean. 'Take this and fill it with the blood of Stormcasts for me. Bring it back to me, and I will raise you high in my councils.'

Hulmean stared at the goblet. 'Why?'

Bakhos laughed and turned away. There were preparations to be made. More dull champions to be raised up and sent to their well-deserved dooms.

'Because I desire it, my friend. No other reason is necessary.'

'Madness,' Chaell the Unborn said, softly. The Chaos warrior watched as beastmen flooded the streets below and spilled towards the Azyrite emplacements. 'They hurl themselves into death with such abandon.'

'They honour the gods,' Ghosteater growled. He crouched nearby, studying the enemy defences. 'Our souls, for yours. That is our lot.' They stood atop the shattered roof of something that might once have been a temple, or a guildhall, watching the assault below. Ghosteater's guards were scattered about them, on the slope of the roof. Chaell heard the roar of guns and the crash of thunder. The smell was strong on the air.

'I sense that you do not believe that, my friend.'

Ghosteater shrugged. 'Who can say what the gods truly want?' He tapped his chest. 'They do not speak directly to us, save in here. In our hearts.' He glanced back, to where Wyrm-hoof, Blacktongue and the other shamans had gathered, to work their magics. Chaell studied the beast-witches, wondering what savagery they were brewing. Whatever it was, it made the air stink and twist. 'Or else they whisper through the lips of shamans.'

'You don't trust them.'

'Do you trust witches?'

'No.' Chaell turned. He'd never trusted magic, save when it was wrought in iron. Magic had a nasty habit of deserting you when you needed it most. Silver shapes suddenly darted into view, high above the streets, and he tensed, ready to draw his sword.

'They cannot see us,' Ghosteater said, not looking at him. 'That is what the spell is for. Keeps us hidden, so that we can ob... ob... *observe* enemy positions.' The beastman drew out the word, as if it were unfamiliar to him.

'Just us?'

Ghosteater twitched. 'Others as well. All across the city. We must watch and wait – see where the enemy is strong. Where they are weak.' He scratched his armpit. 'Must watch and wait, like the Maiden's Son says.'

'You are calm, for one who sends his folk to their doom.'

'Not mine. Manglepaw's herd. They worship the Blood God. If I did not send them, they would go anyway. And others would wonder if I was as strong as they had thought.' Ghosteater glanced at the shamans again, as he spoke. Chaell shook his head.

He'd always thought of beastkin as simply... beasts. Ambulatory, perhaps. Capable of swinging a sword or an axe, but essentially what they resembled. Primitive, unthinking brutes. Fit only for the vanguard, or to be bent over a stone altar. Many thought as he did, and not just in Bakhos' horde.

Chaell had served more masters than he could recall. His

memories were scattered things, flitting into prominence at the unlikeliest of moments. For instance, at the moment his strongest memory was of the day he had first pledged himself to the service of the Dark Prince. He had heard the echoes of the Absent God's voice, thrumming from a stone the colour of night, and been caught by its beauty. A single word only, a hum of intent. *Please,* the god had said. And Chaell had been lost.

All that he had been before – a lifetime lived well and honourably – had been washed away, in a baptism of vice. He remembered being old – his hands aching, his eyesight weak – and the voices of his children, and his grandchildren. All gone now, some by his hand. Sacrifices to his own pleasure. To the perfection of his true self.

That was the nature of the Dark Prince. To ever seek that which could not be found. To ever desire that which could not be had.

And so too, he realised, was it with this albino beast. It desired what it could not have. What it could never have. And that desire drove it, even as his own drove him. 'If only I could remember what that desire was,' he murmured.

Ghosteater looked at him. 'What?'

'I said, what do you desire?'

Ghosteater looked up, gaze unfocused. This happened often. Chaell knew that the beast was talking to whatever enslaved spirits guided him. It was not an unfamiliar state of affairs – he had known many warriors who shared their minds and souls with daemons. The beastman shook his shaggy head and growled, 'What do *you* desire?'

Chaell laughed. 'I do not know. I left my desire – and all memory of it – in the Glades of Silk.'

Ghosteater started. 'You – have been there?'

Chaell nodded. 'Of course. All of us Blessed Ones have, in

one form or another. Some go in dreams, others in person. I went by a roundabout way, caught up in a dance of daemonettes, drawn deep into their realm by their caresses.' He smiled, as the memory grew firm. 'Oh, that was a time. I was brought before the Perfumed Throne, with its long-empty cushions, and there I bowed in prayer for six days and nights, seeking some sign of the Absent God.'

'Why?'

'I thought I had been chosen. Like Bakhos. I thought myself a lord in the making, and that I would take up the quest to find the lord of the land. That I would be the one to find him and bring him back to us, his loyal servants.'

Chaell turned and watched the dying below. After a moment, he continued. 'But instead, I was given an epiphany. The Absent God does not wish to be found, I think. For in seeking him, we are driven to heights undreamt. So I turned to other pursuits.'

'What were they like?' Ghosteater rumbled. 'The Glades?'

Chaell paused. In truth, he could not recall. The memory of them was all gossamer and dust, slipping through his fingers as he tried to grab them. He had vague impressions of banners rustling in a sweet wind, and the soft singing of the flowers beneath his feet. He shook his head. 'The Glades of Silk are places of great beauty and peace. For in them, all desires are fulfilled, and new ones conjured.' He sighed. 'What do you desire, my friend?' he asked again. 'Not this, I think. Or not simply this.'

Ghosteater was silent, his great leonine features as still as those of a statue. Then, he shook himself. 'I wish to be more than this.'

'A good dream.'

'Not a dream.' Ghosteater gestured. 'This city was ours. Our folk took it and were gifted it by the gods. A place to grow, and grow strong. A forest of stone for our very own.' He looked at Chaell. 'But then, you came. You Blessed Ones. And so, we thought we must fight – but how to fight those blessed by the gods?'

'You did not fight. I remember. I was there, when Bakhos first arrived. He challenged those long-dead beast lords for control of the city, and they bowed to him. Like cattle, they surrendered all too willingly.'

Chaell heard nearby beastkin growl at that, and his hand dropped to his sword. Ghosteater twitched an ear, and the growling died away. He looked at Chaell, and for a moment, the Chaos warrior thought that more than one person was watching him from behind that pink-tinged gaze. The albino had changed, somehow, after killing his rival. Not physically, but mentally. As if he were more sure of himself now. Not just a chieftain, or Bakhos' pet, but a warlord equal to any Chaell had ever had the misfortune to serve.

Ghosteater bared his teeth in what was almost a smile.

'Not surrender,' he growled, softly. 'Watching. Waiting.'

Funny, isn't it?

'What is?' Mannfred asked. He leaned back on his cot, trying to re-establish contact with Ashigaroth. The dread abyssal was proving frustratingly uninterested in doing as it was told, however. He could feel crumbling rooftops and powdery mortar beneath its claws, but could see nothing save vague flashes of colour.

How every time we come to Caddow, there's a war on.

Mannfred grunted. 'That's not funny at all, Vitalian.'

You only say that because your sense of humour is as withered as your heart.

Mannfred frowned. 'Go away, Vitalian. I'm not bored enough

to talk to myself right now. Even if I am pretending to be you.' The ghost fell silent, and Mannfred caught the faint flicker of Ashigaroth's consciousness. He seized on it with a predator's swiftness, and felt the dread abyssal thrash suddenly, infuriated at this unwelcome intrusion. 'No,' Mannfred snarled. 'No, I must see, and you must be my eyes, you stubborn brute.'

Mannfred felt the echo of the beast's shriek in his bones. But Ashigaroth subsided. Mannfred settled behind his steed's eyes and looked out over Caddow. Something ugly and dead hung from the dread abyssal's claws, its blood staining the stones. Ashigaroth had already devoured whatever passed for the beastman's soul. At Mannfred's nudge, he let the body tumble away, into the ruins below, and took flight.

The dread abyssal swooped over the city – the docklands, Mannfred realised. He could see beastmen loping through the streets in greater numbers than he'd ever seen. Something had mobilised them – not Bakhos, he thought. Ashigaroth snarled and landed on the remains of an onion-shaped dome.

'Ah,' Mannfred murmured. There, below him, on another roof, he saw a group of beastmen crouched, hiding beneath a net of crude magics, watching the battle far below them. One of them was an albino. 'Ghosteater. Curious.' He'd fully expected the creature to have run afoul of one of Bakhos' temper tantrums by now.

Ashigaroth tensed, ready to attack. The stink of the shamans' magics offended the dread abyssal's senses – they were weak. Primitive. Ashigaroth wanted to devour their puling souls, but Mannfred restrained the creature. 'Patience, my friend. Patience.'

A crack of thunder caught the dread abyssal's attention, and at Mannfred's urging it flung itself into the air. There were battles going on all across the city's eastern and southern districts.

Wherever the Azyrites had set themselves, Bakhos' forces raced to meet them.

He's sending his forces in piecemeal, Vitalian murmured. *Bad strategy.*

'Only if you intend to win. Bakhos' idea of victory is more elastic than most.' Mannfred could see the sense of it, from Bakhos' perspective. His army was too large to use effectively – only around a third of it had managed to participate in the initial assault, before they had been driven back.

So instead, he hurled the chaff into useless battle. He would bleed the defenders, keep them busy repelling assaults instead of fully shoring up their defences. Then, when he had identified a weak point – he would attack. That was Bakhos' way. The way of Semele, and its phalanxes. They had been effective, in part, because they swamped their enemies with armies of slaves first, before grinding the battered survivors under their sandalled feet.

Ashigaroth shrieked suddenly as a flare of cerulean light split the sky. Mannfred caught a glimpse of a Stormcast driving the ferrule of his battle-standard down against the street. Comets of celestial energy struck the advancing enemy, hurling burning bodies in all directions. The air shook with the echoes of the magical summoning, and Ashigaroth peeled away, screeching in pain. The energies bit at the dread abyssal's unnatural substance, and Mannfred reluctantly allowed the beast to flee. He slipped out of the dread abyssal's skull and back into his own.

Magnificent, Tarsem murmured.

'You would think that,' Mannfred said. His head ached. The reverberations of the celestial magic had stung him as much as they had Ashigaroth. 'In retrospect, it is unsurprising that the God-King plucked your soul from its husk and remade you in his image – you were already halfway there.'

And yet, we were friends.

'Nagash and Sigmar were friends, once.' The words slipped out. They tasted wrong. 'So they say,' he added, quickly. He was annoyed with himself for even thinking it. Nagash had forbidden such statements.

They were. You witnessed it yourself – you were there, in those dim, ancient days, fighting at the forefront of the first great wars. Don't you remember?

Mannfred shook his head. 'Nagash says it did not happen, and thus… it did not.' He grimaced as he spoke. There was ache in him, where memories had once been. They had been torn from him, like rotten teeth. Or maybe they had never been there at all.

There is a hole in you, brother. An abyss, where once there was history.

'Some things are best left forgotten.'

Is that why you told Ramus you could lead him to me?

Mannfred fell silent.

Why did you say that, Mannfred? If you've known where I was, why haven't you tried to rescue me yourself? There is no opportunity here that you could not have conjured long before now…

'You know why,' Mannfred snarled. His voice echoed tauntingly, and he heard the Stormcasts guarding the chamber stiffen. They murmured to each other in low, concerned voices, and he wondered if they thought him mad.

You are mad. As mad as Neferata and Arkhan. Nagash has shattered and rebuilt your mind more times than even he knows. With every failure, every revolt, he pulls you apart and makes you anew. To purge you of weakness.

'Just like them,' Mannfred muttered. 'Just like the Stormcasts.' Nagash and Sigmar were more alike than either would admit. He ran his claws over his scalp. He'd had hair, once. A jet-black mane, worn in the fashion of – of… of some kingdom, now long forgotten. But he had shaved it, hadn't he? 'Vanity,' he murmured.

Or because it reminded you of someone. It made you look like someone.

As Tarsem spoke, Mannfred saw the faces of other, silent ghosts… a young woman with a leopard's smile, a nobleman with eyes like embers. He shoved the heels of his palms into his eyes and tried to push away the faces.

'Quiet,' he said. 'Quiet. I must think.'

Why, Mannfred? What is there to think of? Wondering what you'll do if Ramus refuses you? Or are you worried that he won't…

Mannfred swept out a hand, cutting the air with his claws. When he opened his eyes, he saw nothing. Heard nothing. There was only the darkness of his cell.

And the darkness in his mind.

CHAPTER FOURTEEN

WAYS OF RUIN

In ruin, there is beauty. And in beauty, potential.
– Guym of Megado
The Harmony of Dissonance

'Look upon ruin, and behold its ways,' Albain Lorcus said. He stood atop the ziggurat, watching as a pair of great aurochs pulled a supply wagon down one of the immense ramps constructed by the Ironweld. The ramps – made from timbers and steel plates – had been made in Nordrath, and the first of them had been erected by duardin workgangs within hours of securing the central plaza.

'Guym of Megado,' Lord-Ordinator Taltus said, from behind him. 'You surprise me.'

'Oh?' Lorcus turned.

'Guym was one of the pre-eminent philosophers of the Lantic Empire. Or so he claimed.' Taltus' smile was so quick that

Lorcus almost thought he'd imagined it. 'I wasn't aware any of his writings had survived.'

'*The Harmony of Dissonance* was a… formative text for me.' Lorcus peered at the Stormcast. 'My grandmother spent a fair few comets acquiring copies of what few of his works she could find. Did you know him, then?'

'We moved in similar circles,' Taltus said. 'I recall watching him get thrown out of a tavern, though I do not remember the context. I remember… that such was a common occurrence, where he was concerned.' He frowned. 'I remember that the world was hard, even then, for a man who sought beauty in the ugliness of life.'

Lorcus shook his head. As ever, the sheer age of the being before him was all but impossible to grasp. To have known a philosopher like Guym… impossible to imagine.

He turned back to the ramp. Construction was ongoing, all around the realmgate. The Stormcasts were turning it into a fortress, capable of withstanding a siege. Palisades had already been raised around the edges of the central plaza. Walkways were being built from these outer walls to the heavy frame of wood and stone being raised about the ziggurat. 'Will there even be a plaza here, when you are done?'

'No,' Taltus said. 'The whole of it will be made over into a Stormfort. The city will be rebuilt around it, plaza by plaza, street by street. From catacombs to eyries.'

'It will take years.'

'Decades. Centuries.' Taltus smiled happily. 'Years of work ahead of me.' He looked at Lorcus. 'Of us, I should say.'

Lorcus laughed. 'I fear you'll outlive me, Lord-Ordinator. Perhaps my children will see the final shape of this city, but I doubt I will.' His hand fell to the pommel of his sword. 'I never imagined it would be so much work. I knew there would be some, obviously, but this...' He glanced at Taltus. 'There are troggoths in the sewers.'

'There's a whole jungle down there, according to the Zhu'garaz. An ecosystem all of its own.' Taltus tugged on his moustaches, his gaze unfocused. 'I look forward to seeing what I can make of it.'

'You're not going to simply burn it?'

Taltus shook his head. 'Why? Unless it is tainted in some fashion, it might be well to weave it into the city's cycle, given how long it has had to spread.' He smiled. 'The greatest cities are not those which scrape the earth bare and build on raw rock. Rather, it is those which grow in harmony with the land-scape. A city must be a part of the land, and the land, part of the city.' He interlaced his fingers, as if for emphasis. 'The land and that which stands upon it are not separate things. You see?'

'Is that another of your host's canticles?' Lorcus asked. The Hallowed Knights seemed to have a saying for every occasion. Taltus laughed. Before he could reply, thunder rumbled, echoing over the city. They turned, and Lorcus saw lightning flashing over the eastern district. He sighed. 'I should be down there.'

'Where?' Taltus asked.

Lorcus gestured. 'Somewhere. Anywhere. Leading the defence.'

'You have lieutenants for that.'

Lorcus nodded. 'That doesn't mean I shouldn't be there as well. This city is mine, Lord-Ordinator. That is why I came.' He waved a hand, forestalling Taltus' reply. 'I know. To risk myself now, when there is no great need, would be foolish. That does not mean that I do not feel the urge.'

He sighed and watched the flare of distant lightning. Storm-casts, fighting and dying, buying this city back for him in blood. His own soldiers would be there as well. Unlike the Stormcasts, they would not rise again. He tugged on his noose. It felt tight.

He'd insisted on being allowed to head up part of the defence – a foolish thing to do, he knew – and been reprimanded for it. That Gardus had done so in kindly fashion, rather than as a chastisement, only made it worse. The Steel Soul had no interest in risking mortal lives, especially lives as important as Lorcus'. But Lorcus knew that was a mistake. He could not simply be given the city – it would never truly belong to him, then.

No, he had to earn it for himself. At some point, he would have to shed blood with his own blade, and shout himself hoarse in the front line. That was why he had come. To earn the title his father had thought to buy for him.

His father, the duke, had never understood what such power meant. He thought in terms of land and revenues. Of influence in distant courts, and connections to powerful folk. He saw it all as a game, rather than a duty. But maybe it was both.

Lorcus' head was full of figures and notes. Reminders to speak to this sergeant, or that quartermaster. To re-read this contract, or redraw that one. The hard graft of empire building. Rather than trading blows with beastmen, he was poring over ledgers and parsing land grants. Still important, but lacking in glory.

'I was a boy when my father first told me of Caddow,' he said, idly. 'He told me such stories – of the great soulblight lords and their entourages who would occasionally journey to Azyr, or the deathrattle kings who came to test their lances against those of the Nordrathi aristocracy, in friendly tournaments. Wondrous tales. The glories of the past.'

Taltus said nothing. Lorcus sighed again. 'Legends, even then. When the gates closed, our sister-city was lost. The kings and queens of the dead vanished into myth. I barely credited such tales, until I saw my first deadwalker.' His stomach clenched at the sudden memory of cold, dead hands reaching out of the turgid waters of a Ghyran fen to grip and tear. He closed his eyes. The old scars on his legs and belly twinged.

'Too, he told me of the sky-ships that would dock at the highest eyries, and the great trade-barques that slid across the Sea of Dust. Of the sounds of the Carnival of Crows, at the turning of the seasons. A single celebration, stretched across two cities. Stories his father had passed on, and his father before him. Stories of how it was, when the Lorcus family had influence in two realms. When a Lorcus sat upon the Grand Conclave of Azyrheim, as well as Nordrath. When a Lorcus ruled Caddow…'

'And now, a Lorcus rules Caddow again,' Taltus said.

Lorcus frowned. 'Caddow is dead. The more I see of it, the more I realise that this place will never be as it was in those old stories. Caddow is dead. A new city – a new people – will arise from its ashes.' He looked down, towards the great, open-air tents that covered the ground around the base of the ziggurat. 'Is Gardus down there?'

Taltus nodded. 'He is organising the defences.'

'And Cassandora?'

Taltus smiled. 'Where do you think?'

Cassandora raised her tempestos hammer. 'Shields… *up!*'

Her voice echoed across the narrow square. Liberators raised their shields, locking them together. They were a loose wall of sigmarite, stretching across the width of the open ground. Long-dead trees clattered in the wind as the Stormcasts readied their weapons. Behind them, three cohorts of Judicators knelt in prayer, awaiting the signal to judge the enemy in their own fashion.

The square sat on the edge of the western district, near the grand thoroughfare that linked the district to the ziggurat.

Streets curved away from it in a rough wheel pattern. The sound of the enemy echoed along these thin passages, and the air throbbed with the sounds of their approach. Chariot wheels creaked as iron-shod hooves struck the cobbles. Lunatic screams split the dawn. Daemonic shadows stretched far ahead of their owners, as if eager to reach the foe.

The enemy were on the move everywhere, not just here. Disparate warbands, hurling themselves against newly erected emplacements or hastily assembled battle-lines like this one. At the other end of the square, Ironweld engineers and Freeguild soldiers worked swiftly to raise the last of their defensive bulwarks in this part of the city. Her task was to buy them the time they needed to do so.

'Just as the vampire predicted,' she murmured. It was a trifle unsettling, to realise that the creature hadn't lied. She wondered if Ramus was right, and they ought to have dispatched Mannfred as soon as he fell into their hands.

Thinking of the Lord-Relictor made her wonder where he'd vanished to. Ramus had never been what one could call sociable, but it wasn't like him to miss a war-council. That he'd sent his Lord-Castellant in his place was surprising. Messengers had failed to find him. Whatever the Lord-Relictor was doing, it seemed as if he didn't wish to be disturbed.

'No time to worry about that now, though.' She drew her rune-blade and scraped the sword's edge against her hammer. 'Steady, brothers and sisters,' she said, her voice carrying easily along the line. 'Who will weather the storm?'

'Only the faithful,' came the response. Hammers struck the insides of shields, mimicking a roll of thunder. Cassandora nodded in satisfaction.

'We have stood in this place before, haven't we?' she called out, walking behind the line. 'Whatever the realm, whatever the cause, we have always stood in this place. We will always stand, whatever comes. That is our glorious burden.' She clashed her weapons. 'Who will endure the winds of Chaos?'

'Only the faithful,' her warriors roared. The thunder of hammers and shields increased in volume. 'Only the faithful! *Only the faithful!*' With every shout, they grew louder. The storm of Azyr, swelling with fury.

'A righteous fury,' she murmured, as the enemy boiled into the plaza – a disharmony of colour and shapes. Strange songs sawed the air, and strange scents teased her senses. They came in a rush, like filth spewing from a burst aqueduct. 'No discipline,' she murmured. 'No control. No chance.'

There were armoured Chaos warriors on unnatural steeds, and nomadic riders, galloping atop horses daubed in gaudy paints. Chariots, pulled by mutants with the bodies of stags and the heads of women, rattled over the broken cobbles, their riders loosing arrows with more enthusiasm than skill. Among these wild riders loped beastmen and mortal warriors, all howling out praises to their daemonic patrons.

The air about them seemed infected with colours without description, and the odour of rotting meat grew pervasive. Eerie lights danced about them, flickering in time to their cries, purposeless and directionless. The crash of cymbals and the winding of horns made the plaza throb with sound. Cassandora felt a murmur of unease go through her battle-line.

'Hold,' she said.

At her word, the shield wall stiffened. Gaps vanished as a wall of blue and silver formed. She turned. 'They're close enough. Calypias – loose! Aim for their steeds!'

As one, the Judicators rose and readied their boltstorm crossbows. 'Low,' she shouted, dropping to one knee. The shield wall sank down with a clatter of sigmarite, opening up a clear line of fire for the Judicators. Boltstorm crossbows hummed, and a scythe of celestial energy struck the foe's battle-line. The Judicators fired again, and again, reloading with inhuman speed. Chariots flipped as the beasts pulling them died, and horse-things squealed in agony. It was a brutal tactic – but necessary.

The massed cavalry charge was blunted in moments, as the dying front ranks became tangled with those racing behind. A fifth and final volley further muddled things, erasing any momentum the enemy might have had.

'High,' Cassandora cried. Her Liberators rose, shields still locked. Chaos warriors charged out of the confusion, attacking alone or in small groups. Something with a woman's face squealed as it lashed out with gilded hooves, dragging the broken remains of a chariot in its wake. Nomads shrieked prayers as they tried to break the line. Liberators absorbed the impacts on their shields, and replied in kind.

'Who will meet the enemies of heaven, and cast them back?' she called out, as her sword split a multihued helm. 'Who will walk in glory and wonder, forever after?' Her hammer crashed down, buckling a shield embossed with a leering, daemonic countenance. Around her, the Stormforged set their shields – and held.

'Only the faithful.'

'Only the faithful!'

'Only the faithful!'

The great, open-air tent was one of several that had been raised in the plaza about the base of the ziggurat. Freeguild soldiers and Stormcasts moved back and forth among the great wooden slats that had been set up at irregular intervals beneath it. Each slat was taller than a man, and twice as wide. Upon each, a rough field-map of part of the city had been stretched. Flocks of scribes and cartographers busied themselves making annotations to each.

Gardus stood in the midst of this organised confusion, arms crossed, his eyes fixed on the map before him. 'Report,' he murmured. Behind him, Knight-Venator Enyo crossed her wrists and bowed her head.

'Horsemen along the eastern thoroughfare,' she said. 'They're supported by scattered herds of beasts, but only in the loosest sense.'

Gardus turned. 'How many?'

'A few hundred.' Enyo removed her helm, revealing olive features, and close-cropped dark hair. 'No discipline,' she added, after a moment's consideration. 'A few bows, mostly blades and spears.'

Gardus gestured, and a scribe made a note on the map. 'Take your huntsmen – break their assault. Then continue on to the southern defences. The Gold Gryphons are hard-pressed there, according to their last missive.' He looked at Enyo. 'Go with Sigmar, sister.'

Enyo nodded. 'Always, Lord-Celestant.' As she turned to depart, Albain Lorcus entered the tent, and made his way through the crowd of scribes and messengers. The young captain-general looked about, expression bewildered.

'How you can stand all of this, I don't know,' he said, by way of greeting. 'I have never seen the like. Don't you fear missing something?' He came to stand beside Gardus. 'Taltus sends his regards, by the way. He told me he's heading out to check the northern emplacements.'

Gardus nodded, and gestured for a scribe to make note of the information. 'When I was mortal, I learned early on that success often came with organisation.' He motioned sharply, and a pair of soldiers lifted the slat before him and moved it to the side. Another map soon replaced it, this one of the western district.

The Lord-Celestant motioned to a dishevelled young man in the uniform of the Nordrathi Red and Blacks. Jon Cruso's horsemen were responsible for harrying the beastkin in that part of the city. 'Report.'

The young harquebusier swallowed and stepped forward, helmet under one arm, his repeater handgun slung across his back. 'Milord, Jon says – I mean, Captain-General Cruso sends his warmest regards and asks – ah…' He hesitated, glancing at Lorcus. Gardus smiled.

'Go on.'

'Jon says if you could please send us some sodding infantry, that'd be darling.' The youth spoke quickly, shooting glances between Lorcus and Gardus. Lorcus laughed.

'That sounds like him.' He borrowed a piece of parchment and a quill from a nearby scribe and scratched out a missive. 'Take this to Lieutenant Reffa, in the western district. There's three cohorts of Gallowsmen stationed there, to act as support for the Ironweld. Handguns and halberds. They'll move up in support.' He handed it to the harquebusier, and Gardus dismissed the youth.

'Well done.' Gardus was pleased by Lorcus' quick thinking. It showed an aptitude for command that would be sorely needed in the years ahead.

'These attacks – it's as if they're not even regrouping,' Lorcus said, looking at the maps. 'How many warriors do they have, to throw them away so casually?'

'More than us. But not enough.' Gardus stared at the maps, parsing them in his head. Slowly, he was building a whole picture of the city in his head. But it wasn't complete. Not yet. He glanced towards the rough maps of the city's outer districts – Sathphren's scouts hadn't managed to get that far, yet. Until they did, he would only be able to guess at the enemy's numbers.

'What do you do?' Lorcus asked, in the moment of quiet.

Gardus looked down at him. 'What?'

'What do you do, when you are not doing this?' Lorcus gestured to the maps. 'Some say you Stormcasts are concerned only with war. That when you are not at war, you are training for war. Is that true?'

Gardus chuckled. 'For some of us, certainly.'

'For you?'

'No.' Gardus frowned. 'I… read. Medical treatises, mostly. Though I have a growing fondness for Verdian poetry. A bit bucolic, but soothing in its way.'

'Medical treatises?' Lorcus looked startled.

Gardus nodded. 'It has been almost three hundred years since I last oversaw a hospice. Some few advances have been made, and I felt it necessary to familiarise myself with them.' He smiled. 'I should like to write my own, at some point. I have made a thorough study of the folk traditions of Verdia and I feel that many are of great value with regard to a number of common ailments. But that will have to wait, I fear.' He turned, as Knight-Vexillor Angstun entered the tent.

He strode towards Gardus, his meteoric standard in hand, and his helm under the other arm. His heavy war-plate was smudged with soot and blood. 'Angstun – what news?' Gardus called out.

'We have repulsed the beasts on the eastern flank.' Angstun glanced at Lorcus as he spoke. 'Your soldiers acquitted themselves well. A Lieutenant… Dashos conveyed her greetings, though her language left something to be desired.'

Lorcus laughed. 'That would be my cousin, Rena. Her father

sailed with the sky fleets. He taught her how to swear like an aetherjack, much to my aunt's chagrin.'

Angstun nodded. 'She will require reinforcement. They are short on powder and shot. My cohort stands in support, as does the Shieldborn's. I have ordered Iunias forward, along with Feros and his cohort, to flush out any beasts yet lurking in the streets near the emplacement. The docklands will be clear by dawn.'

Gardus nodded. The Retributors would make short work of any enemies waiting there.

'Good. Press forward, if you can, and establish a temporary bulwark on the northern wharfs. Use whatever you can find – collapse a building, if you must. Our foe has given us an opportunity, and we would be remiss to ignore it.' Gardus turned to a scribe. 'Inform the quartermasters that the Gallowsmen are in need of resupply.'

'I can take it,' Lorcus said, still looking at the map.

Gardus looked at him. Lorcus met his gaze, after a moment. 'At some point, I must be seen at the front,' he said. Gardus frowned.

'If you perish, this endeavour–'

'Will continue, Lord-Celestant. You will do your duty, and someone else will assume mine. That is the nature of our work.' Lorcus glanced at Angstun. 'Besides, I am sure the Knight-Vexillor will provide a capable escort.'

'It would be an honour,' Angstun said, in a tone that implied it was anything but. Gardus swallowed a laugh and nodded.

'Very well. Gather your men, captain-general. I will see that supplies are ready within the hour.'

Lorcus saluted, turned and marched out. Angstun watched him go. 'He seems competent enough, for a mortal.' The words were grudging.

'More than competent, I think. Otherwise Sigmar would not have granted him the fief-rights for this city.'

Angstun grunted. Not quite agreement, but not disagreement, either. A philosophical noise – acknowledgement, with no hint of judgement. Gardus did laugh, this time. 'Something bothering you, Knight-Vexillor? Out with it, please.'

'The Bullhearts,' Angstun said, after a moment.

'What about them?'

'The Lord-Relictor has not been seen since the clearing of the eyries.'

Gardus motioned for another map to be brought forward. 'Ramus has his duties, and he attends to them,' he said. Angstun wasn't the only who'd noticed Ramus' absence. The Lord-Relictor had sent others to represent him in war-councils, and the Bullhearts performed their duties as well as ever, but of Ramus himself there had been little sign.

'The God-King should not have sent him,' Angstun said, softly. 'Not here.'

Gardus stiffened, and looked at his Knight-Vexillor. 'Why do you say that?'

Angstun grunted again. His blunt features were seamed with scars, some vivid, some faint, and they flushed slightly as he spoke. 'The Bullhearts keep to themselves, and speak little to those not of their Chamber. But some among them think this duty is not an honour but…' He trailed off.

'An insult,' Gardus said.

Angstun nodded. 'It seems so, to some among our own Chamber as well. Given Ramus' petition to seek out Nagash…'

Gardus sighed, and looked back at the maps. 'Ramus has suffered much. His warriors have suffered as well. Almost an entire Chamber – nearly annihilated and Reforged, twice over. The veterans among them have a right to question their reasons for being here, especially Ramus.'

'They can question all they like, so long as they do their

duty,' Angstun said. 'But Ramus – the Lord-Relictor – does not appear to be doing his. And I am not the only one to notice, and wonder.'

Gardus frowned. He stepped close to Angstun, and pitched his voice low. 'What have you heard, Angstun?' The Knight-Vexillor was closer to the rank-and-file than other officers. He heard things those in the upper echelons might not. If he felt it necessary to say something, then it was only wise to listen.

Angstun looked straight ahead. 'Some question Ramus' fitness to hold his rank. If he will not command, then why not elevate another who will?'

'That is not for us to decide.'

'We may soon have to, my lord.' Angstun met his gaze. 'Why is he not here, my lord? Why is he not in the front line, like Cassandora? Why is he even here at all, if his presence contributes nothing to our efforts?'

'Because Sigmar wanted him here, Knight-Vexillor. That is enough.' Gardus turned back to the maps. 'Find Lord-Castellant Grymn before you go, and send him to me. He can handle the defence as well as I. And I will seek out the Lord-Relictor, wherever he secretes himself, and learn what keeps him from his duties.'

Osanus stepped down into the smithy. 'You are hiding, yes?' he rumbled.

Ramus stopped, warhammer raised over a molten chunk of silver. 'No. Merely busy.' He had claimed the small smithy for himself, after its discovery by a Freeguild patrol. It was a simple thing, set low into the street. Several anvils, now coated in rust, and a forge that had been cold for centuries. Racks of rusty tools – farm implements and the like – hung from the stone walls, waiting for owners who would never claim them.

'Hiding,' Osanus said. The Knight-Heraldor sat on a nearby anvil and took off his helm. 'Always hiding of late, mine brother. Why?'

Ramus struck the silver, turning it with the tongs. Nearby, blue flames crackled in the forge, filling the air with the smell of clear water and cold winds. He manipulated the silver, crafting the ancient death-mask into a spike with deft strikes of his hammer. He'd found it in the catacombs. 'I am not hiding, Osanus. Attend your duties, and leave me to mine.'

'There is a battle going on,' Osanus said.

'Am I required?'

'Hardly,' Osanus snorted. 'But Khela worries about you, Lord-Relictor. So does Osanus. Though not as much.' He held his fingers apart a fraction. 'Only a bit, yes?'

Ramus grunted. 'Worry elsewhere. I need to concentrate.' He struck the silver again, and murmured a prayer, working the words into the metal with his will. He heard Osanus begin to hum behind him and felt his war-plate vibrate in sympathy with the other Stormcast's voice. He sighed and turned.

'Speak, then.'

'What do you do here?' Osanus asked, coming to stand beside him. 'Why do you hide yourself from your brothers and sisters? You gave orders to Sagittus that none were to disturb you…'

'And yet here you are.'

Osanus grinned and nodded. 'Osanus thought you might be lonely, yes?' He looked around. 'What do you do here, Lord-Relictor?' he asked again, more sombrely this time. He gestured to the silver. 'What is this that you make, and weave prayers into?'

Ramus lifted the half-formed spike and studied it. 'It is necessary.' He thrust it into the flames, and sent a pulse of lightning rippling down through the tongs to inundate the metal, speeding the process.

'You are not answering my question.'

Ramus shook his head. 'No. I am not. I am not answerable to you, or to the Lord-Castellant. Not yet, at least.' He had prayed for a night and a day, seeking relief from his doubts, but no answer had come. Sigmar was silent. And so, he had decided to act. Even if it was the wrong course, better to try and fail than to wonder.

Osanus chuckled. The Knight-Heraldor tugged on his beard and looked into the flames. 'Perhaps never will be, eh?' He glanced at Ramus, his expression sly. 'Sagittus said you were up to something.'

'Sagittus talks too much.'

Osanus nodded. 'He's worried as well. Stories fly like crows. They say you plan to kill the vampire, yes?' He leaned forward and prodded Ramus in the chest. 'Greedy, brother mine. That is a kill best shared, yes?'

Ramus frowned. He drew the silver from the fire and set it on the anvil. 'I am not planning to kill the beast.' He struck the silver, again and again. Find the rhythm. 'Not yet, at any rate.'

'Then what is this?'

Ramus paused. He looked at the Knight-Heraldor. For all that he liked to think that Osanus was a fool, the Knight-Heraldor was anything but. Neither was Khela, more was the pity. They knew he was planning something, just not what. 'Have you spoken to anyone else about your... concerns?'

Osanus shook his head. 'It is for us – for the Bullhearts – to worry about you. Not others. No one outside the Chamber's command cohort knows anything.' He prodded Ramus again. 'We have been covering for you, brother. Gardus and Cassandora have both sent runners while you have been sequestered here. Luckily, they are too busy to question your absence in person.'

Ramus felt a flash of guilt. He should be out there, he knew. Doing his duty. Not here, not doing this. He struck the silver again, with more force than was needed. 'I am sorry,' he said. 'It is all necessary, I swear to you.'

'Then explain it, yes?'

Ramus did not look at him. 'It is best you do not know.' He held up the silver spike, and nodded in satisfaction. It was thin, shaped by muscle and magic into something unique. 'If I fail, someone must remain untainted by my decisions.'

Osanus' eyes narrowed. 'You intend to free him,' he said, flatly. 'Why?'

Ramus hesitated. 'He claims that he can lead me to Tarsus' soul.' He gestured with the spike. 'This... is my way of ensuring that he does so.'

Osanus smiled. 'When?'

'When what?'

'When will you leave?'

Ramus shook his head. 'You are not going with me.'

'I am. To see that your foolishness doesn't cost you dearly, yes?'

'I am defying Sigmar, Osanus. I will be punished, even if I succeed.' As he said the words, Ramus felt, for the first time, the weight of what he intended. It was a crime to defy Sigmar's edicts. Mortals had died for doing so. To his knowledge, no Stormcast had ever set himself in the God-King's path. Ramus wondered what would be said of him, in the centuries to come. Would he be remembered as a fool, a cautionary tale? Or would he be forgotten entirely, erased from the ledgers of history?

It didn't matter. It had to be done regardless. His grip on the spike tightened. 'I will be punished,' he said again, more softly.

Osanus nodded. 'Yes. As it should be. Can't defy the gods and escape unscathed.' He crossed his arms and grinned. 'But one must try, on occasion. Keeps them honest.' He looked into the fire again. 'When?'

'As soon as the opportunity presents itself. We will need a vessel.'

'And a crew,' Osanus said. 'Others will wish to come.'

'I will ask no one to accompany me.'

'Don't worry,' Osanus said. 'I will.' He clapped Ramus on the shoulder. 'When the time comes, we will be ready.' He thumped his chest. 'Zig-mah-HAI.'

Ramus looked at him. 'Are you certain of this, Knight-Heraldor?'

Osanus stepped past him, heading for the door. 'If I do not accompany you, I must stop you, yes? You are mine brother, Ramus. And mighty Osanus will be ready.'

He left Ramus standing there, in the middle of the smithy. Ramus looked down at the silver spike in his hand.

Suddenly, it felt very heavy.

CHAPTER FIFTEEN

ESCAPE

In the final days of Caddow, many of its people chose to escape over the Sea of Dust. To them, the unknown was preferable to the certainty of destruction.

– Tuman Wey
The Shadow-Routes: Trade in Eastern Shyish

'Fall back,' Sathphren Swiftblade cried, as he hauled back on Gwyllth's reins. 'Break off – fall back!' Chaos warriors flooded the central avenue, pounding towards the newly erected defensive emplacements in a wave of iron and hate.

The Chaos warriors weren't alone. Strange, yowling beasts flapped overhead, swooping on leather wings and clawing at the Stormcasts with hooked claws. Great malformed ogors lumbered ahead of their armoured masters, swinging heavy blades. A solid wedge of monsters, punching into the bulwarks like a mailed fist. Stone cracked and toppled as the Ironweld defences collapsed.

Freeguild soldiers, in the heraldry of the Gold Gryphons, retreated in good order, firing handguns and crossbows as they fell back across the plaza. Stormcasts formed up between the mortals and their pursuers, but the silver warriors were outnumbered and soon overwhelmed. Lightning surged upwards, again and again, as the last warriors of the cohort fell. Sathphren cursed. 'Who was that?'

'Tolmeus, of the Bullhearts,' Feysha said. She levelled her boltstorm pistol and fired at one of the winged beasts, plucking it from the air. Freeguild soldiers retreated around the Vanguard-Palladors, falling back to the secondary emplacements. 'We've lost Cassel's cohort as well. We underestimated them.'

Sathphren growled softly. He didn't want to admit it, but she was right. Whoever was in charge of this sortie wasn't the usual dullard. He turned in his saddle and saw that the last of the Freeguild had made it to the secondary emplacements. 'Come on. We need to buy the mortals time to regroup. Follow me!'

He hauled Gwyllth around and raced towards the edge of the plaza. 'We go for the flank,' he shouted, pointing towards the entrance to a side street. 'Strike hard, but keep moving. Don't stop!' Feysha nodded, and relayed his intent to the others. They sped down the twisting street, moving with the speed of lightning.

The side streets of Caddow were like scars carved into the body of the city – they wound about with little rhyme or reason, ending as suddenly as they had begun. The Vanguard-Palladors erupted into the enemy's flank, bowling over mortal warriors and Chaos horsemen alike. The gryph-chargers surged through the mass of the foe, shrieking and snarling. Their riders laid about them, seeking to wound, rather than kill. Wounded men made better obstacles than the dead.

Sathphren urged Gwyllth over the top of a chariot. She slammed into the cart and scrambled over its side, moving with unnatural agility. Sathphren fired his pistol into the team of mutated beasts pulling it, killing them, even as Gwyllth bit the head off the driver. Then they were moving again, leaving the chariot to flip onto its side.

Boltstorm pistols cracked and shock handaxes snarled as the Vanguard-Palladors rampaged through the Chaos formation. They were moving too quickly for all but the most monstrous of Chaos champions to follow. Sathphren's warriors ignored the bellowed challenges that rose in their wake as they sped on.

Out of the corner of his eye, Sathphren saw the looming shape of a Chaos war-altar, pulled by a team of monstrous horses. The malign construct creaked loudly as it ground forward, great wheels cracking the paving stones beneath it. Thousands of censers, steaming with cloying incense, swung from its scalloped sides, and the front was all of gold, and had been wrought to resemble dozens of bodies, locked in orgiastic excess.

Standing atop it, a heavy, black-armoured warrior raised a single-bladed axe and roared out something that might have been a prayer. Or perhaps a curse. He gesticulated with the axe and winged beasts swooped low, clawing for the Stormcasts. Sathphren ducked aside as a daemonic talon sliced through the spot where his head had been. 'Fall back and regroup,' he bellowed, turning Gwyllth about.

As they raced back the way they'd come, the warrior atop the war-altar raised a great, curved horn to the mouthpiece of his helm, and blew a single, quavering note. The plaza shook as an immense shape, bound in chains, rose from behind the altar and slouched into view. Dozens of mortal warriors sought to control its lumbering movements by tugging on the chains or striking it with goads.

'They have a gargant,' Feysha shouted.

'Yes, thank you, I can see that for myself – keep riding,' Sathphren snarled.

The gargant gave a booming cry and lumbered towards them, jerking its handlers from their feet. A bellow of animal rage shook the plaza as the creature crushed slow-moving beastmen and mortals beneath its feet, and snatched at the Vanguard-Palladors. The gargant thudded after Feysha, groping for her as she turned in her saddle to fire her pistol.

'Feysha – leave it! Let Thalkun earn his keep,' Sathphren shouted. But to no avail. She was too close, and the gargant was faster than it looked. It slammed both fists down, splitting the ground, and knocking Feysha and her steed sprawling.

Sathphren cursed and brought Gwyllth around. He shot towards the gargant, firing his boltstorm pistol. Vanguard-Palladors followed him, swirling about the gargant, trying to keep it distracted as Feysha hauled herself back into the saddle.

A moment later, the thunder-crack of longstrike crossbows split the air. The gargant jerked and reeled as the shimmering bolts struck it, and it staggered against a building. The brute bellowed again and swept out a hand, casting a nearby statue from its plinth. It groped for the statue, and dragged it up as if it were a club.

The gargant swung the statue at the Vanguard-Palladors, knocking one from her steed. Her broken body rolled limply across the street as her beast screeched in outrage. Gryphchargers leapt onto the gargant, clawing and pecking. The gargant roared and flung the statue, smashing part of the secondary emplacements.

Sathphren urged Gwyllth forward and she leapt, slamming full-tilt into the gargant and knocking it back. It stumbled out into the plaza, crushing ogors and Chaos warriors beneath its great feet. It swiped blindly at its attackers, and sent a beast-man flying. Gwyllth avoided its groping fingers and climbed the gargant as if it were a tree.

Sathphren slipped from the saddle and caught hold of the chains draped over the brute's scarred chest. Swinging himself around, he raced beneath its arm even as he drew his star-bound blade with his free hand. Seeing an opening, he thrust his sword into the creature's armpit and sought its massive heart. The gargant roared in pain and clawed at him, forcing him to adjust his strategy. He whistled, and Gwyllth went for the beast's eyes, as Sathphren, still holding on to the chain, dropped towards its legs.

Swinging himself out, he hamstrung the gargant with a single, economical slash. The gargant keened shrilly and wobbled, sinking to its knees. Boltstorm pistols cracked as the other Vanguard-Palladors took advantage of its sudden weakness. The creature wailed piteously as lightning punctured its skull and neck. It collapsed onto its face, shaking the plaza.

Sathphren turned as an arrow bounced from his helm. An ogor barrelled forward through the dust of the gargant's fall. He avoided the sweep of a serrated blade, and Gwyllth pounced on its wielder, tearing out the ogor's throat. As Sathphren hauled himself into the saddle, more ogors charged into view, bellow-ing guttural war-cries. 'Back to the emplacements,' he roared, parrying a blow that would have removed one of Gwyllth's forelegs. The gryph-charger shrieked and clawed at the ogor's face, staggering the brute. Before she could press her attack, Sathphren urged her away.

With some relief, he saw the others following his example. As he rode towards the emplacements, he glanced back towards the war-altar. The heavily armoured warrior standing atop it thrust his blade in the direction of the rooftop. He bellowed something, and the flapping, daemonic shapes broke off from pursuing the Vanguard-Palladors and swirled towards the rooftops like a maddened cloud.

The crack of crossbows faded as the Vanguard-Raptors fought to defend themselves. Lightning sawed upwards, staining the sky blue for a brief moment. Sathphren turned away.

'Thalkun's position has been compromised,' Feysha said, as she pulled abreast of him. 'They'll have to pull back.'

'Can't be helped,' Sathphren said. He turned back towards the secondary emplacements. A hastily assembled line of Freeguild soldiers was doing what it could to hold the foe back with volleys of gunfire. Behind them, Ironweld crews were shoving artillery into position. He could only hope he'd bought them enough time.

Gwyllth leapt easily over the emplacement, and Sathphren dropped from the saddle. A Freeguild soldier in the uniform of the Gold Gryphons, with a golden helm in the shape of a gryph-hound's head, saluted him. 'My lord, what are your orders?'

Sathphren hesitated, but only for a moment. 'Pride is the flaw in the shield of faith,' he muttered. The tenth canticle of the Hallowed Knights.

'My lord?'

'Send word to the Steel Soul. We need reinforcements, and swiftly.'

'Where is he?' Gardus asked. 'Where is Ramus? I was told he was here.' He looked around the smithy, noting the simmering coals in the forge. He tossed aside a scrap of metal, and turned. 'Well, Lord-Castellant?'

Khela did not answer him immediately. 'Praying,' she said, after a moment. Gardus did not glare or shout. It would have been preferable if he had. The weight of the Steel Soul's dis-appointment was barely tolerable. When she had learned he was looking for Ramus, she had made to intercept him, as had been her duty since the Lord-Relictor had sequestered him-self. She had no idea where Ramus was – or what he was up to – but she had her suspicions. But she didn't intend to share them with Gardus – not unless he ordered her to. Whatever Ramus was planning it was for the Chamber alone to deal with.

Granted, that would be easier had Osanus not chosen to disappear as well, along with thirty of their best warriors, including Sagittus and Cassos, the Decimator-Prime in charge of Ramus' bodyguard.

The warriors of the cohorts under her direct command knew nothing. But others – those veterans who had fought in Shy-ish – seemed to be taking pains to keep something from her, and the rest of the Chamber. It was irksome, and worrying. She had not yet confronted them. There was no way to do so without word getting around. The other Chambers already questioned the capability of the Bullhearts, and she wished to add no more fuel to that particular fire if she could possi-bly help it.

'I have sent runners to every temple in the secured areas of the city,' Gardus continued. 'He was not in any of them. Then, I was told he was seen here.' He thrust a hand into the coals, stirring them. He lifted a handful, and crumbled them between his fingers. 'It does me no good to have a Lord-Relictor if he cannot be found when I need him.'

'And do you need him, my lord?' Khela tried to keep her voice even. She bristled at the implication of his words, even as she suspected he was right. 'Is there some task that requires his wisdom?'

Gardus looked at her. 'Always. There are dead things stirring in the deep. Reconciler Ahom and the others could use his help in putting the dead to sleep. Or binding them more tightly. Instead, they struggle without him. Where is he?'

Khela looked away. 'Praying, as I said.'

'Where?'

Light flared, driving back the gloom of the smithy. A soft light, but pervasive. She felt its warmth through her war-plate. Gardus glowed like one of the beacons of Sigmaron, radiant with starlight. She looked into the light without flinching. 'I do not know.'

'Because you do not wish to know.'

It was not an accusation. Merely a statement. 'I…' She trailed off. 'Yes. Because I do not wish to know. He has been… distracted, since the vampire was captured.'

'Since before that, I think.' Gardus shook his head. 'Since the day he returned empty-handed from Ghur. Since he came to me, seeking my support…'

'Why didn't you?' The question came as a surprise to both of them. Khela considered taking it back, and then decided against it. She set her feet. She would not be moved. Gardus didn't reply. 'Why didn't you?' she pressed. 'One word from you, and surely Sigmar would have listened…'

'I did,' Gardus said, softly. 'I did ask why.'

Khela stared at him. His light filled the smithy, illuminating every stone and crevice. 'When I returned from Ghyran – from my second sojourn into the plague garden of Nurgle – I asked Sigmar why. He did not answer me. But now, I think perhaps he did. I think his silence was an answer. Just one that Ramus did not wish to hear.'

He reached up and removed his helm, revealing features which shimmered. There was nothing human in his face, save the general outline. It was simply… stars and light, in the rough shape of a man's head. Khela stared, unable to look away, to pull her gaze from the infinity where Gardus had once been. 'Sometimes, I think we only ever hear that which we wish to. Does Sigmar truly think as we do? Or is he but a reflection of us, magnified to divine proportions?' His words echoed strangely, reverberating through her, like the rushing of the winds between the stars. 'The thought unsettles me.'

Khela tore her gaze from him. 'Yes,' she said, her voice hoarse.

'Look at me, Lord-Castellant.'

Khela did. Gardus smiled. His face was his again – no stars, merely the same bluff, familiar features she'd expected. The light was still there, but dimmer now, hidden behind his eyes and beneath his skin. 'If Ramus is planning something, I must know.'

She cleared her throat. She wanted then to voice her suspicions. But she didn't. Whatever Gardus was, whatever he had become, he was not her Lord-Celestant. She straightened. 'If I knew, I would deal with it myself, Lord-Celestant.'

'Yes. I know.' Gardus sighed. 'I do not wish to see harm come to the Lord-Relictor, of his own making or otherwise. If you learn of anything…'

'If it is necessary, I will alert you,' she said, stiffly.

Gardus pulled on his helm. 'I trust that you will…'

A shout from outside the smithy alerted them both to something amiss. Khela was first outside. A Liberator of her Chamber strode towards them. 'Lord-Castellant – word from the central plaza,' he said. As Gardus stepped out of the smithy, he bowed.

'What is it?' Gardus said, impatiently.

'The enemy has come in force. The Swiftblade calls for aid. We are needed.'

Gardus glanced at Khela. 'Gather who you can. And find

Ramus!' He started towards the central plaza. 'I have a feeling we may need him in the coming hours.'

Khela watched him go. She turned to the Liberator. 'Where is Osanus?' she said. Whatever Ramus was up to, Osanus would know. Indeed, he was probably involved in it up to his eyebrows, by now. Wherever there was trouble, the Stormwolf would be there.

The Liberator hesitated and she felt a flare of irritation. He was a veteran, his helm marked with an orruk tusk, scrimshawed with sigils of death and penance. She let the flat of her halberd tap against his shoulder-plate. 'I will not ask again,' she said. 'You will tell me, and quickly, or I will tear this city apart until I find him.'

'Lord-Relictor,' one of the guards said, respectfully, as Ramus entered the chamber. Both were Liberators from the Bullhearts. He'd insisted that his warriors be a part of the rotation. 'Sagittus told us you were coming.'

Ramus studied them a moment, before replying. 'You understand what is about to happen?' he asked, harshly.

The two exchanged a glance. 'We do, lord.' The one who'd spoken took a breath. 'We were with you, at the Bridge of Seven Sorrows. We were there, when Tarsus sacrificed himself so that our souls might rise and be Reforged. If there is any chance that creature can help us free him...'

'Then we must do what we can to help,' the other Liberator said, softly.

'Even if it means defying Sigmar's will?'

The two were silent. Ramus shook his head. 'You know where to go?' he asked, after a moment.

'We do,' one said.

'Then go. I will bring the vampire.'

'But–'

'It is better this way. If I am caught, no blame will fall on you. And I can handle him myself. Go. I will see you at the meeting point. And tell Osanus to make ready.' Ramus gestured, and the two Liberators departed. He waited until the sound of their footsteps had faded, and then entered the vampire's cell.

'I am here, vampire,' he called out.

'Come to kill me at last, then?' Mannfred said, from a pool of shadow. Ramus could only barely discern the vampire's shape, reclining on his cot. 'Your need for vengeance burns in you like a torch in the darkness. You are disappointingly single-minded, Ramus of the Shadowed Soul.'

'A crooked mind leads to a crooked soul,' Ramus said.

Mannfred laughed. 'Another of your pious homilies? How droll.' The vampire leaned forward, his bald head gleaming in the light of Ramus' staff. 'Will you talk me to death, then? Or shall you lay me to waste with storm and drive?'

'If I had my way, neither. Instead, I would take you to Azyr, and seal you in a vault of celestine and sigmarite, there to howl unheard for all your eternities. You would be forgotten, and the realms would be the better for it.'

Mannfred cocked his head, smiling. 'But…?'

Ramus stared at him. 'Tarsus. You can lead us to him.'

'Better. I will help you free him. As I said, I owe him a debt.' Mannfred's smile faded. 'And whatever else, I pay my debts.' He slid forward with boneless ease. 'Free me, and we shall go. Together, we shall dare Death's domain, and rescue our friend.'

Ramus studied the vampire, seeking any sign of deception. But for once, there was nothing. Mannfred was telling the truth, however unlikely that seemed. Certain now he was making the right choice – the only choice – Ramus gestured. 'Stand back.'

Mannfred retreated, and Ramus lifted his warhammer. He

dashed the cell bars to fragments with a single blow, as ragged threads of broken enchantment swirled about him. Mannfred hesitated as Ramus filled the cell. Another blow shattered the vampire's chains. 'Up,' the Lord-Relictor said. 'Quickly.'

'Unsubtle, but effective,' Mannfred said, following his rescuer out of the cell. He rubbed his wrists. 'My weapons and armour.'

'Waiting below. We don't have much time. The city is under attack, but I have no doubt Gardus will beat our foes back. The sooner we are gone, the better.'

Mannfred laughed. 'Bakhos has come again, has he? I did warn you he was persistent. Almost as single-minded as you.'

Ramus spun, and the head of his hammer caught Mannfred in the throat, driving him back against the wall. Before Mannfred could react, Ramus set aside his staff, and drew the silver nail from the pouch on his belt. Mannfred's eyes widened. 'What...?' he gurgled.

'A bit of magic of my own, vampire. Hold still.'

Ramus thrust the nail into Mannfred's breast, just above his heart. The vampire shrieked, but Ramus ignored his struggles. He shifted his grip, holding the vampire pinned with his free hand, and lifting his hammer over the nail. One blow was sufficient to drive it in. Mannfred choked on his own scream, as the blessed metal sank into his flesh.

Ramus leaned forward, until he was staring directly into Mannfred's wide eyes. 'Betray me, betray our cause, and the nail will split your heart. Do you understand?'

'–e–esss,' Mannfred choked out. Steam rose from the wound, but it was already healing over. He grimaced and fumbled at the wound, as if fighting the urge to claw it open. 'What – what is that?'

'Azyrite magic. Old and mostly forgotten. It will ensure your loyalty – or your doom. Either is satisfactory.' Ramus stepped back, and Mannfred slumped, clutching his chest. 'Now come. We must be swift, if we are to depart without being found out.'

Mannfred rose unsteadily and followed him down, his expression uncertain. Ramus felt a flush of pleasure at having worried the vampire. Mannfred liked his games, but Ramus had learned how to play them as well, since their last encounter.

When they reached the lowest chamber, the vampire retrieved his war-plate, cloak and sword and made himself ready for battle, as Ramus kept a watch on the street. Troops moved across the plaza outside, hurrying towards pre-determined mustering points. The air throbbed with the grumble of artillery. 'I trust that cloak of yours has a hood?' Ramus growled, as they left the eyrie.

'Even vampires like to keep the rain off,' Mannfred said, with mocking cheerfulness. He flipped a ragged cowl over his head, casting his narrow features into shadow. He glanced up at the dark sky. 'I do hope Ashigaroth hasn't wandered off again. He gets bored so easily, if there's no prey to be had. I once lost him for a week, found him hunting skaven in some detestable slum north of Shardlake.'

'Like master, like beast,' Ramus said. 'Now be silent.'

They hurried across the plaza. No one tried to stop them, though a few mortals cast wary glances their way. Ramus could hear the clash of weapons and the cries of the wounded. Lightning streaked upwards from elsewhere in the city, and he flinched with every flash and growl of thunder.

Mannfred laughed softly. 'Regretting your decision already, Ramus? It's not too late. I can go myself, and you can stay here – hands clean, as it were.' He touched his chest. 'After all, you have my loyalty.'

'You'd like that, wouldn't you?'

'Immensely. You are not an ideal travelling companion.'

'Nor are you.'

'No, I suppose not. Needs must, eh?' Mannfred's grin was a slash of white in the dark. 'Where are we going, by the way?'

'The docklands.'

CHAPTER SIXTEEN

EMBARKATION

Constructed from fossilised wood, dredged from the tar pits of the Starmere, each dust-barque was crafted by artisans to the specifications of their owner...

– Tuman Wey
The Shadow-Routes: Trade in Eastern Shyish

Clouds of powder smoke rolled across the plaza. Carrion birds circled, their shrieks mingling with those of the winged daemons that perched on the heights.

Dame Suhla Morguin raised her sword. 'Twelfth Cohort – face... *shields!*' Her golden helm felt heavy. Sweat rolled down her face. She ignored it, blinking the stinging droplets from her eyes. Ahead of her, the secondary emplacements were all but hidden by the smoke. But the enemy were still there. She could hear them.

With a crash of steel, the Gold Gryphons swung their pavises around and planted them. The shield-bearers crouched, bracing the pavises. Behind them, pikes lowered with a sound like the crash of felled trees. Handgunners moved to take up position behind. The broad, rectangular shields had firing slits set into them – a duardin innovation that the regiment's armourers had seized on.

'Volley primus – *fire!*'

Handguns gave a rolling bellow as the air filled with another layer of powder smoke. The first line of handgunners stepped back, already reloading, as the second line moved to take their place. 'Volley secundus – *fire!*' A third line replaced the second, and a third volley roared. Three volleys in as many moments, Morguin noted, with no small amount of pride. Still, they could be faster. Smoother. She resolved to double their firing drills. The Gold Gryphons had a reputation to maintain, after all.

'Still coming,' her second-in-command, Chutehk, said. He tapped the leather hilt of the obsidian knife thrust through his belt. He was Chamonian, like Morguin, but from the southern jungles, rather than the highlands around Vindicarum.

'And we'll be here to meet them,' Morguin said, flatly. 'And stop playing with that bloody knife. There's no hearts to be cut here, you serpent-worshipping bastard.' She paused and glanced at him. 'No offence.'

'Great Sotek forgives you your blasphemy,' Chutehk said, idly. 'And he wouldn't take their hearts anyway – rotten all the way through.' He smiled, displaying teeth capped with turquoise. 'He prefers the hearts of heroes.'

'I already told you, I'm not interested.'

'It is a high honour, dame.'

'Then you do it,' Morguin snarled.

Chutehk sighed. 'I would, but I am not a hero. Merely a second-in-command. Ah well.' He laughed. 'However shall I live with myself?'

'You won't have to worry about that if this line doesn't hold – *did I say stop firing?*' she bellowed, pointing her sword at an unfortunate handgunner. 'Get that gun up, or I'll feed it to you piece by piece, soldier!'

The sound of cracking stone brought her around. She squinted, trying to see through the smoke. The secondary emplacements were made from great slabs of stone, set into a semi-flexible iron frame. The Ironweld strung them out like strands of rope, from one side of a street to another. They were durable, and quick to set up, but were easy enough for a determined enemy to clamber over.

And the Slaaneshi were certainly that. They came on, not as a horde but as knots of individuals, each striving to outdo the others. The only glimmer of discipline came from the wedge of ogors who chopped and tore at the emplacement, trying to cast it down. The rest – mortal and otherwise – simply climbed over and hurled themselves at the Gold Gryphons' lines, screaming obscenities or prayers, or things that were both.

Twelfth Cohort was holding them back, but that would change once the ogors finished with the emplacements. Then it would be a game of numbers and blades, and the Gold Gryphons didn't have enough of either. She glanced back, towards the far end of the street. The Ironweld were dragging their artillery to their fallback positions, and trying to set up a new defensive line. Twice now they'd been pushed back.

'There won't be a third time,' she muttered. The Gold Gryphons had never been broken in battle and that wasn't going to change here. Not on her watch. She looked around, seeking any sign of reinforcements.

'They're on the way,' someone growled, as if reading her mind. Morguin tensed and turned. Lord-Aquilor Sathphren Swiftblade approached, his gryph-charger padding silently in his wake. The Stormcast loomed over her soldiers, taller and broader than any mortal. One hand rested on the pommel of his blade, and the other on the boltstorm pistol holstered opposite. 'Cohorts from the Steel Souls and the Stormforged are advancing from the north and the west.' His remaining Vanguard-Palladors stood among the ranks of her soldiers, each Stormcast acting as a silver bulwark for the mortals around them.

'They'd best get here soon,' Morguin said, turning back to the emplacements. She paused. 'I'm sorry about the others. About Thalkun.'

Sathphren inclined his head. 'He will be Reforged. As will we all, one way or another.' He glanced at her. 'Perhaps even you, Dame Morguin.'

Morguin felt a chill race through her at the thought. The idea of being remade, of being other than what – who – she was, terrified her in a way battle could not. She swallowed and looked away, not wanting to meet Sathphren's gaze. Not wanting him to see the fear in her eyes, as she imagined being like him.

There were stories – every regiment had them – of soldiers caught up by a hammer-stroke of lightning, during some battle or other. Of good men and women, snatched away by the hand of Sigmar. And of them returning, months, years later, clad in sigmarite. Changed, in mind and body. Sometimes they recognised old comrades, but mostly, they didn't. It was always worse when they did.

Sathphren cursed, and Morguin pushed the thought aside. Through the powder smoke, she saw an ogor lumber towards her battle-line. A second brute followed the first, and then a third. She turned and bawled, 'Pikes... *extend!*'

With a rattle, the line of pikes lowered, forming a wall of steel. Handguns roared, and an ogor toppled over, body torn apart. 'We're not going to get a third volley,' Chutehk said, drawing his sword. He turned and waved a line of swordsmen forward, as the third and first ranks of handgunners fell back.

'Then we'll have to make the second one count,' Morguin said. She glanced at Sathphren. He'd drawn his sword and bolt-storm pistol. He nodded, and she returned the gesture. 'Brace… *shields!* Not one more step back.

'Whatever comes… the Gold Gryphons will hold!'

'From the sound of it, we're just in time,' Angstun called out, as he crushed a beastman's skull with a blow from his hammer. The Knight-Vexillor's standard crackled with barely restrained power, casting a blue haze over the street.

Gardus said nothing. Ichor dripped from his runeblade, and his hammer was encrusted with gore. They'd encountered moderate resistance as they moved towards the central plaza from small packs of beastmen or mortal Slaanesh-worshippers. The street was now hidden beneath a carpet of broken, smouldering bodies.

Behind them, a cohort of Retributors, led by Feros of the Heavy Hand, made short work of the remaining beastmen. Overhead, Prosecutors drove back a flock of daemonic furies, skewering the creatures with javelins, or casting their broken bodies down with hammer blows. One of the leathery monsters flopped to the ground before Gardus. It half rose, bat-like features twisted in a grimace of rage.

Gardus removed its head and kicked the dissolving body aside. 'Keep moving – the plaza is just ahead.' A pair of beastmen loped to meet him through wafting clouds of incense and gun-smoke. He barely slowed. The first fell, skull crushed. The second fled, clutching its slashed abdomen. The smoke thinned and cleared, revealing the end of the street and the plaza beyond. As he stepped into the plaza, Gardus saw masses of beastmen, mortals and Chaos warriors, advancing towards him – or, rather, towards the wall of pavise shields erected by the Gold Gryphons. Behind them came the creaking, nightmarish shape of a Chaos war-altar. Furies swooped in screeching flocks, all but filling the sky.

A knot of ogors and mortal warriors had already reached the Freeguild lines, and were fighting with the Swiftblade and his remaining warriors. But it wouldn't be long before the bulk of the enemy reached them.

'Angstun,' Gardus said.

'As you command, Steel Soul,' Angstun said. He stepped in front of Gardus and slammed the ferrule of his meteoric standard down. The energies contained within it arced outwards and upwards, blistering the air and shaking the surrounding ruins with a thunderous boom. The energies of the standard blazed, tearing the sky to tatters as blazing meteors of celestial force hammered down, splitting the plaza in two.

Many of the foe died, burnt, smashed or torn apart. The rest drew back, as horns sounded, and overseers howled commands. Atop the war-altar, the black-iron reaver in charge of the host blew his horn, and those daemons not consumed in the conflagration drew back. Gardus extended his hammer. 'Feros – advance.'

Quickly, the Retributor-Prime led Gardus' forces into the plaza. Liberators and Judicators formed up between the Gold Gryphons and the foe. Retributors swiftly took up a staggered formation in front of the shield wall. At Feros' bellow, they swung their hammers down and sent shock waves rippling through the shattered plaza, further disorientating the foe. The war-altar creaked to a halt, as the creatures pulling it stumbled and reared. The Chaos horde fell back, trying to form themselves up into something like a battle-line.

Gardus and Angstun joined the other Stormcasts. 'More of

them than last time,' Angstun murmured. 'You were wise to pull us away from the docklands.'

Gardus smiled. 'I thought that standard of yours might come in handy.' He studied the foe, through the fading smoke and dust. 'At least they've stopped moving.'

'For the moment.'

Gardus frowned. There were hundreds of them, packed into the plaza. A chaotic mass of colours and sounds. No discipline, no organisation. Just a wave of angry meat. And atop the war-altar, the one who led them. 'Think that's Bakhos?' Angstun asked.

'I doubt it. Just one more warlord. Tegrus and the other Prosecutors reported that there are still thousands of warriors in those encampments. If this were Bakhos, those pavilions would be empty.'

'Whoever he is, he appears to be upset,' Angstun said.

Gardus raised his hand, gesturing for Angstun to be silent.

'I am Hulmean of Dath,' the Chaos champion bellowed. 'Hulmean Cancreson! I have wrestled ogors and wooed the daughters of kings!' His voice shuddered out across the plaza, setting the furies to shrieking.

He leapt down from the war-altar and stalked across the broken ground, gesticulating with his axe. 'I have endured the caresses of the Mother of Daemons and swum in seas of excess. My bones are iron, and my hair is steel! Who will face me in honest battle?'

Angstun began to step forward. Gardus stopped him. 'No. This one is mine.' The Knight-Vexillor made as if to argue, but fell silent as Gardus stepped forward.

The rite of challenge was one of the few that the enemy respected. Whatever monstrous god they served, few of them would falsely issue such a challenge. The Dark Gods were like decadent nobles, eagerly wagering on the skill of their chosen gladiator. Unless it served some other, esoteric, purpose, an honest challenge was the surest, simplest way to catch the eye of a daemonic patron.

All this Gardus had learned through decades of war. Decades of death and slaughter, treated as a game by malign entities, crouched on the threshold of the realms. Treated as a game, by men and women who might once have fought against such darkness.

The old anger – the anger that had seen a humble physician lift a silver candlestick in defence of the sick and the dying – flared anew, kindled by the arrogance on display before him. As if a battlefield were nothing more than a stage for such creatures to strut and declaim their worth to an invisible audience. Light swelled, leaking from the joins of his armour.

Hulmean had seen him now. He laughed harshly, and his warriors laughed with him. 'One has courage, at least,' he shouted. He lifted his arms. 'We shall dance the dance of blood and steel. We shall worship at the altar of war, and offer up our souls to the Absent God!' The horde cheered as he spoke.

Gardus did not stop. Other might have. Others – Zephacleas, Vandus, others – might have stopped. Might have met the enemy's words with their own. They might have traded boasts the way swordsmen traded blows.

But Gardus was not them. Gardus had no tongue for boasts, no skill with words. No wit to prick his opponent's pride. He had only his faith. Only his certainty. That would have to be enough. So he did not stop.

His implacability seemed to infuriate Hulmean. He cursed and shouted, and his warriors shouted with him. He threw words like caltrops. Gardus did not stop, did not slow, did not speed up. But his light swelled.

'I am Hulmean the Hero, Black Son of Dath,' the warrior roared, as he loped to meet Gardus. 'Daemons weep at the touch of my gaze, and mortal souls wither at the sound of my voice.' He pounded across the broken ground, trailing boasts in his wake.

Gardus said nothing as he moved to meet the Chaos warrior. He blocked the creature's axe and brought his hammer down, pulverising his opponent's knee. The blow was swift, almost surgical. Hulmean staggered, roaring in shock and pain. Gardus gave him no time to recover. His next blow carved through Hulmean's shoulder-plate, and knocked the Chaos warrior to his knees. 'No,' Hulmean bellowed. 'No, this is not–'

'Quiet.' Gardus said. His hammer snapped out, crunching into the side of Hulmean's helm. A gnarled horn snapped off and black metal crumpled as Hulmean toppled over. Gardus looked down at his opponent as he twitched in his death-throes, then back up at the waiting horde. He raised his weapons and clashed them together. Lightning snapped and screamed about them, crawling along his arms.

'Who will carry the storm into the heart of Chaos?' he roared.

'Only the faithful,' came the response from the shield wall behind him.

'Who will walk into the long night, blades bared?'

'Only the faithful!'

'Who will stand, though the realms crumble?'

'Only the faithful! *Only the faithful!*'

The cry beat against the air. It drowned out all other sound. Gardus swept his weapons apart, and cried out, 'Only the faithful!' He took a step towards the enemy, and the shield wall – mortals and Stormcasts both – advanced slowly in his wake.

Slowly, but surely, the Chaos battle-line began to crumble.

Those at the back were the first to retreat, falling back along the avenue. Individual warriors backed away, shouting to their followers. Soon, even the most fanatical adherent of the Ruinous Powers was recoiling from the advancing Stormcasts. At Gardus' gesture, Liberators began to strike their shields, adding to the thunderous cacophony of their march.

By the time the shield wall reached Gardus, the last of the Chaos warriors were slinking away, shouting insults over their shoulders as they ceded the field. Gardus sheathed his runeblade and waved Angstun and the shield wall on. They would push forward to the edge of the plaza and ensure that the enemy didn't regroup.

Sathphren galloped towards him, laughing. 'Well done!' he shouted, as he swung himself out of the saddle. They clasped forearms. Sathphren's armour was tarry with ogor blood. He and his warriors had dispatched the last of the brutes while Gardus fought his duel.

Gardus shook his head. 'I have had too much practice at this.' He looked back at the war-altar. Feros and a group of Retributors were breaking it apart with steady, precise blows. 'But it is done, for the moment. Casualties?'

Sathphren pulled off his helm and frowned. 'More than I like. We lost at least three cohorts from the Bullhearts, as well as Thalkun.'

Gardus frowned. 'The Bullhearts... but no Ramus.'

Sathphren shook his head. 'No Osanus either.' He looked at Gardus. 'That bodes ill.'

Gardus was silent for a moment. Then, softly, 'Yes. Yes, it does.'

'You are an even bigger fool than I imagined, Osanus.'

Osanus turned as Khela climbed the gangplank, halberd

thumping against the fossilised wood. 'Lord-Castellant, you do mighty Osanus a great honour,' Osanus said, seemingly pleased to see her. 'Come to see us off?'

'Not even going to attempt to lie, are you?' Khela asked. Osanus shrugged. His helm hung from his belt, and his wide face split in a grin.

'Why lie? You are here, yes? You would not be, if you did not know... So.' He clapped his hands and sat on the rail. Khela made to reply when a boom from further down the wharfs caught their attention. Osanus whistled, and Khela frowned.

'I cannot believe you are considering abandoning the city, while it is under attack.'

'The Steel Soul has it in hand. And the Stormforged as well.' Osanus gestured. 'The Steel Soul once fought a god, yes? That is what they say. What is Osanus, next to that, yes? Yes.' He crossed his arms and studied her. 'Besides... if it is so important, why are you not there?'

Khela frowned. 'Because the Steel Soul sent me to look for you and Ramus.'

Osanus looked around. 'I do not see the Lord-Relictor. You should keep looking.'

'Do not play the fool with me, Osanus. I do not know what you are planning exactly, but I know it's nothing good.' Khela looked around the barque. More than two dozen Stormcasts sat on the rower's benches, or worked to adjust the sails. None of them met her gaze. They were all veterans of Shyish and Ghur – the first to fall, and be Reforged.

Despite the outward appearance of stolid homogeneity, Chambers and Stormhosts were full of divisions – not just by rank and conclave, but by status. The first to carry war to the enemy, the first to fall in battle – these things carried weight, among the chosen of Sigmar. It was no different among the Bullhearts. Those warriors who had followed Tarsus into Shyish, and then Ramus into Ghur, had an unspoken cachet among the rest of the Chamber. Where they went, the rest followed.

To see so many of them here, like this, unsettled her. And to see Osanus here – even worse. She slammed her halberd down, and the grin on Osanus' face slipped. 'These barques are ancient,' she said. 'They will not sail. They will crumble to dust, and you will find yourself lost among the dunes.'

'They will sail,' Osanus said. 'It is the nature of this realm… It preserves some things, even as it erodes others.' He thumped the rail. 'It will carry us far, I think.'

'If I do not stop you.'

Osanus grinned. 'You could come with us, eh? It will be a glorious thing, mine sister.' He crossed his arms. 'They will sing of us in Sigmaron.'

'Only if you succeed. Maybe not even then.' Khela looked around. 'All of you are a part of this foolishness, then? Sag-ittus… Cassos… Even you, Iunias?' None of them met her gaze. 'All of you. Not one of you has thought better of this?' She looked at Osanus. 'And you – them, I understand. They're all veterans – they all fell at the Bridge of Seven Sorrows, and fought their way through Cartha and the hordes of Great Red. But you?'

Osanus shrugged. 'I have faith.'

Khela stared at him, and knew he was speaking the truth. Of course Osanus had faith. If he didn't, he wouldn't be help-ing Ramus.

'You should not be here, Lord-Castellant.'

Khela turned. Ramus stood on the gangplank, Mannfred just behind him. The vampire sneered at her, but she ignored the creature. She strode to meet the Lord-Relictor, letting her halberd thump with every step. 'What was it I said to you, in Nordrath?' she asked.

Ramus looked at her in puzzlement. 'What?'

She stopped, a short distance away. 'You are not my superior, Ramus. Do not think to command me. We are equals, you and I.'

'I have never said otherwise.'

'And yet, you have kept me at arm's length since this began.' She shook her head. 'Did you doubt my loyalty?'

'Never, sister.' Ramus leaned against his staff. 'The fewer who knew, the better. Only those of us on this vessel will be at risk of punishment. Whatever comes of this, the Chamber will survive. Whether as the Bullhearts or... something else.'

'You risk everything. For what?'

'Tarsus,' Sagittus said, from behind her.

'*Tarsus,*' the others repeated, murmuring the name as if it were a prayer.

Khela studied them, and then turned back to Ramus. 'If Tarsus were here...' she began. Ramus cut her off with a sharp gesture.

'But he isn't,' he said, harshly. 'He is trapped in some underworld, rather than here, with us. We – I – failed him, Khela. We had the chance to free him, and we failed. I will not do so a third time. One way or another, this ends.'

'Enough talking,' Mannfred growled. 'Shove her off the barque and let us be gone!' He gestured, and Khela heard a monstrous shriek from somewhere above. A great skeletal, almost feline, shape dropped suddenly to the deck of the barque, scattering Stormcasts. The dread abyssal shrieked again, its bat-like skull ablaze with witch-light. It stalked towards Khela, tail lashing. She swept her halberd up and braced herself.

'No!' Ramus roared. Mannfred screamed, and the dread abyssal staggered. It screeched in confusion and sprang to the mast, where it clung, claws embedded in the wood. Khela turned to see Mannfred on his knees, one hand clutched to his smoking chest. Ramus stood over him, hand outstretched.

'What did you do?' she demanded.

'A rite of warding,' he said. 'There are many ways to control the dead. For the moment, Mannfred von Carstein is mine to command.'

'F-for the moment,' Mannfred growled, as he stumbled to his feet. 'But not forever, Stormcast.'

'Nor would I wish it to be so,' Ramus said. He looked at Khela. 'I – we – must do this, Khela. Mannfred knows of an entrance to the underworlds. We will storm Nekroheim and free Tarsus' soul…'

'And lose your own in the process.'

'No,' Mannfred said. 'No. Not if we act quickly.'

Khela looked at the vampire and then glanced at the dread abyssal, still clinging to the mast. The skulls within its monstrous frame seemed to be whispering. She looked back at Ramus. 'Answer me this, at least – is this because of Tarsus? Or is it because you cannot bear failure?'

Ramus did not reply. He looked away, out over the distant dunes. She sighed.

'Maybe it doesn't matter, at that.' She looked at Mannfred. 'You would be a fool to attempt the same trick twice. Then, only a fool would have fallen into our hands.'

'It is no trick,' the vampire began. Ramus silenced him with a gesture.

'As I said, Mannfred is under my control, Lord-Castellant.'

Khela looked at him. Ramus met her gaze this time. 'You will tell them,' he said, after a moment. He didn't sound surprised. She nodded.

'Of course.' She could tell he was frowning, beneath his

skull-helm. 'It isn't as if they're not going to notice, Lord-Relictor. Gardus already suspects something. At least this way, we maintain some illusion of being in control of our destiny.'

'You could come with us.'

'And abandon my duties here? Abandon our responsibilities?' Khela laughed. 'The only reason you are even considering this is because you know that I will stay and do my duty. I will stay, while you hare off in pursuit of your obsession. That is the duty of a Lord-Castellant, after all.'

She strode down the gangplank towards him. 'And I do not need to be reminded of my duties.' As she passed him, she added, 'Unlike some.'

Ramus watched the Lord-Castellant go, and felt anger warring with regret within him. He wanted to follow her, to argue his point, but knew that she was right.

'We should go,' Osanus called out. 'While we've got the wind.'

'Yes.' Ramus looked at Mannfred. 'If you ever try to attack one of my brothers or sisters again, I will set your heart alight, and see you consumed in celestial flame.'

'Ashigaroth would not have harmed her.'

'True. Though she might well have killed it. Khela once fought her way through an entire Alfrostun to claim a frost-lord's head. Once she sets her mind to do a thing, there is little that can prevent her from seeing it through.'

'A common trait among your breed of Stormcasts, I find. All bull-headed and convinced of your own righteousness.' Mannfred's smile slipped. 'Like Tarsem.' He pulled his cloak about himself and whistled. Ashigaroth launched itself from its perch and landed lightly beside him.

He made to climb into the saddle, but Ramus stopped him. 'Why did you offer to help me?' he asked.

Mannfred was silent, for long moments. Then, just as Ramus was beginning to think that he wouldn't answer at all, the vampire said, simply, 'He was my friend.'

Ramus laughed. Mannfred glared at him. 'Laugh if you will, Stormcast, but it is the truth. I do not have friends. Some among the dead do, perhaps, but not I. And yet, Tarsem of Helstone was my friend.'

'And you left him to Nagash.'

Mannfred looked away. 'I left Tarsus Bullheart to Nagash. A different man. I help you now, in memory of the one I knew. I owe Tarsem a debt. Perhaps this will go some way to clearing it.'

'What you owe him cannot be paid back so easily, vampire.'

'Let us see what he says about it, shall we?' Mannfred climbed into Ashigaroth's saddle. 'Now, we must hurry. Our route takes us past the Chaos encampments. Bakhos is tenacious, but no fool. This assault will fail, and he'll retreat. We don't want to be in his way when that happens, do we?'

'Do you fear him, then?'

'No. But I worry.' Mannfred hauled on Ashigaroth's reins. 'As should you. After all, what do you think will happen when the Steel Soul discovers what you've done?' He smiled thinly. Ramus fell silent. Mannfred laughed. 'Yes. I thought as much. Come! The hourglass empties, and our time runs short.' He thumped the dread abyssal's bony flanks and the creature shrieked, setting Ramus' teeth to itching. The creature loped forward and hurled itself skyward, clawing for purchase on the air.

Ramus turned and climbed aboard the barque. Osanus peered up at the circling form of Ashigaroth and snorted. 'Does think highly of himself, yes?'

'I will indulge his vanity if it gets us one step closer to Tarsus.' He looked at the Knight-Heraldor. 'I hope you have figured out the function of this craft.'

Osanus laughed. 'Wind and muscle, mine brother. Very traditional.' He turned and clapped his hands. 'To your benches, brothers and sisters!' He drew his blade and started towards the rear of the barque. 'I'll weigh anchor.'

As Osanus cut through the chocks holding the barque in place, the vessel began to slide down its ramp with a clatter of wood and sail pulleys. Ramus thumped the deck of the barque. All eyes turned towards him – scarce thirty of his Chamber, those he could trust implicitly: Sagittus, Iunias a few others. Enough to do what must be done, but not enough to weaken the defences.

'You heard the Knight-Heraldor,' he said. 'Ply your oars, brothers and sisters. We have a long journey ahead.'

CHAPTER SEVENTEEN

EASTERN WIND

Reason is for the weak. Explanation is for the weak.
Do, or do not.

– Heygruel Martch
The Hammer of Azyr

There was jubilation in the pavilions of the Blessed Ones. Hulmean's fall had precipitated a hundred small wars of influence, and wagers flew fast and thick among those observing the fallout. The Black Son of Dath had been much respected, and quite wealthy by the standards of the Blessed Ones. And now that wealth was being stripped from his encampment by greedy slaves and subordinates, all eager to buy themselves new positions in the hierarchy of Hulmean's rivals.

'He died well, at least,' Chaell said, as a slave ran past them, clutching a jade statuette that glowed with a sickly radiance. 'In battle, like a true hero. His soul will be welcome in the Glades of Silk.' More slaves ran in all directions. Some sought freedom in the wastes. Others went to beg for sanctuary from the servants of Hulmean's peers.

Ghosteater snorted. The air stank of blood and fear. Not all of Hulmean's slaves were brave enough to seek their own fortune. Many huddled in growing terror, awaiting the coming of new masters – or of death. Either was a possibility. *Or both,* Herst murmured. *Death and slavery, the two inevitable pillars of Shyish.*

Herst had strong opinions about Shyish, Ghosteater had discovered. The old man's ghost wasn't shy about sharing them either. *Because you listen,* Herst said. *An apt pupil, as I said. A rare thing to find, at this stage of my existence.*

'Are you listening to your ghosts again?' Chaell asked. Ghosteater looked at him. Chaell gestured apologetically. 'Your gaze went a bit vague. Has one of them at last counselled you on the foolishness of this decision?'

'No,' Ghosteater growled.

'You know what will happen, if you tell him.' Chaell stepped in front of him, forcing Ghosteater to stop. 'It will be just the excuse he's been looking for. Bakhos will leave, and all this – all that you have worked for – will come apart, in an instant.'

'He will leave,' Ghosteater said.

'But they won't. Not all of them.' Chaell swept out a hand. Around them, the sound of fighting swelled and faded with the wind. Applause sounded, somewhere, as someone died. 'And they may well decide to rid themselves of you. Especially if you follow through with the other reason you came...'

'Mine,' Ghosteater thumped his chest. 'I am chief-of-chiefs. Mine by right.'

'But they are not of your herd. They are not your property, and you have no claim here. No matter what Bakhos says.' Chaell leaned forward. 'I owe you a debt, so I am forced to speak only truth – if you do these things, you will die. Maybe not here. But soon. Without him, you have no protection…'

Death is not so bad, Herst whispered. *Indeed, it is quite free-ing, in a sense. To join the great majority sees untold vistas of perception open to one.*

Ghosteater twitched his ears and roughly forced Chaell aside. 'I will tell him what we have seen. What happens next is up to him.'

'You know what his reaction will be.'

Ghosteater said nothing. He tasted the air, seeking one of the scents he was in search of. When he found it, he loped after it, Chaell trailing in his wake. He threaded through the encampment, avoiding the knots of struggling warriors and fleeing slaves.

I am reminded of the scrums whenever one of my academic colleagues died – everyone wanted first crack at their library. Books are as good as gold, you know.

Ghosteater, who had no use for either, snorted. The air in this part of the camp stank of wine and blood. Someone had broken into Hulmean's stores. Even so, he could detect the musky odour of one of his own. The drunken beastman staggered into view, weaving between tents, braying sing-song obscenities.

The gor was not of the Caddow tribes, but one who'd followed Hulmean across the Sea of Dust. He wore the dead champion's brand on his flesh, and his horns were notched with golden rings. More rings rattled in his nostrils, and golden chains stretched from these to the ones set into his ears. He wore silks and tarnished armour over his piebald limbs – a sign of status. If he wasn't a chieftain, he was close.

Hulmean had impressed half a dozen herds into his service before arriving at Caddow. None were very large, or powerful. They were all but slaves, regarded as little better than chattel with blades by the Blessed Ones. With Hulmean dead, they would wander away, or be enslaved by some other champion.

Ghosteater growled softly.

The beastman stopped, jug halfway to his lips, and peered blearily at Ghosteater. He grunted interrogatively, half in challenge and half in worry. Ghosteater didn't bother to answer. His first blow knocked the gor onto his backside. The second dashed the jug from his grip. Ghosteater dropped into a crouch over him, and set a hand about his throat, stifling his bray of protest. 'How many?' he growled.

The gor stared at him in drugged incomprehension. Ghosteater tightened his grip. 'How many?' he asked again.

The gor made a sound that might have been an answer. Ghosteater dragged him upright, satisfied. He looked at Chaell. 'Where is Bakhos?'

'He'll be at the heart of the encampment, overseeing the festivities.'

Ghosteater snarled and shoved his captive forward. 'We go.'

Bakhos was easy enough to find, sitting under the largest tent – once Hulmean's own. His eunuchs stood arrayed protectively about him, as he ran his hands through the contents of a chest, marked with the sigil of some Azyrite city. Other warriors and champions sat or stood around, heaps and piles of plunder scattered about them. Slaves huddled in the corners of the tent, watching the gathered warriors like mice watching cats.

Bakhos glanced up as they entered the tent. 'Do you know what armies such as this run on, my friend?' he said, without preamble. He let gold coins drip through his fingers. He gestured to the coins with his free hand. 'Not this. But close.' Bakhos tossed coins all about. Warriors scrabbled to collect them, while Bakhos watched, smiling. 'This. See?'

Ghosteater shook his head. Bakhos sighed. 'Favours,' he said. 'Gifts, doled out by the influential to the unimportant. The gift of gold, of slaves, of spices, of battle. Gold has no value to us, for we take what we wish, when we wish. But it is pretty, and a sign of favour. The more of it you have, the more important you are. Hulmean had much. I am told he liked to roll around in it, on occasion. He gave it away to his favoured slaves and concubines, he draped it about those warriors loyal to him – he even gave it to beasts such as the one squalling in your grip there.' He looked at Ghosteater. 'Why is he squalling, by the way?' His eyes narrowed. 'Why did you come?'

'Claim what is mine.' Ghosteater shoved the gor to his knees and caught the brute's horns. 'This is mine. All of them. My claim.'

Bakhos laughed softly. 'Brave.' He gestured and turned back to the gold. 'Take them, if they'll have you. My gift to you.' His words elicited a murmur from the warriors around them. They fell silent at a glance from Bakhos.

Ghosteater looked down at the gor and dragged the beastman's face up. 'Call them. Bring them to me. They will bow. You will bow. Or you will be meat. I will make you meat. Understand?' He let the gor go, and the beastman scrambled out of the tent. Chaell coughed, and Ghosteater looked around.

The champions were watching him. So were the slaves. Judging him. *They are wondering if you are to be raised up to their level,* a ghost said. *Men are the same, whatever their god.*

Seek to kill-murder you, yes-yes, another ghost piped up.

He shook his head, and realised that Bakhos too was watching him. The Maiden's Son was smiling slightly. 'I have taught you much over the past days, my friend. But now comes the greatest lesson.' He scooped up a handful of gold coins from the chest before him and carefully flicked one back into the chest.

'Do you understand what it requires to hold a morass of such disparate souls as this together for longer than a week?' Bakhos tossed another coin into the chest. 'More than will. More than intelligence. More than favours.' He looked at Ghosteater. 'Luck. Luck is required. Look at what is going on outside this tent.'

Ghosteater did, almost against his will. Everywhere, the encampment was in an uproar. Tents were burning and treasures lay strewn across the sandy ground. Slaves had been strung up from tent poles, and their shadows danced in the light of the flames. Warriors, blood-drunk and sated, sat or lay nearby, murmuring amongst themselves. 'Look at them,' Bakhos said, gesturing to the closest of the warriors. 'Drunkards and fools.'

The warriors set up a slurred cheer at this. Chaell snorted derisively. 'Even him,' Bakhos said, pointing at Chaell. He tossed another coin into the chest. 'Fools, madmen and monsters. Such an army is held together by circumstance and luck. Since I came here, I have done my best to keep them inebriated and inward-looking. By luck, I have succeeded.'

More coins fell into the chest. Ghosteater watched them. *A king's ransom in gold,* Herst said. *Some of it gleams red – urgold. A chieftain could buy many dependable allies with that gold.* Ghosteater licked his chops.

If Bakhos saw, he gave no sign. 'But now, my luck turns. Enemies have appeared from the stars, and my commanders eat themselves to the bone, all for the chance at glory. My options narrow – hurl them at our common foe, or risk them turning on me. Neither yields me satisfaction. Both end in this army's destruction.'

'If you were to lead us, O Maiden's Son, victory might be ours.'

Ghosteater turned as the sibilant voice intruded. Lemerus leaned on its maul, dainty fingers tapping against the gems set in the weapon's haft. It bared shark-like teeth in a challenging grin and rattled its spines. Ghosteater stared at the creature, wondering if it had ever been mortal. 'They say Lemerus is the child of a daemonette and a mortal warrior,' Chaell murmured. 'That it is destined for greatness. Or perhaps that is merely the story it has spread about itself.'

Bakhos laughed. 'And it might not mean victory, Lemerus. We might lose. And then, perhaps, either you or Etax would seek my head, eh?'

'Mighty Etax is loyal unto death, O great Leopard of Semele,' one of Etax's slaves spoke up. The hulking champion stood apart from the others, his young translators crouched by his feet. 'Prideful Etax shall ever place himself between you and harm,' the other slave said. Etax merely growled and examined the necklace of shadeglass shards he held.

'And I am but your shadows in all things, O Maiden's Son.'

'There you have it,' Bakhos said, looking at Ghosteater. 'And what about you, eh? How will you declaim your loyalty, eh?'

Ghosteater ignored Chaell's look of warning, and said, 'Saw something.'

Bakhos smirked. 'We all have eyes, my friend. Seeing things is not–'

'Boat. Leaving city. Enemies aboard.'

Technically, it had been Wyrmhoof who had seen them, with his magics. But Ghosteater saw no reason to confuse the issue. 'Stormcast,' he added.

Bakhos stared at him. Then, slowly, his face split in a panther's grin. He let the last of the gold fall from his hands as he stood. 'Well,' he said, softly. 'Isn't that unfortunate. I wonder where they're going?'

'East,' Ghosteater growled, helpfully.

'East,' Bakhos repeated. He ran his hands through his hair,

staring out of the tent. What was to the east? He froze. Nagashiz-zar. Why would they be going to Nagashizzar? Unless… He laughed. 'Oh, how delightful.'

'What is it?' Lemerus asked.

Bakhos turned. 'Everything. Everything I have ever wanted.' He clapped his hands together and laughed wildly. 'Can it be…? Is it possible…? O Dark Prince, let it be so, let it be so.' He danced in a wild circle, all grace and motion. As he slid to a stop, he bowed low to Ghosteater, startling the beastman.

'Come, my friend. Let us speak in private.'

Bakhos slipped his arm around the beastman's shaggy shoulders and walked him out of the tent. Up close, the creature stank of blood and wet fur. He wrinkled his nose, but did not comment. There were more important matters at hand. 'I did not wish the others to hear – no need to start a stampede east, eh? Now, what did you see, exactly? Are they fleeing the city?'

They weren't. He knew it. But he had to make sure. His heart leapt as Ghosteater shook his head. 'One boat only,' the crea-ture said. 'Going east.'

Bakhos laughed again. 'Excellent, excellent. Do you know where they're going?'

'East.'

'Yes, but what lies to the east, eh?' Bakhos saw incompre-hension on the beast's face. 'Forgive me, the world is yet a vast mystery to you, isn't it? Nagashizzar, my friend. The Silent City lies to the east. Or part of it, anyway. They go to make com-mon cause with the Undying King!'

Ghosteater growled softly, ears flattened against his skull. Bakhos nodded. 'Oh yes, my thoughts exactly, my friend. A ter-rible thing – one that cannot be allowed to happen.' He paused. 'I would be… remiss in my duties if I allowed it, wouldn't I?'

Ghosteater's eyes narrowed. Then, slowly, he nodded. 'Must chase them. I will do it.'

'No!' Bakhos said, more forcefully than he'd intended. 'No. It is my duty. I must go. But someone must remain in command here. Someone must keep the rest of the enemy contained. Do you see?'

Again, Ghosteater nodded. 'Who?' he growled. Bakhos paused, letting the moment stretch. He studied the beast, wondering if the creature truly understood.

'It cannot be one of them,' he said, softly. 'You understand?'

'Chieftains fight,' Ghosteater said.

'Yes. Chieftains fight. They would bicker and squabble, because I have favoured them all equally, to keep them happy. And they would turn on one another the moment I left. The army would fall apart, and the enemy would be free to go where they would. So I must pick someone who understands. Someone who is already a chief-of-chiefs...'

Ghosteater's muzzle twisted up into something that might have been a smile. Bakhos nodded, pleased by the intelligence the creature displayed. Perhaps this would be more interesting than he'd thought. 'You will watch the city,' he continued. 'The Sea of Dust is yours, and you will guard it in the name of the Three-Eyed King.'

Bakhos turned back to the tent, flinging the edge of his leopard-skin cloak over his shoulder. 'Do this, and you will be well rewarded.'

Ghosteater licked his muzzle. The beastman cocked his head, as if listening to something. 'Need... authority,' he grunted, after a moment, stumbling slightly over the word.

'Yes. I expect so. Come. Let us establish your claim, eh?'

The others were waiting for them when they re-entered the tent. Most of the war-chiefs he'd brought with him stood in easy silence. They could smell change in the air, and were content to let it play out, as it should. But Etax and Lemerus were too close, if not quite side by side. Each ready to challenge the other for leadership. The war-chiefs would be all but divided between them, by now. Bakhos nodded in satisfaction. As it should be. Unfortunately, if he allowed such bloodshed, his army might well rip itself apart.

'Well?' Lemerus said. 'What did the creature have to say for itself?' It sounded impatient, and its fingers tapped tunelessly against the haft of its maul.

'Ghosteater has brought me disturbing news, my friends – disturbing news indeed. Our foes cross the Sea of Dust, seeking alliance with Nagash. An alliance we must prevent, else Archaon's efforts in this cruel waste will be for naught.'

As he'd hoped, his words provoked an uproar. Champions and chieftains shouted questions, and Etax and Lemerus glanced at one another in obvious consternation. Bakhos smiled. He had no proof of his claim, obviously, but then, they wouldn't ask. The possibility was enough, as he'd known.

Demands flew – some wanted to pursue, others to attack, some even dared suggest flight. A few remained silent. He studied each of them in turn, letting the noise build. When his hand went up, they all fell silent. 'Of course, I must pursue them,' he said. 'It is my duty, as castellan of this place.'

'And who will rule here, in your absence, O Leopard?' one of Etax's translators asked. 'There can be only one choice.'

Lemerus hissed softly. It lifted its maul and bared its teeth. 'Only one choice indeed,' it said. Both champions met his gaze unflinching.

Bakhos put on his widest smile and set his hand on Ghosteater's shoulder. 'I have chosen, and my choice is here.'

A murmur swept through the gathered warriors. Etax and

Lemerus glanced at one another. Etax jangled his translators' chains. 'The Lord Etax will not serve a mere beast,' one of the translators said, in high, musical tones. The other, in lower tones, added, 'He is of the blood of kings, and owed more respect, O Maiden's Son.'

'Just so,' Lemerus murmured, in its soft voice. 'Who is this mangy thing to earn your favour, my lord? What deeds has it done, to be accorded such glory?'

Bakhos smiled. 'You speak of respect and favour, as if I am owed neither. He is in command, because I say it. No more explanation should be required.'

Etax rumbled, his fangs flexing and clicking. One of the translators laughed. 'We are not slaves, Leopard in Summer. We have our own songs, our own stories.'

'But for the moment, you are nothing more than a part of mine.' Bakhos tapped the pommel of his blade. 'Or has the time come for our skeins to part?'

'And what if it has?' Lemerus murmured.

Bakhos drew his sword and darted forward, faster than Lemerus could react. The tip of his blade tickled the hollow of the champion's throat. 'Then you die. Here. Now. Because I will have no further use for you.' He pressed the blade and a trickle of ichor ran down the champion's pale flesh.

He looked at Etax. 'That goes for you as well, Etax. Blood of kings, indeed. *I* was a king. It is no difficult thing.' Without removing his blade from Lemerus' throat, he looked around. 'Have no doubt – I have made my choice. Go against it, and I will butcher you all. There are a hundred like you, waiting for your deaths. They will be more amenable to my whims. And if they are not – there a hundred like them. A thousand.'

Lemerus swallowed. 'Command us, O Maiden's Son.'

Bakhos nodded and stepped back. 'Lemerus, you will come

with me. Etax, you will remain here, and support my chosen regent, until such time as I return. That will keep you two from killing each other, or forcing him to waste time killing you.' He sheathed his blade with a flourish. 'Any others who wish to accompany me may duel for the privilege. Regardless, I will be leaving at first light.' He flung out a hand to his eunuchs. 'Make ready my steeds, and gird yourselves, my friends.

'Glory awaits us all.'

The eastern wind assailed Mannfred as he urged Ashigaroth on. Dust clawed at his bare arms and face. Down below, he could just make out the dust-barque, carrying his new army. He grinned.

Not much of an army. Tarsem's voice, louder now than it had been. Mannfred wondered if that was a good sign. Even if it was only his madness speaking, he found some comfort in it. It had been too long since his ghosts had had anything to add save recriminations.

'Thirty of them is worth three times that number of decrepit skeletons. Though you'll not hear me say that in front of them.' He hunched forward in his saddle. 'And they are motivated, besides.'

By a lie.

'Not a lie. An omission. I simply did not tell them how we were getting you back. And you well know it, being a figment of my imagination.'

Your conscience, perhaps?

Mannfred snorted. 'We both know that's not true. Now be silent. I must think.' He looked over his shoulder, where the thin line of Caddow rode the western horizon. They were not far out, but far enough that pursuit would be difficult. And there would be pursuit, of one sort or another. Perhaps a conclave of winged Prosecutors, or a column of trudging Liberators, but something would come. Reinforcements, by any other name.

It was a dangerous game he was playing, he knew. Trusting in luck and timing, hoping that he had not overestimated Sigmar's need to preserve the status quo. At the moment, Azyr and Shyish were balanced against one another. Neither had made an obvious, open assault against the other.

But that would change in time. Nagash was up to something, in the depths of Nekroheim. He was building something, in the dark. A weapon, perhaps. Or a tool. Something to upend the natural order in his favour.

Mannfred could smell it, on the wind. A hint of distant death, of cold and darkness, like the coming of a long winter. A great silence readied itself to fall over the realms. Mannfred felt the echoes of its approach in his bones. The seers of the Hanging Wood whimpered of nothing else, and in Mortannis, he had witnessed the caged souls of prophets and witches flutter against the glass of their jars, seeking escape from what they saw.

Something was coming.

Things were changing. Not the raw, wild change that followed in the wake of Chaos, but something more glacial. A slow shifting of the realms themselves. As if the great orrery of existence were slowly but surely turning on its head. Change of the sort that even the Ruinous Powers might well fear.

There was opportunity there, if he was but quick enough to snatch it. If he could free himself of the last, cloying tangles of unfinished business.

And is that what I am, brother – unfinished business?

'I thought I told you to be silent.'

Admit it to yourself, if not to anyone else – your opportunism is but a mask for your fear. Fear that you will forever remain as you are. Fear that even with this great change that you sense

on the horizon, you will forever be as Nagash has imagined you.
Fear that the destiny you imagine for yourself is nothing more
than a fever dream...

'I fear only that your voice will not cease to haunt me, once
I have pried your soul from Nagash's clutches,' Mannfred spat.
He shook his head. 'Idiot. Fool. That is what I am. Allow-
ing myself to endanger all that I have built in the years since
Gothizzar, and for what? The soul of a man long since forgot-
ten, save in dusty texts.'

Tarsem's voice did not reply. Mannfred felt no satisfaction at
its silence. He hauled on Ashigaroth's reins, and sent the beast
circling down towards the dust-barque. The vessel ploughed
through the shifting dunes with a steady speed, catching the
wind in its sails and riding it eastward. Scooped oars, manned
by Stormcasts, struck the surface of the dust and lent momentum to the barque.

It was a simple thing. A trader's craft. Constructed for speed,
rather than war. Ramus had chosen well. Once, hundreds of
such craft had plied this silent sea. Now, their wrecks littered
the dunes.

Ashigaroth touched down with a snarl. Ramus stood at the
prow, looking out over the sea. 'There are ruins, rising from
the dust. I have counted almost a dozen, since we started out.
Have we truly left the city?'

'Outposts and waystations. We are well away from Caddow,'
Mannfred said, dropping from Ashigaroth's back. He slapped
the dread abyssal on the flank and the creature shrieked and
leapt skyward. He noticed a nearby Stormcast pulling his hand
away from his weapon, as the beast left. Mannfred smiled. Ashigaroth made them nervous, as he ought. The dread abyssal ate
souls, and for the Stormcasts such a thing meant an unsightly
end to the eternities that Sigmar had gifted them.

Ramus didn't answer, for a moment. The Lord-Relictor had been staring at the horizon since their departure, as if willing the distance between them to vanish. Mannfred laughed, and Ramus turned. 'If I killed you now, would anyone mourn for you?'

Mannfred froze. He was suddenly all too aware of the weight of a silver spike, pressing against his heart. He forced himself to remain calm. 'No. I am an island, in a sea of strangers.'

'Poetic and nonsensical, as I have come to expect from you, leech.'

'Harsh words from an ally.'

'We are not allies.' Ramus turned back to the horizon. 'You do not know the meaning of the word, vampire. Or if you ever did, you have since forgotten.'

'I know what allies are, Stormcast. I have had many, in my life.'

'Yes. When you fought beside them – did they trust you? Or did they trust *him*?'

'What do you mean?'

'The others follow me because they love Tarsus. Not because they hold any particular respect for me. I am not blind to my failings. Indeed, they only add urgency to my cause. Tarsus is our heart and soul. Without him, our chamber is a hollow thing, held together only by dimming faith.' Ramus did not look at Mannfred as he spoke. 'Was it the same for them, when he died?'

Mannfred frowned. 'The others were dead by then. He and I were the last. And now they live only in my memory.' He snorted. 'Though I expect it would have been the case. I was tolerated, but not trusted. No matter how often I proved myself, or Tarsem spoke up for me.' He shook his head, smiling thinly. 'Are we so alike, then? Keepers of a flame neither of us is worthy to bear.'

'I did not say that,' Ramus growled. 'I merely asked a question.'

Mannfred joined him at the rail. 'Do you know that I almost killed him, at our first meeting?' He laughed. 'His father had fallen for some ruse of Neferata's and aligned himself with enemies of mine. When I came for Tarsig's head, Tarsem was there. We duelled for hours, through pillared halls, and more than once I found myself wondering why I did not simply destroy him with an incantation.'

Ramus paused. Then he asked, 'Why didn't you?'

Mannfred sighed. 'I do not know, even now. I suspect it is because heroism of such calibre is rare in Shyish. Tarsem was known to me, even then. Neferata had her eye on him, of course, and no doubt Arkhan did as well. He had fought daemons and wyrms, had rescued innocents, had defended Helstone and its allies in wars. He had gathered heroes to him – Count Vitalian, Aksun Fellblade, the Red Duke – and forged an alliance that gave even my fellow Mortarchs pause. And all before his thirtieth year.'

'He never spoke of such things,' Ramus said.

'Perhaps he did not remember. Do you remember who you were, before you donned that skull helm?'

Ramus looked at him. 'How long before we reach this place?'

Mannfred peered up at the sky, frowning. 'A few days, I expect.'

'That is what you said a few days ago.'

'Shyish is not Azyr, Stormcast. Time and distance are more fluid here. Nagash is under siege, and warps the realm around himself, so that the enemy cannot reach him, save with great determination.'

'And are we enemies, then?'

Mannfred laughed. 'Of course! Just not the ones he's concerned about, at the moment.' He made a show of squinting at the horizon. 'In truth, I am merely following Ashigaroth.' He pointed towards the dread abyssal, loping through the clouds of dust above them. 'The place we are going… undulates. It shifts to the north or the east at Nagash's whim. Only creatures like Ashigaroth can find it unerringly.'

'Then why do we even need you?'

Mannfred laughed. 'Because I control Ashigaroth. Without me, he'll simply leave you here, sailing on an empty sea, with no star to guide you home.'

Ramus grunted. Mannfred studied him, trying to gauge the Lord-Relictor's mood. 'You have not asked me yet where we are going.'

'I know where we're going. Nekroheim.'

'No. Nekroheim is vast, and all but unreachable. Save through Nagashizzar.'

'Nagashizzar?' Ramus' voice was hoarse. 'You intend to lead us into the very jaws of death?' He raised his hand, and Mannfred leapt back, and quickly scaled the mast.

'No, no, no.' He paused. 'Or rather, yes.'

'Nagashizzar is no more,' one of the Stormcast said. The short one – the Knight-Heraldor, Osanus. Mannfred looked at him.

'And where did you hear that?'

'From the songs of the foe,' Osanus said, crossing his arms. 'They sing of Nagashizzar's fall even in Aqshy. And of the eight kings who now rule its ruins.'

'Mmm. I see news travels as slowly as ever – Nagashizzar is once more in the hands of its rightful king. Rejoice!' Mannfred clapped a hand to his heart. 'Rejoice with me, friends!' he called out, loudly. No one did. Mannfred laughed. 'Oh, yes, the retaking of Nagashizzar was a sight to see. Not that it was the true Nagashizzar, of course – just the one Nagash let the Three-Eyed King have.'

'Have?' Ramus said.

'Of course. A cur growls, you give it a bone. Keeps it occupied.' Mannfred let himself dangle from the rigging, one hand tight about the ropes, his feet braced against the mast. He shaded his eyes with his free hand, and peered towards the horizon. 'No, that Nagashizzar was but one grain of sand in the hourglass of Nagash's dominion. It is more than a city – a full ninefold cities bear that honoured name.'

'Ninefold…' Ramus began, staring at the horizon.

Mannfred glanced down, grinning. 'Of course! Wherever Nagash chooses to set his throne is Nagashizzar. Is it not the same for Sigmar?' He dropped lightly to the deck. 'At any rate, when Nagash emerged from the Starless Gate at last, he made straight for those of his demesnes that Archaon had claimed.' He laughed. 'Oh, the blood flowed like wine, and we danced to the sweet music of mortal agony.' He slid forward, dancing a gavotte across the deck, bowing to each Stormcast as he passed them. He spun and fell into a low bow before Ramus. 'Heady days.'

Ramus stared at him, eyes flat within the shadows of his helm. *Remind you of anyone?* The memory of Tarsem chuckled, and Mannfred's smile faded.

'You remind me of Arkhan,' he said. He straightened. 'That's not a compliment, by the way.' He ran his palm over his skull. 'Our destination is Nagashizzar, and it is not. It is a part of the whole, but separate. An outpost, if you will. And beyond it – Nekroheim.'

'And that is where Tarsus' soul is held?'

Mannfred nodded. 'If I am right, that is where Tarsem is.' He frowned. 'We will have to fight our way to the bridge between upperworld and underworld. Archaon set an army to watch these ruins. They lay an eternal siege to the bridge-keep – the

Liche-Gate. It is that siege that I intended to break with the dead of Caddow.'

'We are a match for any army, yes?' Osanus growled, from behind him. 'Show them to me, and I shall sing them a sweet lullaby. Zig-mah-HAI!' The Knight-Heraldor struck his chest with his fist. Mannfred winced as the sound echoed across the deck.

'Why did you bring him again?' he asked, looking at Ramus.

'I didn't really have a choice,' the Lord-Relictor said. 'Why do any of that?'

Mannfred shrugged. 'Nagash defends his demesnes against a thousand such sieges. They distract him from other, more important, matters. I seek merely to relieve him of one of those distractions.'

'Out of the goodness of your heart.'

Mannfred laughed. 'Of course not. I am a Mortarch. I seek influence in the courts of the dead and Nagash's favour, in all things. By bringing him an army, I hoped to gain the Undying King's goodwill.'

'And yet you defy him. You said you intended to free Tarsus. Make up your mind.' Ramus' tone was accusing, and his hand twitched. At the gesture, Mannfred felt the spike in his heart grow unpleasantly warm.

'And do you not defy Sigmar?' he asked, quickly. 'We best serve the gods by serving ourselves. Some philosopher or other said that. I forget his name.'

'You rationalise treachery.'

'All men do, mortal or otherwise.' Mannfred gestured. 'You say, I want this thing. And then you come up with reasons why you should have it. Why you deserve it.' He grinned at Ramus, sensing the Stormcast's growing discomfort. 'You say to yourself, it must be thus. It can be no other way. And you convince yourself of the rightness of your path. But it is always a lie. You serve yourself.'

'I serve Sigmar.'

'And Sigmar said to leave Tarsus imprisoned. To leave him to Nagash.'

Ramus looked away. Mannfred leaned close. 'Nagash is a god, as Sigmar is. But even gods can be distracted. Distraction breeds opportunity. With one hand, I do Nagash a good turn. And in doing that, I also do him a disservice. I distract him with a gift, so that I might plunder his vaults, and steal that which he values most highly.'

'And if he discovers us?'

Mannfred looked away. His next words came softly, and reluctantly.

'Then we will join Tarsus as captives in the black silence of Nekroheim.'

CHAPTER EIGHTEEN

PURSUIT

Responsibility. Duty. These are the keystones of command.

– Archime Dashos
The Middle Span

'He did *what?*' Cassandora shouted. Startled carrion birds rose into the air. 'That insufferable, arrogant, self-righteous...' She raised her fists to the purple skies. 'I'll drag him to the Anvil myself! I'll hammer that stubborn soul of his to dust!'

Gardus tried to calm her. 'It is my fault. I should have expected this.' They stood at the top of the ziggurat, overlooking the city. Around them, duardin laboured to construct the defences that would guard the Corvine Gate. Bulwarks of celestine and heavy celestar ballistae mounted on firing plinths would soon cover every approach to the realmgate.

'Expected him to go mad, you mean?'

'Yes.' Gardus could feel the heat of her anger. It was even

greater than his own, as if Ramus' actions had somehow personally offended her. And perhaps they had. Ramus had endangered them all, whether he knew it or not.

Cassandora snorted. She flexed her fists, as if wanting to strike something. 'Idiot. He's an idiot. He's more than an idiot. He's...'

'Convinced of the rightness of his cause. As we all are.'

She looked at him. 'Who told you about this?'

'Khela.' The Lord-Castellant had come to him in the aftermath of the battle for the central plaza, and told him everything. Of how Ramus had freed Mannfred, and set out across the Sea of Dust. Gardus knew there was only place they could be going – Nagashizzar.

Cassandora shook her head. 'She tried to stop him?'

'Yes.'

'And failed, obviously.'

'I doubt anyone could have stopped him, short of violence.' Gardus sighed. 'I should have expected this.'

'And if you had?' Cassandora laughed. 'What? Would you have talked him out of it? Would you have sent him back to Azyr, in disgrace?'

'No, I would have sent him back with Mannfred, in chains. As he wanted in the first place. As we intended to do.' Gardus looked out over the city. 'Someone will have to go after him. To stop him from...'

'From saving Tarsus,' Cassandora said, quietly.

'From getting himself and the others killed, or worse.' Gardus hesitated. 'Enyo, perhaps. She and her huntsmen...'

'He won't listen to her, and you know it.' Cassandora sighed and sat down on a block of stone. 'He won't listen to anyone – save, possibly, you.'

Gardus frowned. 'Not me. I'm needed here.'

'Yes, because I've never commanded the defence of a city before.'

'That's not what I meant. It's just…' He trailed off, unable to give voice to what he was feeling. 'I don't know what I'm supposed to do,' he said, finally. 'My mind says one thing, my heart another.' He laughed softly. 'Remember Artos? He never worried like this.'

Cassandora looked away. 'He was a good man.'

Gardus hesitated. Then he rested his hand on her shoulder. 'He was. And he would be proud to see what you have made of the Stormforged since then.' He chuckled. 'But he never questioned himself.'

Cassandora snorted. 'No. Very straightforward, Artos. Certain of himself.'

'I used to wish I had that sort of certainty.'

'And now?'

'Now I pray for it.' He looked out over the city. 'Artos wouldn't find his head full of questions. He would know what was right, and he would do it, or be damned.'

'It was his surety that got him killed, and that magnificent soul of his shattered into a thousand pieces by the Queen of Swords,' Cassandora said, flatly. 'I mourn him, Gardus, but I do not mourn that pig-headed stubbornness of his. Not that infamous conviction that claimed his existence, and almost took the Stormforged with him.' She poked him in the chest. 'Our faith must be tempered with wisdom else it is only madness.'

'And am I wise then? For questioning everything, as I do?'

'Wiser than Artos. Wiser than me. And certainly wiser than Ramus.'

Gardus nodded. 'Thank you, sister.'

She snorted. 'Don't thank me yet, brother. We still have a way to go, before we see whether or not I am right.' She looked at him. 'Artos would leave Ramus to his fate. But that has never been your way. You've never let a soul slip your grasp, brother. You will go after him, because that is what you always do. You never abandon those who depend on you. Even when it might be wiser to do so.' She punched his arm. 'So go. I will hold this campaign together, while you go rescue our brother from his own foolishness.' She smiled. 'There – certainty. Sigmar will provide, brother. You just have to have faith.'

Gardus laughed. 'Good enough, sister.' He looked down at the sprawling city of tents that now spread out in all directions around the base of the ziggurat. One in particular caught his eye – a small tent, stretched among the ruins of what might once have been a hostelry. Light flickered within. 'Lorcus is hard at work, I see.'

'As he has been since he arrived.' Cassandora said. 'Who will you take with you?'

'Sathphren, I think. If he agrees. He knows the terrain, and I think he'll be glad of a change of scenery. This style of war doesn't suit him.' The Lord-Aquilor had been chafing at the slow progression of things, inventing reasons to lead his Vanguard-Palladors on raids into enemy territory.

Cassandora nodded. 'Good choice. Those gryph-chargers of his will move much faster than any barque. You should catch up with Ramus in no time.'

'Unless he does the sensible thing and uses magic to speed his journey.'

Cassandora thought for a moment. 'Best hurry, then. I'll inform Taltus and the others.' She paused. 'What about Lord-Castellant Grymn? He might not be pleased to see you go haring off, given your past history.'

Gardus started towards the steps. 'Let me worry about Grymn.

Right now I need to speak with Lorcus. Given the situation, it seems only fair that he is told of my decision.'

'How polite of you. I'll find the others,' Cassandora called out from behind him.

Gardus descended the steps of the ziggurat swiftly, stopping only once to allow a group of duardin to troop past, carrying newly cut timbers. Everywhere was the sound of a city's birth pangs. In the hours since the battle in the central plaza, the Zhu'garaz and the Ironweld had redoubled their efforts.

He caught a glimpse of Lord-Castellant Octarion standing atop nearby scaffolding, directing the construction of the western escarpment of what would be the city's Stormfort. Grymn was responsible for the east, and Sango the south. Taltus, though not a Lord-Castellant, was responsible for the north.

Soon, the Stormfort would occupy the entirety of the plaza – a massive citadel of celestine and stone, the axis around which the city would revolve. If all went well. If Bakhos' followers did not swamp the city. If Nagash did not bestir himself to become involved. If things did not go badly wrong. If, if, if.

Gardus stopped, suddenly all too aware of a weight on his shoulders. He closed his eyes, just for a moment. Then he looked up, seeking the stars. They were all but impossible to see in the pale amethyst of a Shyishan dawn, but he knew they were there regardless. 'Much is demanded, of those to whom much has been given,' he murmured.

Lorcus was in his tent when Gardus arrived, speaking to a heavyset warrior wearing an unfamiliar uniform. The mortal looked for all the world like a common sellsword, but something about the way he carried himself said he was anything but.

He left as Gardus arrived, hurrying away with a bemused glance at the Lord-Celestant. 'Lord Gardus,' Lorcus said, half rising from his seat. He sat behind an ironwood desk, brought from Nordrath on the last supply train. The desk was covered in stacks of loose papers, ledgers and scrolls. An ink pot and quill sat balanced precariously on a ledger, and Lorcus' sword was close to hand. An artisan pistol sat opposite the ink pot, hidden beneath loose papers. 'Welcome to my humble abode, such as it is.'

'Who was he?' Gardus watched the heavyset warrior greet one of the guards positioned at the end of the street. 'I do not recognise him.' The two men laughed uproariously at something. Gardus let the tent flap fall, and turned back to Lorcus.

'Tupo Vend, a paymaster, and a friend of my father's. His contacts ensured that we could secure the services of Morguin and Cruso's soldiers, as well as Mahk's engineers. He makes his money that way – helping others forge armies. If you need ten men or a thousand, he can get them for you, for the right price.'

Gardus had a vague recollection of such things, from his time as a mortal. Demesnus had had its share of Freeguilds, though most of them had been small bands – barely more than forty or fifty soldiers under arms at any time. 'Why is he here?'

Lorcus looked at him with a tired smile. 'I need more men, my lord. Morguin and Cruso are only here for the duration of this campaign. After they leave, we'll be stretched thin. I need to swell the Gallowsmen's ranks, and quickly.' He poured sand on the parchment and carefully blew it off, drying the ink. 'I've just signed a contract for thirty-odd warriors from the mountains of Ghur. Their clan is in debt to Tupo, and all they've got to pay him back with is their own flesh and blood.'

Gardus frowned. 'That sounds like slavery.'

Lorcus paused. 'They will be paid for their service. And a

fairer wage, I suspect, than they would get elsewhere.' He looked up. 'I need warriors, my lord. You will not be here forever. And this city must stand on its own eventually.'

Gardus had no reply. Lorcus' pragmatism was a necessary thing, but it sat ill with him. Sometimes, he forgot that victory was only the beginning. The true work came after the last trumpet had sounded, for good or bad. 'I came to tell you that I'm leaving Cassandora in command.'

'You're going after the Lord-Relictor, then?' Lorcus sounded unhappy. Word had spread quickly among the mortals that Ramus had departed. Gardus could sense their unease, and the worry of the civilians. He wondered what unrest his leaving would bring. Hopefully, between them, Cassandora and Lorcus could handle it.

'Someone must, and it is my responsibility.'

'One might argue that this city is, as well.' Lorcus sighed and stood. 'But I understand.' He stretched, grunting slightly. 'Stiff.'

'I remember those days,' Gardus said, chuckling. 'I used to regularly put my back out, poring over alchemical treatises.' His smile faded. 'No need to worry about that of late.' He picked up a ledger. 'Water stores?'

'Fresh water, brought in from Nordrath at no little expense. It will be used to flush out the cisterns, once Mahk gets them in working order. Failing that, we'll use it as drinking water.' He stepped outside, and Gardus followed him. Lorcus looked up at the Corvine Gate. 'Things are easier than they might be, thanks to the realmgate. I dread to think about what things might be like without it.'

'Its presence was one of the reasons this expedition was allowed. So long as we hold it, we have a foothold in this part of Shyish.' Gardus watched as a troop of Gallowsmen marched past, carrying tools, ropes and barrels of gunpowder. He could hear other soldiers heading to the mess tents, and the lowing of the great aurochs as their tenders fed them. The camp was waking up, as the last shadows of night faded.

Lorcus sniffed the air. 'Fried troggoth for breakfast. Again.' He grimaced. 'Maybe I'll just have bread and wine.' He ran a hand through his hair. 'Why did he do it?' he asked, after a moment.

'I don't know.' Gardus looked at the ground. 'Ramus… Ramus has endured much. Perhaps he thought it was the right thing to do. Or perhaps he wasn't thinking at all.'

Lorcus looked askance at him, and Gardus smiled. 'We Stormcasts are many things, Albain, but we are neither all-knowing nor all-wise. His reasons do not matter. All that matters is that he is brought back.'

Lorcus laughed, suddenly. Gardus peered at him, and the man gestured apologetically. He tapped one of the papers before him. 'That is almost word for word what this letter from Gaspar Twayn says.'

'That name sounds familiar.'

Lorcus nodded slowly. 'It should. He's a member of the Grand Conclave of Azyrheim. He runs one of the largest sky-fishing fleets in Azyr.'

'No. I met a priest by that name earlier.'

'A priest?' Lorcus frowned. 'Young?'

'Yes.'

Lorcus shook his head. 'So he is here. Gaspar's youngest son. His father is demanding we send him back to Azyr at the first opportunity.'

'His son is a priest?'

Lorcus shrugged. 'He felt the calling, as is often the way among we Nordrathi. A second child stands to inherit little. My own sister – well.'

'Will you send him back?'

Lorcus sighed. 'I may have to. Gaspar Twayn is not an enemy I'd like to have. Still…' He trailed off, but Gardus understood him well enough.

'But until you see the boy with your own eyes, it's a worry you can safely set aside. For the moment, there are more pressing matters.' Gardus clasped his shoulder. 'Come. One last council of war before I go.'

The building had once been a temple of Sigmar. It seemed fitting, then, that it had been turned into the nerve centre for the rebuilding of one of his cities. Lord-Ordinator Taltus and the Lord-Castellants had taken it over, and the walls were plastered with hand-drawn maps. Makeshift tables occupied the floor, and mortal scribes – both human and duardin – sat at them, working diligently to update the older schematics of the city.

Khela studied a set unrolled across three easels. She tapped a symbol, indicating the city's aqueducts. 'If we reroute the water flow here, we might be able to get pressure to the new valves the Ironweld have devised.'

Grymn leaned over her shoulder. 'That might mean building a new cistern, directly under the Stormfort.'

Octarion, standing nearby, looked up from the handful of schematics he was holding and said, 'You were planning to do that anyway, Lorrus.'

'Yes, but I have a schedule.'

'So we change the schedule,' Khela said.

'Change the– We can't change the schedule,' Grymn spluttered. 'It throws off all of my calculations!' He turned. 'Taltus, are you listening to this?'

'I heard,' Taltus said, from where he leaned over a scribe's workstation, making corrections to the sweating mortal's notes.

'Your calculations are off,' he murmured to the mortal. 'Not by much, though.'

'And?' Grymn demanded.

'Change the schedule, Lorrus. Practicality must be our guiding star in all things. We need water, and we need it drinkable. Too, we can use the larger tunnels to transport materials without risk of ambush.' Taltus looked at Grymn. 'Change the schedule.'

Grymn frowned and looked at Khela. 'What are you grinning at?'

'Nothing,' Khela said. 'Shall I change the schedule?'

Grymn glared at her, and then laughed. 'Yes, fine. A new cistern it is.' He paused. 'There is a new intake system I've been tinkering with. Now might be the time to try it.' He turned. 'Finally,' he muttered.

Khela turned as a murmur ran through the seated scribes. Lord-Celestant Gardus had entered the temple, followed by Captain-General Lorcus, Lord-Celestant Cassandora and Lord-Aquilor Sathphren. Reconciler Ahom arrived a few moments later, accompanied by Cogsmith Mahk. An entourage of junior officers, battlemages and engineers followed, all waiting to carry word back to their commanders.

Khela felt a flicker of unease. She had been dreading this moment since Ramus had left. Would she be called to account for his actions? If so, how would she answer? How could she answer? She glanced at Grymn, who clasped her shoulder supportively.

'You did nothing wrong, sister. The burden is not yours,' he murmured.

Khela nodded in thanks, and turned her attention back to the newcomers. Gardus had stopped before an easel, and was studying a set of schematics. Taltus coughed politely, and Gardus turned. He tapped the paper. 'A hospice?'

'With an isolated cistern, to prevent outbreaks of plague,' Khela said. 'As well as a communal garden, and a quarantine area.'

Gardus smiled. 'I recognise the designs.'

'You talk about it often enough, I decided to make use of your ideas,' Grymn said. He shrugged. 'Most of them were impractical, but there were a few of some worth.'

Gardus laughed. He looked at Khela. 'I am going after Ramus. I will bring him back safely, sister. Of that you have my word.'

'To face trial?' she asked, before she could stop herself. 'And what of those with him?' She shook her head. 'Forgive me, but perhaps I should be the one to go. He is my responsibility. It is my Chamber.'

'It is your Chamber,' Gardus said. 'You are in command now. But it is not your responsibility, it is mine. Your responsibility is to this city. To this campaign. Mine is to you – to all of you.' He turned. 'I am not in command of this campaign. I am in command of you. So I will go. And I will find Ramus and the others. And I will bring them back.'

'And who will be in command while you are gone?' Taltus asked. He looked at Cassandora as he spoke. Gardus followed his gaze.

'Lord-Celestant Cassandora will act in my stead. You will follow her, as you would me.' Gardus looked at Grymn. 'I trust you can do so with no complaint?'

'No more than usual, at any rate,' Cassandora said.

'How many will go with you?' Sathphren asked. 'Have you decided?'

'Just a few. A handful, at most. We cannot afford to strip the defences.'

'One of us could hold this place from such rabble,' Grymn said. He glanced at the other two Lord-Castellants. 'Three of us – pfaugh. The gods themselves would find it hard to shift us.' He looked at Gardus. 'Go, Steel Soul. Bring him back.'

'I will. Swiftblade – will you accompany me?' Gardus looked at Sathphren. The Lord-Aquilor grinned and nodded.

'Gladly. It will be nice to see something other than stone.'

'Gather your huntsmen, then. I would leave as soon as possible.' Gardus turned to the others. 'I will leave you now in Cassandora's hands. Except you, Khela. I would speak with you, if I might.'

Khela nodded and joined the Lord-Celestant. He led her from the temple and out onto the street.

'Tell me,' he said, after a moment.

'Tell you what, my lord?'

'Your thoughts, Khela.'

She frowned, and turned, watching as the horizon slid from violet to lilac over the tops of nearby buildings. 'Ramus and I have never seen eye to eye, my lord,' she said. 'He has become the ring in the bull's nose, pulling us in his wake.' She leaned on her halberd. 'But this is not like him. Something drives him. Something more than the grief we all feel.'

'Mannfred,' Gardus said.

She frowned. 'It could be. He released the beast. But that is not all there is to it.'

Gardus looked away. 'No. I expect not. I do not think Ramus has fallen under the creature's sway. Others, perhaps, but not him.' He looked back at her, and she remembered his face in the smithy. The stars moving beneath it. They were not visible now, but she could feel them – feel their light. She had told no one of what she had seen.

'Is Ramus a fool?' he asked, softly.

'I do not think so.'

'No, nor do I. Perhaps we are the fools for denying him.'

Gardus sighed. 'Either way, he must be brought to heel.' He smiled sadly. 'You will make a fine leader for your Chamber, Khela.'

'Until Ramus returns,' Khela said. 'I do not desire command.'

'That is how I know you will make a good leader.' She looked at him, and Gardus laughed. 'I know. A nonsensical saying. But true nonetheless.' He paused. 'Did you really hew your way through an Alfrostun?'

'Not the entire Alfrostun,' she said, smiling. 'Did you truly drive your sword into Nurgle's eye?'

'No.'

Khela paused. 'I know why you must pursue him, my lord. But a part of me hopes that you fail. A part of me… A part of me wishes that I had gone with him. That he succeeds in this madness. Does that make sense?'

Gardus nodded. 'If you did not feel that way, sister, I would wonder why.' He looked at her. 'I will bring him back.'

Khela nodded. 'I know, my lord. I have faith.'

Sathphren checked Gwyllth's saddle. She chirruped and scratched his shield-plate with her beak. 'Easy, girl. Almost done,' he murmured. Feysha whistled, and he turned. Gardus was coming. He stood, and patted Gwyllth on the head.

'Are you ready?' Gardus called out as he entered the ruin that the Vanguard-Palladors had claimed for their camp. Feysha and the others watched him warily. They'd all seen him kill Hulmean, and it lent a certain veracity to the stories about the Steel Soul. Gardus was not just a Lord-Celestant. There were many Lord-Celestants. There was only one Gardus – the warrior who'd spat in Nurgle's eye, and led the war in Ghyran.

Gardus of the Steel Soul. A legend. Sathphren smiled. Gardus did not seem to realise he was a legend. Nor did he seem to wish to be one. In fact, he seemed tired. Not beaten. Just… tired. Then, given what they were doing, perhaps he had a right to.

Sathphren glanced around. Feysha nodded, and he looked back at Gardus. 'All but one last task. We need to get you a mount.'

Gardus stopped. 'A… mount?'

'Did you think you were going to plod along in our wake?' Sathphren laughed and slapped him on the back. 'No, no – if you're riding with us, you're doing it the right way, brother. Now come, there's someone you need to meet.'

Sathphren led Gardus through the ruin. Several gryph-chargers stood or sat, gnawing on hanks of meat or stripping bones. Gardus stopped as the beasts looked up. 'Are these…?'

'For the moment.' Sathphren clucked his tongue, and one of the gryph-chargers rose. Turquoise feathers rustled as the blue-furred beast padded forward. 'Their riders perished. I doubt they'll mind.'

Gardus looked at him. 'I was more concerned with the gryph-charger's opinion.'

Sathphren laughed. 'Probably wise. Put out your hand.'

The gryph-charger screeched as Gardus extended his hand. Sathphren chuckled and took hold of the creature's reins. 'Easy does it, brother. Let him get to know you.'

Gardus nodded and reached up to stroke the beast's wide skull, allowing it to take in his scent. The gryph-charger studied him with a knowing gaze as the tip of its beak scraped against his shoulder-plate. 'What's his name?'

'Squall, I believe. It's the name he answers to, at any rate.' Sathphren slapped the beast affectionately on the flank. Squall glanced at him, eyes narrowed.

'Will he allow me in the saddle?'

'He'd better, if he knows what's good for him,' Sathphren said, meaningfully. He grabbed a handful of the gryph-charger's feathers, and dragged its head around to face him. 'You understand, you great brute?' The gryph-charger screeched, full in Sathphren's face. He patted its beak and laughed. 'He understands.'

'They are intelligent,' Gardus said.

'For beasts,' Sathphren said. Squall snapped at him, and he punched the beast in the side of the head. 'Squall here a bit less than some.' He looked at Gardus. 'A bit like me, in that regard. Is this a reward, or a chastisement?'

Gardus looked startled, and Sathphren laughed. He liked Gardus. There was something innocently affable about the Lord-Celestant. He hid a keen mind, and very well. 'Why me? Why not Enyo or an Angelos Conclave?'

'You are a hunter. You think like a hunter. And the gryph-chargers are faster than even the Prosecutors, especially over long distances.' Gardus turned. 'Too, if I fall in this endeavour, I trust you to do what must be done.'

'To stop Ramus,' Sathphren said, softly. He crossed his arms and leaned back against the wall. 'And if he will not let me stop him?'

'Stop him anyway.' Gardus stroked Squall's head. 'Put him in chains if you must.'

'Why?'

Gardus did not look at him. 'Ramus' actions will alert Nagash to our presence. It will force a response, one that we will not be able to endure.'

'But if we could?'

Gardus laughed. 'Then we would start a war, Sathphren. A war over one soul.'

'That war started the moment Sigmar forged the first of us, Gardus. Nagash has betrayed us time and again…'

'Yes. And one day, I have no doubt the hosts of Azyr will march on Nagashizzar. But at the moment, there is peace. Or at least no overt hostilities. Nagash wages war on Chaos, as do we. And it serves Sigmar's purpose for that state of affairs to continue.' Gardus shook his head. 'We are stretched to the limit, Sathphren. The soul-forges burn like stars as more and more of our brothers and sisters are Reforged. Thousands of us, every day. And how many mortal lives are snuffed, because even now there are not enough of us.'

He turned. 'Chaos had more than a century to bring the realms to their knees. There are kingdoms that have never known the light of Azyr, and they resent our coming. We are not liberators to them – we are invaders. And they will fight us to the last. As the armies of the Ruinous Powers will fight us. As they fight us even now. And if we must fight Nagash as well – not just his minions, but the Undying King himself? What hope is there?'

'There is us,' Sathphren said. 'Who will stand, when all others fall?'

'Only the faithful,' Gardus said. He patted Squall again, and the gryph-charger squawked, as if in agreement.

'Only the faithful,' Sathphren said. 'Come, Steel Soul. I fear we have a long ride ahead of us, before the end.' He smiled. 'Try your best to keep up, eh?'

'A sea of dust,' Ramus murmured. 'It seems inconceivable.' Though he had seen wonders and glories aplenty in his time among Sigmar's chosen, this was not one of them. Instead, it seemed to him emblematic of this realm. A vast, rolling waste, obscuring all that might once have existed here.

'It gets larger with every passing century,' Mannfred said, joining him at the rail. 'There are whole cities drowned beneath these dunes. Entire civilisations lost but for a footnote in some tome or other. I once fancied attempting to plunder them, but it was not to be. Whatever secrets they hold, they keep, for now.'

Despite the irritation he felt at the vampire's proximity, Ramus was curious. 'What caused it? The dust, I mean.'

'Nagash. Always Nagash.' Mannfred looked at him. 'Nagash's coming twisted the underworlds. Not at first, but eventually.' He shook his head. 'He did not see it – could not. And cannot see it now. But we did – Arkhan, Neferata and I.'

'And abetted him even so.'

'As Sigmar abetted him, in the days of myth. Nagash did not conquer alone, no matter what he claims. He fought side by side with the God-King to bring order to the Realm of Death. The underworlds of Shyish were home to a thousand and one petty godlings, some beautiful, some terrible. Together, Nagash and Sigmar slew the Lord of Dust, and chained Mother Night. They drove back the First Shadow, and released the souls in its great larder. These and a hundred other deeds that few dare speak of now.'

Ramus looked away. 'You are lying.'

'Sigmar would tell you these things himself if you but asked him, fool. They are alike in that respect. Too certain of their own truth to lie.' Mannfred smirked. 'As you are too blinded by it to question.'

'Better a blind man than a fool.'

Mannfred turned, still smiling. 'A fool, am I? How so? Do explain, revered teacher.'

'You are here. Helping me. And thinking that I do not see the treachery that lurks in you.' Ramus jabbed a finger into the vampire's chest. 'I *know* you. As well as I know myself. You are a traitor to every cause, and your hand is turned against every man. One against all. That is how you see yourself.'

'What of it? At least I am certain in my loyalties. How many can say that, eh?'

'You have no loyalties!'

'Exactly. Which makes me incredibly trustworthy.' Mann-fred paused. 'Tarsem knew that. That is why we were friends, I think. He never saw me as anything save what I was, and accepted it as what must be.'

'That is not friendship.'

'And how would you know? Do you have friends?' Mann-fred turned and sat on the rail, arms crossed. 'Duty and hon-our don't count.'

Ramus glared at him. 'I should slay you where you stand.'

Mannfred laughed. 'You've tried that before and failed. What makes you think this time would be any different?' He pointed at Ramus. 'No. We are allies now, for good or ill. Boon compan-ions, bound on a glorious quest. You need me, and I need you.'

'And Tarsus needs us both.'

Mannfred nodded. 'Yes. More than you can know.' He looked over his shoulder, out over the dunes. 'Nagash is intent on finding the secret to your existence. What Sigmar has done... infuriates him. More, it challenges him on his own ground. Nagash has never been one to let a challenge go unanswered.'

'We will challenge him and win.'

Mannfred snorted. 'If your God-King is with us, we might have a chance.'

'Even if he is not.' Ramus straightened. 'Much is demanded of those to whom much is given. What we do, we do it not just for Tarsus, but for Sigmar as well.'

'Whether he realises it or not, eh?'

Ramus hesitated. 'Even as you act for Nagash's benefit,' he said, after a moment. Mannfred's smile slipped. He pushed away from the rail.

'What would you know of it?'

'You serve a mad god,' Ramus said, catching hold of the vampire's arm. 'But not willingly. You speak of the Nagash of old as we speak of Sigmar, but heap scorn on him as he is now. That tells me much, Mannfred von Carstein. It tells me that maybe, just maybe, Tarsus was not so great a fool as I have believed.'

Mannfred pulled his arm free and stalked away without reply.

Ramus watched him for a moment, and then turned back to his contemplation of the dunes. He stiffened as he caught sight of something flashing in the distance. The wind shifted, carrying a discordant piping to his ears. Osanus joined him at the rail.

'We are being followed.'

'Yes. Keep an eye on them.' Ramus turned away.

'We are too close to be stopped now.'

CHAPTER NINETEEN

WILD HUNT

*To hunt... to stalk your prey... This is the stuff
of dreams.*

Felg the Mad
Confessions

Something – many somethings – emerged from the dust.

The air trembled as a groaning rose to fill it. Many voices, mingling in a wordless cry of need and frustration. Mummified hands fumbled at the hull of the barque as it slid forward. Mannfred stared down at the sea of dead faces that peered up at him blindly.

The deadwalkers were all but submerged, and unable to do more than thrash about. To a traveller on foot, they could prove deadly. But to those safely aboard a vessel, or a fast steed, they were little more than a curiosity. Hundreds of hands and faces, swaying on the surface of the dust like fleshy algae. Below them were hundreds more, and a hundred more below that. A reef of dead flesh, twitching and clawing in the dusty depths.

'What is this?' Ramus growled. Mannfred smiled. He could hear the disgust in the Stormcast's voice. The vampire sat atop the rail, fingers twitching as if in time to a melody. His sheathed sword sat close to hand.

'A corpse-reef. Hundreds of dead bodies, all blown together by the slow shifting of the sands, until the concentration of death causes a unique reaction.' Mannfred swept a hand out. 'There are thousands of these in the Sea of Dust – the detritus of a hundred armies, marking centuries of war.'

'Can you not silence them?' Ramus demanded.

'Why? Don't you care for the tune?'

'They are in torment.'

'So they are. And for good reason. They defied Nagash, and sought to cast down the pillars of Nagashizzar. An army more than a million strong – stretching from horizon to horizon. Lords and peasants, knights and bandits. The highest to the lowest, joined in common cause. An army of liberation.' Mannfred's smile was ghastly. 'I warned them, of course, that mighty council of rebels. I told them what awaited them.' He leaned over the side and called out, 'Didn't I, my Lord Pharrok?'

A groaning deadwalker, clad in rags that might once have been fine robes and armour, reached up towards him. The creature wore a spiral helm, its ruined features hidden behind a veil of rotting silk. Mannfred drove the end of his sheathed blade down, dislodging the helm and punched through the deadwalker's skull. The deadwalker tumbled back and vanished beneath the slow tides of dust.

Was that truly Pharrok? Tarsem murmured. *Or are you being hyperbolic again?*

Mannfred ignored the memory and looked at Ramus. 'I

warned them. I tried to help, I really did. But they wouldn't listen. That is my curse. My wisdom is dismissed, and what I fear always comes to pass.'

'Perhaps people only dismiss you because you are so blatantly treacherous,' Ramus said, flatly. 'There are entire sagas devoted to your betrayals, you know. I spent months digging through mouldy parchments and dusty tomes, following your trail through history.'

'I'm flattered.' Mannfred frowned. Annoyance flared. Ramus had been baiting him since they'd left Caddow. It was as if the Lord-Relictor wanted to provoke him. Then, maybe he did. He rubbed his chest.

Ramus studied him. 'Don't be. It was necessary, but exceedingly tedious. Every story with you ends the same, Mannfred. Treachery is in your bones. You are a lightning rod for dissent. Where you go, Nagash's eye is soon drawn. One might almost suspect that such is your purpose, in the grand scheme of things.'

'What do you mean?'

You know what he means, Tarsem said. *And you know he's right. My father suspected as much. You are a stalking horse, and where you go, death follows.*

'You foment dissent, vampire,' Ramus said. 'You are a spark on the wind, and it was Nagash who kindled you. Wherever you stir up trouble, there Nagash turns. Rather than waiting for rebellion, he creates it and crushes it, as an example to everyone who comes after. And you are his tool in this.' Ramus laughed. 'You are his slave.'

Mannfred's face darkened, as he pushed himself to his feet. Black veins pulsed, and his lips peeled back from long fangs. 'I am no slave,' he said, softly. 'I am a Mortarch. I sit at his left hand, by dint of my cunning and power. If anyone is a slave here, it is you – what are you but a puppet-soul, stuffed with lightning and unleashed on an unwitting realm?'

'And you are nothing more than a fragment of a mad god, given unnatural life.'

'We have that much in common, at least.' Mannfred turned his attentions back to the dead. 'If you think I am a puppet, then why follow me?'

'Hope.'

Mannfred grimaced. 'How naive of you. I expected better, Ramus.' He heard a shriek from above and saw Ashigaroth circling, something clutched in his jaws. 'What is this?' He gestured and Ashigaroth dropped heavily to the deck. In his jaws something at once simian and lupine twitched and screamed.

'A daemon,' Ramus growled. Stormcasts rose from the rowers' benches, reaching for their weapons. Osanus joined the Lord-Relictor.

'A fury,' Mannfred said, dropping to his haunches. 'A type of minor daemon. They congregate like barnacles about Bakhos' pavilions. Drop it.' He directed this last at Ashigaroth. Reluctantly, the dread abyssal spat out its prey. Mannfred caught the daemon before it could squirm away and examined it. The thing hissed and squealed, clawing at him. He ignored it and stood. 'Yes, this is one of them. That's unfortunate.'

'Why? Could it not simply have followed us?' Ramus leaned close, and the fury shrank back, unable to bear the tang of celestial magics.

'That would require a sense of curiosity, which these creatures do not possess. They are elemental. Basic. No. It would not be out here unless there was someone pulling its strings.' Mannfred turned and stared back the way they'd come. Dust filled the air, whipped up by the winds. He could hear the groans of deadwalkers – more corpse-reefs. Their presence was why he had guided the barque on this course.

Unfortunately, it seemed as if their pursuers were more determined than he'd first thought. 'We are being followed,' he said.

'I know. I have known for the last day.' Ramus met his startled gaze with a cold glare. 'I am no fool, Mannfred. Nor am I blind. They were on our trail the day of our leaving. Likely thanks to that creature you hold.'

Mannfred glanced down at the fury and tossed it to Ashigaroth. The dread abyssal delightedly tore the daemon apart and gulped down its essence. 'Not just one. Never just one.' He peered up, into the dust-wracked sky. He could feel the sting of Shyish's distant, wan sun, but ignored it. Shapes darted through the roiling clouds of dust.

He heard a familiar scream. More than one. A cacophony of hellish yelps, dancing teasingly across the air. 'The Hounds of Slaanesh,' he muttered. Bakhos – or his servants. No. No, it would be Bakhos himself. He wouldn't be able to resist. The flash of reflected metal caught his eye, and he saw a line of distant shapes, growing larger. He flung back the edges of his cloak. 'The enemy is soon upon us. I shall deal with them now, so that we do not have to do so later.'

Without waiting for a reply, he caught at the skeins of death magic binding the corpse-reef and began to change it. Without a mind to guide them or freedom of movement, deadwalkers would simply sit in one place. But give them a direction – give them a scent – and they would not stop until they had tasted flesh.

Before he could release the spell, he felt a flare of silver pain and screamed. An ugly heat ripped through him, burning his thoughts to cinders and sending him to his knees. Ashigaroth screeched and spun, lunging for Ramus. The Lord-Relictor stepped back as two Liberators interposed themselves. Dimly, Mannfred heard the telltale whine of Judicators nocking arrows. He flung up a hand. 'Stop,' he croaked. 'Stop, Ashigaroth.' The dread abyssal subsided, tail lashing.

'Fool,' Mannfred snarled, glaring at Ramus. 'Allow me to use my magics, or we shall lose our heads!'

'No,' Ramus said. 'You are on my leash, vampire, and I will not give you any more freedom than I must–'

Ashigaroth roared, interrupting him. They all looked up. Furies filled the air, descending through the wind and dust with hateful shrieks. Mannfred hissed and snatched his blade from its sheath as the Stormcasts leapt to arm themselves.

Mannfred's blade cleaved the first of the daemons in two. He ripped the wings from the second and chopped through the spine of the third. But there were more. Dozens. Two dozen. Three. They swarmed the Stormcasts, shrieking and screeching. The silver-armoured warriors fought back, despite being unprepared.

A Stormcast was dragged bodily from the deck by several furies and dropped into the corpse-reef. The warrior's curses were lost as he was quickly dragged beneath the dust by hundreds of clutching hands. A moment later, a snarl of lightning erupted upwards, turning the dust to brittle glass, and setting nearby deadwalkers alight. Another Stormcast pitched backwards over the rail, but was saved from a similar fate by Sagittus. The Judicator-Prime smashed a fury from the air with his bow, wielding it like a club.

Osanus roared and bisected a fury with his blade. He raised his horn and blew a single note. The air convulsed and furies fell, their unnatural forms pulverised. Ramus raised his reliquary staff and slammed it down. Blue fire shot out in all directions, limning every board and post on the barque. Mannfred felt the sting of celestial magics, and knew that however uncomfortable it was for him, for the furies it was worse.

Many of the daemons burst into flame, and were reduced to greasy motes before they even had a chance to screech. Others took off like comets in reverse, rising even as they burned. Mannfred swept ashes from the air and looked to the dunes. The riders he'd glimpsed earlier were closer now, and gaining.

'We've slowed,' he called out, alerting the Stormcasts to their danger. 'Look, fools! The enemy is almost upon us – look!'

'Ride,' Bakhos roared. 'Ride for your souls, and for the pleasure of the hunt!' He bent low in the saddle, as his steed galloped across the wind-blown dunes. Clouds of dust twisted and danced in his wake, forming faces that screamed silent entreaties to the riders.

The horse was no match for the steed he'd lost in Caddow, but it would do well enough. It was a lean beast, with mottled scales and a spiny mane the colour of smoke, taken from the herd Hulmean had brought to pull his war-altar. It snapped wolfish jaws as he jerked on the reins, and loosed a savage squeal.

Six of his eunuchs rode in silence alongside him, mounted on similar steeds, and Lemerus followed close behind, trailed by its warriors. It had brought nearly two dozen of its followers, champions all – the most trusted blades at its command. Overhead, furies rode the winds, and daemonettes, riding serpentine steeds, galloped wildly all around them. The daemons laughed and sang as they rode.

The enemy was just ahead, speeding east, carried by the wind. Their vessel was an ungraceful thing, square and low, but swift. Swifter than he'd expected, and the wind hid their trail. It was only thanks to the furies that he'd even been able to find them. But the flock of lesser daemons had spotted them, and now dogged their trail.

Even if the furies hadn't been able to find them, Bakhos knew where they were going. If he couldn't catch them, he would simply meet them there. But he needed to make the attempt, at least. If he was going to earn the gratitude of the Three-Eyed King, he needed to bring a proper gift. A prisoner or, failing that, the head of a Stormcast, was what was called for. He licked his lips, eager to meet them in battle. Eager to stretch his limbs.

He glanced back at Lemerus. The androgynous champion seemed pleased enough to be included. No doubt it thought that this would be an ideal opportunity to rid itself of him and perhaps make itself known to the Three-Eyed King or his lieutenants. Of the two of them, he trusted Lemerus more than Etax. Etax had always had airs above his station. But Lemerus was wiser. It kept its intentions to itself unless provoked by Etax.

Smiling, Bakhos slowed his steed, and allowed the champion to catch up with him. 'See, Lemerus?' he called out. 'As I said. Despite the wind, the furies have their scent.'

'Let us hope that they do not lose it, for I can barely see them in this dust.' Lemerus bared its needle fangs in what might have been a grin. In that moment, the champion resembled the daemonettes that rode close by. Bakhos laughed.

'I have always been curious,' he said. 'Are you truly the child of a daemon and a mortal? Or is that simply something the skalds say, when deep in their cups?'

'It is the truth insofar as I know, O Maiden's Son,' Lemerus said with some pride. 'I am the child of divinity. The blood of a god runs in my veins. In time, I might ascend to my father's kingdom, as a true prince of the realm – if I prove myself worthy.'

Bakhos looked away. 'I was a prince once, before I was a

king. The anticipation was all but unbearable. Your patience is commendable.'

Lemerus laughed. It sounded like bells. Bakhos wondered if he ought to remove the creature's head now and save himself the trouble later. Like Etax, Lemerus was on the cusp of relevance – either could pull together an army on their name alone. Either would make a natural successor to him, as the marcher-lord of Caddow. But which would it be?

As if reading his thoughts, Lemerus asked, 'Why did you invite me, my lord?'

'To keep you from murdering Etax in my absence. Or vice-versa.'

'Then the beast is not your chosen heir?'

Bakhos laughed. 'The beast is a beast.' He glanced at Lemerus. 'It is a test, Lemerus. As this is a test. I wonder... which of you will pass it?' A shriek split the air. He turned back to the distant barque. 'There, Lemerus – see? The furies have caught them.'

'Yes, as you said they would,' Lemerus said. 'Should we call them off?'

Before Bakhos could answer, a flare of azure light split the dusty air. Daemons screamed as they were consumed. Bakhos cursed. It had cost him a hundred slaves – fertile ones, virgins unmarked and unharmed – to summon the furies. To see so many of them killed so easily was infuriating. 'Go!' he snarled.

Daemonettes screamed and urged their unnatural steeds forward, across the dust. They seemed to fly across the dunes, not quite touching the ground. The dust-barque had slowed noticeably, and the daemonettes drew abreast of it quickly. But as the first of them reached it, Bakhos heard the hum-snap of Stormcast bows. Lightning danced across the dunes and daemonettes shrieked in pain. Daemonic steeds fell, spilling their riders.

Even so, a few reached the rear of the barque. Their monstrous steeds leapt, scrabbling up the back of the vessel, barbed tails lashing. Stormcasts met them at the rail, and the sounds of battle filled the air. Bakhos grinned and urged his horse on. He heard Lemerus shout something, but ignored the creature, intent on reaching the barque.

He noticed the shadow a moment later. It grew, swelling to envelop him. He looked up and saw a monster of iron and bone falling towards him. He sprang from the saddle, even as the creature crushed his horse beneath it, snapping the animal's spine. He rolled to his feet, snatching his blade from its sheath. The monstrosity faced him, iron scraping iron. Atop its back, its rider laughed mockingly. 'How many times, O Maiden's Son? How many times will you race ahead into the jaws of disaster?'

The voice was familiar. Bakhos rose to his feet. 'Vlad?'

'There is no Vlad. There never was. Only Mannfred.' The vampire leaned over the head of his steed and grinned. 'Mannfred, and the fool he led into defeat. Hello, my lord – it has been some time.' With a kick, Mannfred urged his steed into motion. 'Ashigaroth – take him!'

Bakhos flung himself aside as the creature pounced. He was on his feet in moments, his blade scraping across his attacker's flank. He recognised it, if dimly – a dread abyssal, they were called. And its rider, one of the Mortarchs of Nagash. Shame warred with excitement within him. He leapt away from a sweep of black talons and laughed.

'You will have to be faster than that, whatever your name is. I have fought leopards with naught but my hands, and senators with only words – this… this is but child's play!' Beyond the beast, he could see Lemerus and the others darting towards the barque, eager to come to grips with their prey. Bakhos was content to let them have it – a Mortarch made for greater prize than any Stormcast.

His eunuchs circled the beast, their steeds shrieking and hissing. Bakhos waved them back with a gesture. 'This one is mine, children. Stay back.' He dodged the beast's next lunge, gauging its speed. 'I am glad to see you, Mortarch – your presence is proof of that which I suspected. The enemies of Varanspire seek alliance. Archaon will reward me well for bringing him your head.'

'Ah, Bakhos, always one to count the wine drunk before the grapes have ripened,' Mannfred said. His sword flashed, and Bakhos parried the blow. Mannfred laughed. 'It was that arrogance that allowed me to hide among your warriors for months on end.'

Ashigaroth leapt again, and Bakhos dropped beneath it, blade flickering along its underbelly. Ashigaroth screeched in what might have been pain, and jerked away from him, nearly spilling Mannfred from the saddle.

Bakhos spread his arms as the beast took to the air. 'No stomach for it then?' he cried out. 'Did you think me easy prey, Vlad? Or are you afraid of me, perhaps? Is that why you hid, rather than challenging me openly?'

'My name is Mannfred,' the vampire spat, as he hauled on the reins. 'A name you shall remember, in whatever underworld awaits the black tatters of your soul.' The dread abyssal galloped through the air, turning back towards Bakhos. Bakhos readied his blade, eager to face the beast, and its rider both. But instead of attacking him, the beast swept past, towards the embattled barque.

Bakhos turned, cursing. Mannfred's steed crashed into the back of the barque, casting daemons aside with feral urgency. Mannfred himself leapt onto the rail to aid the Stormcasts. He saw Lemerus bring its steed up short as Mannfred raised his hand to the sky and began to chant. 'What is it?' he called out. 'What is–?'

Lemerus began to ride back towards him as amethyst lightning played across the dunes. Bakhos' eyes narrowed. The wind seemed to gather itself, and the faces in the dust became distorted and monstrous. The dust shifted beneath his feet, as if something was moving beneath him.

Bakhos looked down. Lemerus was shouting. Something brown and crumbling burst from the dust – a hand. Followed by another, and another. He heard screams and yells, and saw several of Lemerus' followers fall as their steeds were pulled to their knees. Dead things erupted from the dust and clambered over the thrashing animals. Rotting fingers pried at the gaps in baroque armour, as the warriors fought against the numberless hordes intent on dragging them beneath the dunes.

Bakhos swept his sword out, slicing through grasping claws. Dead bodies heaved themselves up, the tatters of their ancient robes and armour encrusted with centuries of dust. Amethyst lights filled the eye sockets of every skull, and they lurched towards him, or crawled, dragging broken spines in their wake.

All over the dunes, the dead rose. Hundreds of them, perhaps more. He felt the first tickle of fear at the base of his skull. He turned, seeking some escape, but everywhere he looked, the dead looked back. He cursed and slashed out, smashing a deadwalker from its feet. Two more took its place, crowding him.

One of his eunuchs galloped towards him, arm extended. The eunuch burst through the dead, knocking corpses aside. Bakhos caught the arm, and with a simple motion dragged the eunuch from the saddle and tossed him to the dead. He pulled on the reins, turning the horse away, as the eunuch disappeared beneath the dust.

The wind picked up, howling now. It sounded like laughter. Bakhos turned, but saw no sign of the barque. Lemerus rode towards him, its face streaked with ichor. 'They got away!'

'No. We know where they are going.' Bakhos pointed his steed east. 'Come. If we ride hard, we will be there to greet them!'

Ghosteater stared at the bodies hanging from the wooden frame. Slaves, mostly. A hundred, butchered and made ready for the evening's feast. The camp's cook, an obese giant, clad in stained silks and bejewelled war-plate, gestured with a cleaver.

'Not enough, milord. They've all taken to the hills, little rabbits. Saw Bakhos' leaving as a sign they were free, eh? Sad, sad. We will find them, eventually – why, Lord Etax leads a hunt even now! – but not enough in the larder. Not enough!'

The cook had no name that Ghosteater was aware of. His kitchens were a foul-smelling tent that sprawled at the rear of the encampment. Vats of boiling fat and barrels of bones cluttered the interior. Great firepits were tended by scarred, mutilated slaves. Sacks of spices, looted from caravans, lay in out-of-the-way corners. A slave scuttled by, carrying a heap of dead rats by their knotted tails. Others dumped spices and bone-meal into cauldrons while the froth within was slowly stirred.

'I must have more, milord – more meat, eh?' the cook burbled. 'More bone to make my bread, more fat to crisp, more meat to char and spice. The horde is a beast, milord, and a hungry one, yes? This is not enough, oh no.'

Ghosteater peered at the giant, perplexed. 'Why tell me?'

You are in charge, Herst said. *Exactly where you wanted to be, I remind you.*

'Bakhos provided banquets and wine every evening. His followers have become… accustomed to a certain level of comfort.' Chaell stepped up. 'That said, they all likely have their own stores set aside for lean periods. Failing that, they can eat each other. As your folk do, I'm told.'

'Quite good, beast-meat. Properly cooked, the fats, they–'

the cook began, jowls rippling as his fanged jaws flapped. He stopped short, as Ghosteater looked at him.

'You told Lord Etax before you told me,' Ghosteater growled. The cook glanced at Chaell, who stepped back, head bowed.

'I–' the cook stammered.

Ghosteater's khopesh severed the hand holding the cleaver. His next blow opened the giant's throat to the bone. The cook sagged with a piteous wheeze, and toppled onto his face. Ghosteater looked at Chaell. 'Now there's enough meat.' He gestured to the nearby slaves.

Chaell laughed. 'I suppose so.' He stepped over the body and joined Ghosteater as they left the cook's slaves to harvest their master's flesh. 'That's not going to sit well, with some. Bakhos' cook was considered… communal property.'

'Don't care.' Ghosteater looked about the camp. It was quiet. Many of Bakhos' subordinates had retired to their camps in a fit of pique. Others had launched unplanned assaults on the enemy. Ghosteater had allowed all of it.

Your friend thinks you are being a fool, Herst murmured. *He will challenge your decisions. Tell you that you are wrong. You must not kill him. While he lives, he acts as a buffer – you understand this term?*

Ghosteater grunted in the affirmative. He felt the ghost's sigh of satisfaction. Herst continued. *You need him. They will listen to him where they will not listen to you. You buy yourself a day with every hour you spare his life.*

'You are being foolish in allowing them to ignore you, as they are. You should have burned Etax's pavilion the first hour after Bakhos' departure. Set loose your curiously absent beastherds on him and established your authority.'

'Too many dead. Need warriors.'

'For what?' Chaell shook his head. 'What are you planning?

You order attacks on random points – attacks your beasts could conduct more quickly – and then pay little heed to the results. You haven't even asked how they went, yet.'

Ghosteater looked at Chaell. 'The attacks?'

'Failed. As expected.' Chaell looked at him. 'You've launched a dozen attacks since Bakhos left. None of them have got as far as Hulmean's assault. There are… mutterings.'

Ghosteater nodded. 'Bakhos made me lord.'

'Then you must act like it. This army frays beneath your feet. Bakhos has been gone but a day and already Etax is planning to nail your ivory pelt to his throne. You must confront the others, force them to see you as regent.'

Ghosteater nodded, as if considering this. In reality, he was studying the camp. Studying the way the Blessed Ones lived. He had not truly thought of it, until he had seen it. They lived like beasts. No, worse. Beasts lived in ruins. They did not build, for what beast needed a tent or a door? They did not have these things because they did not need them.

But the Blessed Ones did. Like the men they had once been, they surrounded themselves with walls and trenches. They shed blood to ward off ghosts, lit fires to drive back the night. They let their waste fall where it would, rather than where it would best mark their territory. They rolled in filth, not to mask their scent, but out of… laziness.

Everything beasts did was of purpose. But the Blessed Ones had no purpose, save pleasure. The more he saw of them, the more he realised where his own pleasure lay. The storm-things were not the real enemy. They were merely… prey. Savage prey. Strong prey. But prey all the same.

He looked at Chaell. The Blessed Ones were the enemy. And to be free, beasts must defeat the enemy. 'Are you listening?' Chaell demanded.

'Yes,' Ghosteater said. 'Army is breaking. Bakhos will be displeased.'

Chaell snorted. 'I doubt that. I doubt that he's coming back. Responsibility is a trap, my friend. One you fell into all too willingly.'

He is right, of course. You are being used.

'Yes,' Ghosteater said, answering them both.

'You have not even called for a council of war,' Chaell pressed. 'Etax will see that as a sign of weakness. As proof that you are not fit to lead.' He shook his head. 'Is that your plan? Do you wish him to challenge you?'

Ghosteater laughed. 'No. Would lose.'

'Yes, you would. Etax is a vainglorious oaf, but a dangerous one. Watching and waiting will not serve you here.' Chaell stepped in front of him. Ghosteater stopped, but restrained his instinctive snarl. 'If you wish to be more than what you are, you must think as one of us.'

'Why help me?' Ghosteater growled.

'I told you. I owe a debt. Too, my fate is tied to yours now. If you fail, I will fall alongside, whether I will it or no. But for the moment, you rule here. So rule!' He lowered his voice. 'Indeed, you have the opportunity to do more here now than Bakhos has done in an age. You have an army – use it!'

'Not my army,' Ghosteater said. 'Won't listen.'

'They will, if you make them. Let me call them together. Etax and the others… We can show them that you are no mere puppet. You have a cunning beyond theirs. Let us show them what sort of war-leader you can be, eh?'

Ghosteater considered. In truth, this time. It was tempting. Among beasts, such a thing was common. There was an honesty to it. But the Blessed Ones did not think that way. They saw weakness in strength, and would continue to bite, even after being beaten. Despite Chaell's words, such a council would convince them of nothing.

But it will buy you time, Herst murmured. *Always important, time. Never enough, and always too much. The longer it stretches, the worse things will be when it finally... snaps.*

Ghosteater looked at Chaell. 'Call them,' he growled. 'Time for watching is done.'

CHAPTER TWENTY

PERSISTENCE

A leader must be true to themselves, above all others.

– Padraig Glymm
The Glymm: A Concise History

Deep in the catacombs beneath Caddow, Reconciler Ahom traced astromantic sigils upon the stones, tightening the mystic wards that already existed there.

The wards were primitive, by the standards of the Collegiate Arcane – barely more than ritualised hedge magics. The tomes and scrolls recovered from elsewhere in the city by his assistants and apprentices showed that whatever else, the mages of Caddow had certainly not been the equal of the sorcerer-kings of the Lantic Empire. They were barely the equal to the warrior-mages of the Glymm.

Ahom knew himself to be a master of the ancient rites. He had read the Starbound Tomes, and studied the ancient cosmological scrolls of the great library of Sigmaron. He had forgotten more about magic than most men learned in their lifetime. For that reason, he had been designated the rank of reconciler. To him fell the task of acquiring and reconciling the lost mystic lore of fallen kingdoms, and adding the worthiest to the Great Repository of the Collegiate Arcane. Ancient magics such as this were the whole of his purpose.

And yet, the tighter he wove these new wards, the more quickly the old ones slipped from his control. They defied him, when, by all rational thought, they should have been as the softest clay in his hands. A ward flared, erasing the last few moments of work, and he cursed. He stepped back and an apprentice mopped at his sweating features with a handkerchief.

'Something is wrong,' he said. When no one replied, he turned. 'Are you listening?'

Jerob, his colleague from the Amber College, grunted. 'Are you saying anything worth listening to?' Jerob was a brute, and more interested in studying the shamanistic rites of the savage tribes of Ghur and Aqshy than in the more civilised magics of the fallen kingdoms. As if such savages knew anything about the mystic arts.

'My every utterance is worth the deepest attention.'

'Save it for your apprentices, Ahom.'

Ahom snorted and looked at the third member of their expedition. 'Ilesha – you sense it, I trust? Jerob might be blind, deaf and dumb, but your sensitivities are more nuanced.'

'Listen to them. The guns are pounding day and night. Death seeps through the stones.' Ilesha stared upwards at the ceiling of the chamber. 'And the sleepers awaken.' Ilesha, a mistress of the Amethyst College, was a more convivial companion than Jerob, but only just. She spent so much time among the dead that she often forgot how to talk to the living. Even so, she was right. He could hear the dull thump of Mahk's toys. The Iron-weld were outdoing themselves as far as noise was concerned. He glanced back at the walled-up archway. The wards shifted eerily, throbbing with power.

He could feel the dead stirring, somewhere behind them. They sensed the battle above them, the way a sleeper might yet detect an unusual sound, despite not being awake. They had not awoken yet, but it was getting more difficult to ensure that they never would.

'Always so cryptic,' Jerob growled. 'Say what you mean, woman, or be silent.'

Ilesha looked at him, and adjusted her spectacles. 'And why should I have to explain myself to you, Jerob? Are your wits so dull, then?'

Ahom sighed. 'Quiet, both of you.' Tempers – never the best – had begun to fray. They all had other duties they would rather be attending to, but the wards had demanded their full attentions. Whatever else happened, they could not allow the wards to weaken.

'Be quiet yourself, Ahom,' Jerob said, turning on Ahom. 'My wards bleed away like sand between my fingers. This place eats magic. It is a hibernating bear, and we drag raw meat across the mouth of its den.'

'Which is why we must figure out a solution,' Ahom said.

'Which is why we should leave it, and lend our efforts to the battle above,' Jerob snarled. 'The quicker it ends, the quicker the dead go back to sleep!'

'Quiet,' Ilesha said, suddenly. Then, more softly, 'Quiet.'

Ahom turned. The wards were burning amethyst. They shone brightly, like evil stars. He swallowed and stepped back. Jerob stared. 'Do they awaken?'

'No,' Ilesha said. 'I do not think so. But...'

A sound. Soft, at first, but growing louder. The click of bone on stone, echoing from all around them. How long had it been hidden beneath the thunder of the guns? 'What is it?' he whispered.

'Digging,' Jerob said, harshly. 'It's the sound of digging.'

'But from where?'

'Does it matter?' Ilesha said. 'They stir from the sleep of ages, and claw at the stones which entomb them.' She looked at Ahom. 'Jerob is right. The longer this campaign goes on, the greater the risk. To soothe the dead, we must cease adding to their number.'

Ahom shook his head. 'Impossible. There is an army on our doorstep, and beasts in the ruins. Would you have us leave?'

Ilesha frowned. 'I do not have an answer, Ahom. I can only tell you what I know.'

Ahom looked away. 'A few more days, perhaps, and we will have it.'

'Or we will be up to our shins in dead men,' Jerob growled. 'Listen to her, fool. You must speak with the Lord-Celestant – and swiftly.'

Ahom opened his mouth to argue, more out of habit than any real sense of disagreement. But the sound stopped him. The soft click-click-click of fleshless fingers, digging away at the stones. He swallowed his objections and gathered his robes and dignity about him.

'I will go,' he said. 'And I pray it is not too late.'

From her seat at the top of the ziggurat, Cassandora studied the western emplacements. She made notations on the slate she held with a bit of chalk, gauging distance and position with an acuity that was more than human. She hoped the notes would help Lord-Ordinator Taltus in his preparations. And if not, they at least kept her busy.

Great bonfires were kept lit, casting back the night's gloom. She could see Freeguild patrols moving through the long shadows, keeping watch. The air throbbed with the grinding of Ironweld artifice as heavy emplacements of stone and gromril were fixed into place by the engineers, in preparation for future assaults.

The whole of the city's centre had become a fortress. Inviolate and unbreakable. Or so Mahk swore, up and down. Then, he'd sworn that before they'd nearly lost the central plaza.

'Business as usual,' she murmured. It was almost dull.

In the early days, in those first deadly wars for control of the realmgates, it had been a close thing. The warrior chambers had been thrust into war with no reinforcements, no supplies. Only themselves to count on. Chaos had nearly overwhelmed them. *Had* overwhelmed them, more than once.

But now, a new status quo had been achieved. The armies of Azyr had made war into a science. A thing of routine. Set the shields, prime the guns and watch the enemy die. Sometimes, the science failed. But mostly, it worked. Especially against foes like these. Brutal. Simplistic. They charged, because charging had always worked.

Eventually, they would learn their lesson. But until then, she intended to take advantage of the situation as often as possible. She looked back down at her calculations. Such things were not strictly her responsibility, but she felt the need to step into Gardus' shadow. The Steel Soul liked to keep his hand in, as the saying went. Cassandora preferred calling him what he was – a busybody. Her fellow Lord-Celestant rarely just… sat. He thought, constantly. He meditated, prayed and sought counsel. And he never stopped working, training, *doing*.

'What will become of you when the war ends, I wonder,' she

murmured, making a notation. Then, what would become of any of them? Would there be a use for them, in the realms to come? She stopped and stared, watching the fires. Or would the war never end? Would watchfires burn eternal and Stormcasts stand ever on guard?

She didn't know which thought disturbed her more.

'Lord-Celestant?'

She glanced back. 'Ah, Octarion. How goes it?'

Lord-Castellant Octarion approached slowly, his warding lantern lighting his path across the top of the ziggurat. 'Slowly, as ever. Lorrus argues for the sake of arguing, and Khela is as stubborn as her Chamber's namesake.'

'Having fun, then?'

Octarion chuckled. 'Some, I suppose.' He looked out over the city, his face hidden beneath his war-mask. But she could tell what he was thinking. Octarion spoke volumes with the set of his shoulders. 'I remember when this city was alive.' He sat beside her.

Cassandora looked at him. 'You were from here?'

'No. From a city called Palewater. To the north of here. Or it was, centuries ago. I expect that it's gone now, as so much is.' Octarion looked down at her. 'But I remember travelling with my uncles to Caddow. They were merchants – booksellers, I think. I remember... a certain flavour of crushed ice, served in clay cups by street vendors. Black lime, I think. I had never tasted it, before that day.'

'Do you remember? The taste, I mean.'

He shook his head. 'No. What about you, sister? What do you remember?'

'I remember so many things, all out of order and tangled up with each other,' Cassandora said. 'The sound of a baby's first breath, and a young child's cries... The light of the moon, and a promise made under the sun. But that is all I have. Fragments and pieces of who I was, and who I might have been. Growing fainter with every century.' She shook her head. 'Soon, I fear I will not have them at all.'

'Would that not be for the best, my lady?' Octarion said. 'What use such ephemera in the days to come, save to weaken your resolve? We are the storm, and what need has the storm of memories?' He ran a thumb along the blade of his halberd. 'Let us shed all mortal weakness so that we might carry the light of Sigmar, unencumbered and unhindered.'

'What you call weakness, I call a whetstone.' Cassandora looked at him. 'Without the memory of mortality, what are we save articulate weapons? It is the memory of something better that kindles the light which guides us. If we lose that, then we trade faith for servitude.'

'And are we not his servants?'

Cassandora paused. 'Because we choose to be, Lord-Castellant. Because we believe in something greater than ourselves. Without that choice, we are no better than the beasts who break themselves on our shields.' She turned, as alarm bells sounded from the Ironweld emplacements to the east. 'Speaking of which.' A few moments later, she heard the crackle of handguns, and the doleful boom of artillery.

'They are persistent.'

'Yes.' She watched the flicker of handguns in the dark. 'How many attacks since Gardus left? A dozen? More?'

'About that. Why?'

'Previously, the attacks were slow. Measured. Always in threes. But now – erratic.' New calculations filled her head. As a Lord-Celestant, her task was to read the battlefield and act accordingly. Something had changed. Their strategy would need to change as well.

'Lord-Celestant! Lord-Celestant! I must speak with you.' Reconciler Ahom hurried into view, moving as quickly as he could in his robes. He was followed by a gaggle of scribes and apprentices. The battlemage looked wan and haggard.

Cassandora rose to her feet. 'What is it, reconciler?' She had little of Gardus' patience for the fussy astromancer. Ahom had contributed little so far to the war effort, as far as she could tell. If he was here with more complaints…

'The dead,' he said, flatly.

Cassandora stiffened. 'They awaken?'

'They are in the process of doing so, we believe. The death toll of this campaign… It awakens them. Like calls to like.'

'How soon?'

Ahom shook his head. 'Impossible to tell. We did warn Lord-Celestant Gardus…'

Cassandora gestured sharply. 'Gardus is not here. I am.' She looked at Octarion. 'I need to speak to Enyo.'

'She is on patrol, I believe.'

'Find her.' She thumped Octarion's arm with the side of her fist. 'Get Grymn and Sango as well. I will find Lorcus. The situation has changed, and we must change with it.'

Albain Lorcus sat at his campaign desk and laid out the world to come. The thunder of the Ironweld's guns kept him company as he laboured over his books and papers. Conquest required more paperwork than he'd been led to believe. Certainly more than he preferred. He pushed aside a pile of scrolls. 'Marta?'

Marta ducked beneath the archway and peered at him. 'Yes, my lord?' She was taller than most Azyrites, with a spattering of freckles across her round features. Her red hair was cut short, and her uniform was smudged with dust, much like his own. One of her arms was in a sling. She'd been wounded in a skirmish – not by an enemy blade but by a chunk of loose masonry, thrown up by the impact of a Prosecutor's hammer – and had been seconded to serve as Lorcus' aide.

'Have you seen my maps of the western district?'

'Under the letters of marque,' she said, pointing.

'Thank you. Has Vend come back yet?'

'Not yet.'

'Let me know when he does.'

Marta nodded and stepped back outside. Lorcus moved aside the stack of letters, all bearing his family's personal seal, and retrieved the maps. They were rough things, drawn by field cartographers. Later, he'd compare them to the old maps of Caddow, and see what sense could be made between the two. The city had changed much, in the centuries since contact had been lost. He studied the hasty sketches. 'Cisterns, cisterns... Where are they?' he murmured.

'Look, children – it is Sigmar at his labours.'

Lorcus looked up sharply. Vend sat in the corner, smiling.

'Marta,' Lorcus called out.

'Yes, my lord?'

'Never mind about Vend. I've found him.'

'Very good, sir.'

Vend followed the exchange with a bemused expression. 'Looking for me, were you?'

'I am paying you to act as a consultant and I wish to consult.'

Vend spread his hands in a gesture of invitation. 'Ask, and you shall receive.'

'What are your thoughts on the situation?'

Vend grunted and his expression became serious. 'You'll need more men. More than thirty, certainly. Two hundred to start with, maybe more. Not hillmen. You'll need experienced garrison troops. Are the Stormcasts staying?'

'The Lord-Castellants are already setting the foundations for a Stormfort. The engineering gangs will be working day and night for the next few weeks.'

'That'll do, for a time,' Vend said, stroking his chin. 'Can't order them about, obviously, but you chose well. The Hallowed Knights are a bit more... flexible than some of the others. They don't interfere too much.'

'You sound like you've had experience with them before.'

'Not them. Knights Excelsior.' Vend shuddered. 'Not so friendly, them.' He leaned forward, slapping his knees with his hands. 'Enough about that. I hear you've got troggoths in the sewers.'

'Yes. And?'

'What do you want for them? They'd fetch a pretty price in Excelsis. They'll make excellent fodder for the fighting pits.'

'You want me to... sell them?'

Vend leaned forward. 'If it helps, we'll call it a down payment, shall we?' He smiled. 'Plenty of fat Azyrite nobles would love to own such a creature, even if only to kill it and mount it in their foyer. That way they could pretend that they too were at the forefront of Sigmar's glorious crusade. I could make you a deal for the teeth of the dead ones as well, if you can stop the Stormcasts from burning all of them.'

Lorcus stared at Vend. He'd known that there was a going rate on the shadow market for such things, but knowing and seeing it in action were two different things. 'I'll keep it in mind,' he said, after a moment.

Vend shrugged. 'You could also keep your eye out for a few beasties of unusual size. There's always some, lurking in ruins like this. Harpies, chimeras, that sort of thing. Those are worth a pretty mote, to the right buyer.' He rubbed his thumb and finger together. 'And you need money, my friend.

Your war chest is rapidly emptying. Caddow has no realm-stone, no prophecies, nothing special to it. Nothing to attract the right sort of people. You need to think wide and deep, or this expedition is doomed to failure.'

'Your optimism is appreciated.'

'You asked for my opinion.' Vend stood and leaned over Lorcus' desk. He tapped the letters of marque. 'These, for instance. Who are you giving these to?'

'No one, yet.'

'I have a list of names. Unpleasant bastards the lot of them. Aelves, mostly. Scourge privateers. They live to hunt monsters. Give them the letters, let them hunt. They get paid, you get a cut, the region is pacified in half the time. The quicker you clean the beasts out of the ruins, the quicker trade routes can be re-established.'

'And of course, you would receive compensation for the recommendation.'

Vend spread his hands. 'A man has to make a living.'

Lorcus sighed. 'Give me the list.'

'I'll have a scribe draw it up.' Vend flipped a ledger open. 'Speaking of which, you should hire someone to look at your regimental accounts. I can recommend—'

Someone cleared their throat. Vend turned, and paled. Lorcus rose hastily to his feet. 'Lady Cassandora. Is something amiss?'

'No,' the Stormcast said. Her voice was a silken rumble, and it sent a chill down Lorcus' spine. She stepped into the chamber, one hand on the pommel of her runeblade, her helm cradled in the crook of her arm. 'Master Vend. How good to see you again. I'm sure you must have something to do, elsewhere.'

Vend swallowed and nodded. He hurried past her without a backward glance. Cassandora watched him go, and then turned back to Lorcus. 'I wasn't aware you knew Master Vend.'

'It seems he is no stranger to you, either.'

Cassandora smiled. 'Master Vend is very useful.'

'Too useful, sometimes.'

Cassandora nodded. 'That too. Now come. We have important matters to discuss.'

Lorcus caught up his cloak and sword. 'Such as?'

'We are going to win you your city.'

'Mahk says there are troggoths in the tunnels below us,' Khela said.

'I don't care about troggoths below us. I care about the enemy in front of us. These attacks... Do you see the pattern?' Grymn asked, gesturing. 'This one, the one earlier, yesterday, the day before. Different spots on the line, every time.'

Khela nodded. 'They're counting the guns. I saw orruks do something similar, on the Amber Steppes. But why?' She and her fellow Lord-Castellant stood atop one of the Iron-weld's mobile emplacements, watching as a group of warriors launched themselves across a crater-riddled plaza into the very teeth of Azyr's artillery.

It was the third attack of the night. A small sortie, no more than a hundred or so warriors. Savages, mostly, clad in plundered raiment and armour, their flesh marked by obscene symbols. But they were led by a great, bellowing warrior clad in hell-forged armour.

The warrior stood a safe distance from the guns, herding his followers on like sheep. Khela watched him, and wondered how old he was. You could tell, sometimes. The truly ancient ones were always clad in archaic war-plate, their forms barely human. Like trees, warped by the turning of innumerable seasons. 'He's an old one. That style of plate was ancient when I was a girl.'

Grymn nodded. He reached down and stroked the head of his gryph-hound. The creature chirped and scraped his beak against Grymn's gauntlet. 'That explains his tactics. Pre-Lantic Empire, at best. There are tribes in Ghur that show more cunning.' He grunted dismissively. 'They don't learn, you see. Can't. Something about them... about what they are... It's like becoming trapped in tar. Or so I've been told, by one who would know best.'

'Tornus the Redeemed,' Khela said, looking at him. The Knight-Venator was famous, or infamous, depending. Once a servant of Chaos, he now fought for Azyr, clad in the silver of the Hallowed Knights. 'You have spoken to him?'

'Often.' Grymn sighed. 'He remembers how they think. Or, rather, how they don't think. They live in an eternal dream. They fight the same battles, over and over again. That is why we can do this to them.' He indicated the emplacements, and the Ironweld handgunners firing from atop it. 'They do not learn, do not question. The gods command, and they obey. The Dark Gods demand blood and souls – it does not matter whose. It – this – is but a game to them. A hideous game.'

He pointed. 'Look.' Khela saw the ancient warrior hewing at his own followers as they retreated in disarray. The Chaos warrior's roars of frustration echoed over the street. 'They kill each other when no one else is to hand. But for every ten willing to clog our guns with their bodies, there is one who does something unexpected. And that one can kill so many of us, because we have become complacent.' He looked at her. 'They are millions strong, and can afford to lose a hundred times to earn one victory. Because one is all they need.'

'Do you think that's what they're doing here?' Khela asked. The thought of such monstrous calculation repulsed her. 'Sacrificing a thousand, to earn the one?'

'Maybe. They're looking for weak spots in our defences,

I'm sure of it.' Grymn pounded his fist against the top of the emplacement. 'I was hoping to fight idiots, for once.'

'So far they don't seem to have done anything with the information.'

'Something's changed over there. There's a new strategy unfolding here, and it's one I don't like.' He sighed. 'Damn Ramus and his foolishness. And damn Gardus for following him.' He shook his head. 'Fools, the pair of them.'

'You'll get no argument from me, regarding Ramus at least. He is like the child who swallowed the foxberry, and is now being eaten from inside out.'

Grymn looked at her. 'What?' Down below, horns blew, as the enemy readied themselves for a new attack. More bodies, hurled into the guns. The street was shaking with every roar of the cannons, as they spat fire through the gun-slits built into the base of the emplacement. She wondered if there would even be anything left of the city, when they had finished winning it.

'The foxberry,' she said. 'Old Ghyran fable.' She watched as engineers wheeled a cannon back and swiftly cleaned the barrel, in preparation for another salvo.

'Ah.' Grymn looked at his hand. 'Ghyran,' he said, as if that explained everything. He flexed his hand. 'I miss Ghyran.'

'Do you?'

'No. Not in the least.' Grymn frowned. 'Something else I've noticed. No beastkin.'

Khela blinked. 'What?'

'No beastkin. No warherds. They went from participating in every attack to… none. Curious, don't you think?'

'Perhaps we killed them all.' She watched the enemy mass. There was no discipline to their advance. It was a tide of lunatics lapping against a fiery shore. She watched the Chaos warrior, still standing back. Waiting – but for what?

Grymn laughed. 'You know better than that.'

Khela nodded. For every beastman you saw, there were five you didn't. 'Something has changed, as you said.'

'That bodes ill.'

Octarion coughed politely. Khela glanced at Grymn and turned. The Lord-Castellant of the Stormforged nodded in greeting. He had his helm under one arm, exposing a haggard, seamed face. Octarion looked old, even in good light.

'Something's changed,' Grymn said, without preamble.

Octarion nodded. 'Cassandora said much the same.' He peered over the top of the emplacement. 'Maybe they're building a rampart of bodies. I saw the worshippers of the Blood God do as much in Aqshy.'

'She intends to take advantage of it,' Khela said, reading his expression. 'Of whatever is going on over there?' She gestured towards the distant pavilions.

Octarion nodded again. 'That's what she does best. She wants to see you both for a council of war.' He tilted his head, listening to the thump of the guns. 'We should alter the firing patterns. That might confuse any calculations they're making.'

'Assuming they're making any at all,' Grymn said.

'There's no fault in overestimating the enemy's competence,' Khela said. 'If something has changed… If someone new is in charge over there, then we'd best prepare ourselves for a change in their tactics.' She turned back. 'What is he waiting for?'

Grymn followed her gaze. 'Maybe he's just a coward.'

Octarion snorted. 'You know that's the one vice these creatures do not indulge.'

Shouts drew Khela around. She saw that the stones of the street behind the emplacement were buckling and shifting. Engineers scattered, trying to pull their war-engines away from the disturbance. 'What is it?' she called out. 'Is the street collapsing?' That had happened more than once – whole streets dropping away beneath newly erected defences. Caddow itself had claimed more lives than the foe.

A moment later, three troggoths erupted from beneath the street, roaring. Disturbed by the reverberations of the guns, Khela thought at first – then she saw the brands on their flesh and the chains of gold that decorated their skulls and torsos. She knew then what the Chaos warrior had been waiting for. A glance at Grymn showed her that he understood as well.

'I told you,' he said harshly. 'There's always one.'

The troggoths were ungainly creatures, at once froglike and simian, with distorted, fang-filled maws and bulging, fishlike eyes. Long, knobbly arms swatted engineers aside and warty fists slammed down on a cannon, knocking it askew. One of the troggoths vomited a stream of boiling filth across a group of engineers, reducing them to screaming heaps.

The third beast barrelled towards the temporary camp at the other end of the emplacement as the engineers there scrambled to mount a defence.

'Pikes, you fools,' Grymn bellowed. 'Pikes!'

'They're not listening,' Khela said, drawing her helm on.

'I see that. Talon!' Grymn gestured, and his gryph-hound leapt from the emplacement and loped after the third troggoth. He turned to the Ironweld gunners on the emplacement. 'Keep firing, or Sigmar help me, I'll take it out of your hides.'

Khela leapt from the emplacement as one of the troggoths hefted a cannon over its head and hurled it across the street. Engineers scattered. Artisan pistols barked, and impact craters opened on the troggoth's rubbery hide. The beast roared and snatched at an engineer, yanking him off his feet. The creature bit the man's head off and tossed the body aside. Khela cursed and pounded towards the beast, halberd raised.

Her first blow rocked the troggoth on its heels. The second pulped the side of its skull. The troggoth staggered, whining. Undaunted, it swept an arm out, forcing her to duck. It lunged, the wound in its skull already healing. As she backed away, she caught a glimpse of Octarion confronting the second beast, and Grymn charging after the third.

The beast lumbered after her, blubbery mouth champing mindlessly. She interposed her halberd as it closed in, and its great hands closed on either end of the haft. She was driven back, against the bottom of the emplacement. The creature's rank odour caused her eyes to water. It glared at her and leaned forward, seeking to crush her. Khela released her halberd and drove her hand into one of the beast's bulging eyes. With a shout, she tore the gruesome orb from the socket, causing the troggoth to reel back with a high-pitched shriek.

It released her and staggered back, wailing. She cast the eye aside and swung her halberd out, catching the beast in the neck. Hooking it, she dragged it off balance, and toppled it to the ground. The troggoth flailed in agony, but she stood atop it, pinning it down. She thrust the ferrule of her halberd down, striking it between the eyes. Bone crunched as the weighted end of the staff punched through its skull and into its brain.

The troggoth jerked and fell still. Khela reached down through the hole and tore its brain loose, just in case. She'd seen such beasts get up from worse before. She turned, and saw that Octarion, alongside several handgunners, had put down the second beast and that Grymn and Talon had done for the third. From behind her, she heard a hiss, and saw that one of the Slaaneshi warriors was crawling through an unguarded firing slit.

She swung her halberd out, crushing his skull. But there

were more behind him. Atop the emplacement, the handgunners were forced to wield their weapons like clubs.

'The troggoths were a distraction,' Octarion called out, as he helped several engineers drag their cannon out of immediate danger.

'Yes, thank you for pointing out the obvious, Octarion,' Grymn snarled, as he stalked towards the emplacement. There was a roar above, and Khela saw the Chaos warrior clambering over the wall, a brutal-looking axe in his hand. She took a step towards him, but Grymn's shout brought her up short.

'No time for heroics,' he said. 'Let them burn.'

She unhooked her lantern, as he raised his own. Together, they flipped them open, and azure light washed across the emplacement. Octarion joined them a moment later, and the light swelled, filling the street. The Chaos warrior staggered, screaming and clawing at his helm. His followers cowered back, their mutilated flesh bubbling where the light touched it. Some fled, while others collapsed where they stood, their forms burning in the cleansing light. The three Lord-Castellants advanced, driving the enemy back, until only the Chaos warrior remained. He bellowed something – a challenge maybe, or a curse – but slumped, even as the words left him.

Smoke boiled from his armour as Khela climbed the steps of the emplacement. Down below, Grymn and Octarion advanced to the gun-slits. The Chaos warrior had fallen over as she drew near. He clawed weakly for the haft of his axe. Khela kicked the weapon aside, and looked down at him.

'Who were you?' she asked, softly. 'Do you even remember?'

The warrior heaved himself up, with a snarl. He lunged at her. She stepped back, and raised her lantern, bathing him in its glow. He burst into flames and stumbled blindly towards the edge of the emplacement. With a final, despairing scream, he fell. She closed her lantern and turned. Somewhere close by, horns sounded.

More were on the way. Always more.

CHAPTER TWENTY-ONE

THE SILENT CITY

Nagashizzar is a state of mind.

– Whelm Chaell
A Song for Graveyard Flowers

Gardus rose in his saddle and peered across the dusty wastes. They had stopped to rest the gryph-chargers in the lee of a fallen ruin – a scattering of pillars and jumbled stones, with a single jetty of fossilised wood, half buried by dust.

It was possibly an old outpost of Caddow's mercantile empire, now lost and forgotten. Or perhaps one of the nine hundred watchtowers of Nagashizzar, once said to dot these lands. There was water, still, in the iron-plated cistern at the centre of the ruin. Feysha and the other Vanguard-Palladors doled out helms of brackish liquid to their steeds, or else investigated the ruins. Sathphren eased Gwyllth towards Gardus. 'We'll rest here for a bit, then go on.'

Gardus reached out and scratched his steed's head. 'I defer to your wisdom.' Starlight played strangely across the soft dunes, and he thought he heard singing, on the night wind. 'Do you hear that?' he asked, glancing at Sathphren.

The Lord-Aquilor nodded. 'Best not to listen too closely,' he said. He did not elaborate, and Gardus didn't press him for answers. Instead, he concentrated on the dunes, seeking any sign of their quarry.

'It's been three days. We should have caught them by now.'

'It's been four.' Sathphren stretched. 'And we are not trying to catch them.'

Gardus looked at him, startled. 'What?'

'Hunters do not chase prey. Animals chase prey. Hunters go to where prey will be, and wait. That is what we are doing. We know where they are going. Or at least, I do. So we're going to get there first.' He shrugged. 'Simple. The question is, should we?'

Gardus looked at him. 'What do you mean?'

'They tell stories about you, you know. How the Steel Soul entered the realm of the Dark Gods not once, but twice, carrying the light of Azyr into the deepest shadows.'

'One of those times was not by choice.'

Sathphren waved the excuse aside. 'Ramus follows your example, whether he admits it or not. Do we go to stop him – or to aid him?'

Gardus shook his head. 'I don't know,' he admitted. 'I know only that we must pursue him.' He sighed. 'I think... I think it is not the same. When I entered the plague gardens, I was not acting on my own. Sigmar's hand was at my shoulder. He wished me to go, so I went.'

'Perhaps his hand is also on Ramus' shoulder.'

'Then why deny him so often?'

'Better to ask why send him here, into the very mouth of temptation?' Sathphren shrugged. 'There are some who believe

Sigmar tests us. They believe that the soul is a blade, tested and sharpened by the hand of the God-King.'

'And what do you believe, Swiftblade?'

Sathphren was silent for a moment. 'I think Sigmar is a hunter. And like any hunter, he waits for his moment. Let the arrow fly too soon, or too late, and you miss your prey.' He chuckled. 'Do you know what the most annoying thing about you is, Steel Soul?'

Gardus peered. 'No, but I have the distinct impression you're going to tell me.'

'All the questions,' Sathphren said. 'You question the way the suns rise, the way your shadow falls, what you're meant to do, what you're meant to be. Questions and more questions. You handle faith like a dog with a bone.'

'Is that a compliment or an insult?'

Sathphren laughed. 'It's an observation. Your faith shines for all to see, but you turn certainty to doubt. You think yourself in circles, worrying over what you know to be right. Now, for example. You know we must follow Ramus, but you worry about why.'

'And you don't?'

'No. We'll figure that out when we get there.'

Gardus stared at him. Then, he gave a rueful laugh. 'I suppose we will at that.' He stopped as the wind picked up. Dust rose in swirling clouds as the gryph-chargers screeched in alarm.

Sathphren cursed.

'What is it?' Gardus asked.

'Something's coming.' The Lord-Aquilor turned in his saddle and whistled sharply. Around them, his Vanguard-Palladors stiffened to attention. They were in their saddles in moments. Gryph-chargers squalled, pawing at the dust. They scented something on the wind, and they were clearly agitated.

'Are we under attack?' Feysha asked. She urged her steed towards them.

'Not if we move quickly. Come on.' Sathphren thumped Gwyllth's ribs and the gryph-charger shot away from the ruins. Gardus and the others followed close on her heels, their steeds moving swifter than the mortal eye could follow.

'Don't look back,' Sathphren called out. Despite this warning, Gardus turned in his saddle, looking back at the ruins.

He felt a chill as something massive wavered into view near the dock. It came in silence, sliding over the dust. An ancient barque, with tattered sails and a shattered hull. Witch-lights danced across its rails, but no crew was visible. It slowed as it reached the dock, and for a moment, Gardus thought he saw indistinct shapes moving to and fro across the jetty. Pale hints of human movement that appeared and faded at random.

Time seemed to slow as he watched. He felt the moment become elastic and stretch. The sound of his steed's claws striking the ground became as thunder, and the harsh rasp of its breath was like the scrape of a whetstone across a sword. He felt cold – a bone-deep chill that filled him from fingertips to spine.

There were shapes on the deck now – not human. Not mortal. He could not perceive them clearly, but he could hear… music. Singing. The same singing he'd heard earlier, he thought. The passengers flickered with an unearthly light, and descended in an orderly line down a gangplank to the dock. One stopped at the deck rail and turned. Eyes like dying stars met his own, and his heart felt as if it were being squeezed in his chest. He heard a voice, calling to him out of the dark, calling him back.

They had come to see *him*. They had sailed across centuries, all for this moment. He knew it, though he could not say how or why, only that it was so. Whispers fluttered across the edge of his hearing and he strained to catch the words. Why did their voices sound so familiar? The cold hand on his heart tightened. He felt himself hauling on the reins, as if to turn his steed, but the gryph-charger resisted, with a screech. The sound sawed through him, driving back the whispers. He wrenched his gaze away from the ruins.

The wind rose, casting up waves of dust, and the ruins were momentarily lost to sight. When the dust cleared, the ship was gone, as if it had never been there at all. The cold faded, as did the compulsion to return. Gardus turned back around, unsettled. He saw that Sathphren was watching him. The Lord-Aquilor rode close beside him, and Gardus realised that Sathphren had been ready to grab the reins from his hands. 'I said not to look.'

'My... apologies.' After a moment, Gardus asked, 'What was it? A ghost?'

'A memory,' Sathphren said. 'These wastes are full of them – forgotten moments, one tumbling over the next with every gust of wind. There will be more of them, the closer we get to Nagashizzar.' He bent forward, over Gwyllth's neck, urging the animal to greater speed. 'It's best to avoid them, when possible, else you risk being caught up in their wake.'

Gardus didn't reply. He still felt the lingering chill on his heart, and wondered at it. He'd felt no malign intent in the whispers, no fear... only a strange sort of calm. As if he were being called home, by old friends. An enchantment, perhaps. He glanced back, almost against his will, but the ruins, and whatever secrets they held, were soon lost to sight.

Ramus looked back, across the dunes. There was no sign of their pursuers. No sign of any pursuit at all. 'Where are you, Gardus?' he murmured. He expected to see the glint of silver on the horizon at any moment. But it had been almost three days. Or perhaps more. Time was a strange thing, here. It flowed like water, and eddied in places. He looked at Sagittus. 'How many days?'

'Six,' the Judicator-Prime said.

'I count three,' Ramus said, looking at him. Sagittus shrugged. 'Shyish,' he said.

Ramus laughed. 'Indeed. Perhaps we should ask the native. Well, Mannfred? How many days has it been?'

The vampire, sitting at his accustomed spot on the rail, turned. 'What is time to an immortal?' He peered up at the darkening sky. 'It's been almost four days, as the crow flies. One of them was slightly longer than the others, however.'

'Four days. Is that all?' Ramus frowned. 'I expected… months. Weeks, at least.'

'I told you, Nagashizzar is vast. It stretched to all corners of the realm. Where we go is but the farthest corner of the black pyramid.'

'The what?'

Mannfred smiled. 'A jest. It is what we Mortarchs sometimes call Nagashizzar… the black pyramid.' He leaned forward. 'You see, Nagash built a pyramid. Only he did not simply build it in one spot. He built it everywhere. One pyramid, but with nine sides, each visible in one of the ninefold Nagashizzars.'

Ramus stared at him. 'Why?'

Mannfred shrugged and sat back. 'Who knows? Vanity? Such are the unknowable whims of a god, I suppose.' He gestured over his shoulder, back the way they'd come. 'The great ziggurat of Caddow was carved in its honour, as were the smaller pyramids of Gez and Harrowshank. It was, as the saying goes, the style at the time.'

Ramus shook his head. Behind him, he heard Osanus begin to sing. The Knight-Heraldor had a need to fill the air with noise. He had been singing since the fight with the daemons, as if in challenge.

'*Gilead was an aelven king... of whom the harpers sadly sing... whose realm was between the forests and the sea...*' Osanus sang, his voice echoing out over the wastes. Ramus growled softly, irritated despite himself.

Mannfred tapped his knee, seemingly enjoying the tune. 'And here I thought all your sort could do was fight. You Stormcasts are full of surprises.'

'*His sword was sharp... his arrows keen...*'

Ramus did not look at him. 'I had thought you would understand us better, by now.'

Mannfred frowned. 'I understand *you*, at least. Failure eats at you, like acid.'

'*For into darkness tumbled his light...*'

'Enough, Osanus. Enough.' Ramus thumped the deck with his staff.

The Knight-Heraldor looked at him. 'Would mine brother prefer a duardin song, eh? Or a wail of mine own kinband?' He clapped his big hands together. 'I shall sing of the worm's thunder, yes.' He looked around. 'Very stirring, for mine brothers!'

'I would prefer no songs at all, Knight-Heraldor.'

'No songs?' Osanus seemed aghast. 'But this is a holy quest!'

Mannfred sniggered, and Ramus thrust up a hand, silencing the vampire. 'Yes, but there is a time and a place, brother. Now is not it.'

'No?'

'No.'

Osanus smiled widely and clapped Ramus on the shoulder. 'You will tell me when is the time, yes? Then, I shall sing!' He turned towards the rowers' benches. 'Someone move. Mighty Osanus would ply the oars!'

'Mighty Osanus isn't the brightest star in Sigmar's heavens, is he?' Mannfred murmured, coming to stand beside Ramus.

'Do you know what Osanus said, when I told him what my plan was?'

Mannfred smiled. 'No, but I'm sure it was amusing.'

'He told me to cut off your head and stick it in a cage, because you didn't need a body to guide us, only your tongue. Offered to do it himself.' Ramus looked at him. 'Sometimes, I suspect Osanus is the wisest of all of us.'

Mannfred blinked. 'Yes, well.' He looked away.

Ramus smiled and turned towards the prow of the barque. 'The wind is changing. I can taste more than just dust on it.' It smelled of smoke and blood. Of death, sudden and violent. The smell of war.

'Smoke,' Mannfred said. 'Ashigaroth scents it as well.' Ramus glanced back to where Mannfred's steed lay sprawled near the mast. Its tail curled and thrashed, and he could hear the great bellows of its lungs working.

'Is that thing even alive?'

'Much in the way you are,' Mannfred said, fondly. 'A shard of something greater, beaten into a new shape and girt in iron.' He made a fist. 'And all mine.'

'Until Nagash decides to take it from you.'

Mannfred looked at him. 'And we were getting along so well.'

'We are not getting along. We despise one another.'

'Yes, but honestly and openly. There are worse ways to conduct an alliance.'

'Speaking from experience again?'

Mannfred sneered. 'Always. And such is the bounty of my wisdom, that I offer it to you freely.' He gestured. 'You and I are bound together, like it or not. We are joined in a glorious endeavour. Why, some might even call us heroes...'

'No one would ever confuse you for a hero, vampire.'

Mannfred snorted. 'What you don't know about me could fill a book, Stormcast.'

'Then illuminate me.'

'I could have been a good man, once,' Mannfred said, after a moment. 'I think – I dream, sometimes, of another world. Of a time when my path was not set before me. When the chains of fate did not weigh me down.'

'Spare me,' Ramus said. 'Introspection does not suit you, vampire.'

'It suits neither of us,' Mannfred said, looking at him. 'Yet we continue to gnaw at the roots of past decisions. In this case, it is the same decision, if from opposite ends. We abandoned him.'

'I did not abandon him.'

'You did. As surely as I did. Else you would have stormed the gates of Nagashizzar long before now.' Mannfred laughed. 'We abandoned him, Ramus.'

Ramus looked away. 'But no longer.'

'No. No longer.' Mannfred ran his hands over his bald pate. 'If I had saved him in Helstone, things would be different. I like to think that.'

'He would still have died. All men die.'

Mannfred snorted. 'Maybe not. Maybe he would have accepted the gift of un-life. Better a blighted soul than a broken body.'

It was Ramus' turn to laugh. 'You don't honestly believe that.'

Mannfred frowned. 'No. But at least I would have given him a choice. Tell me, Ramus – did Sigmar give you a choice? Do you even remember the moment, or who you were, before you were draped in silver and self-righteousness?'

Ramus hesitated. 'No.'

'Pity. It might have made you more interesting.' Mannfred

looked out over the rail. 'We are close. I can feel the shadow of the city on my soul.'

'Good.' Ramus sighed and looked up. Night had fallen swiftly, and through the clouds of dust he could just make out the stars, shining in the dark. 'Is this what you wanted of me?' he asked, softly. 'Or have I made another mistake?'

Mannfred frowned. 'He cannot hear you here, Stormcast. This realm is not his. It will never be his, no matter how many underworlds you colonise or cities you plunder. Nagash is all, and all are eventually one in Nagash.'

'You do not sound pleased by that.'

Mannfred laughed. 'I am not! Do you think I look forward to that black silence, stretching for an infinity? Nagash will make a graveyard of every realm. He will make order out of disorder, and every soul will be a cog in his great machine...' He trailed off. 'But I am his servant, his slave, as you said. My path is predestined, as is yours. We are but pawns of the gods, playing out a game whose end we shall never see.'

Ramus nodded. 'The expected answer, from one of your kind.'

Mannfred looked at him. 'And what is your answer, eh? Are you serving Sigmar or yourself? Is this what he wants? If so... what are you but a puppet? And if it is not, what are you but a failure?'

Ramus looked away. For a moment, he wondered if the vampire was right. If all of this, all he had undergone, had been predestined from the beginning. If every failure was a part of some great plan he could not see, or understand. He looked up. The clouds cleared for an instant, just one, and he saw the stars overhead.

'Once... once, there was only the dark,' he began. 'And then, there was light. The light of a single star. And from that star came others. One became a hundred. A thousand.' He pointed at the sky. 'Look, vampire. See. The eternal void is riven by light. For every star that is snuffed out, another is born. That is my answer. Whatever is happening, whether it is planned, or not… we are *winning*.'

Mannfred shook his head. 'You see victory in– in starlight? You're madder than I thought, Stormcast.'

'Maybe. But better to be mad, than to be without hope.' Ramus leaned against his staff. 'Better to lose yourself in a story – a dream – than to walk knowingly to a bitter ending. At least in the dream, there is the chance of victory, however slim.'

'Is that what this is, then? A dream?' Mannfred smiled a slow, cruel smile. 'Do you imagine Sigmar will forgive you for your trespasses, and that all will be as it once was?'

'That is not my dream,' Ramus said, softly. 'I dream only that my friend will stand beside me again, and that the world will once more make sense.'

Mannfred fell silent. Ramus looked at him, and knew, in that moment, that the vampire understood his meaning. Perhaps more than either of them cared to admit. Mannfred sighed, and looked out over the tides of dust. 'That is a good dream,' he said, finally. 'But it is one I cannot share.'

'Then why help me?'

Mannfred laughed. 'I told you… I owe him a debt. And I cannot bear its weight any longer.' He tapped the side of his skull. 'I have a head full of ghosts, Stormcast. I would lessen that number by one, if I can.' He turned. 'There,' he said, softly. 'Nagashizzar.'

Ramus turned. His breath caught in his throat as he saw it. At first, he thought it was a ruin like the thousands of others he'd seen. Then, he saw the statues rising out of the dust – enormous, seated giants, with skulls for heads. Nagash, staring west.

Great pylons of stone dotted the dunes, marking the path. The dust-barque navigated them slowly, and the serpentine curve of the wharfs became visible through the clouds of dust. Pillars and broken temples, half hidden. And above it all – a ziggurat. A pyramid. Three times the height of the one in Caddow, and so wide as to fill the horizon – all but impossible to comprehend. A black mountain of stone and stairs, falling upwards. But there was something wrong with it. Something he could not quite put into words.

'Is it… upside down?'

Mannfred chuckled. 'That depends entirely on your perspective.' He looked out at the city, and his smile faded. 'Nagashizzar is nothing but a temple – albeit one the size of a city. Nine cities. Even then, in the days before it all went wrong, it was nothing more than a single, grandiose monument to Nagash's ego. Now, if anything, it is worse.' Mannfred spoke softly, as if afraid to attract the attention of the ruins around them.

Ramus thought he saw amethyst light flare in the depths of a statue's eyes. Will o' the wisps of purple and green danced in the ruins, and he could hear, if faintly, the sounds of war. 'Archaon's forces wage a never-ending siege.'

'And you thought to break it?'

'For a moment, at least.' Mannfred turned away. 'Just a moment. Until it all begins again. And again and again.' He fell silent. Ramus almost felt pity for him, in that moment. However much he did not wish to admit it, they were alike in one fundamental way – for them, the war would only end when their god decided that it had.

'Mine brother,' Osanus said, from behind him. Ramus turned. Stormcasts readied themselves on the deck, while others plied the oars. 'We must speak.'

'Are they ready?' Ramus asked.

'Soon.'

'We must be ready. There is no telling what awaits us.'

'Did you ever listen to the tale of Gardus, in the gardens of plague?' Osanus asked, softly. 'Osanus thinks that you did not, brother.'

'I do not have time for cryptic questions, brother – come to your point, and swiftly.'

'Stories repeat. Only the endings change. You seek to do as he did, but you have made an error.' Osanus eyed the approaching wharfs with a grim expression. Impatient, Ramus gesticulated.

'Well? What is my error?'

'You are not Gardus.'

'I am well aware, thank you.'

'I do not think that you are.' Osanus looked at him. 'You see only the similarities in the story. Not the differences. It was a test of faith. Gardus had faith, and so came out victorious. But you, brother…'

Ramus stared at him. 'Me what?'

'Where is your faith, brother?' Osanus smiled sadly. 'Gardus questions, but never loses faith. You lost yours long ago, I think. This is not about Tarsus. Not solely. It is about fixing what you see as broken. You think we are broken.'

'I… I do not…' Ramus trailed off. He watched as the great stone pillars marking the path to the wharfs slid past, silent and morbid. 'Aren't we?'

Osanus gripped him by the shoulder. Ramus looked at him, and Osanus shrugged. 'That is your purview, not mine. Mighty Osanus is but a singer of songs. Not a judge of souls. Still… something to think about, eh?'

'You could have picked a better time.'

Wood scraped against stone. Mannfred stood.

'We're here,' he said, in a low voice.

CHAPTER TWENTY-TWO

SLAVES OF DARKNESS

To say that those who serve the Ruinous Powers are
of one mind is to say that an orruk and a duardin
might find common ground. While possible, it is,
at best, unlikely.

– Karl Logrim
Memoirs of a Witch-Finder

'Beautiful, is it not?' Bakhos said. Around him, the broken husk of Nagashizzar spread out – a sea of pillars, fallen temples and shattered statuary. A monument to the vanity of a demigod, unrolled like some immense carpet across the dusty wastes.

'You see beauty in strange places,' Lemerus said.

'The eye of the beholder, yes?' Bakhos laughed and reached down into his saddlebag for a skin of wine. It had taken them six days – as near as he could tell – to reach Nagashizzar. A good omen, he thought, six being the number of the Absent

God. Philosophers had taught him that, among other bits of sacred numerology. 'My own wife was acclaimed the greatest beauty in the land – but only after our wedding.'

'Your… wife?'

'Does that surprise you?' Bakhos smirked. 'I was a king, Lemerus. Is it not fitting then that I have a queen?'

'Have,' Lemerus said. 'She still lives, then?'

'She– no. No,' Bakhos said, after a moment. Old memories rose up, as painful as the first time he'd experienced them. Her face, her eyes – the sound of her last cry. It ratcheted through him, and he bent forward in his saddle. 'I desired her, and I made her mine. That is the heart of the story, the only thread that matters. She was mine, and death took her. So I came to find her, leading my phalanxes…' He trailed off, lost in that moment. Glorious and foolish, all at once. He had left them all in the dust, one way or another. The phalanxes of Semele were nothing now, save memory and regret.

Lemerus looked at him. 'And?' The champion sounded eager. Stories, like memories, were a form of currency among the daemonkin. 'What happened?'

'I failed. Death cannot be beaten. Not with weapons.' Bakhos twitched his head, trying to shake the webs of memory away. 'I made a bargain with Archaon. I would serve him until he found her soul.'

'But you have left Caddow,' Lemerus said.

'And yet, I have reason – one enemy goes to make common cause with another! A thing that cannot be allowed. If Archaon is here, he will thank me. And if he is not, well, then he need never know.' He tipped back his wine skin and drained the last dregs. 'Besides, Caddow is in good enough hands.'

'The beast,' Lemerus muttered.

'Indeed. Who better? The monotony of the task will not

bother such a dull-witted creature, and its aggression will help keep the foe penned in.'

'And it angers Etax.'

Bakhos smiled. 'So it does.' He turned. 'Ah. There – look. Between those pillars. See?' He pointed towards the distant base of the black pyramid that dominated Nagashizzar's skyline. Its shadow shrouded this part of the city in a semi-permanent twilight. At its base was a high gatehouse, banded on either side by two massive stone sphinxes with skulls for heads. The gatehouse was immense, the equal of any great citadel, but it stood alone save for the sphinxes. To either side of it stretched the edges of an abyss that plunged down into lightless depths.

Bakhos knew that the abyss encircled the pyramid in its entirety – an impossible expanse, traversable only via the great bridges of stone which extended from the gatehouses like the one in the distance. Those gatehouses, and the bridges beyond, were defended by the legions of Nagash. The rest of the city was left to the invaders, or the unbound dead.

'The gates of the underworld,' Bakhos said.

'It is unguarded,' Lemerus murmured.

'It only seems so from here. I–'

His steed reared with a shrill scream as an arrow sprouted from the dust before him. More arrows fell, creating an artful barrier between his forces and the path through the ruins ahead. Bakhos grinned as he fought to bring his mount back under control. 'You have my attention,' he called out.

His surviving eunuchs bunched up around him, drawing their weapons. Lemerus hissed an order, and its warriors spread out, readying themselves. Bakhos gestured. 'Be still. They don't mean us any harm – do you, my friends?' he called out. 'We are all servants of the Three-Eyed King, after all!'

'Above us,' Lemerus murmured, as it urged its horse closer to him. Bakhos glanced up and saw shapes crouch-walk across the top of a looming archway. Savages in buckskins and scaly hide-armour. Ash coated their bare flesh, and they carried bows.

More shapes lurked in the ruins around them – warriors in crimson silks and brass cuirasses, wearing spiral helms and masks wrought in the shape of daemons leering. They advanced slowly, barbed spears balanced on the rims of their round shields. Behind them, malformed creatures clad in rags and brass chains, their heads sealed in iron-bound boxes, crept closer, trailing clawed hands across the stones.

There were others – dozens more, no two alike, save in their obvious devotion to the Ruinous Powers. Flyblown blightkings stumped forward, the stink of their maggoty flesh causing the horses to paw the ground. Warriors clad in bejewelled armour and iridescent robes watched Bakhos over the fluted barrels of arcane jezzails.

'What have we here? A true conclave of champions, eh?' Bakhos slid from the saddle and plucked the arrow from the ground. He examined it and tossed it aside. 'How interesting. Who's in charge here? Quickly, quickly, some of us have things to do.'

'I am,' a deep voice growled. 'Who are you?' A tall, gangling warrior, clad in crimson war-plate that resembled raw flesh, stepped into the open. He wore a helm shaped like a daemon's skull, and a mane of dirty white hair spilled outwards from behind it. He carried a heavy, cleaver-like axe in one hand, its blade marked with sigils that glowed faintly. A deathbringer of Khorne, Bakhos thought, a champion of the Blood God.

'Who are *you*?' Bakhos countered.

The warrior stared at him for a moment. Then, 'Stulakh.'

Bakhos waited. When no appellation seemed forthcoming, he gestured. 'Is that it? Just… Stulakh?'

'It is my name.' Stulakh raised his axe. 'Tell me yours.'

'Bakhos.'

'Is that it?'

'It is enough,' Bakhos said. 'Do you speak for the Three-Eyed King? I see the mark of Varanspire on your war-plate, and that of your followers. I too serve the Grand Marshal.'

'Easy enough to say.'

'And yet, who would dare claim such, were it not the truth?'

Stulakh paused, thinking this over. Bakhos felt a flush of impatience. Finally, Stulakh nodded. 'Come. We talk. Just you.' He turned and made his way back through his warriors. With a warning glance at Lemerus, Bakhos followed.

Stulakh led him up a set of crumbling spiral steps to a free-standing space that had once been an enclosed structure of some sort. Now it was open to the elements, the stone floors covered in heaps of dust. Rusty gibbets hung from the shattered roof beams. Inside each, a deadwalker twisted and fumbled, moaning softly.

'You are leader of the garrison?' Bakhos asked, without preamble. Stulakh pushed one of the gibbets and watched it spin slowly.

'One of them. There are many.'

'The ruins are silent. When last I was here, they were full of the noise of war.'

Stulakh gestured. 'To the south and the west, today. The fight… moves. The enemy is everywhere. They come from catacombs and pits. They creep in the dark. Warbands vanish in the night, and return empty of life but still hungry for battle.' He banged the gibbet, and the deadwalker inside thrashed, moaning. 'But still, we fight.'

'Archaon would be pleased. Where is he?'

'Not here. Why did you come?'

Bakhos paused. 'We've come to reinforce you.' The lie came easily to his lips. He looked towards the distant pillars and the bridge beyond, stretching to the strange contours of the black ziggurat. It seemed so small a thing to be so well defended. 'Though I cannot imagine why we are needed to lay siege to a bridge.'

'Nekroheim,' Stulakh grunted. The deathbringer bared jagged teeth in a grisly smile. 'The black pyramid is its entrance.'

'The greatest of the underworlds,' Bakhos murmured. He'd heard the stories, but never thought it was so close. His hand slipped to his sword. Was she there, then? Across that bridge, at last? Even if not, he had no doubt this was the road his quarry sought. The only question that remained was whether or not he had beaten them to their destination. 'Why do you not attack now, then?' He looked around. 'Why huddle in these ruins, accosting your fellow warriors? The bridge is there. I see no siege engines, no armies massed for the attack. I see no defenders, even.'

Stulakh growled. 'Ordered to keep watch only. Archaon comes soon. He will lead the assault.' His displeasure at this was obvious. Bakhos smiled.

'Of course. When is he coming?'

'Soon.'

Bakhos nodded. That could mean hours, or days or months. Centuries, even, given how time flowed in this realm. 'Perhaps we should begin without him.'

Stulakh shook his head. 'I swore an oath before his throne.' As he turned away, his voice was almost wistful. 'Archaon commands, Stulakh obeys. That is Khorne's will.'

Bakhos sighed. 'So it is. But I serve the will of another.' His sword was in his hand an instant later. Stulakh spun, a snarl rippling from him as he heard the hiss of steel. Bakhos' first blow tore the axe from Stulakh's hand. His second opened the brute's throat and sent his helm clattering away. Stulakh staggered, one hand clamped to his torn jugular. With a guttural roar, he swept his free hand out, catching Bakhos on the chin.

Bakhos stumbled back, ears ringing. Stulakh followed him, blood streaming between his fingers, turning the dust to mud. Down below, he could see his warriors surging to meet Stulakh's. The sound of fighting filled the air. He needed to end this quickly, while there was still an army left. He avoided his opponent's next clumsy blow and rammed his sword through a gap in the deathbringer's war-plate. He twisted the blade and tore it loose.

Stulakh sank down, wheezing. Bakhos stepped back and raised his sword over the deathbringer's exposed neck. 'My apologies, friend. But needs must.'

It took two blows to remove Stulakh's head, in the end. When it was done, Bakhos retrieved the gory trophy and raised it. 'Hold,' he cried out. Then, more loudly, 'Hold!'

Down below, the fighting slowed. Lemerus and the others retreated. Warriors turned, necks craned to see. Bakhos flung Stulakh's head down among them. 'By the ancient rites of Varanspire and the laws of all the gods, I claim my opponent's domain – and all within it – for my own. Will any here argue with me?'

Silence fell. Bakhos smiled and nodded. 'Good. Now… ready yourselves. I have an underworld to besiege.'

'Where is the beast?'

The voice of Etax's translator echoed through the silent pavilion. Without Bakhos, there was no music, no debauchery, here.

Just silence. Chaell looked around, meeting the gazes of the champions he'd summoned. More than thirty of the greatest warriors ever to walk the realms, and all of them angry at him.

It was *invigorating*. But also worrying. Chaell accounted himself a good warrior. But he wasn't good enough to fight his way through all of them, much less Etax. The malformed champion sat on Bakhos' throne, his translators crouched by his feet like hounds. That alone told Chaell that things had taken a turn for the worse, and swiftly.

Etax had wasted no time. Then, knowing Bakhos, he hadn't expected it to. Ghosteater had been used to prod Etax into making his move. Bakhos expected Etax to tame the beast-herds and ravage the enemy – or die in the attempt. Either way, a problem was solved. When Bakhos returned, if he returned, he would simply remove Etax's head and retake his throne. Backed, no doubt, by Archaon.

Such had always been the way of it. An eternal rut, and all of them following it blindly to their predestined end. But Chaell had begun to wonder if that was as it should be. Just because it was, didn't mean it must be. Slaanesh was a patron of the transgressive, as well as the hedonistic. The Absent God encouraged his followers to flout and upend the rites and traditions that bound a soul to mediocrity. To seek something more than the commonplace.

And yet here they were, once again angry that the world was not bending into a familiar shape. He looked around, suddenly annoyed with them. They'd grown fat on easy victories and unearned debauches, and forgotten the pleasure to be had in loss. They learned nothing, wanted to learn nothing. And so, they would perish.

Chaell cleared his throat. 'He is... late.' He had no idea where Ghosteater was, though he dearly wished it were otherwise.

The beastman – all of the beastmen, in fact – had seemingly vanished. Even those that had served Hulmean and the other fallen warlords had slipped away.

'He steals the Lord Etax's chattel,' one of the youthful interpreters murmured. 'Beasts branded with mighty Etax's sigil have fled. Others have lost their warriors as well.' Etax gestured and other warlords nodded grimly. 'Beasts serve men, Chaell the Unborn. That is the way of it. The will of all the gods.'

'Perhaps the gods have changed their minds,' Chaell said.

'The hedge-witches are dead – or have fled,' a chieftain growled, baring golden fangs. 'Ghosts haunt our camps, and prey on our slaves.'

Chaell hesitated. He had not known about the witches. 'How did they die?'

'What does it matter? Something savaged them as they slept,' one of Etax's interpreters snapped. 'Hungry beasts, perhaps. Without them, the entrails cannot be read. We walk blind into the future.'

'Is that fear in your voice?' Chaell asked. 'I thought only Bakhos gave credence to the mutterings of sorcerers. Is mighty Etax not brave enough to take the world day by day?' He laughed. 'Even the beast can do that.'

'The beast is a fool,' Etax's interpreter shot back. 'It sends us to our deaths – and for what? Where is the glory we were promised, Chaell?' Warlords and chieftains murmured at this. Chaell could read their dissatisfaction on their faces, in the set of their bodies. They were impatient. Bakhos had forced patience on them. But Bakhos wasn't here. They wanted an excuse – a reason. An opportunity.

Chaell frowned. 'There for the taking, unless you are blind as well as dumb, Etax. Shall we find you a slave to see for you, as well as one to speak?'

Etax chortled. 'The Lord Etax sees well enough,' his slave said. 'The Lord Etax sees you, Chaell. He wonders where the beast you have sworn yourself to is, at this moment? Why is it not here, with us? Why is it not leading us in glorious battle?'

'A good question. Shall I go ask and him?'

'Perhaps the Lord Etax shall go with you.'

'That is not necessary,' Chaell said, hurriedly. He heard the rattle of weapons and the creak of armour. Chieftains moved, cutting off avenues of retreat.

'Do not be a fool, Chaell,' one of the interpreters said, softly. 'The Lord Etax has use for a factotum such as you. Your lack of ambition is your saving grace.' Etax gestured and gurgled. His translators nodded in unison, and one said, 'The Lord Etax would offer you a place at his side. Serve him as he has served Bakhos, and he will elevate you to the limits of your desire.'

'And if I refuse?'

'Then he will kill you and scatter your parts from his chariot, as he goes to do what Bakhos refused to do and what the beast could not. But first, he will kill the beast and mount its head on his banner pole.'

'That will be more difficult than you think, Etax. Ghosteater is cunning.' Chaell backed towards the entrance to the pavilion. He glanced to the left and saw a brazier. It was burning merrily, lit by Etax's slaves. The pavilion stank of old wine. It would catch fire quickly. 'Would you really fight a war on two fronts?'

'The Lord Etax will fight on as many fronts as there are stars in the sky, and emerge victorious,' the translator half sang. Chaell nodded.

'Of course. How silly of me.' He spun, caught up the brazier and hurled it like a spear towards Etax. He didn't wait to see what happened. He hit the entrance and ran, moving smoothly.

For a moment, he considered finding the closest horse and

escaping. There was nothing for him, here. He had little ambition, and no urge to lose himself in battle. But he owed a debt – one he would pay. Ghosteater had saved him, and there was little Chaell valued more than his own life.

If Ghosteater were warned, perhaps something might yet be salvaged.

The fire roared up from the pit, casting an orange glow across the broken stones. The ruin lay on the far edge of the city, near the pavilions of the Blessed Ones. Once part of the city wall, it was now nothing more than a circle of standing stones. Ghosteater had taken it for his own. Etax and the other champions hadn't argued.

Beastmen basked in the warmth, sprawled around the fire, jugs of Bakhos' wine clutched in their hairy paws. Ghosteater watched them as they growled and muttered among themselves. They were his chosen subordinates. The chieftains and champions of those warherds most loyal to him, after the winnowing of the past few days.

Some were newcomers to the city, their flesh still marked with the brands of their former masters. He had sent Wyrmhoof and Blacktongue among the warherds that served the Blessed Ones and had them whisper the forbidden word – freedom.

In the coming days, he would begin to teach them. To show them new and better ways of waging war. Some of them would learn. Those that couldn't – or wouldn't – would be culled in battle. Something new was being born here.

Ghosteater tore a chunk of meat from the bloody mass hanging above the fire and bit into it. Redness stained his jaws and spilled down his chest as he ate. Cooked meat tasted strange. Not unpleasant, exactly, but... odd.

Wait until you learn the art of spices, Herst murmured. *In the proper hands, even the basest ingredients become a work of art.*

Ghosteater grunted and took another bite. The scholar's ghost had become the loudest of the voices in his head. Once, that might have annoyed him. Now, he found a confusing pleasure in the dead man's lessons. He had even sent scouts out into the ruins, seeking the ancient libraries of Caddow. Now, piles of books and scrolls littered the ground, many with pages missing. Herst read them to him, filling his head with new thoughts.

It is strange. I had many students in life. But in death, I have found my best one. And he's not even human. Fate is a mocker.

Ghosteater chuckled hoarsely and tore a length of bone from the mass. Thick strips of muscle and meat shrouded it, and he growled in pleasure as he took a bite. The hedge-witch had been plump, fattened on the scraps of the Blessed Ones' tables. His newest warriors had brought them as gifts – witches and seers. None of which he had any need for. But even so, they had their uses.

The ghosts shifted within him, muttering disconsolately. They did not like it when he ate man-flesh, except for one or two, who seemed amused by it. Herst was one of these.

I am not so much amused as I am philosophically resigned. You are a beast, and lack the morals of a man. Those may come in time, of course. Every day brings new lessons to the willing student.

Ghosteater turned as a scout slunk into the firelight. The ungor was scrawny, and eyed the meat hungrily. Ghosteater growled softly. 'Speak.'

'They come,' the ungor said, shuffling nervously on his hooves. 'The silver ones and the fire-throwers. They fly on wings of lightning.'

A murmur of concern rippled around the fire. Ghosteater

waved them to silence. 'Good. Spread the word. No fighting. Let them pass.'

'Let them…?' a gor growled. The beastman rose, goatish features twisted in an expression of bewilderment. 'They attack!'

Ghosteater turned. He considered the gor. There had been no challenge in his words. Only confusion. 'Yes,' he said. 'But not us.'

'So… that is how it is, is it?'

Chaell's voice echoed among the stones. Beastmen made to rise, snorting and snarling. Ghosteater stilled them with a gesture. Chaell had approached from downwind. The Unborn was more cunning than he appeared.

'Come to the fire, if you wish to speak,' Ghosteater growled.

Chaell stepped into the light. The soft hues of his war-plate seemed washed out in the glow of the flames as he approached. 'I came to warn you. Now I wonder why I bothered.' He looked around, his unlined features stiff with anger.

'What warning?' Ghosteater asked. He turned back to the fire.

'Etax has lost patience. Too many warriors litter the ruins. Our numbers shrink by the day, and we have nothing to show for it. Etax comes for your head. The other warlords will rally to him.'

'Not many left, now,' Ghosteater said, idly.

'No,' Chaell said. 'But enough to paint these ruins red. These attacks – you've been feeding us to the enemy, one warband at a time, haven't you? Just like Bakhos, only worse.'

Ghosteater turned from the fire and looked up at the Chaos warrior. He offered Chaell the bone he'd been gnawing on. There was still some meat on it. 'Hungry?' he growled.

Chaell slapped it from his hand. 'Answer my question.'

The others looked up, nostrils flaring. Warning growls filled the air, and Chaell looked around, suddenly aware of the danger he was in. Ghosteater let him worry for a few moments longer, then rose unhurriedly to his feet. 'Yes,' he said.

'Why?'

Ghosteater gave a rumbling laugh. 'They want to fight. I let them.'

'They are idiots,' Chaell said, his voice harsh. 'You are not. You throw your army away – for what?'

'Not my army,' Ghosteater said. 'Bakhos' army. Your army.'

Chaell licked his lips. 'He put you in command.'

Ghosteater laughed again and tore the remainder of the meat from his bone. He chewed thoughtfully. 'No,' he said, a moment later. He broke the bone and dabbed at the marrow inside with a claw. 'He made me leader. Different.'

Chaell shook his head. 'You don't understand.'

Ghosteater tossed the bone aside. 'I understand,' he growled. 'The gods need blood, yours or ours. I choose yours. We will not be meat. But someone must be. That is you.' He spread his arms and bared his fangs. 'For beasts to rise, men must fall.'

'You're mad. Etax and the others – they're not fools. They see what you're doing. They will usurp you.' Chaell gestured. 'They are coming here. Now. Coming to kill you and take command'

Ghosteater shook his head. 'Command of what?' He turned and gestured. The others around the fire rose and departed, silently. He let his hand fall to his khopesh. 'No army.'

Chaell's eyes widened. 'This was your plan from the beginning, wasn't it? To use us.'

Ghosteater looked up at the pale stars. 'Meat,' he said, again. 'The gods need meat. Bakhos wanted us to be meat, but tough. Wanted us to choke the silver skins. Wanted us to be phalanxes.' He looked down at his hands. 'I wanted us to be a phalanx, too.' He shook his head. 'We are not.'

He could hear it now. The crash of thunder. He could feel the ground tremble.

The storm of Azyr comes, Herst murmured. *Best find cover.*

'But we will serve the Absent God better than any Blessed One,' Ghosteater growled. He stepped back, into the shadows between the stones. Chaell made as if to follow him, but stopped. He heard the sounds of the approaching enemy as well. He turned, features gone pale. Ghosteater felt a flicker of pity for the warrior. Chaell had helped him. He was honourable, for one of his sort. But there was no place for him in the kingdom Ghosteater envisioned. He left Chaell there, to live or die as the Absent God willed.

In the ruins around him, he could hear the horns of the warherds, signalling retreat. They would fade away, into the outskirts and the hills. They would fall back, and leave their old territories. Let men rebuild the city, if they would. In one year, or a hundred, Ghosteater's people would return – not as a horde, or as a herd of mindless beasts, but as something better. The kingdoms of men would fall, to be forgotten.

In their ruins, the beasts would rise.

And rule all, in the name of the gods, forevermore.

CHAPTER TWENTY-THREE

PROVOCATION

An easily baited foe is an easily defeated one.

– Arcudi Fein
A Soldier's Life

Enyo arced through the air, Periphas by her side. Below her, the pavilions of the foe spread out across the wasteland – a small city of tents with a crooked tangle of makeshift streets. A fire was burning among them already.

'Nice of them to light our way,' Tegrus called out, from her left.

'Perhaps they wish to welcome us,' she shouted back. Smoke rose into the air from the burning tents, and her wings sliced through it, opening a path for the Prosecutors who swooped in her wake. Around her, the Angelos Conclave spread out in all directions, each cohort claiming a portion of the enemy encampment for itself. At her signal, they would commence an assault from on high.

'We should have done this from the beginning,' Tegrus continued, drifting close. 'Gardus is too cautious.' His voice was harsh, almost akin to the screech of a bird of prey.

Enyo glanced at him. 'Gardus did not wish to risk unnecessary deaths for no appreciable gain,' she said, firmly.

'We are meant to die and live again.'

'And what of the mortals? What if we were not enough to break the enemy? How many of them would die, when we were overwhelmed?'

Tegrus twitched his head. 'Soldiers die.'

'But to make them die for no other purpose than your impatience is foolhardy, at best.' Enyo let her wings snap out, carrying her ahead of him. Tegrus' temper was short, of late. Perhaps Azar and Mathias' deaths had something to do with it. The other two huntsmen had perished in the battle for the central plaza, torn from the sky by screaming daemons. Tegrus had almost followed them.

Down below, horns wailed. Someone had seen them, or had heard the thunder of their massed wings. She smiled, pleased. Part of her agreed with Tegrus, despite her chastisement of him. Gardus was cautious, and at times that did not sit well with her. She understood, but this sort of war was her preference. Swift. Decisive.

She banked and let gravity pull her towards the ground. She nocked an arrow as she fell, wings folded. Below her, ants ran in all directions. They swelled, becoming warriors. A rain of arrows lifted into the air, and fell far short. The servants of Chaos had even less patience than Tegrus. They lived in an eternal moment, stretched between damnation and death. She was pleased to give them the release of the latter.

She loosed the arrow. It struck home, puncturing the helm of a warrior clad in gaudy plate. Then her wings spread with a crackle, and the soles of her boots were connecting with the skull of another enemy. She dropped to the ground as he fell, neck snapped, and nocked a second arrow. The ground shook as Tegrus hurled his hammers from far above. There was movement all around her – warriors running in all directions, shouting and brandishing weapons. Her silver armour acted as a beacon, and they came rushing in from all sides. Some were mortal, but others were not.

She loosed, nocked and loosed again. Her wings snapped, carrying her backwards over the ground. Explosions shook the air. Overhead, silver shapes swept past, crackling hammers whirling towards the ground. Wherever the enemy sought to stand, hammers scattered them. Prosecutors crashed down, and waded in, crushing skulls and flinging bodies aside before rocketing back into the air to attack somewhere else.

Periphas shrieked and she turned, blocking a sword with her bow. The force of the blow staggered her. She lashed out with a kick and sent the weapon's wielder staggering. He roared and lunged again – a giant in baroque plate stained the colour of rotten plums. His sword was an executioner's blade, square-tipped and so heavy that he had to use both hands. His helm was featureless, save for two curved horns jutting from either side.

He roared again, shouting his name perhaps – declaiming his pedigree. She twisted aside, snatched an arrow from her quiver, nocked and loosed. It took him high in the chest, and he stumbled. The second arrow knocked his head back. He toppled over and lay still. Smoke boiled in thick bulwarks to either side of her. Fires raged through the pavilions.

She heard screams – mortal ones. She whistled for Periphas, and the bird shot past, searching for the origin of the sound. She followed, walking rather than flying. None tried to stop her.

She could hear the rattle of chariot wheels, and the scream of horses. Something massive lumbered towards the Sea of Dust, bellowing in pain, its form hidden by the smoke.

When she reached the source of the screams, she found Tegrus had beaten her there. 'I found them,' he said. 'There are a hundred other cages like this, scattered all throughout the encampment.'

'Someone must do the work.'

The cage was made of bone and sinew. It was large, and stank of years of death. Inside, slaves cowered. Mortals, branded and scarred, all but naked, save for rags and tatters, their eyes fixed on the silver forms staring at them. Tegrus raised a hammer, ready to smash the cage asunder, and the mortals drew back. He paused and looked at her. She nodded. He struck the cage, shattering a hole in it.

The slaves huddled back, moaning. Tegrus stepped through the hole, hand extended. 'Come,' he rumbled. 'It is safe now.'

A slave stepped forward, her face scarred and cut, as if by many blades. She licked frayed lips and reached for his hand. Then, with a wild scream, she lunged, a piece of sharpened stone in her hand. The makeshift knife shattered on Tegrus' war-plate, and he stepped back, startled. 'What–?'

'Fall back. Leave them,' Enyo said. The rest of the slaves surged forward, crying out the name of Slaanesh. Some had weapons – sharpened bones, rocks – while others had only their bare hands. Tegrus backed away, trying to fend them off.

'What's wrong with them?' he snarled.

'Nothing we can fix. Take to the air.' Enyo loosed an arrow between Tegrus and the closest mortal. Startled, the slave fell back. Tegrus shot upwards with a snap of his wings and Enyo followed, Periphas at her side.

As she rose into the air, she looked down. The mortals stared up at them, expressions hungry and savage. Then, a curl of smoke hid them from view, and Enyo turned back to the stars. She rose past Tegrus, who was still staring down.

'Come,' she said, her voice harsh. 'We have work yet to do this night.'

'What is going on over there?' Jon Cruso asked, as he stepped into the command tent. Cassandora waved him over as the last of the maps were set into place by the scribes. 'The horizon is on fire. Did the Ironweld decide to destroy the city and not tell anyone?'

'If we did, it'd make a bigger fire than that,' Mahk said, chewing on an unlit cheroot. The cogsmith stood with a group of human and duardin engineers, studying a set of maps. He glanced at Cassandora. 'Ask this one.'

Cassandora snorted and eyed the duardin. He met her gaze, unperturbed. The command tent was crowded with scribes, junior officers and cartographers. Scouts moved through the tent, reporting to the latter, who then made adjustments to the maps. Gardus had designed an efficient system to keep track of the flow of battle, and Cassandora had seen no reason to change it. Reports were coming in from across the city – assaults faltering, the enemy in disarray. Enyo's attack had done exactly as she'd hoped.

'What did she do?' Cruso asked, as he joined Lorcus and Morguin. The Freeguild commanders stood near the representatives from the Ironweld and the Collegiate Arcane. Ahom leaned on his staff, looking older than his years. The reconciler twitched slightly, at every stray sound.

'Put us in the soup,' Morguin said. She glanced at Cassandora. 'Begging your pardon, my lady.' Cassandora inclined her head, showing that she'd taken no insult.

'Lord-Celestant Cassandora did as she thought best,' Lorcus said. 'And she acted with my full knowledge and agreement. The time has come to bring this affair to its natural conclusion.'

'Oh, well, in that case, we'll just tell the enemy to pack up and go home, eh?' Cruso said. 'Only those beastkin my lads and I have been chasing around the western district for the past four days don't seem the type to give up and leave.'

Cassandora turned from her study of a map of the central plaza and looked at Cruso. His uniform and armour were stained with soot and blood, but his moustaches were clean. The harquebusiers had been fighting running battles in the western districts since their arrival, using their speed and mobility to harass the beastmen and drive them from their lairs.

'Only that's exactly what they've done, isn't it?' Grymn said, from where he sat. 'I'd bet you've not seen hide nor hair of the creatures since Gardus left, eh?' The Lord-Castellant was looking over the newest maps of the city's edge, alongside Octarion. Khela stood nearby, adding her own observations to that of the cartographer Tulla Mir.

'Plenty of other things out there needing killing,' Cruso said, sourly. He looked at Cassandora. 'But aye, he's right. They have been scarce.' He looked at Lorcus. 'I'm guessing that means something, then?'

'It means that things have changed,' Cassandora said. She turned to face them all. 'I thought – I hoped – that we would be able to simply follow Gardus' strategy. Unfortunately, that hope has become untenable.'

'Meaning?' Cruso said.

'That fire on the horizon was the Angelos Conclave at work. I sent them to raze the enemy's camps.'

Mahk nearly swallowed his cheroot. 'You did what?'

Cruso crowed and slammed his fist down on a table. 'At last!'

'That's a gamble,' Grymn said, looking at the other Lord-Castellants. 'We know that they outnumber us. Even now, they outnumber us. Provoking them when we can simply wait them out…' He shook his head. 'I don't like it.'

Cassandora nodded. 'I don't expect you to.' She looked around. 'The fact is, with every day that passes, we run short on time. If Gardus fails…'

'He won't,' Grymn said, harshly.

'If Gardus fails,' Cassandora continued, meeting his glare with her own, 'then we must prepare ourselves for the worst.'

'What do you mean?' Cruso asked. The Freeguild commander looked around. 'What am I missing?'

'The dead,' Lorcus said, softly. 'The ones in the catacombs.' Cruso looked at him, realisation dawning on his features. He turned pale.

'But surely they still sleep,' Mahk said.

Ahom rubbed his face tiredly. 'They do. But they stir regardless. Despite my earlier assertions, I now believe Von Carstein had already begun to wake them up when he was caught. We've done what we could to repair the wards, but…'

Cassandora frowned. 'We may well face a war on two fronts. If Nagash's eye should be drawn here, there is little we can do to prevent him from awakening those ancient legions. They will rise, and we will be forced to match them. So best we are done with old foes before these new ones arise.'

'So a gamble, but a calculated one,' Grymn said, sitting back. 'What's the plan, then?'

'It has already begun. Once the Angelos Conclave finishes its work, the enemy will be faced with two choices – retreat…'

'Or attack,' Lorcus said. He rapped a knuckle against one of the maps. 'They will come in force this time. A larger assault than any other. And we will turn it back on them.'

'How do you propose to do that, then?' Mahk growled.

'That's where you come in,' Cassandora said. 'The Ironweld emplacements, reinforced by the Gold Gryphons and the Steel Souls, will be the anvil. The enemy will break themselves on you.' She turned. 'The Stormforged and the Bullhearts will advance into the teeth of the foe, supported by the Red and Blacks–'

'And the Gallowsmen,' Lorcus said. Cassandora looked at him, a denial already on her lips. But it faded unspoken, as she saw the look on his face. 'You know I must, my lady. This battle will decide the fate of the city, and the Gallowsmen must fight at its forefront. *I* must fight at its forefront. Else my authority will always be suspect.'

Cassandora nodded grudgingly, seeing the truth in his words. 'Fine. But you will advance in our wake – we will bear the brunt of the fighting. Do you understand?'

Lorcus smiled. 'Happily, my lady. I have no intention of throwing my life away. Just so long as I can say I was there.'

Cassandora chuckled. 'Good.' Before she could continue, a commotion outside drew her eyes to the side of the tent. A Prosecutor strode in, his war-plate stained by smoke and dust. He sank to one knee before Cassandora.

'My lady, the pavilions of the enemy have been razed,' the newcomer said. 'Their tents burn and their slaves run riot. We slew many before returning.'

'And?' Cassandora said.

'Many remain,' the Prosecutor said, reluctantly. 'The attack seemed to… to excite them.' He seemed uncomfortable with the concept. Cassandora gestured for him to rise.

'Good.' She looked around, meeting the grim gazes of Lorcus and the others. 'They will come. We will meet them. And then we will break them, once and for all.'

* * *

Lord-Ordinator Taltus climbed onto the scaffolding and greeted the workers there. The duardin returned his greeting gruffly before turning back to their labours. In the distance, Taltus could hear the thud of Ironweld artillery. Clouds of dust and smoke rose over the city. Beneath that thunderous fusillade, he could detect the whine of enemy horns as they launched another futile assault.

He had made note of the recent attacks, using them to calculate the location of future assaults. Reinforcing those positions had enabled the forces of Azyr to pre-empt their foes, driving back their attacks in good time. He had begun to wonder if the enemy commander was entirely lucid. Each attack seemed designed not so much to achieve an objective, as to get as many of the enemy warriors killed as possible. Then, knowing the foe they faced, that might well be the goal.

He had considered that the attacks were nothing but a massive blood sacrifice, but there was no pattern that he could detect. He had made a study of such things and knew the signs, but there were none here. Either their foe was a fool, or totally mad.

'Or there's something going on that we're not seeing,' he murmured, watching as plumes of smoke rose over the city. When it came to the Ruinous Powers, one could not trust the portents, no matter how favourable they might seem. He was certain that something was happening, just out of sight, and the thought unsettled him.

Around him, the duardin workers suddenly stiffened, and bowed their heads. Taltus turned. '*Kvin* Hruna,' he said, bowing shallowly to the newcomer.

Hruna Kollok returned the gesture. 'Lord-Ordinator,' she said. The head overseer of the Zhu'garaz workgangs was tall for a duardin, and broad, beneath her overseer's leathers. Heavy bracers of gold covered her forearms and a circlet of the same held her dark hair back from her round, freckled features. A stonemason's hammer and a fyresteel throwing axe were thrust through her belt, where she could get to them swiftly.

'How goes it?' he asked.

'We have the outer palisades erected on the northern approach.' She pointed the edge of the central plaza, where a palisade of flat, stone pillars now rose, blocking the city from view. Gantries and walkways of iron and wood had been assembled behind it, and Judicators patrolled along its immense length. 'Good ground there. Solid. Mostly bedrock.'

'And the west? Lord-Castellant Grymn had some concerns…?'

Hruna leaned over and spat. 'Sour ground. Soft. There's water in the rocks. A cistern burst and flooded the tunnels of the western district. We'll need to drain them and reinforce the tunnels below before we raise anything heavier than a wooden wall.'

'Leave it for now,' Taltus said. 'Cassandora is planning something, and we need to concentrate on keeping the realmgate safe.' He peered up at the ziggurat, taking note of the structure being built around it. Often, Stormforts were built near a realmgate, rather than around it, to enable ease of access. In this case, the Stormfort would be built around the base and lower levels of the structure, leaving the uppermost plateau open. A network of causeways would be built from the top, allowing for access to the rest of the city, and enabling the Hallowed Knights to stand vigil without impeding the flow of trade.

'Four, I think,' he murmured. 'One to each plaza… splitting into eight from there, and then twelve, so as to create a celestial latticework…' His fingers twitched and he reached for his parchment and quills. 'A fractal pattern? No… a wheel? Hmm.'

Hruna coughed politely. Taltus blinked and looked down at her. 'My apologies, Hruna. I lost myself for a moment. Something concerns you?'

'What are my people to do when the fighting begins? We are not contracted as warriors.' She frowned at him, her hand resting on her throwing axe. 'And it will be impossible to continue work without adequate protection.'

'The enemy won't get this far,' Cassandora said, before Taltus could reply. The Lord-Celestant joined them, followed by Lord-Castellant Octarion. 'You have my oath in that regard, Kvin Hruna. Your workgangs will be safe enough.'

Hruna nodded. 'I accept your oath, Lord-Celestant. But if the situation should change…'

'You will be the first to know,' Cassandora said. She looked at Taltus. 'I need to speak with you, Lord-Ordinator.'

Taltus made his apologies to Hruna and allowed Cassandora to pull him to the side. 'What is it?'

'I need your gifts, Taltus. You can read the ebb and flow of battle better than any of us, and I need you to put that talent to use in the coming attack. We need to break them here and push those that survive into the Sea of Dust.'

Taltus frowned. 'You mean to launch an assault.'

Cassandora nodded. 'I mean to win this war. I can't do that without you. Our scouts have read the signs – the enemy is coming again, and this time we are going to break them.' She looked away, watching the workforce hard at their labour. 'Then, when we have them on the run, I intend to press our advantage. We will raze whatever is left of those pavilions to the ground and shatter their standards.'

Taltus looked away. 'Yes.'

Cassandora paused. 'You don't sound convinced. Have you seen something in the smoke? Some omen of disaster?'

'No. Not as such.' Taltus shook his head. 'Merely a feeling. As if we are serving the ends of another.' He looked at her. 'But what will be, will be. Would you have me with you, Lord-Celestant?'

'Always, my friend.' Cassandora clasped his shoulder. 'You will be in command of the defence, Taltus. I need the artillery to cut off the enemy's line of retreat. Keep them boxed in, so we can beat them bloody.'

'Like a blacksmith's tongs,' Taltus said, approvingly. 'An old-fashioned stratagem, but effective.'

'I thought you might approve. When they are caught fast, then the faithful will march. With the Gallowsmen in support, we will smash them.'

'You hope.'

Cassandora smiled. 'I have faith.' She looked up at the stars and nodded. 'Let us go, brother, and set the foundations for this city's future.'

Lorcus looked towards the distant fires, and felt a chill go through him. He stood on the steps of one of the many temples that dotted the heart of the city. He could hear the Ironweld guns, and smell the smoke.

'Tomorrow, then,' Vend said, taking a swallow from a clay jug he held. He sat on the bottom step. The paymaster offered it to Lorcus. 'Cider, straight from the orchards of Stormvault. Have a taste.'

'No, thank you.'

Vend shrugged. 'Suit yourself. Tomorrow. And you at the forefront.' He smiled. 'Very smart. That'll raise your stature some.'

Lorcus ignored the implication. 'And where will you be?'

'Back here. Safe. I've had my fill of battlefields. I'll stay behind the guns, and enjoy a drink to your continued health, Lord Lorcus of Caddow.'

'I think I am going to change the city's name,' Lorcus said, idly. He looked up at the temple doors. There was a light within. 'Caddow is dead. A new city needs a new name, don't you think?'

Vend laughed and stood. 'King's prerogative, I suppose.'

'Duke,' Lorcus corrected.

'Much the same, this far from Azyr's light.' Vend raised his jug in salute. 'I'll speak to you again when the battle's done, my lord.' He stood and wandered away, whistling a merry tune. Lorcus watched him for a moment, and then turned to the temple. Slowly, he went inside. Candles had been mounted in every nook and cranny, and the nave was lit by a soft orange glow.

Stone benches lined the nave, leading to an altar. It was new – made from solid celestine, hewn from the peaks above Azyrheim. The first of many to be brought to the city, and at no little expense. In time, the building would be rebuilt, enlarged and made grand. It would be the first temple of the city, laying in sight of the realmgate as it did. A lector would be sent from Azyrheim, to take matters in hand.

But for the moment, it was a simple chapel, a place of quiet prayer for desperate men and women. During the day, it was often full of soldiers, asking awkwardly for Sigmar's grace. Lorcus had only rarely felt the need to pray, himself.

Someone knelt before the altar stone, murmuring softly. A priest, clad in blue robes and golden armour. He stopped as he heard Lorcus enter.

'My apologies – I wasn't aware that anyone was in here.' Lorcus sat down on one of the stone benches. The priest rose to his feet.

'No need to apologise. The temples of Sigmar are open to – oh! Captain-General Lorcus. I wasn't expecting you.'

Lorcus smiled slightly. 'It's Twayn, isn't it? Cullen Twayn?' Briefly, he considered passing along Gaspar Twayn's message. Then, he pushed the thought aside. There would be time for that later, if there was a later.

Twayn nodded jerkily. 'Yes, my lord.'

Lorcus went to the altar stone. 'Were you praying?'

Twayn nodded. 'It provided no answers, sadly.' He sighed. 'I wonder... I wonder if his silence is a sign?' He looked at Lorcus. 'If my answer is there, in the stillness.'

Lorcus shook his head. 'That is beyond the limits of my wisdom.' He looked down at the altar stone. It was a simple thing, unadorned save for the marks of hammers. He traced his fingers across the impact points, almost feeling the power and prayer that had gone into each blow. 'I know only that I came here to build a city.' He looked at Twayn. 'What about you?'

Twayn was silent. Then, 'I came to teach.' He looked at Lorcus. 'There are places, in the wastes, where the light of Azyr has not yet reached. I would go and carry the word of Sigmar to those who would hear it. I would teach them.' He laid his hand on the altar stone, and smiled. For a moment, Lorcus thought he saw a flicker of the same light that Gardus possessed within the young priest. But it passed as quickly as it had come. 'You came to pray, didn't you? I shall leave you to it.' He turned to go. Lorcus stopped him.

'Would you pray with me, priest? I find I have no tongue for it, at the moment.'

Twayn smiled. 'Of course. What shall we pray for?'

Lorcus knelt before the altar.

'Victory.'

CHAPTER TWENTY-FOUR

NAGASHIZZAR

Nagashizzar is, as I am. It is wherever my shadow stretches.

– Nagash
The Epistle of Bone

The ruins echoed with the clamour of war, of drums and clashing steel. Strange scents hung heavy on the still air. Ramus murmured a prayer. Around him, his brothers and sisters knelt in wary readiness. A grove of pillars, each adorned with a bust of Nagash, loomed around them, sheltering them from sight.

They had left the wharfs behind them, and, with Mannfred guiding them, had carefully navigated the tangled streets, moving steadily towards their destination. They had been forced to stop often, to wait for patrols of yowling beastkin or silent Chaos warriors to pass by. 'That's the fifth patrol we've seen,' Ramus said, as a group of reavers in black iron vanished down a side street, singing an abominable hymn.

'There are whole legions in these ruins,' Mannfred said, peering around the edge of a pillar, eyes narrowed. 'I sent Ashigaroth ahead, to spy the way. A dozen camps or more, all directly in our path, waiting for the least excuse to ride to war. We will need a plan.' He smiled. 'A bit of sorcery, perhaps?'

'No,' Ramus said. He gestured. Mannfred winced and touched his chest. 'No. We will smash through them, if we must.'

'We have only twenty-odd warriors,' Mannfred said. 'Doughty fighters as you are, that is not enough. Even with my magics, that is not enough. We have to distract them...'

'Ha! A song, perhaps,' Osanus said.

Mannfred looked at him. 'What are you blathering about?'

'A song...' Ramus murmured. He glanced at the Knight-Heraldor. 'That might work. Your horn will echo through this place like thunder. Every daemon and warrior in these ruins will be drawn to it, if they're as eager as Mannfred claims.'

Mannfred was nodding now, a sly expression on his face. 'They will. Or enough of them to clear us a path. It's boring, fighting the dead. We make it so – dullness and repetition are the millstones that grind down the enemy's will to fight. Bones, marching forward forever. They will be drawn to the promise of new foes like a maggot to meat.'

Osanus gave his horn a fond pat. 'A good plan. Only one body is needed.' He turned and pointed. 'There, I think. That old fane we passed. Good wide space. A proper stage, eh?'

'You are not going alone,' Ramus began.

'Only I can play my horn,' Osanus said. 'And you will need every sword and hammer in the underworld. We can only spare me.'

'I can spare no one,' Ramus said. The words felt hollow.

'Osanus will go, yes?' Osanus caught Ramus by the back of the head and forced the Lord-Relictor to look at him. 'Osanus

420

will stand firm, mine brother. I will give you time. I will draw
the gazes of all the daemons in this dusty place. Go. Save him.'

'I cannot let you do this, Osanus...' Even as he said it, he saw
no other choice. One more life, lost to his foolishness. If he
had not come, if he had killed Mannfred the first time they'd
seen him, if, if, if...

'It is not your choice,' Osanus said, grinning. 'I would make
a poor Lord-Celestant, I think. Too many songs in my head,
not enough wisdom. But this? Ha! This, the Stormwolf can
do, and gladly. I will play them a song, and make them fall
asleep, gentle as lambs, eh?' His grin turned savage. 'Then I
will butcher them, yes?'

He clapped Ramus on the neck once more and turned away.

'Go with Sigmar, brother,' Ramus said. 'May he stand with
you.'

'And you, mine brother. Mind you succeed though, eh? Or I
will feel very foolish.' Osanus turned to look at Sagittus and the
others. 'See you on the Anvil, mine brothers and sisters.' Then,
with a cheerful wave, he turned and departed, horn in hand.

Ramus watched until the Knight-Heraldor was lost to sight.
Then he looked at Mannfred. 'Another brother gone,' he said,
heavily. He made a fist, and the vampire looked away, rubbing
his chest. 'This had better be worth it, vampire.'

'It will be,' Mannfred said. 'It must be.'

They waited in silence. Moments passed. A succession of
heart beats. Ramus counted them, reciting the canticles to himself. They moved through his head, a litany of faith that seemed
to become more hollow with every passing hour. What was
faith, that he had discarded it so readily? Or perhaps Gardus
had been right – that this was Sigmar's will, in some fashion.
That all he had endured had been nothing more than a test.

Was that it, then? Was faith a blade, to be honed until it was sharp enough to shed blood? He bowed his head, wanting to beseech the stars. But there were no stars visible here. Only dust and stone, and a carpet of broken bones.

'Is this a mistake?' He did not realise he had spoken out loud, until Mannfred laughed. The vampire looked at him.

'A bit late to be asking that, don't you think?'

Ramus didn't reply. The vampire was right. Too late now for anything but jamming the blade in, and hoping it hit something vital. His grip on his staff tightened as the air was split by the first note of Osanus' last song.

The note quavered on the air, shaking the ruins to their roots. The drums stopped. Carrion birds took flight, screaming in protest. Crude horns sounded a few moments later, as if in mockery of that single, silver note.

A second note, as if in reply to the mockery of the Chaos horns. Not an announcement, but a challenge. *Here I stand,* it said. *Come and meet me, if you are brave enough. Here I stand.*

'Vitalian,' Mannfred murmured.

'What?'

'Count Vitalian. An old comrade of mine and Tarsem's. He bore a war-horn made from something he'd hacked from a beast chieftain's head. Despite its origins, it gave off the most... haunting notes. Like the cry of the wind one moment, or the roar of a beast the next.' Mannfred closed his eyes. 'You could tell help was coming, when you heard it. Many were the battles where the clarion call of that horn was all that stood between victory and defeat.'

'And what happened to him?'

'He died, Stormcast. All men die. Only the soulblighted go on forever.'

More notes now, shaking the air, a song of war and jubilation – a hymn to the God-King. Ramus had heard that song often on the fields of the Gladitorium. The streets shook with the tread of many feet, and hooves. The patrol of black-armoured warriors they'd seen earlier spilled back into view, hurrying in the direction of the sound. They were no longer singing.

'How long?' Mannfred murmured.

'What?'

'How long can he hold them?'

'Long enough.' Ramus rose to his feet. 'Come. It is time to bring this to an end.'

'A city,' Gardus said, sitting up in his saddle. 'Where no city should be.' The Vanguard-Palladors and their gryph-chargers crouched in the lee of a dust-dune, a safe distance from the place. He could see the dust-barque Ramus had taken resting in a berth, and hear the thump of drums. There was fighting going on, somewhere close by. But no lightning, no thunder. That came as a relief. That meant Ramus hadn't announced his presence yet. 'What is this place?'

'Nagashizzar,' Sathphren said, harshly.

'Nagashizzar is far from here, to the east.' Even as he said it, his eyes were drawn to the immense ziggurat that dominated the city's skyline. Larger than the one in Caddow, it's black surface seemed to shimmer with an unholy light.

'Not always.' Sathphren looked back the way they'd come, as if he'd spotted something on the horizon. 'The Silent City moves. It creeps and crawls like the shadow of the Undying King himself. Wherever you least expect it.' He turned back. 'That is Nagashizzar. Part of it, at least. And there – the black pyramid, rising from its heart, like a tombstone for all the realms.'

Gardus studied him for a moment. The Swiftblade's normal

ebullience had faded the closer they'd come to this place. All of the Vanguard-Palladors seemed on edge. He could feel it himself – like an indescribable miasma, clinging to every particle of dust and stone. This place belonged wholly to Nagash. It had been made from him, drawn from the blackest reaches of whatever passed for his soul. And it was *angry.* Angry at the hordes that assailed it. Angry at the temerity of the living to walk its streets. Angry at life itself.

'Was this what you felt, when you entered Nurgle's realm?' Sathphren asked, softly.

Gardus hesitated. He did not like to think of that time, of that moment of desperate hubris and faith. It had been like drowning in a mire, every breath a struggle, every movement a war. He had seen the Plague God rise from the underside of the realms, a mountain walking, groping towards him. A voice like sour thunder, shivering through him, too immense to be understood save as a roar of noise.

He shook his head. 'Not like this. But similar.' He looked at Sathphren. 'Gods invest something of themselves in all that they create. As we each have a mote of Sigmar's grace, so too does this place have something of Nagash in it. But it is… diffuse. As if his mind is not here. As if his eyes are elsewhere.'

'Perhaps that is a good thing.'

'It is a lucky thing. If Nagash were here…' He trailed off. 'If Nagash were here, we would know. It would be like standing at the edge of an abyss, where all light and hope dies.'

'What if he returns?'

'We must pray that he won't. We must find Ramus and bring him back before we reach that precipice.' Gardus paused. 'I will not ask you to go any further. If I fail, it is entirely likely that I will once again face a god in battle. And this time… this time Sigmar will not save me. This time, I will suffer the fate

I should have suffered before.' He pointed upwards. 'Because that is what he wills.'

Sathphren shook his head. 'I do not believe that.'

Gardus smiled. 'Neither do I. He does not wish us to fail, brother. So we will not. We must not. But I will not force you to ride into the maw of death.'

'Nor could you,' Sathphren said. 'But I will go. I have taken you this far, Steel Soul. It would be churlish of me to leave you here.' He turned. 'Don't think the rest of you are getting a choice, though. I am your Lord-Aquilor and I say get up, brothers and sisters. We have one last ride, either to victory or death.' Sathphren nudged his steed to her feet. 'Which of these it will be depends entirely on our speed.'

A familiar note punched the air.

'Wait,' Gardus said. 'Listen.'

Another note – the winding call of a Stormcast war-horn.

'Osanus,' Sathphren said. 'That's the Stormwolf's horn, I'd bet my life on it.'

'But is he calling for aid – or sounding a warning?' Gardus urged his own gryph-charger up. 'Either way, we must answer.'

'No,' Sathphren said. He looked at Gardus. 'No – think, Steel Soul. Think like a hunter, not a hero. If you were Ramus, and you were trying to sneak through a city full of monsters and madmen, would you signal your presence in such a fashion?'

Gardus frowned. 'A distraction?'

'A necessary sacrifice. Osanus is drawing away whatever forces lay between Ramus and his goal. It's what I would do. And...'

'And he's inadvertently clearing our path as well,' Gardus said, grimly. He shook his head. Sathphren was right. As much as it pained him, the choice was clear. 'We keep pursuing Ramus. We find him and stop him.'

Sathphren nodded. 'Lead the way, Lord-Celestant. The gryph-chargers have the scent. They will take us where we need to go as swiftly as they can.'

'What is that noise?' Bakhos demanded. He turned in his saddle as the note bounced from ruin to ruin, ripsawing through the air. More followed – a song, some hateful hymn to the god of starlight. It shivered through him, and he felt a moment of unease.

'I think it's coming from that direction,' Lemerus said, pointing south.

Bakhos smiled, suddenly. 'Ah. Wait. I know that sound. It's a battle-horn. I heard it in Caddow, when our foes first arrived.' He turned his steed about and galloped in the direction he thought the sound had come from. 'Come, perhaps they've been caught by one of Stulakh's rivals.' He hoped not – or if so, that he was in time to claim the glory of the kill. His new army, such as it was, followed. Warriors riding daemonic discs hurtled past, trailing motes of warpfire, and heavyset blight-kings plodded in the wake of the horses, chanting doleful hymns to Grandfather Nurgle.

Khornate warriors, in their crimson silks and brass armour, loped through the ruins with a surety that reminded him of the phalanxes he'd once led. Fifty warriors or more – not many, but enough to earn him the victory he desired.

The sound of the horn echoed again. His steed leapt a fallen archway and he found himself riding along a narrow procession. To either side of him, skull-faced statuary glared sightlessly down upon those who passed beneath them.

His steed reared as the procession widened suddenly, and he saw the remains of an ancient temple spread outward in all directions. Great statues and pillars marked the expanse. Once, it had been a monument to the Undying King. Now it was the haunt of night-birds, full of dust and shadows.

A warrior stood alone among the broken pillars of the ancient fane, blowing his horn. Clad in silver, and bearing a great broadsword in his other hand, he blew a final blast and lowered the horn. Bakhos saw that his forces were not alone in investigating. Warriors of all shapes and sizes crowded the streets and doorways around – hundreds of them. Armies.

'Is he mad?' Lemerus said.

'Yes. Gloriously so.' Bakhos studied the distant warrior, wondering what the purpose of this stand was. Defiance? Heroism? Or something more practical? He looked towards the pyramid. 'Oh, of course.' He laughed. 'A distraction.'

Lemerus looked at him. 'What?'

'A distraction, Lemerus. We came following a boatful of his fellows – where are they? Not here.' He pointed to the pyramid. 'There. They slip past, while this one draws every eye. Bored warriors make for an attentive audience.' He made to turn his steed. 'Come. This is but the sideshow. I wish to see the true performance.'

Lemerus hesitated. 'What is he waiting for?'

Bakhos turned, impatient. 'Death, most likely. They seek death, in general and in particular. Have you not realised that by now?'

'Yes, but what is he going to do, save be torn apart?' Lemerus urged its horse closer to the fane. Bakhos saw many of his newly acquired warriors doing the same. Even his eunuchs were interested. They were all the same – novelty was the headiest intoxicant of all. He glanced back at the pyramid, and then cursed under his breath.

'Fine,' he said, impatiently. 'What is it you wish, Lemerus? Shall we ask him?'

Silence had fallen over the fane, save the murmurs of the curious and the mad. Daemons laughed or snarled. Weapons scraped. Bakhos could see the spheres of influence now – chieftains, champions and sorcerers. All gathering to see who had dared challenge their control of this place. 'Idiots,' he murmured.

Then, had he not done the same? Eternity as a watchman was a hell of dull moments. Battle against the dead had few pleasures.

He straightened in his saddle. The sounds of battle echoed through the streets, but none of those around him reacted. He could not see any sign of it on the horizon, and he wondered if it were happening here at all. Perhaps it was simply the echo of another battle, occurring in another Nagashizzar, elsewhere.

He'd heard stories of such things. And this Nagashizzar did not resemble the one he'd laid siege to, seeking his wife's soul. Perhaps the philosophers were right, and Nagashizzar was not simply a city but the shadow of its ruler, cast across the entire realm.

None of that mattered, of course. Nagash, his city, his legions – simply obstacles. Death was but a wall, keeping Bakhos from that which he most desired. He had intended to cross it with Archaon's help. Perhaps being here meant that he no longer needed that aid. He hauled on his steed's reins. 'Come, the black pyramid awaits. I have no need to watch a silver-plated fool die.'

Lemerus didn't move. 'Look,' it said. 'They're attacking.'

Despite himself, Bakhos turned back. He expected it to be over in moments. Daemons surged towards the lone warrior, cackling and howling. A tide of red flesh and multihued flame. The warrior raised his battle-horn and blew.

The air tensed. Horses reared and stones fell from the tops of the ruins. As the sound reverberated outwards, daemons simply… unravelled. The sound swelled, filling the fane and spilling outwards, its echoes doubling and redoubling in volume.

Lemerus shouted something that Bakhos could not hear for the roar of the horn. Chaos warriors raced across the broken space, brandishing weapons. They surged towards the lone Stormcast like waves lapping at a stone. The horn spoke again. And again. Solid notes, punching out like the hammer of a god. Pillars splintered and fell. Archways collapsed. Bodies were sent tumbling like leaves caught in a wind.

The horses were bucking and kicking. Bakhos clutched at his aching head. The blisters on a nearby blightking trembled and burst all at once as the warrior collapsed. A bird-headed warrior was slapped from his disc and crushed against a broken statue. Bakhos gritted his teeth, and felt them quiver in his gums as another wave of sound beat at the air. He peered at the heart of the fane.

Despite all odds, some of the warriors had reached the Stormcast. They stumbled forward, as if thunderstruck. The Stormcast fought them, broadsword flashing. Whenever he bought himself a moment, the horn sounded again. But the bursts of sound grew less frequent as more foes pressed forward.

Arrows took the Stormcast in these moments where no sound could smash them from the air. For every blade deflected or turned aside, two slammed into silver war-plate so closely did his enemies press him. A blast of the horn knocked them scrambling, or pulped them where they stood. But more replaced them. Bakhos fought the urge to join them. He could see others doing the same, or retreating entirely. They'd realised, as he had, that this was nothing more than a distraction.

The broadsword swept out, smashing a black-armoured warrior from his feet and then the Stormcast was clear. He staggered back against a pillar, his helm gone, blood dripping from the joins of his armour and staining his beard. The bodies of dozens of warriors and beasts lay scattered about the fane.

The Stormcast had begun to speak – no, he'd begun to sing. But Bakhos could hear nothing save the awful reverberation. He shook his head, trying to clear it. He could feel the ground shuddering beneath his horse's claws, and was reminded of what had happened in Caddow – the fall of the buildings, his forces crushed to paste.

He tried to catch Lemerus' attention, and saw blood trickling from the champion's pointed ears. He signalled, gesturing back the way they'd come, even as another burst of sound washed over them. The Stormcast had lifted his horn and was blowing it once more, but without pausing for breath or even to defend himself. Just blowing louder and louder, like the rumble of approaching thunder. Blue sparks danced across his armour, and dropped to the ground like blood. And still the sound grew.

Undeterred, the brave and the foolhardy pressed forward, eager to taste the blood of their foe. Bakhos kicked his steed into motion and galloped away from the fane, trying to escape the sound. Behind him, he felt a sudden wash of familiar heat as the gloom was suddenly pushed aside by a swell of light.

A moment later, he felt as if a great, crushing wind had caught him in its grip, sending his steed rolling. He lunged free of the thrashing animal and narrowly avoided a falling statue. Around him, he saw others scrambling for cover, through the murk of dust. He caught sight of one of his eunuchs rolling limply across the ground, neck at an odd angle.

A hand caught his shoulder, and he rose, half-deaf, sword in hand. He shoved its owner back, and found it was Lemerus. The champion said something, but Bakhos heard only a thin whine. He shook his head savagely, and the world returned slowly to its normal volume.

'You hear that?' Lemerus shrilled.

'I hear nothing except your whining voice,' Bakhos snarled, lowering his sword. He shook his head again. He could see warriors gathering around him, seeking reassurance. Seeking leadership. There weren't many of them left, but there were enough. 'What is it?'

Thunder. He turned towards the pyramid. Lightning thrashed over the rooftops. He shoved Lemerus aside and spat a mouthful of blood.

'Enough,' he said. 'Enough. Time to finish this hunt.'

CHAPTER TWENTY-FIVE

BRIDGE

The bridges to Nekroheim are many and varied in shape, and length. Designed by artisans now long forgotten, each exists as a monument to an extinct style. So much lost, remembered only by the dead.

Palento Herst
The Night Paths

Ramus struck, and the beastman fell.

'That's the last of them,' Sagittus said, lowering his bow. Ramus glanced at the Judicator-Prime and nodded. Mannfred dragged his blade free of a twitching corpse and turned to them. More than a dozen beastmen lay scattered around the narrow street. The creatures had died surprised – with no time to call for aid, or do more than put up a token resistance.

'The gate is just ahead. Hurry!'

Ramus followed the vampire towards the stone archway marking the end of the street. Dust filled the air, and the echoes of Osanus' last song still echoed through the city. Ramus had seen and heard the Stormwolf's soul rise to meet the stars, with one final, titanic note. He wondered, even as he ran, if the being that rose Reforged from the Anvil of Apotheosis would still remember how to sing. Or was that another sacrifice, added to the litany?

As the echoes faded, however, he heard the sounds of battle – clashing swords and cries of pain. The noise slipped through the ruins from all around. 'Have you led us into the middle of a fight?' he demanded.

Mannfred laughed and slowed as they reached the archway. 'No. The battles you hear are taking place in other Nagashizzars – some of them centuries ago. Others, years from now. But most, right at this moment.' He nodded to the pyramid, rising high above them. 'This close to it, time *bends*. It folds in on itself, and all things collapse to a single point. The past and the future are as one in the fortress-city of the dead.'

They passed through the archway and into a wide plaza of dark stone that spread outward before them. Up ahead, the black gates that marked the bridge to Nekroheim rose, their shadow stretching as if to meet the approaching Stormcasts.

'How is that possible?' Ramus muttered. 'It's madness. This place is mad.'

'It is the will of Nagash. Time is a wheel, and Nagashizzar is at its centre. All things that happen inside its walls will always happen, the finale of a thousand lives played out forever. Those creatures we passed – those fiends who lay siege here? They are already dead. Time simply hasn't caught up with them yet.'

Mannfred laughed, and Ramus thought there was a hint of hysteria there. He wondered what creatures like Mannfred felt here, so close to the centre of all that they were. Was it the same as what he felt in Sigmaron? 'But it will,' Mannfred continued. 'All things reach their end, inevitably. And then it begins again. And again. Forever.'

'Unless we break the cycle,' Ramus said. He stopped. Before them the obsidian gates rose, higher than any gargant. Cold radiated from them, bone-deep and numbing, and strange scenes from Shyish's past had been carved upon them. He saw what he thought was the moment that Nagash and Sigmar had burst the Gates of Deepest Night. He saw Sigmar, hammer raised, fighting against a tide of… waves, tendrils, something, as Nagash plunged his blade into a great, staring eye.

'The Dreaming God,' Mannfred said, softly. 'One of the old ones. The gods of those things that existed before the realms themselves. Architects of an order so awful that even Nagash could not bear it.'

'What happened to it?'

'He used part of its corpse to make the foundations of Nekroheim. Or so the story goes. It was before my time – before even Arkhan the Black's time.' Mannfred stroked Ashigaroth's head and stared up at the gates. He extended his hand, and sigils of cold fire appeared on the air. 'Ah. That is why there are no guards. The gates are sealed by great magic. It would take a god to open them.' He smirked. 'Or one who was taught by a god.'

'You can open them?'

'Yes.' Mannfred looked at him. 'I will need time, however…'

'How much?'

'Enough.'

Before he could press Mannfred further, Ashigaroth screeched. From the other end of the courtyard, a gryph-charger shrieked in reply.

'No,' Ramus said, as he turned. 'Not now.'

Half a dozen Vanguard-Palladors prowled towards Ramus

and his cohort. He saw the Swiftblade among them, riding beside Gardus himself.

'You should not have come,' Ramus called out. 'Do your responsibilities weigh so lightly on you, Steel Soul?'

'You are my responsibility, brother,' Gardus replied. He brought his gryph-charger to a stop and slid from the saddle. The Vanguard-Palladors encircled Ramus' cohort, blocking them from getting any closer to the gates. 'I will not let you do this,' Gardus continued. 'It will mean your death, and the doom of what we came here to achieve.' He moved to confront Ramus, his hands empty of weapons.

'You are not our Lord-Celestant, Steel Soul. Step aside.' Ramus faced him. 'We must do this. For our own souls, as much as his.'

'We still have a chance to erase this folly, brother. It is not too late.' Gardus looked past the Lord-Relictor, at the others. 'Turn back, and there will be no reprimand. Iunias, Sagittus – help me make him see reason.'

'I regret that we cannot, lord,' Sagittus said. The others murmured in agreement. Ramus glanced at them, and then back at Gardus.

'Perhaps, brother, if Sigmar did not wish this, he would have stopped me.'

'Perhaps that is why he sent me.' Gardus shook his head. 'You would storm Nagashizzar, and set off a chain of events that will upend all that we have fought and bled for. Succeed or fail, and the result is the same. Nagash turns his gaze to Azyr, and the War of Heaven and Death begins anew.'

Mannfred laughed. 'You are naive if you believe that war ever truly ended. This war here – Nagash's struggle to reclaim Shyish? It is but a prelude. Nagash sees only one rival in all the realms, and that is Sigmar. You need not fear provoking him, for Sigmar himself did that centuries ago. If we but marshal our forces, we can harrow the vaults of Nekroheim and free every trapped soul within.'

'You hear?' Ramus said. 'I do not trust this creature, but I know truth when I hear it.'

'And why does he speak it?' Gardus looked at the vampire. 'Why?'

Mannfred did not reply. Gardus nodded. 'Wheels within wheels. Nagash's pride will not let him ignore an overt assault. If we burst that wall, shatter those gates, then we will have declared war.' He pointed at the vampire. 'Perhaps that is what he wants.'

'War began the moment Sigmar took his first soul and remade it.' Mannfred leaned forward. 'We have always been at war, because Nagash has decreed it.'

'That is not true. Once our realms were the closest of allies – the shield and the sword of the Mortal Realms.'

'No, because Nagash has demanded that it be not so... and so, it never was.' Mannfred shook his head. 'Even now, you do not understand. All things end in Shyish – not just lives, but stories, hopes, dreams. It is a land of bitter endings.'

'Then why all of this? Why lead Ramus here?' Gardus looked at Ramus. 'Why come here? What do you hope to gain?'

Ramus was silent. Then, 'Faith.'

Gardus stared at him, and though he could not see the Lord-Celestant's face, Ramus knew that he understood. Of all of them, only Gardus truly understood. That was why Ramus had all but hated him, since the Steel Soul had turned away from him in Sigmaron. Gardus understood what it was to lack faith. And to know that you lacked it.

'Ramus, I–' Gardus began.

The sound of hooves interrupted whatever he'd been about to say. Howls and screams rose from the ruins about the gate, and armoured riders appeared at the edge of the courtyard. Mannfred snarled in recognition.

'Bakhos.'

Ramus looked at him and then at the enemy gathering. Mortals, daemons – slaves to darkness all. He gestured. 'Open the gates, vampire. Do what must be done. We will hold them back.' He looked at Gardus. 'Faith, brother. I find I am in short supply. I… need help.' He held out his hand. 'I need your faith, Gardus.'

Gardus said nothing. Then, he took Ramus' hand. 'Say the words, Lord-Relictor,' he said, drawing his runeblade. 'Cast your voice to Azyr, that the God-King might hear, and see.' Ramus stared at the Lord-Celestant. Then he nodded and turned to face the enemy.

'Who will see that Sigmar's will is done?' the Lord-Relictor roared.

'Only the faithful,' came the rumble from two dozen throats. Not many. Never many. But enough. Enough for this moment. Ramus struck the ground with his staff.

'A foe of a thousand swords comes fast upon us, brothers and sisters,' he growled. 'Who will meet them, blade to blade?'

Hammers struck the insides of shields. Gryph-chargers shrieked. 'Only the faithful.'

'Who will be the bulwark upon which Chaos breaks?'

'Only the faithful!' Feet stamped as hammers struck.

Ramus slammed his reliquary staff down again, adding his beat to theirs. 'Who will stand fast, in the name of Tarsus Bullheart?'

'*Only the faithful!*' A bellow full of thunder and fury.

'Are you sure about this, Steel Soul?' Sathphren murmured, as the echoes of the battle-cry faded. Gardus nodded.

'I think it is too late to worry about certainty. Whatever

comes next is up to the gods. We will do as we have been made to do. If the battle turns against us…'

Sathphren nodded. 'We will carry word to Caddow, if we can.' He drew his boltstorm pistol and laughed. 'Until then, we may as well enjoy ourselves. It's been a long hunt, and now it's time to loose our arrows, eh?' He turned in his saddle. 'Fey-sha – like we did that time in Grindlemere, remember? Keep them guessing.'

The Pallador-Prime nodded. 'As you say, Swiftblade. One lunatic charge coming up.'

With a snarl, the Vanguard-Palladors split and flowed around the battle-line, moving onto the flanks. Swiftblade urged Gwyllth to leap over the heads of his fellow Stormcasts and land in a crouch before them.

'Insufferable show-off,' Ramus muttered.

Gardus glanced at the Lord-Relictor. 'Good thing he's on our side.'

Ramus snorted. He looked at Gardus. 'You do not have to do this.'

'I think I must, brother.' Gardus paused and looked at the enemy, gathering their courage. 'I think, maybe, that this is why I am here. Perhaps this was always meant to be. Perhaps Sigmar always intended that we two stand here, before the gates of death.'

Ramus was silent. Then, softly, 'Thank you.'

'Do not thank me yet, brother.' Gardus glanced at Mannfred. 'How long?'

Mannfred had turned to the gates. Without looking at Gardus, he said, 'Too long. But I will do my best, with the time you give me.'

Gardus and Ramus traded looks. 'Do you truly trust him?' Gardus asked.

'No. But he is here. And we have no other choice.'

'Your confidence overwhelms me,' Mannfred said. 'Now leave me be – I must bend my mind and will to these gates.' He lifted his hands and began to chant, Ashigaroth curled about him in a protective crouch.

Ramus grunted and struck the ground with his staff. Caged lightning writhed about the head of the reliquary standard, snapping and sparking. Gardus took up a place at the centre of the line, alongside Iunias and the other two Retributors. The handful of Judicators – five in all, counting Sagittus – formed up around Ramus. The Liberators took up positions on either side, ready to move into place to defend their Lord-Relictor.

Before them, the enemy spilled into the courtyard. Blightkings, their obese forms glistening with filth, marched alongside mortal worshippers of Khorne. Avian tzaangors crept through the ruins, screeching. And at the centre, a tall warrior atop a monstrous steed. He was clad in a high, crested helm, and a leopard's skin hung raggedly atop his archaic armour. Bare limbs gleamed with blood and sweat. He was surrounded by a coterie of riders, all bearing the mark of Slaanesh upon their twisted forms.

His laughter echoed across the courtyard, drowning out the shrieks and cries of the small army gathering about him. 'At last,' he cried out. 'At last, I have you. Are you afraid? Can your sort even feel fear?'

His steed reared, as he laughed again, wildly. 'It does not matter, I suppose. I must thank you for such sport as you have provided. Now my hunt is done. The way to the underworlds lies before me, and my quest begins anew! But first – the old stories must be ended.' He turned in his saddle. 'Lemerus – bring me their heads. But remember – the vampire is mine!'

A pale, aelven thing clad in baroque war-plate laughed and brandished its maul. 'Gladly, O Maiden's Son!' With a wordless cry, it kicked its steed into motion. The others followed, galloping past their master, and with a communal howl, the rest of the horde lurched into motion.

'There we go,' Sathphren roared. Gwyllth surged to meet the approaching horsemen, followed by the other gryph-chargers. Even Gardus' steed raced forward, riderless. Boltstorm pistols crackled as the Vanguard-Palladors split up and scattered.

'Shields up,' Gardus shouted. The Liberators stepped forward, shields ready. 'Whatever comes, protect the vampire. Iunias – on me. We'll take the heart from them.'

Iunias readied his hammer. 'An honour, Steel Soul.'

Gardus glanced back at Ramus. 'Fight well, brother.'

'I will see you on the Anvil, Gardus,' Ramus said. 'But not today.' Lightning ripped from his standard, shearing the air into jagged fragments as it sprang to meet the approaching enemy. Chaos warriors were torn from their feet and sent tumbling, armour alight with celestial flames. Tzaangors staggered blindly as their blue flesh crisped and sloughed from the bone. A daemonic disc exploded, and its rider fell, twitching. The lightning snaked through the horde, killing until it faded.

But still they came on, gathering speed. Sagittus barked a command, and a volley of arrows hissed upwards, plucking furies from the sky, or sending horsemen tumbling from the saddle. But not enough.

Gardus leapt forward with a roar, the Retributors on his heels. He avoided the bite of a blightking's pitted blade and crushed the brute's skull with a blow from his hammer. A tzaangor leapt at him, curved blade drawing sparks from his shoulder-plate. He knocked the bird-thing sprawling and Iunias pulverised it with a two-handed blow. Another Retributor struck the ground, sending a ripple of destruction across the courtyard. He staggered as a blood warrior hacked at him with a pair of axes. Gardus shouldered the Khornate warrior back and drove a knee into his abdomen, folding him over. He drove his opponent's head down until it cracked against the stones, and then kicked him aside, in time to parry a spear-thrust from a mortal in red silks and brass armour.

The mortal was snatched from his feet by Sathphren's gryph-charger and sent flying. The Lord-Aquilor and his steed raced past, a blur of silver and azure, heading for the maul-wielding Lemerus. Sathphren fired his boltstorm pistol and the Chaos champion's steed fell as if poleaxed. Lemerus struggled to its feet, maul raised as Sathphren closed in.

There was a crack, and a sound like many voices raised in agony. Gardus saw Gwyllth roll, screeching, as Sathphren was thrown from her back. The Lord-Aquilor shook his head as if stunned. Lemerus raced towards him, weapon raised.

Gardus drove his sword into the ground, caught the edge of his cloak and turned, causing it to flare in the direction of the fallen Lord-Aquilor. 'Sathphren – get down!' The runic enchantments woven into it blazed to life, and a barrage of celestial magics swept out, hammering Chaos warriors and beastmen from their feet. Lemerus staggered back, black eyes narrowed in consternation.

Sathphren was on his feet a moment later, starbound blade in hand. Lemerus' maul slammed down again, striking the ground, and once again, the air was split by many wailing voices. Sathphren staggered back. Then Gwyllth lunged, slamming into the champion. Lemerus screamed as it was knocked from its feet. It swung its maul around, trying to bat the gryph-charger away. Sathphren closed in, blade held low.

Gardus lost sight of them a moment later as the press of battle pulled him away. He heard a bellow, and saw a Retrib-utor sink down, a blade in her back. Four warriors wearing mirrored helms stepped lightly past the dying Stormcast as lightning blazed upwards. Gardus and Iunias met them. The Retributor flattened one of his opponents, but found himself hard-pressed by two more.

Gardus beat aside his own attacker's blade and snapped the warrior's neck with a blow from his hammer. He was momentarily separated from Iunias by a lumbering blightking, and as he dispatched the rotbringer, he saw Iunias erupt into blue lightning. As it cleared, Bakhos stepped through the crackling energies, a wide grin visible beneath his helm. The Chaos lord launched himself at Gardus, and the Lord-Celestant stepped back, forced to defend himself.

Bakhos was fast – faster than Gardus. His sword was never where Gardus thought it would be, and he felt it slam into his armour again and again, seeking weak points. Worse, Bakhos easily avoided Gardus' own blows, and slipped beneath his guard. 'Your silver dogs are disciplined – but I led phalanxes, Stormcast,' Bakhos laughed. 'I know how fragile even the strongest shield wall is.'

The Chaos lord's sword danced across his wrist, and he lost his hammer. Twisting aside, he caught up his runeblade in a two-handed grip, and barely managed to block a blow that might have slid through one of the eye-slits of his helm. Bakhos darted close, giving him no time to recover. His blade thudded into Gardus' chest and knee-plate. He bulled forward, forcing Gardus back, step by step.

'You fight well, for a silver statue,' Bakhos breathed. 'Tell me your name, eh?'

Gardus said nothing. He could feel blood pooling in his armour. Some of Bakhos' thrusts had found flesh. Bakhos clucked his tongue and padded forward. 'I would offer mercy, but there can be no pacts between leopards and their prey.'

He lunged again. Gardus met him, and their blades skidded against one another. They turned in a staggering circle, swords locked. Past his opponent, Gardus saw Ramus, standing tall against a tide of foes. The line had broken, and every Stormcast was an island of silver. Ashigaroth rampaged among the enemy, tearing them apart. 'That you still live is a testament to your skill,' Bakhos said. 'Rarely have I enjoyed such a spirited duel. But it ends now.'

He shoved Gardus back and their blades were wrenched apart. Lightning flashed, once, twice, again, azure strobes piercing the sky. Gardus felt the weight of his armour, the pain of his wounds. He heard a gryph-charger shriek – and then the sound was cut short.

'If I take your head, will it vanish with the rest of you?' Bakhos purred.

Gardus swung his sword up, readying it.

'Let us find out,' Bakhos said, and mirrored him. The din of battle faded away as Gardus concentrated on the foe before him. But before either of them could make a move, there was a sound like the peal of a bell – a great bell, larger than a fortress, and its sound was as black as the spaces between the stars.

Fighting slowed as all eyes turned to the great obsidian gates. They were opening, slowly but surely.

'Nagash,' Mannfred howled. 'Nagash comes – and death follows with him!' He backed away from the gates, arms spread. 'The Black Sun rises, and time itself shudders to eternal stillness. Behold! See, and know fear!'

A mortuary silence fell, choking all sound from the battlefield. Gardus watched the great gates slowly grinding open. Spectral shapes raced between the obsidian doors, trailing eerie screams. Ghostly riders galloped through the gates, the hooves of their steeds making no sound. The gargoyle-like shapes of morghasts, made from bone and black iron, crashed down from on high to perch upon the top of the gatehouse. They brandished enormous glaives, shrieking out inhuman challenges to the living warriors below.

Finally the gates opened to their full width, revealing the stone expanse of the bridge beyond. It stretched away into the shadow of the pyramid, and was lined by hooded statues of enormous size, their heads bowed as if in prayer – or fear.

There was something black on the bridge. For a moment, it resembled nothing more than a flock of carrion birds, all swirling and screaming, and in that scream – a name. A name that reverberated through the cloying silence like the stroke of a funerary bell.

And then, as the birds became more frenzied and their forms seemed to blur, a voice spoke. It rolled across the ruins like the rumble of shifting ice. Bakhos' forces drew back.

'You called, and I have come.

'Nagash has come.'

The birds slammed together in a screeching cyclone, and in a billowing of feathers, a giant rose, a titan of bone and iron, stinking of sepulchral depths, radiating a dark cold. Nagash. Nagash the Eternal. Nagash the Undying King.

'You called,' he said again as he strode across the bridge, each footfall like the boom of distant thunder. 'And I have come. Who seeks to draw my eye to this place?' The great skull turned. Eyes like dying suns fastened first on Ramus, and then on Mannfred. 'You.'

'Me, O great Nagash, lord of all that walks or crawls,' Mannfred called out. 'See how I serve you, my lord! I bring an army to cast back the forces of your great enemy!'

Nagash was silent for a moment. Then he laughed. Gardus felt a chill race through him at the sound. 'You bring one foe to slay another, my clever little prince. Am I to dispense with them both? Very well.' He raised his claw, and the air writhed with dark power.

'Let it be so.'

CHAPTER TWENTY-SIX

BATTLE

A battle is made of scattered moments. Each is pivotal, in its own way. Only when silence falls can their place in the greater mosaic of victory or defeat be determined.

– Arcudi Fein
A Soldier's Life

Cassandora watched as the battle unfolded in the plaza before her. The southern emplacements were high palisades of wood and stone, anchored into the ground and chained to the closest buildings. Walkways and scaffolding stretched back from them, making a temporary fortification. Ironweld engineers wheeled cannons over the walkways, getting them into position. Below the upper rampart, on a second walkway, handgunners from the Gallowsmen, and two cohorts of Judicators, sent volley after volley into the enemy assaulting the palisades. The air was thick with powder smoke and the dust of pummelled stone.

'Report, Gallia,' she said, glancing at the Judicator-Prime waiting behind her.

'We're holding them, my lady.' Gallia commanded the palisades to the north. Not quite so high as the ones Cassandora stood atop, but more heavily defended. Cohorts of Judicators held the walls there, with support from Liberators and soldiers from the Gold Gryphons. 'But they're bringing up siege weapons,' she added.

Cassandora blinked. 'Siege weapons? Are you sure?'

'Improvised, my lady. Pillars, wrapped in chain, or statues. They've not got close yet, but there's no sign they're planning on giving up.'

'They're doing the same down there,' Grymn said, sourly. The Lord-Castellant stood nearby, leaning on his halberd. 'Look.'

Cassandora turned. Down below, despite the smoke and dust, she could see Chaos warriors dragging statues from plinths and hacking at pillars with axes. She frowned and gestured. Grymn thumped his halberd against the emplacement. Down below, Judicators took aim and loosed a volley.

'Be glad that they don't have artillery,' Grymn said. He shaded his eyes and peered east. 'You know... this may well be the last easy battle we have.'

'Easy?'

'You know what I mean.' Grymn shook his head. 'The fools and the mad and the ones that can't – or won't – learn... they're all but gone, now. The ones who survived – they're more dangerous. More cunning. Imagine what a competent leader could have done with an army this size? Or even just a more attentive one?'

Cassandora felt a chill go through her. 'I know. We were lucky.'

Grymn smiled, but there was no mirth in it. 'But for how

long?' He pulled his helm from his belt and put it on. 'I'm going with Gallia to check the defences to the north.' He paused. 'Go with Sigmar, sister. And try not to get killed. I'd hate to have to explain it to Gardus.'

Cassandora nodded. 'I'd hate that as well.' As Grymn and the Judicator-Prime strode away, Grymn's gryph-hound trotting in their wake, she turned.

Jerob stood farther down the emplacement, hairy arms crossed, a scowl on his face. The battlemage had volunteered his services – or, rather, Ahom had volunteered on his behalf – to support the counter-attack. Ahom and Ilesha had remained in the catacombs to ensure that the dead remained quiescent. Studying the scowl on his face, Cassandora wondered if he were angrier about being pulled away from the catacombs, or being put on the front lines. Then, perhaps he was simply impatient.

She glanced at Lorcus. The young captain-general stood some distance away, spyglass in hand. His general staff waited nearby. The mortals were trying very hard not to look intimidated by the hulking Retributors in their bastion war-plate who waited further back along the walkways. Eight cohorts of the hammer-wielding warriors from across three Chambers waited with stolid calm for her command.

When the time came, drawbridges built into the outer emplacements – really, several lengths of wood chained together and operated by a pulley system of Octarion's design – would be lowered, allowing the Retributors to advance down into the plaza.

They would do so under the watchful eyes of the remaining Vanguard-Raptors, and flanked by Vanguard-Hunters. The fast-moving warriors would ensure that the Paladin Conclave struck like the mailed fist it was meant to be. The Gallowsmen would advance behind them, establishing a second battle-line.

Slowly but surely they would advance along the corridor created by the Ironweld barrages, and drive the enemy before them. It would be a single, solid blow to the enemy's centre. From experience, Cassandora knew that was where the leaders would be. Khornates led from the front, but the Slaaneshi were wiser than that. They liked being close enough to smell the blood, but not close enough to get it on their war-plate.

'Different,' Lorcus murmured. His fingers tap-tapped against the pommel of his sword. He lowered the spyglass, a frown on his face. 'It's different.'

Cassandora nodded. 'More focused. Someone new is in charge.'

'Could that be a problem?'

'Too late to worry about now.' She attempted a confident smile. 'I think Ramus did us a favour, odd as it sounds. I think whoever was in charge followed him. And now their subordinates are reverting to type, which is both better and worse. We need to make sure they stay disorganised – that whoever has picked up the reins doesn't get control.'

'And that's where I come in, eh?' Jon Cruso called out, as he stepped beneath a set of scaffolding and ambled towards them. He bowed floridly. 'My lady. My lord. The Nordrathi Red and Blacks stand ready to cast down the enemy with fire and steel.'

'You know what to do?' Cassandora asked. Cruso had a habit of making up his own plans, rather than following those of his superiors.

He grinned and twirled his moustaches. 'Easy enough, my lady. Slash and shoot until it's time to stop.'

'Good. Go with Sigmar.'

Cruso saluted breezily and trotted back the way he'd come, whistling cheerfully. Lorcus watched him go. 'They won't be enough.'

'They don't have to be,' Cassandora said. 'That's what we're here for. Gather your Gallowsmen, Captain-General Lorcus – it is time to win your city.'

Aetius Shieldborn watched as Reconciler Ahom and the other battlemage muttered their chants and filled the air of the catacombs with ghostly, glowing sigils. The sigils flickered like candles in the dark before fading away. He contemplated the glowing motes, wondering what they meant. From the look on Ahom's face, it wasn't anything good.

'Why are we here, Shieldborn?' Ravius muttered. The Liberator – one of half a dozen stationed throughout the chamber – glanced up, towards the tower of wooden scaffolding that led up from the catacombs to the street above. Echoes of the Ironweld artillery drifted down, causing the stones around them to tremble. Ravius slapped his sheathed warblade. 'We should be on the front lines – facing our foes.'

'We are,' Aetius said. He pointed to the sealed entrance to the burial vaults. 'The dead are as much our enemies as the living. And they are gathering their strength. Listen.'

The scratching had grown louder since Aetius had been ordered to bring his cohort to the catacombs. It was a constant, pervasive sound, hiding beneath the clamour of the battle taking place on the streets above. It was coming from all directions, as if an army of the dead were slowly digging its way towards them.

'They're getting closer,' another Liberator – Serena – murmured. 'Stronger.' She looked at Aetius. 'If they burst free...'

'Then we are to escort the battlemages and their assistants to the surface, before setting off the powder-charges along the support pillars.' The Ironweld had planted the charges at Gardus' insistence, just in case Ahom and his fellow mages failed to contain the dead in their vaults – which was looking more likely by the moment.

Aetius could sense the push and pull of magics on the dusty air. Ahom's voice was hoarse as he wove a complex rite from the verbal and the physical. Beside him, Ilesha drew wards on the walls in blood taken from an auroch and mixed with sacred purple salts. Their apprentices added their voices to Ahom's own. Aetius felt a strange pressure, as of a bubble about to burst.

When it did, they all felt it. It was as if someone – something – had spoken. A single, black note that struck the air and shattered all thought, just for a second. A single word, echoing through the space between one moment and the next.

'Awaken.'

Aetius felt it in his marrow. He had heard that voice before, he thought, calling out to him in the instant before his soul had been drawn to Azyr by Sigmar's grace. He looked around and saw that his warriors had been similarly affected. Serena shook her head.

'What – what was that?' she asked, hoarsely.

'Quiet,' Aetius growled. 'Listen.'

The dead had fallen silent. As he watched, the mystic sigils on the walls flared like dying stars, and crumbled away. Ahom looked around, face pale in the torchlight. 'No,' the astromancer whispered. He clutched his head and looked at Ilesha, who had gone grey, her expression one of fear.

'I heard it as well. Like a bell tolling far away in the deep. I know that voice. The amethyst winds respond to it, the way a dog heeds its master's call...'

Stones shifted, scraped and fell, as ancient mortar became powder, and the bricked-up archways crumbled. Portals that had been sealed since before Caddow's fall opened once more. Aetius caught the gleam of bone, and heard the rasp of weapons leaving rotted sheaths echoing from all around them. 'Shields – forward,' he barked. 'Bulwark formation!'

Ravius, Serena and the others fell into formation, lifting their shields and readying their weapons. Aetius stepped towards Ahom and Ilesha. 'It is time to leave, reconciler. You have done what you could. Now we must go.'

'No, I will not be – be chased away by clattering bones,' Ahom said. Cerulean energies swirled about his knotted fists. 'I am a reconciler – this place, its secrets, they will belong to Azyr!' His voice echoed through the chamber, and something in the dark sighed.

The first dead man lunged into the lantern light a moment later – a shape devoid of flesh, wrapped in rags and armour of unfamiliar design, wielding a long-hafted axe. As it emerged from the collapsed walls, Ahom flung out a hand, and spat a single word. Blue lightning erupted from his palm and struck the dead thing full in the archaic breastplate it wore. The lightning ripped through the skeletal warrior, and it arrowed backwards into the darkness it had emerged from.

In the fading azure glare, Aetius saw more of the dead – dozens, hundreds – stirring from biers of stone that seemed to stretch away forever. In great alcoves set along the walls, fleshless soldiers stirred, lifting rusted shields and spears. Amethyst witch-light glowed in empty sockets, and limned blades that had not been drawn in centuries. The royal dead of Caddow were awake at last. An army, ready to reclaim that which had once been theirs.

Aetius caught Ahom by his robes and shoved him towards the wooden steps that led to the street. 'Go – all of you, go! Fall back!'

'Up and at them, you great wazzocks!' Mahk bellowed, holding his grudge-raker over his head. 'Get those emplacements moving.' The street shook as the mobile emplacements ground forward, pushed by men and duardin. The heavy barriers of gromril and stone had concealed celestine runners, allowing them to gouge through almost anything. It made a mess of the street, but that was a small price to pay.

As the emplacements advanced, so too did the Ironweld handgunners sheltering behind them. Whether human or duardin, they wore half-armour over ochre uniforms of stiff canvas and leather, with round, open-faced helms, stamped with the sigil of the Ironweld. Each carried a handgun of their own construction, and enough powder and shot to see them through the fight ahead. They were all apprentices – junior engineers and gunners – and this was an important part of their training. Knowing how to handle a weapon was as important as knowing how to make one, at least to Mahk's way of thinking.

Following in their wake came assorted clockwork contraptions, some shaped like small duardin, others like animals, all carrying replacement parts, and extra powder and shot. All of it would be sorely needed in the hours ahead, if he was any judge.

Most cogsmiths and gunmasters contented themselves with overseeing artillery batteries or defensive emplacements, but Mahk liked to play a more active role in things. He liked to smell the powder smoke and feel the kick of a grudge-raker.

'Oli, watch the rooftops,' Mahk snapped, gesturing to one of his apprentices. 'Put that rangefinder of yours to use, boy.' The duardin nodded as Mahk turned to another engineer, this one a human, sitting atop a clockwork steed of his own design. 'Gatz – I want you and that infernal contraption of yours to ride over to the western emplacement. See if Dront has shifted his fat rear yet. If he hasn't, give him a kick. Lady Cassandora wants them held fast, and I intend to give her what she wants.'

He turned back to the emplacements. 'Right – hold position,' he growled. 'Bring up the guns!' At his order, two steam-wagons rattled over the broken cobbles, iron-shod wheels casting up sparks. The wagons were little more than narrow frames of iron and wood, driven by boilers housed beneath the driver's cupola. At the front of each was a wide bed on which sat a piece of artillery – in this case, Helblaster volley guns.

Mahk grinned. He'd always liked the Helblasters. Quantity over quality, perhaps, but they did make a fine mess of whatever was unlucky enough to be in front of them.

The wagons stopped a safe distance from the emplacements and their crews hurriedly set down chocks to keep them from moving when the guns fired. 'Hurry it up,' Mahk shouted. 'They'll regroup in a moment, and I want to greet them properly.'

From the other side of the emplacements came a bellow. It might have been a name, erupting from hoarse throats. It sounded more like a curse – two nonsense syllables, chanted by demented warriors. From within the smoke that shrouded the street came the thud of heavy, running feet. The chants grew louder, and Mahk squinted, trying to see.

The Chaos warrior burst from the smoke, running full-tilt towards the emplacements. He was larger than the others, larger even than a Stormcast. His tread cracked stone, and reverberated like cannon-fire. Handguns barked but he didn't stop. Didn't slow. A chill ran through Mahk, and he gestured. 'Brace! Brace, damn you!'

The Chaos warrior struck one of the emplacements. It creaked and swayed. The Chaos warrior struck it again, using his body as a ram. The emplacement fell, and handgunners scrambled back with cries of alarm. The warrior rose, roaring. He had a single-bladed axe in either hand, and his armour was the colour of a bruise gone green. A horned helm hid his features, save for his glaring eyes. He pivoted, bisecting an unlucky handgunner with a single blow. He split the skull of another. Behind him, the rest of the warband began to advance, racing towards the breach.

'Keep them back!' Mahk bellowed. His shouts attracted the attention of the Chaos warrior. Shaking the gore from his axes, he advanced. Handgunners tried to stop him but were smashed aside almost casually. 'Out of the way,' Mahk shouted, trying to get a clear shot at the Chaos warrior. Fire from the rooftops struck him, but he only twitched. Whatever his armour was made of, the guns couldn't pierce it.

'Maybe this will do the job,' Mahk snarled. He fired the grudge-raker, and the Chaos warrior staggered back with a hollow roar. The smoke cleared, and Mahk saw that he'd barely done more than scratch the giant's armour. With a rumbling growl, the Chaos warrior took a step towards him, axes raised.

'Down!' a voice roared. Mahk ducked as a silver shape leapt over him, hammers snapping out with meteoric force. The Chaos warrior fell back as Taltus attacked with a fury Mahk had never seen the Lord-Ordinator display before. His astral hammers slammed down, and celestial energies blazed as a wave of force crushed his foe back against the shattered emplacements.

The Chaos warrior lunged forward again, and Taltus was forced to leap aside. He kept moving, backing away, circling. It took Mahk a moment to realise that Taltus was leading his opponent into position for–

'Now!' Taltus shouted, as he dropped flat. The Helblasters roared as one. The Chaos warrior tottered, armour smoking. He took a step, and then sank to his knees with a groan. Taltus rose, hammers in hand. He raised them both and struck. The Chaos warrior toppled forward and lay still. 'Are you still in one piece, cogsmith?' Taltus asked, looking at Mahk.

'Clearly I am. Move, you sluggards – get that emplacement fixed!' Mahk gesticulated as engineers hurried to replace the broken emplacement.

'I came to tell you that you need to recalculate the angle of fire on the northernmost batteries,' Taltus said. 'We need to drive them together. Clump them up in the central thoroughfares.'

Mahk laughed. 'All in one stew pot, eh? Fine. If that's the way the lady wants it. I–' He stopped, his eyes widening. 'Grungni's thumbs – he's not dead!' Taltus spun as the Chaos warrior dragged himself to his knees, an amethyst light dancing in his eyes.

Shouts from nearby soldiers said that same was happening up and down the line. Even the handgunners the Chaos warrior had killed were beginning to twitch and flop, as if possessed of a new and malign life.

'What is this?' Mahk growled, looking around. 'What's going on?'

'Time has run out,' Taltus said, grimly, as the dead began to clamber to their feet.

'For the Great Mountain!' Jon Cruso roared. 'Red as blood, black as night!'

Behind him, the Nordrathi harquebusiers galloped down the ancient thoroughfare in a wedge-shaped formation, their handguns barking. The enemy flank disintegrated, and warriors previously intent on reaching the palisades ahead of them instead fled back into their own ranks. Cruso laughed. 'That's the way! Give them a taste of Nordrathi steel!'

He had been all but born into the saddle, trained to ride and shoot from an early age. This was what he lived for. He raised his repeater handgun and took aim. The gun roared, peppering the foe. Bodies fell and his steed trampled them, as it had been trained to do. Nordrathi stallions were among the finest horseflesh in the celestial realm – the equal of any Azyrheim destrier.

More repeaters growled as his harquebusiers followed his example. Cruso reloaded without looking, his hands guided by instinct and training. The Red and Blacks crashed through the fraying lines, never slowing. Some of his warriors drew repeater pistols and fired wildly, whooping and singing as their steeds leapt over the fallen pillars and statues that littered the plaza.

In moments, the enemy vanguard – mostly mortals, poorly armed and armoured – came apart and reeled back, ceding the ground. The Ironweld barrage had done its work. The bulk of the enemy army had been forced into a narrow corridor of streets and cul-de-sacs, with only the central plaza ahead of them. Slowly, but surely, they'd been cut off from the rest of the city and boxed in by advancing Stormcasts. Not that it seemed to bother them.

The enemy's strength was in numbers. They could overwhelm any defence, burst any gate, because there were always that many more of them. Block one route, they'd simply take another. But they could be slowed down and their strength bled away, if you were quick enough. The Nordrathi Red and Blacks specialised in quick. They would blaze away at the foe, and then reposition themselves before the enemy could react.

As he galloped along the plaza, Cruso studied the foe. Their advance hadn't slowed. To the contrary, they'd picked up speed upon spotting the harquebusiers. He'd have time for two volleys, maybe three.

Cruso hauled on the reins, bringing his steed to a halt. 'Ready – *volley!*' he roared, signalling. Harquebusiers turned in their saddles, and took aim at the approaching enemy ranks. Repeater handguns had a middling range, but the enemy was close enough – and so tightly packed – that it wouldn't matter. 'Hold,' Cruso growled, letting his steed canter behind the gun-line. 'Make every shot count, my lads, or I'll be wondering why you wasted Sigmar's blessed ammunition, eh?'

He used the barrel of his handgun to adjust a rider's aim. 'Up a bit, Stainlaus – there.' He turned. 'Bellam, finger off the trigger until I say, girl. There now... hold... hold...' Silently, he thanked Sigmar and all his saints that this foe seemed disinclined to archery. He'd seen what warp-arrows and balefire could do to a gun-line.

He glanced back towards the palisades on the other end of the plaza. He could see silver gleaming in the light of torches and storm-lanterns. The Stormcasts were there, waiting for whatever was left when he got finished. He grinned and turned back to the enemy. 'Not much, by the stars,' he murmured. 'Not much left at all.'

The horses stirred, whickering softly. There were low, lean shapes loping among the foe – malformed hounds, or things that ran on four legs. And other things as well, capering, flickering shapes, barely visible among the great mass of bodies charging across the broken ground. The sight of them sent a chill through him, and the horses stamped and snorted. He patted his steed, trying to calm the animal.

'Mad,' one of his warriors said, his voice hushed with fear. 'They see us – they must.'

'They don't care, lad,' Cruso said. 'They think they'll live forever, these beasts. Think their heathen gods have blessed them, made them immortal.' He forced a grin and tweaked his moustaches. 'But we'll show them different, eh?' He raised his handgun. 'Close enough – on my mark, send them Sigmar's greetings... *fire!*'

Repeater handguns roared along the line, and the front ranks of the enemy fell. Not all of them, to be sure. Some staggered on, their armour enabling them to weather the fusillade. But not many. 'Reload,' Cruso said. 'Quickly!'

New cylinders were clicked into place, already loaded and primed. 'Ready... aim... *fire!*' Cruso snarled, as he pulled his own trigger. Another grinding roar, more of the enemy falling in heaps and piles – but not enough, never enough. The rest came on, surging ahead with reckless abandon. Fallen standards were picked up, and raised anew. It wasn't courage, Cruso thought – it was lunacy.

The front ranks crumbled apart, and the advance frayed. As the smoke wafted thick, a massive shape burst through the wavering ranks, scattering many. A chariot, Cruso realised, as the smoke thinned.

It was a monstrous thing – a wide platform, set atop two enormous, crushing wheels of iron and wood, drawn by a team of mutated beasts. A tangle of chains, tipped with barbs and hooks, thrashed in its wake, like the tail of some great beast. A wedge of shields, trophies of past battles, had been hung from the sides and front of the platform, and a plethora of captured standards and banner poles jutted from the back. Aboard the chariot, a massive warrior crouched – a bestial nightmare, clad in golden war-plate, with a flat, wide head that was little more than a fang-studded maw.

Two slim mortal servants crouched beside the brute, both wearing armour, both chained to the creature. They each carried a massive shield, leaving their hideous master free to wield the heavy, wide-flanged mace it held. To Cruso, the mace resembled nothing so much as the head of a siege-ram. The brute raised the weapon over its malformed head and the warriors loping alongside the chariot began to chant.

'*Etax... Etax... Etax...*'

More chariots followed the first, rumbling through the press. No two were alike, save in size and speed. Some trailed smoking censers or glowed with an ugly, unnatural radiance. One was accompanied by a flock of multicoloured birds, while another was drawn not by beasts but by a hunched gargant, its head hidden in an iron cage wrought in the shape of a horse's head. There were ten of them in all – too many to stop.

Cruso cursed as his horse reared. 'Back, back,' he roared. He yanked on the reins, hauling his steed around and galloping down a nearby side street. His warriors followed suit, and in moments they were surging away from the approaching enemy. 'Just like harrying a cave bear, my lads,' he called out. 'Don't waste time with the jaws and the claws – go for the flanks and belly.' His warriors cheered.

There was a crossroads ahead. The harquebusiers turned, following Cruso's lead, flowing smoothly north. They couldn't stop the chariots, but they might be able to slow them down. 'Shoot and slash,' he shouted. 'Don't stop, don't slow!'

They entered the plaza from the side. A Chaos warrior roared out commands, and mortals armed with spears and round shields attempted some semblance of a shield wall. 'Fire!' Cruso shouted, loosing the reins to raise his weapon. The shield wall disintegrated and the harquebusiers burst through the scattered survivors. The Chaos warrior swung a heavy blade, and one horse tumbled, shrieking, spilling its rider into the street. Cruso didn't stop. Couldn't stop. He heard repeater pistols bark, and the Chaos warrior howl in either pain or anger. Then, a man's scream. 'Sorry, lad,' he muttered.

The harquebusiers' charge had caught the enemy by surprise. Their advance stalled and broke up into eddies of movement. It wouldn't last, but the damage would be done. The riders galloped through the enemy, trusting in their speed to see them through. Firing and reloading as they went, they wheeled towards the chariots, still rumbling towards the palisades.

'After them,' Cruso shouted. If they could catch the chariots from behind, they might be able to stall them, or at least steal their momentum.

The explosion came as a shock, echoing from somewhere behind the palisades. His horse reared, whinnying. The street shook and collapsed in places, sinkholes forming. Clouds of dust spewed upwards, filling the air. Cruso shook his head, all but deafened.

His horse squealed suddenly and staggered, nearly throwing him from the saddle. Cruso saw that one of the bodies he'd been galloping over wasn't quite dead. Hands gripped his steed's foreleg. The animal bucked and kicked, but to no avail. As he fired at the ground, he realised that he'd been wrong – they were dead, after all. But moving nonetheless.

His horse stumbled as more bodies lurched up, clawing at the animal's withers and neck. Cruso drew a repeater pistol from his saddle and fired, trying to free his steed, but to no avail. The animal fell, taking him with it.

Cruso cried out in pain as the horse fell on him, pinning his leg. The dead swarmed over the screaming animal, ripping handfuls from its flesh. As he fought to free himself, he saw that it wasn't a localised incident – the dead were rising everywhere, lurching up, attacking anything that stood near them. He saw a harquebusier dragged down, and heard the screams of the enemy as cold hands clawed at their legs.

And then the dead were upon him, and there was no time to see anything else.

CHAPTER TWENTY-SEVEN

BITTER ENDINGS

*Await not the end, for it comes unseen and
unheralded.*

– Nechris Litharge
The Black Wisdom

The dead rose.

Gardus turned, his heart cold in his chest. The groaning
of the newly stirred dead set claws dancing along his spine.
'Sigmar preserve us,' he whispered, as broken bodies began
to drag themselves upright. He spun, splitting the skull of a
corpse as it clawed for him.

Bakhos cursed gutturally and darted past him, heading for
Nagash. 'At last,' he roared. 'My story's end – glorious and–'

Mannfred slipped between them, his blade flashing. Bakhos
skidded back, a snarl on his lips. The two traded blows, moving with quicksilver speed. Nagash didn't seem to care about
the Mortarch's efforts on his behalf. He continued to advance.

His morghasts crashed to the ground on either side of him, as if they were an honour guard. Wherever his shadow stretched, the dead began to twitch and rise.

'This is my place,' Nagash said. 'My ground. Where I walk, the earth gives up its bounty.' Each word was a death knell. Chaos warriors fell to their knees, clutching their heads and howling in pain. Spectral forms swirled across the courtyard, whispering, pleading, laughing. 'Who are you, to challenge me here?'

Gardus shoved aside a stumbling corpse and found his path blocked by dozens more. They forced him back, as Nagash continued on. A great hand shot out and caught up a screaming warrior. Nagash turned him this way and that, studying him as if he were an insect. 'I smell the stink of Varanspire on you. Is he here, then? Has the Three-Eyed King come again?' The massive skull, lit by internal fires, turned. Searching for something. For someone. 'No. Just his rabble. His curs, sent to gnaw at the bones of my kingdom. How disappointing.'

Nagash flung his prisoner aside. The gesture was casual, but its force was undeniable. The screaming warrior hurtled across the courtyard and struck a pillar with a wet crack. He tumbled down, leaving a red stain at the point of impact. Nagash's gaze fell on Ramus, who stared up at him with seeming determination.

The Lord-Relictor didn't move as Nagash closed in. The Undying King stopped and looked down at him. 'I know you, do I not? A soul I have held in my grasp before. Rightfully mine, and stolen. One of Sigmar's slaves, wrapped in the flesh of a dead world. What do you have to say to me, little slave? Have you come to challenge me again?'

'I have,' Ramus cried. 'I will challenge you as many times as it takes.'

Gardus bulled through the corpses, trying to reach the

Lord-Relictor. He could not – would not – allow Ramus to stand alone. If Nagash noticed his approach, he gave no sign. But his morghasts had. One of the gargoyle-like monstrosities turned towards Gardus and raised its shimmering halberd.

It shrieked and took a step towards him, fleshless wings flaring. Gardus slid to a stop, blade ready. The morghast's claws scraped the ground. Its ebon armour gleamed with an amethyst radiance, and the souls of the slain clung to the blade of the halberd it levelled. They moaned and wailed, reaching out to Gardus as if begging him to set them free.

Past the creature, he saw Nagash stop before Ramus. The Undying King looked down at the Lord-Relictor as if curious. 'And what would tempt you to do this?' Nagash sounded almost… amused, Gardus thought. 'Do you yearn for the peace of my realm? Or perhaps you seek freedom from the servitude enforced upon you by the God-King? Is that it, little slave? Would you have me break the chains of starlight that bind your soul to its imperfect flesh?'

Nagash paused, the hell-lights in his sockets blazing like dark stars. 'I sense a black mote of bitterness on your soul. You would make a fine warrior for my cause. Yes… is that it?' He tilted his head. 'Is that your desire, Ramus of the Shadowed Soul?'

Ramus faltered, as if struck by a sudden, strong wind. Nagash chuckled, a sound like falling ice. 'Yes, I know you. I can read your soul as easily as you might read a scroll. I see to the heart of you, and find much that pleases me. The God-King has betrayed you, as well.' He extended an iron talon. 'Come. Bow before me, and I will raise you high in my councils. I will give you all that you desire, and more besides.'

Ramus stared up at the Undying King, and seemed unable to speak. 'I–' he began, his voice hoarse and hollow. Gardus could feel the cold heat of Nagash's radiance – the blistering chill of a black sun, burning and freezing all around it. What man's will could resist such a thing? He could feel the echoes of Nagash's words insinuating themselves in his mind, even here on the periphery of the god's attentions, and knew that it would be so much worse for Ramus. Like being drawn inexorably towards the edge of unending abyss.

'Ramus – no!' Gardus shouted, trying to shock the Lord-Relictor from his fugue. Nagash glanced at him and gestured. The morghast lunged with a guttural roar. Gardus barely avoided the bite of the halberd. His own blow struck the morghast in the abdomen, cutting deeply into the bone. He tore his sword free as the morghast struck at him again, and managed to parry its second blow.

As he stepped back, he saw Ramus raise his reliquary standard and slam it down. Lightning blazed, and Nagash stepped back. 'No,' Ramus croaked. He leaned against his standard, obviously exhausted by his effort. 'No.'

'Very well.' Nagash made to reach for him, but a cry of pain stopped him. Mannfred staggered into view, pursued closely by Bakhos. The vampire matched Bakhos blow for blow, but the Chaos lord was relentless. Every attack drove Mannfred back another step. Nagash straightened. 'And what is this? Can you not even handle one simple mortal, my Mortarch? Is this too beyond your meagre skill?'

Bakhos laughed and shoved Mannfred back with a final, ringing blow. 'Simple? I am anything but, O Lord of Bones. I am Bakhos, last king of Semele, and I come to claim your skull in the name of the Three-Eyed King!' The Chaos lord lifted his blade in challenge, and tore off his crested helm, exposing wild, handsome features. 'Perhaps you will prove the challenge these others failed to be.'

'No,' Nagash said, simply.

Bakhos frowned. Then, with a roar, he sprang past Mannfred and leapt at Nagash. The Undying King's eyes blazed, and Bakhos staggered, his roar becoming a strangled groan. He took another step and Gardus saw that his flesh had withered, losing its sheen of health. Another step, and his armour had rusted, the leopard pelts becoming rotten and tattered. His sword corroded, even as he lifted it. 'No,' he croaked. 'No – my story…'

'This is Shyish,' Nagash said. 'Where all stories end.' He gestured, and Bakhos cried out. Amethyst light blazed from within his mouth and eyes as his body contorted in obvious agony. Smoke boiled from the Chaos lord's pores, and he fell with a dismal thud. Nagash stared down at the smouldering carcass for a moment, and then looked at Gardus.

'Perhaps you will prove more interesting. I see the hand of the Azyrite barbarian on you. He whispers to you, does he not? Or has he fallen silent at the last?' Nagash stepped towards Gardus, and the ground shook.

'I see your past as clearly as the present, Stormcast,' he continued. 'Echoes of you travel ever backwards, showing me all I need to know. Caddow, City of Crows. The Corvine Gate has opened, and Azyr exposes its underbelly to me once more. Shall I claw out its guts with a hundred thousand hands? Shall I send the dead of untold centuries stumbling up into the stars?' Nagash laughed, and Gardus felt his mouth fill with blood. The Undying King glanced down at Mannfred. 'Tell me, my Mortarch? What shall I do?'

'Nothing, my lord – save perhaps give thanks,' Mannfred said, eyes averted from the awful immensity of his master.

Nagash paused. 'What?'

Mannfred looked up, and smiled.

* * *

Lorcus swept his sword out, chopping through a corpse's grasping hand. It had all gone wrong. There was an adage – no plan survives contact with the enemy. Then, who could plan for the dead suddenly standing up and attacking everyone in Caddow?

He'd lost his horse, somewhere. Around him, Gallowsmen and Stormcasts fought against living enemies and dead ones alike. Lorcus caught a blow on his shield, and turned, slashing blind. The organised assault had become a wild melee – every man for himself. The streets were choked with dust and powder smoke, rendering everyone the same, muddled colour. The catacombs had been collapsed, leaving many of the streets unstable.

He staggered as an axe-wielding warrior with a face like melted wax and a torso wrapped in silver chains struck his shield. The warrior howled, casting spittle in all directions. Lorcus beat aside his attacker's axe and thrust his blade through the creature's throat. The body fell away, nearly dragging his sword from his hand. As it hit the ground, it began to twitch. Amethyst light blazed in its eyes.

A hammer slammed down, crushing the corpse's skull. 'Destroy the heads,' Cassandora coughed. Her armour was streaked with ichor and dust. She looked him up and down. 'Are you hurt?'

'In one piece,' Lorcus wheezed. 'More than I can say for your plan?'

'It was working well enough.' Cassandora turned. 'The dead are waking up all over the city. We may need to fall back.'

'To where?'

'Nordrath,' she said. 'If we can't hold out, we'll have no choice but to retreat.' Lorcus was about to reply, when he heard a roar and saw a monstrous shape loom up out of the dust. A stunted gargant, wearing a cage-helm in the shape of a horse's head, burst into view, dragging the broken remains of a chariot in its wake. The beast smashed a Stormcast from its path with a wild sweep of its arm. It roared, and Lorcus winced.

Another roar answered it. Lorcus turned and saw Jerob stalking through the dust, a pale amber radiance illuminating him. The battlemage picked up speed, shoving through the melee, his body swelling, growing larger and larger, until he wasn't a man at all but one of the great cave bears that haunted the peaks above Nordrath.

The bear slammed into the gargant, tearing and biting. The two great beasts stumbled from one side of the street to the other, causing the smaller combatants to scatter. Lorcus lost sight of them as the dust swirled, stirred by the battle. He caught a glimpse of something gold, moving towards him. The dust thinned.

The hulking Chaos warrior, his circular maw gnashing, slammed a heavy mace down, crushing an unfortunate soldier. The monster dragged the bodies of two slaves behind him, their dead forms chained to his chest-plate. They twitched and flailed, clawing at anyone who drew too close, even their unheeding master. Lorcus recognised the beast – the enemy commander, or as close to one as they'd had.

'I think we found the one in charge,' he said. Cassandora nodded. The Chaos warrior bellowed as a Retributor confronted him. He swung his mace around, smashing the Stormcast from his feet in a spray of blue lightning.

'Fall back,' she said. 'Signal the withdrawal.'

'And what are you going to do?'

'I'm going to make sure that they don't follow us. Go!' Cassandora started towards the beast. The creature warbled savagely, as it caught sight of the Lord-Celestant.

Cassandora avoided its first blow, and her sword sliced through the chains binding the dead slaves. The broken bodies tumbled away as the creature lunged for her again, mace swinging. Its blow shattered a pillar, sending a spray of broken stone across the street. Cassandora staggered as one of the chunks struck her helm.

She stumbled away from her opponent as it closed in, mace raised. Without thinking, Lorcus raced towards it, blade held low. His blow took the brute in a gap between the golden plates of its armour. It whirled, shrieking. Its blow cracked the street, and a shard of stone sliced across his thigh. He fell onto his back, barely interposing his shield to block a glancing blow. The force of it numbed his arm and shoulder, and he knew he wouldn't be able to block a second blow. The creature loomed over him, mace held over its lumpen head.

'No. We're not done yet.'

The Chaos warrior spun, snarling unintelligibly. Cassandora kicked it in the gut, and brought her hammer down across its head, as it bent forward. The creature yowled and lurched at her, tackling her from her feet. Lorcus hauled himself towards them, knowing there was little he could do, but knowing he had to try.

But Cassandora shoved her attacker back and lunged up, driving her runeblade through its midsection. Turning past the brute, she ripped the sword free in a spray of tarry gore. The Chaos warrior sank to his knees with a wet gurgle, and finally fell.

'Fool,' Cassandora breathed, looking at Lorcus. She stomped on the brute's skull, crushing it. 'I told you to call for the retreat.' She looked around as the roar of a triumphant bear echoed along the street. Dead men stumbled out of the dust, reaching. Retributors smashed them down, forming a ragged battle-line.

The surviving Gallowsmen were forming up as well. Lorcus

caught sight of Lieutenant Dashos cursing and gesticulating, forcing her soldiers into formation. His cousin saw him and raised her sword in salute. He nodded and winced as pain shot through his leg. The enemy – the living ones, anyway – were falling back, retreating. The dead ones were... hesitating. The dead stood, as if listening to some faraway voice.

'Did we win?' he asked.

'Close enough,' Cassandora said. She helped him to his feet. 'We'll pull back to the palisades.' She looked at the unmoving corpses, and shook her head. 'If we can hold them – if we can outlast the dead – then we may yet see the dawn.'

'And if we can't?'

Cassandora shook her head. 'Have faith, Lorcus. Whatever else, we must have faith. Now signal the retreat, before the dead remember we're here.'

'What?' Nagash said, again. His voice seemed to echo through Gardus' bones.

'Surely, my lord, such ingratitude is beneath one as mighty as yourself?' Mannfred asked, obsequiously. He dropped to his knees. 'Here, see – this creature, Bakhos by name, sought to breach the gate to Nekroheim. And I brought an army to prevent him. These warriors – weak though they are – fought to protect this place from the servants of the Three-Eyed King. They have done Shyish a good turn, my lord.'

'And so, I should forgive their trespasses?' Nagash sounded amused, again. 'I should blind myself to the impertinence of my enemy?'

'Why not? What is one city to you, my lord? What is a realm to you, who rules all realms, in truth? Show them your munificence, my lord – gift them a tiny plot of land, in thanks for this favour.' Mannfred looked up, all slyness gone from his

471

face. 'Whatever else, let it not be said that you are not the just god I know you to be.'

Nagash stared down at him. Then, with a twitch of one talon-tip, the dead... stopped. The risen corpses stood as still as statues, unmoving even as the surviving Stormcast extricated themselves from their clutches. 'I am just. I am *justice*. The final justice.' That awful gaze turned to Gardus. 'Caddow is mine. All dead things are mine. The little prince has stated your case – would you add to it, before I make my judgement?'

'I have nothing to add,' Gardus said. 'Save to say that you struck foul when we extended the hand of friendship. Perhaps there is fault on both sides for that. But now we stand here again – allies, if not friends. Together, we might drive back–'

'Together?' The word hung on the air like the sigh of a dying man. 'Together. Do not speak such homilies to me, little slave. You who serve a betrayer. A liar. *A thief.*' Nagash leaned low, and his shadow seemed to swallow Gardus up. Frost formed on his armour, and the cold bit him to the marrow. 'Would you have me give up still more to one who has already taken so much?'

'It would be a gift, my lord, a true gift,' Mannfred said, quickly. 'A worthy reward for these who helped you. A sign of your magnanimity.'

Nagash glanced at him. 'And do you seek a reward, my Mortarch? Do you think me ungracious?' The Undying King spread his arms. 'What would you have of me, then?' Nagash glanced at Ramus. 'Ah. I read it on the surface of both your thoughts. Such a little thing, but so precious. You wish me to give up my rightful property. Would you beg it of me, Mannfred? *Would you dare make this request?*'

Mannfred hesitated. Before the vampire could respond, Gardus spoke for him. 'We would.' He forced himself to meet

Nagash's gaze. 'You call Sigmar thief. What then are you, O Undying King? A thief who steals from another thief is still a thief.'

Nagash rose to his full height. 'And what if I deny you this? Will you fight me? Will you unleash that light I see burning in you, to counter my own?' He peered down at Gardus. 'Then, you have always been my enemy, Garradan of Demesnus. How many souls did you snatch from my rightful grasp, before Sigmar did the same? Like master, like slave. And here you are, seeking one more.'

Gardus had no reply. He could feel the light, responding somehow to Nagash's voice. It thrashed within him, seeking release. Nagash laughed.

'No. I misspoke. You are not a slave. Even a slave has more free will than you, little weapon.' Nagash reached out and dragged a claw across Gardus' chest-plate, etching the sigmarite. 'Would you like me to tell you what you are? Would you like me to tell you the truth of the light burning in you, little weapon? The truth of what you are fated to be?'

Gardus stared upwards, unable to tear his eyes away from Nagash's own. 'No,' he said, forcing the word out. 'Much is demanded of those to whom much is given.'

Nagash snorted. 'A pretty statement.' He glanced at Ramus. 'But here is one who does not believe in it. You denied me… What if I were to ask you again? Your soul for that of Tarsus Bullheart?' The words were teasing. A spiteful taunt.

'Yes,' Ramus said, softly.

Nagash looked at Gardus. 'What about you?'

'Yes,' Gardus said, without hesitation.

'We all would make that trade, monster,' Sathphren called out. 'Ask any warrior here. Our soul for his. A worthy trade.'

Nagash nodded, as if considering. Then, he looked at Mannfred.

'And what about you, my Mortarch? Would you trade your soul for his?'

Mannfred looked at the ground. For long moments, he said nothing. Then, 'What use is that? You already own my soul, O Undying King.'

'Indeed. But I am generous, as you said. I am merciful.' Nagash turned towards the bridge, one arm extended. The surface of the bridge seemed to waver, like a mirage in the desert. Then, as if emerging from out of the very air, shapes appeared. Twenty dead men hauling rusty chains in their wake, clattering over the stones of the bridge. They were old things, and withered, their armour corroded and their clothing merely tatters. Behind them, wrapped in the chains, was a broad shape – human, but large. The size of a Stormcast.

'I foresaw your arrival, and knew the reason for this invasion before you even entered this realm, little souls,' Nagash said. 'Thus, I prepared accordingly. Look. See. Your lost brother comes.'

The prisoner wore no armour, and only the basest rags, beneath the loops of chain. He rolled and slid across the stones, with seemingly no impetus to stand or move on his own.

'Tarsus,' Ramus said, his voice a whisper. 'He lives. He truly lives.' The hope in his voice was agonising in its intensity. He took a step towards the approaching corpses, but Mannfred stopped him.

'Wait.'

The dead men reached the gateway and stopped. They let the chains go slack, and stepped aside, revealing their prisoner. Gardus bit back an oath, and heard Ramus mutter a prayer. Mannfred turned away. Even the vampire was sickened by what lay before them.

Tarsus was a broken thing. Whatever he once might have

been, he was now a maddened husk, body twisted by agonies Gardus could not even imagine. The dusky flesh was striped by raw, red marks, like the scars of a surgeon's knife, and the once handsome features had become blunt and brutish from privation. The shaggy hair was colourless, as were the wide, staring eyes. The thing – Tarsus – heaved himself to his feet with a curious, mewling wail. It was the cry of an animal tortured beyond its endurance.

'There. See how he greets you,' Nagash intoned, black amusement evident in every word. 'He has missed his brothers dearly.'

The dead strained to hold their prisoner back, chains stretched to their utmost. Gardus saw that the links were barbed and hooked into the captive's flesh. Trails of tarry blood streaked his crooked limbs. Tarsus stared at them, mouth wide, but only that strange, thin wail emerging.

'Tarsus,' Ramus said, hollowly. He took a step towards his Lord-Celestant. 'No...'

'My lord, what – what have you done?' Mannfred stared at the broken shape.

Nagash laughed. It was an ugly sound, like the creak of some great mausoleum door opening. 'Did you think me some petty king, to keep my captives in state? He was no honoured guest. Merely the answer to a minor puzzle. One I have solved.'

At a wave of his talon, the chains burst, and Tarsus Bullheart surged free with a shrill roar. The maddened warrior lunged, bloody, raw fingers spread like talons. Ramus stumbled back, unprepared. Tarsus, still screaming, caught at his Lord-Relictor's throat.

Gardus moved swiftly. His fist hammered home, catching Tarsus in the side. Tarsus spun, eyes bulging, teeth snapping. Gardus hit him again, across the jaw, this time. Tarsus fell with a whine. 'Hold him,' he said. Stormcasts snapped from their horrified reverie to do as he ordered. Tarsus thrashed and screeched like a wild beast, as they held him down.

Nagash's laughter rolled over them like a gust of foul wind. 'I tore his secrets from him, flayed soul from flesh, and flesh from bone,' he intoned.

'Monster,' Gardus said, flatly.

'No. I am a god. And he was my subject. As you all are my subjects. Whatever the God-King has claimed, you are all mine.' Nagash looked down at him, and Gardus stepped back, his hand falling to the hilt of his runeblade. He could not meet the Undying King's gaze, and he did not try.

'What did you do to him?' he demanded.

'I broke him into a thousand pieces and built him anew, to learn that which was kept from me. Then I broke him again. And again, just to be sure I had the answer I sought. And now I am done with him.' Nagash looked down at Gardus, and the rictus of his skull seemed to widen. 'As I am done with Caddow. I have made my decision. You wish to have these ruins – the one of flesh and the other of stone – in recompense for your efforts? Then have them.'

'We are free to depart?' Gardus asked, unable to believe it.

'I am no thief, Garradan of Demesnus, whatever you think. You may go, and take Sigmar's broken toy with you.' Nagash gave a hollow, rattling laugh. 'Besides, it is enough for me that you know that I could take either back any time I wish. Whatever Sigmar claims, all things belong to me, in the end. As he is well aware.' He looked down at Mannfred, and the vampire quailed back from the heat of that pulsing, black-sun gaze. 'As for you, my *faithful* servant...'

Nagash's great talon twitched and Mannfred gasped. Gardus saw molten silver suddenly seep from the joins in the vampire's armour. It hissed as it struck the ground, and Mannfred stumbled to his knees, clutching his chest. 'Beaten and bound. Are you so weak then, little prince? Perhaps I should put you out of your misery at last. What say you?' Nagash raised his claw, and Gardus felt the air twist in anticipation.

'Without him, this day would not have been a victory,' Ramus croaked, looking up from Tarsus' squirming form. 'You sent him for an army and he brought you one.'

Nagash turned. 'Who are you to speak to me so, little necromancer?' he asked, after long moments. 'You, who hate him above all others? You, whom he betrayed and slew?'

Ramus drew himself up. 'You killed me. Not him.' He spread his arms. 'Kill me again, if you wish. Prove yourself an ungrateful god, as well as an unjust one.'

Nagash's gaze flickered. Flared. Gardus tensed, waiting, wondering if he would again have to face a god in battle. The prospect was no more pleasing the second time around. Then, with a rattling sound, which might have been a chuckle or a sigh, the God of Death turned away with a dismissive gesture. 'You have served me well, Mortarch. Go, and continue to serve.'

Mannfred glanced at Ramus, and bowed low. 'That I am allowed to serve you is reward fit for any prince,' he said, his voice harsh. Nagash gave no sign that he'd heard. It was as if, having passed his judgement, the Undying King had already forgotten them.

The awful immensity moved away, back over the bridge. Where he walked, the heaps and piles of the dead not already on their feet twitched and lurched upright, and fell into step behind him. Gardus shuddered as corpses stumbled through the ranks of the Hallowed Knights, their sightless gazes fixed on the shadow of their new master.

Among them was Bakhos, his rusted sword still hanging loosely from his withered fist. The dead man staggered towards

Gardus, his hair lank, eyes empty of all but the barest dregs of their former fire. Something in his slack expression made Gardus wonder if, somehow, the Chaos lord was still aware – if he *understood* what had happened to him. He stepped aside, and the corpse passed him by, mouth working soundlessly.

'Do not weep for him,' Mannfred said. 'Bakhos was a mad dog. He killed his own bride, you know. On their wedding night. Then used her lost spirit as an excuse to invade the lands of the dead.' He turned, looking at Ramus. At the mewling, broken thing on the ground before him. His face became stiff and empty. Like that of a corpse, Gardus thought.

'What did Nagash do to Tarsus?'

Mannfred said nothing. Gardus wondered what was going through his mind as he stared at the man he'd called friend. Finally, the vampire shook himself and said, 'Nothing that you or I can fix, Stormcast. Nagash has broken him, in body and soul.' His voice was hoarse.

'Why?'

'Why does a child tear the wings off a fly? To see what will happen.' Mannfred turned and watched as his master strode across the bridge. 'He has done worse, in his time. And will do worse still.'

'Then why serve him?'

Mannfred laughed – a harsh, almost piteous sound. 'What makes you think I have a choice, Stormcast? Do you have a choice?'

'Yes,' Gardus said, softly. 'There is always a choice.'

Mannfred started, and looked at him. A moment later, he turned away. 'Not for me. And there is no choice here. You cannot help him. You can only put him out of his misery.' He reached for his sword. 'I can do that much for him.'

'No,' Ramus said.

Mannfred whirled, a snarl on his face. 'Idiot! Do you think he would want to live this way? Are you so blind that you would force him to exist in this – this half-life, merely to satisfy your own need to have him back?'

Ramus shook his head. 'I meant that I would do it, vampire. It is my duty.' The words came slowly, painfully. Mannfred made as if to argue, then, with a sigh, he looked away.

'Do it, then. Do it and be damned.'

'I am that already,' Ramus said.

'Ramus…' Gardus began, reaching for the Lord-Relictor.

'I said, I will do it.' Ramus lifted his hammer. He looked down at the writhing, broken hulk of a man. Tarsus met his gaze without recognition. The brute snarled, teeth champing spasmodically. 'I am sorry,' Ramus said, softly. 'I failed you again. I failed us all.'

As the words left him, he struck.

Thunder rolled.

When the flash of lightning had faded, the Lord-Relictor cast aside his hammer and his staff. He wrenched his helm from his head and cast it to the ground at Gardus' feet. With a trembling hand, he tore the mirrored shield from his shoulder-plate and flung it away.

'I am ready to face judgement,' he said, all trace of bitterness gone from his voice. Behind them, the obsidian gates closed with a groan.

'Ramus…' Gardus began. Ramus shook his head.

'No. I knew I would have to face Sigmar for my crime. I disobeyed him… abandoned my duties… freed a prisoner… led my warriors into death. My crimes are my own, and I do not shrink from them.' He held up his hands. 'Take me to Azyr, brother. Let the God-King judge me, if he would, or cast me into the void as a warning to others. I do not care which.'

Gardus hesitated. Then, nodding, he gestured for Sathphren to take the Lord-Relictor into custody. Mannfred peered up into the sky, where the glare of Tarsus' ascension faded. 'Will he return, do you think?' he asked, watching as Ramus was led away.

Gardus looked at him. 'Only Sigmar can say.'

Mannfred laughed. 'I doubt he'd tell me.' He looked at Gardus. 'Well. What now, Stormcast? Am I to go back in chains with Ramus?'

Gardus studied him. 'If I say yes?'

'I will fight you.'

Gardus nodded. 'I have had my fill of fighting today. Go in peace, vampire. For when next we meet, there will be none.'

Mannfred smiled, but there was little humour in it. He turned away, but stopped and sank down. He picked up the mirrored shield Ramus had discarded and rose to his feet. 'Something to remember this moment by,' he said, before striding to the waiting form of his dread abyssal. He climbed in the saddle and kicked the beast into motion. It took two great, lunging steps and then was climbing into the air and away.

'We should have killed him,' Sathphren said. Gardus turned. Ramus stood, staring away from them, head bowed, shoulders slumped. What would become of him, Gardus could not say. He only hoped Sigmar would not judge Ramus harshly. Gardus sighed and clapped Sathphren on the shoulder.

'There has been enough killing, brother. It is time to go home.'

Cassandora walked through the sea of tents, accompanied only by the groans of the wounded, and the thunder of guns. The broken remnants of the enemy had mostly fled, but some had forted up in the ruins. They had burrowed in, like ticks, and refused to be moved. The Ironweld had these areas cordoned off now, and were slowly pounding them to rubble. Cohorts of Stormcasts waited to advance, and deal with any survivors.

The dead had fallen still and silent, as if by some unknown signal. Cassandora thought she knew what it might have been, and said a silent prayer in thanks. Wherever Gardus was, she was sure he was responsible in some way.

The explosion in the catacombs had gutted part of the city, and undone much of Taltus' work on the city's foundations. Despite this, the Lord-Ordinator had not seemed altogether displeased. In fact, he seemed to relish the chance to strengthen the city's roots, or so he'd claimed. Grymn and the other Lord-Castellants had not seemed so enthusiastic.

Around her, work continued on the Stormfort. With the battle done, Octarion and the other Lord-Castellants had returned to their tasks, as had Taltus. Great slabs of rock were raised on pulleys as the first of the foundations were at last set by the Zhu'garaz.

When the Stormfort was finished, the Hallowed Knights would garrison it. While initially the duty would be shared between the three Chambers involved in the campaign, others would take their turn. The city would never be undefended, so long as one of the faithful lived. Of course, neither would it be unthreatened.

She looked up into the pale lavender sky. Though the stars were not visible in the light of day, she could feel them. A sign of Sigmar's satisfaction, perhaps. A sign that all was well. That all was as it should be.

Cassandora sighed. Too many warriors had perished to account it anything other than a glorious victory. Too many souls, gone back to the forges.

'Are you well, Lady Cassandora?'

Cassandora stopped. Dame Morguin strode towards her, her helm under her good arm. The leader of the Gold Gryphons had a bandage around her head, and one arm in a sling. Seeing Cassandora's expression, she said, 'No worry needed, my lady. I'll live.' She nodded back towards the medical tents. 'So will that great fool of a Nordrathi.'

'Cruso? Good. He's a good soldier.' Cassandora felt a flicker of relief. Soldiers like Cruso were hard to come by, and his skills would be sorely needed in the future. 'How is he?'

'Broken leg. The healers think it'll mend well enough. He's unhappy with being confined to a cot, though. Stupid fool. Trying to take on the enemy by himself.' Morguin smiled. 'Speaking of which, the other Nordrathi fool is back that way, if you're looking for him. Feeling sorry for himself, I think.'

'Lorcus? Why do you say that?'

'A hunch.' Morguin shrugged. 'He got a taste of what it means to be king, today. Seeing so many die, and for not much more than a few yards of broken ground.'

'But it doesn't bother you?'

'I'm not king, am I?' Morguin bowed. 'I must go now, my lady. There's fighting yet to be done, and coin yet to be earned.' Cassandora watched her go, and then turned in the direction she'd indicated.

She hadn't gone far before she spotted Lorcus, sitting alone on the bottom step of the ziggurat. His wounded leg was stretched before him, and he held a cup of something that steamed in the cold morning air. He smiled wearily as she drew close. 'Good morning, my lady. I trust you are doing well?'

'As well as can be expected.' She looked down at him. 'I have spoken to both Ahom and Taltus. The catacombs will be sealed, and the dead of Caddow left to sleep in peace. According to the Lord-Ordinator, there is a Lord-Castellant in Glymmsforge who has made certain discoveries in how best to contain such things. Taltus is certain that he can come up with a similar solution that will serve the city well.'

'And yet, they still might awaken at any time.' Lorcus sipped from his cup and plucked at the bandage on his leg. 'A bad business. Tell me, my lady – what did we truly win here today?'

'Time,' Cassandora said, simply. 'Time to build, to grow, to learn. Time is the most precious commodity, no matter the realm. And now, you have it.'

'Do I?' Lorcus gestured. 'Our enemies are still here. They still claim parts of this city for themselves. How many will die, rooting them out? And there is always the chance that we will not get them all. That the monsters of today will simply return tomorrow, when our attentions have turned elsewhere.'

Cassandora frowned. 'Then do not let your attentions lapse. This city is yours. We will build it for you, roots to roof. But you must fight to keep it.'

Lorcus took another swallow and licked his lips. 'I suspect there'll be plenty of that to come in the days ahead. The beast-men vanished into the hills and wastes – likely they will be a problem for years to come. And the dead, of course. Waiting for Sigmar knows what.' He laughed. 'Victory feels remarkably like yesterday.'

Cassandora nodded. 'It always does.'

Lorcus sighed. 'Someone once said that Shyish is a land of bitter endings.'

'Sometimes I think that is the only sort of ending there is,' Cassandora said, softly. She looked down at him. 'But you are alive. And I am alive. And this city rises wild, dead or no. Like a forest, in need of taming.'

Lorcus laughed, suddenly. 'That's what I'll call it, then.'

Cassandora looked at him in bemusement. 'What?'

'Caddow is dead. And the dead should be left to history, especially in this realm.' He raised his cup, as if in salute. 'In the tradition of Hallowheart and Glymmsforge, I shall name this city Gravewild. Long may it stand.' He laughed again.

With a creak of war-plate, Cassandora sat beside him. 'I cannot tell you that it will be better tomorrow. I can only say have faith. Have faith in us. In Sigmar. And in yourself. Every day won is a victory. Never doubt it, Albain.' She looked at him. 'And never lose faith that we will stand with you, whatever comes.'

'Only the faithful, eh?' he asked, looking up at the sky.

She nodded, and smiled.

'Only the faithful.'

EPILOGUE

WHAT WILL BE

A city is the reflection of its people. And in time the people become a reflection of the city. Thus, what was, will be.

– Palento Herst
Groves of Stone

Ghosteater knelt, and looked down at the camp below. The priest sat before the fire, his hammer propped against a stone. He read from a book. Ghosteater growled, puzzled.

He is reading, Herst murmured.

'I see that. Reading what? Why here?'

About Sigmar, and the light of distant stars, I imagine. And why not here?

Ghosteater shook his head, and looked towards the distant city. It had been three days since he had ordered his folk to desert Caddow. Smoke still rose from the city, and the smell of blood was still strong on the wind.

Do you regret it?

'No.'

Then why do you keep looking back? That is the past. You must look to the future.

Annoyed, Ghosteater growled low in his throat. Herst had been getting louder, since they'd left Caddow, as if his ghost were growing stronger, rather than weaker, like all the rest. In fact, Ghosteater could barely hear the others, now. Perhaps they had told him all they knew. Or perhaps he no longer needed them.

It didn't matter. There were always more ghosts to be had. The priest, for instance. Ghosteater licked his chops, both at the thought of fresh meat and a fresh ghost. He turned and gestured. The warriors who waited in the rocks around him began to creep down through the rocks, encircling the priest. Ghosteater slunk after them, one hand on his khopesh to keep it from clanking.

As Ghosteater drew close to the fire, the wind turned. Weak as his nose was, the human recognised their scent. He was on his feet in moments, lunging for his hammer. Ghosteater leapt from the rocks and landed in the camp. With a roar, he plunged towards the priest. He could see now that the human was young, as they judged such things.

His khopesh met the hammer's iron haft, and the priest cried out as he shoved Ghosteater back. 'No,' the human shouted. The rest of Ghosteater's warriors emerged from the rocks, weapons in hand, howling and braying. The priest turned, brandishing his hammer.

'Kill him,' Ghosteater growled.

Wait.

Ghosteater paused. 'What? Why?' The priest stared at him, as if he were mad.

Mercy is the sharpest blade, Herst said. The ghost sounded amused. Ghosteater paused, thinking this over. He twitched an ear in annoyance. *Besides,* Herst continued, *you can learn more from the living than the dead.*

With a grunt, Ghosteater waved his followers back. They did so reluctantly, sliding back into the rocks and vanishing from the human's sight. Ghosteater knew that they were still close, but to the human, it would be as if they had vanished. He used the tip of his khopesh to pick up the fallen book.

'What is this?' Ghosteater asked.

The priest frowned. 'A book of prayers,' he said, after a moment. He straightened. 'The words of Sigmar Heldenhammer.'

'Your god speaks to you?'

'Doesn't yours?'

And that is the question, isn't it? Can a god who is absent still speak? Herst's voice echoed in Ghosteater's skull. *And if your god is silent... do you truly serve him?* His words had an unpleasant weight to them. Ghosteater wanted to ignore them, to push them aside as he did the voices of the other ghosts, but he could not.

He knew too much now. He had a taste for the new, and a hunger beyond the physical. He growled low in his throat. This was another trap. But he was already in it. And perhaps the priest was, as well. The gods offered only tainted meat to the hungry.

'Am I to die, then?' the priest asked. He lifted his hammer. 'If I am, I warn you that I will not do so easily.'

Ghosteater laughed and sat down opposite the priest. He laid his khopesh across his knees. 'What is your name?'

'Twayn. Cullen Twayn.'

Ghosteater nodded. Like all human names, it made little sense to him. He gestured. 'Sit. You will not die. Not yet. First, we will talk. You will tell me of your god. And I will tell you of mine.' He bared his fangs in a ghastly smile.

'And we will see what will be.'

ABOUT THE AUTHOR

Josh Reynolds is the author of the Horus Heresy Primarchs novel *Fulgrim: The Palatine Phoenix*, and the audio dramas *Blackshields: The False War* and *Blackshields: The Red Fief*. His Warhammer 40,000 work includes *Lukas the Trickster, Fabius Bile: Primogenitor, Fabius Bile: Clonelord* and *Deathstorm*. He has written many stories set in the Age of Sigmar, including the novels *Eight Lamentations: Spear of Shadows, Hallowed Knights: Plague Garden, Nagash: The Undying King, Soul Wars* and *Shadespire: The Mirrored City*. His tales of the Warhammer old world include *The Return of Nagash* and *The Lord of the End Times*, and two Gotrek & Felix novels. He lives and works in Sheffield.

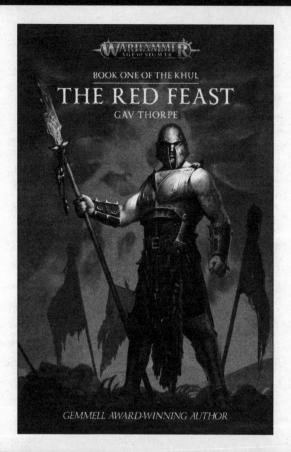

An Extract from
Khorgos Khul: The Red Feast
by Gav Thorpe

Outside, Athol stopped in the shadows for a few moments. The season of Hotwind had only just started and it had been thankfully cool by comparison to previous seasons. When the winds turned and brought the north-burn the air would be like a furnace draught, its movement doing nothing to ease the stifling heat, the dryness stealing the moisture from the eyes and mouth. Shielding his eyes, he glanced up. Broad-winged scavenger birds circled on the hot air just below scant clouds, keen eyes searching the scrubland around the royal city.

The city was not so grand as the name suggested, of little comparison to the stone edifices raised by the likes of the Bataari and Aspirians, or the lifetombs of the Golvarians. A few hundred tents was miniscule when measured against the mighty duardin stronghold at Vostargi Mont. The capital of the Aridians lacked even the strength of the fortified wooden settlements of the other tribes with which they shared the Flamescar Plateau. Even so, it had one great strength the others could not match; it could move across the plains to seek water and verdant growth. Within the turn of a day, the whole of the royal city could be packed upon wagons pulled by gargantuan beasts known as whitehorns, akor in the tongue of the Aridians. Should the winds veer, a river dry or a herd migrate, the whole of the Aridian tribe could adapt, the royal city and its satellite settlements travelling for days on end until they found a new home.

For thirty days now the capital had not moved. Athol was no windwatcher, but it seemed that the mild weather would not hold for much longer. The watercourse that snaked through the centre of the tent city would run low and the whitehorns would move on, heading to cooler climes in the east and south. When that happened, the Khul would follow, for even as the Aridians followed the herds that brought them prosperity, so too did the Khul shadow the Aridians, who paid in milk, meat and hides for their blade-hands. A greedy Bataari thief was of little threat, but when the herds moved the Khul would be needed, their presence dissuading raiders from other tribes.

'A disappointment.'

Athol looked around, recognising the voice of Khibal Anuk, the Prophet-Queen's older half-brother. He stood in the shelter of the door-awning, fingers hooked into the thick belt that bound tight around his considerable waist. A small hammer pendant hung from a gold chain about his neck, the symbol of his calling.

'What's that, Sigmar-tongue?' said Athol. He used the honorific out of respect for the Aridians' traditions, though he cared little for Sigmar himself.

'No trial by arms today,' explained Khibal Anuk. 'I had thought to see you use that spear.'

'It would have been little spectacle,' Athol assured him. 'His champion will provide a better contest, I am sure.'

Khibal Anuk nodded and stroked his stubbled chins.

'You like to fight?'

'I was born to fight – it isn't a question of what I like or dislike,' Athol replied. He brandished his spear. 'Does this like to slay, or is it simply what it does?'

'You are not an inanimate object, Athol. You have feelings.'

'I do, and I share them with my wife and son.' Athol glanced away, his thoughts drawn to the distant encampment where his family waited for his return. 'The queen claims only my blade-arm.'

'You would have been at home at the Red Feast. Days of challenges and combat between the tribes, settled by champions like you.'

'I know of it. I was in the entourage of my uncle when he attended as our champion, back when I was a youngster. He killed five men and women to defend the honour of our people.' Athol frowned. 'You speak of the Red Feast as a thing that has passed, and there has not been one called since we travelled to the gathering at Clavis Volk.'

'The tribes settle their differences in other ways now, through the wisdom of Sigmar.' Khibal Anuk touched a hand to his sacred amulet. 'Better to be united than divided, and settle with peace what once was settled by war.'

'The Red Feast existed to avoid war, I thought. To give the tribes a way to fight without butchering each other and destroying their homes. A better way to keep their honour.'

'If one dies or a hundred, is honour worth killing or dying for?'

'You seem troubled, Sigmar-tongue.' Athol planted his spear in the dry earth and took a step towards the priest. 'I hope my decision to accept the trial of arms did not displease the Prophet-Queen.'

'Oh, I am quite sure she agrees with your course of action. She would not have offered the choice if she did not.'

'If she had ordered me to fight the man's champion, I would have done so.'

'She is the Prophet-Queen. By rights she should have made Williarch fight. She must obey the law, after all, and he had not followed it.' Khibal Anuk shrugged. 'But that's not what has troubled me. There have been a few members of the court that have suggested we sever our relationship with the Khul.'

'I see. Does Humekhta know that you speak to me?'

'Do not be alarmed. It is just whispers – I'm sure they fall on deaf ears. My half-sister knows the value of the Khul, even if others do not.'

'Why? Both our tribes have benefited from the partnership.'

'They speak of being beholden to outsiders, of our sword arms growing weak beneath the shield of the Khul.'

'Your warriors are trained by us. They have never been better.'

'I think that is part of the problem, Athol. It has been three generations since your people came to the lands of Aridian. Greedy minds forget how vulnerable they were before. Now we can fight for ourselves, they think. They see the price paid for your company and wonder if it is necessary.'

'Perhaps you can defend yourselves.'

'For a while. But the name of the Khul is a surer ward against attack than any number of our own soldiers.' Khibal Anuk clasped his hands, almost resting them on his prominent gut. 'You protect us doubly so. The very threat of fighting the Khul keeps our rivals' hands from their sword hilts.'

He shifted his weight from foot to foot and back again, eyes regarding Athol closely.

'Speak plainly what gnaws at your ear, Sigmar-tongue,' Athol told him. 'I will not pass on what you say to any other.'

'It might be necessary to prove the worth of the Khul again. A reminder to those with short memories.'

'I don't understand what you think I can do.'

'The peace we enjoy is a lie, Athol. You know it. We will be tested again, as soon as the herds thin, or when the hot wind blows long. It is in the nature of our people to settle matters with aggression, but a few years of bounty have dulled that temper. I am worried that without a… display of your people's vigour the voices that question your presence will grow bolder and louder.'

'You want me to start a fight? Wage a war?'

Khibal Anuk coughed nervously and gestured for Athol to keep his voice low.

'Not start a war, no. Of course not. But should our enemies decide to test the queen's mercy, it might go well to make an example of them. To show what happens when the anger of the Khul is stirred.'

Athol remembered that he was speaking to a high member of the court and held back the first thought that occurred – that should the full wrath of the Khul be slipped, the Aridians would be swept away by that unleashed storm. It would serve no purpose to alienate him.

'I will remember what you have said, Sigmar-tongue. I am sure there is wisdom in your words.'

The Sigmar-tongue said nothing more but laid a hand on Athol's arm before stepping back into the queen's tent. Athol waited there for a few moments more, agitated by the priest's words as he stared into the shadowed interior. He had no reason to distrust Khibal Anuk, but the Sigmar-tongue had never before tried to involve Athol in courtly politics. The champion had been robust in keeping himself clear of such entanglements and was annoyed that the priest seemed to be trying to draw him into the unfamiliar battleground.

He retrieved his spear and headed out into the tent city,

sun gleaming on his armour as he passed between the rows of brightly coloured canvas structures. The respectful call of nakar-hau followed him along the streets, which he met with a raise of his weapon or nod of the head.

Spear-carrier. A simple phrase but one that conveyed heavy connotations for the Aridians. He was the bearer of the Prophet-Queen's honour, responsible for protecting her reputation even as her personal guards shielded her body. In deed he was an extension of the queen, his actions reflecting upon her. It was no surprise that, even after three generations of service by the Khul, there were still some elements within Aridian society that considered it a dishonour for the nakar-hau to be an outsider.

He remembered his great uncle, the first to swear to the line of the Prophet-Monarchs, and how Orloa described the day he had bent his knee to the ruler of another tribe. It had brought peace, an end to fighting that the Khul had waged for two generations before. It was acceptance of a sort, not only by the Aridians but also the other tribes of the Flamescar. The Khul had both proven their martial prowess and earned the respect of the hardy plains people.

The smell of the akor pens grew stronger as he reached the outskirts, mixed with the musk-stench of the smaller noila the Aridians used as personal mounts. He did not turn towards the corrals but passed the last ring of tents on foot, for the Khul did not ride. They could march for days on end, or run for a full day and still fight a battle at the end of it. Steeds were simply more mouths to feed.

He walked slowly, the sun setting to his left. He followed the slow-flowing river towards the camp of his people, his thoughts weighing more heavily than the spear on his shoulder.